ANGEL ON THE INSIDE

Suddenly discovering that your partner has been married before might come as a shock, especially if the ex-husband appears, fresh out of prison and waving a gun. Even streetwise Roy Angel is a bit staggered by this one. Lots of people are interested in Keith Flowers: the police, several former residents of HM Prisons, two gangs of criminals – in fact the only one not interested is the ex-Mrs Flowers, who is giving nothing away, certainly not to Angel. Then Angel's ferocious feline Springsteen is assaulted and put into cat hospital – and it's too late for counselling. It's war!

ANGEL ON THE INSIDE

ANGEL ON THE INSIDE

by

Mike Ripley

Magna Large Print Books
Long Preston, North Yorkshire,
BD23 4ND, England.

British Library Cataloguing in Publication Data.

Ripley, Mike
   Angel on the inside.

A catalogue record of this book is
available from the British Library

ISBN   0-7505-1989-4

First published in Great Britain in 2003
by Constable, an imprint of Constable & Robinson Ltd.

Published in Large Print 2003 by arrangement with
Constable & Robinson Ltd.

Magna Large Print is an imprint of Library Magna Books Ltd.

Printed and bound in Great Britain by
T.J. (International) Ltd., Cornwall, PL28 8RW

One day, God is walking the boundaries of Heaven when he comes to a section of fence which has fallen down. On one side are the green fields and sweet air of Heaven, on the other are the sharp red rocks and sulphurous clouds of Hell. God is furious at the broken fence and shouts for Satan to get his arse up here quick. When Satan appears, God tells him that the upkeep of the boundary fence is his problem and he'd better get it repaired quick. Satan just laughs and says 'Or else what?' and God fumes: 'Or else I'll get my solicitor on to it.' Satan really laughs this time.
*'Where are **you** gonna find a solicitor?'*
– Anon, HMP Belmarsh.

*So there's this Good Ole Boy Texican out riding in the desert and suddenly he's confronted with a rattlesnake ready to strike, Osama Bin Laden with an AK47 and a lawyer. **But** he's only got two bullets left in his trusty Colt Peacemaker. What does he do?*
Shoots the lawyer twice.
Just to be sure.
– Anon, San Quentin.

THIS ONE
is for a lot of people:
Stephen Habgood of HM Prison Service;
the Governor and staff of HMP Belmarsh;
John Hopes of Essex Police; Margaret and
Joe Maron, my spies on the London Eye;
Michael at Gerry's Club; Tim Coles (again)
whose book *A Beginner's Guide to Model
Steam Locomotives* was an eye-opener;
Frankie Fyfield for dubious legal advice;
George Rivers of the Association of British
Investigators; Sian Best-Harding for vital
research beyond the frontier; and especially
Amanda 'Quisling' Stebbings for cultural
advice above and beyond the call of duty.
Oh, and for Jessamy for use of the tattoo.
Sorry about that.

MR

Chapter One

What was your approximate speed when the accident happened?

That was easy enough: 15 m.p.h.

Bulldozers don't do more than 15 m.p.h. flat out.

Position of other vehicle(s) involved. Use sketch plan if necessary.

Bang in front of me, side-on, to begin with. Through ninety degrees and up on its side after I hit it.

Speed of other vehicle(s) involved.

Nil. After I'd hit it though, I nudged it sideways for a bit with the bulldozer.

Road conditions at the time of the accident.

Not on a road. In somebody's front garden, actually.

Place and location of accident.

Lat. 52'22" N; Long. 0'45" E. (Approx.)

Were occupants of other vehicle injured?

Sole purpose of exercise.

Were the emergency services called to the scene?

You bet.

Which ones?

All of them.

'You can't send that in,' said Amy. 'They'll think you're a nutter.'

'I was hoping they'd reserve judgement on that until they got to the bit where I told them that it was our car I trashed with the 'dozer,' I said reasonably.

'*My* car,' Amy pointed out.

'So why am I the one filling out all the forms, then?'

God, she could be really childish at times.

'Because you think you were put on earth to make life hell for insurance claims assessors.'

'It's a calling. Of sorts.'

Of course I wasn't doing any of this just to annoy the insurance company, though that was an added incentive, nor to prove a point about the vulnerability of BMW Series 7s when hit broadside by seventeen tons of bulldozer just because it's the one test they *don't* do in the wind tunnels over in Munich. (Actually, knowing BMW, they probably do.)

It was after all, a pretty straightforward case. The car had been stolen from our – Amy's – house in Hampstead and later used, miles away up in Suffolk, in the commission of a crime, as they say. Crime in question: abduction of said Amy at gunpoint. All I had been doing was prevent a getaway by using whatever means were at hand and, I think the jury will agree with me

10

on this, with the minimum of force necessary. I put it to you: it is impossible to stop a BMW 7 when it gets up to speed with simply the use of harsh language.

You could, of course, if you wanted to be pedantic, mention the fact that I must have known full well that the driver could be injured during such action. Too bloody right, I say. After all, he had just tried to abduct Amy and he'd pinched the car in the first place – it was almost the first thing he'd done after getting out of prison, after buying a gun that is.

Oh yes, he was a villain. A right jailbird. He had form, a record. He was also totally psychotic. I knew all that.

What I hadn't known was that he was Amy's husband.

Well, her first one.

So all this fun I was having filling in whacky insurance claims was a way of getting Amy to talk about it, because everything else I had tried had failed. (Threats, anger, sulking, more threats, bribery, offers of counselling, romantic restaurants, a few more threats, the silent treatment, the going-on-and-on-about-it treatment, double sulking.)

'I'm not signing the claim and it is my insurance, so why don't you just let it lie,' she said. 'The warranty will cover it.'

'I don't think so. I think it becomes invalid

if you deliberately remove mechanical parts from their factory mountings,' I said, pretending to read the small print on the claim form.

'What, you mean like a wiper blade or something?'

'I was thinking of the engine.'

'Oh fuck it, just get rid of it, sell it for scrap. I don't want to know.'

'Amy, dearest, that's thirty-five grand's worth of car you're writing off.'

'We can afford it.'

'We *can?*' I hadn't meant to shout.

'*I* can,' she said icily.

'Look, we've got to talk about it some time,' I pleaded, all the time thinking about how many accounts she must have hidden away.

'Why?'

'Well, what if there's a hearing or something. I mean, there could be.'

Even as I said it I knew it sounded lame.

'So there's a hearing; so there's a trial at the Old Bailey; so there's a Royal-fucking-Commission. What? You stopped my car getting stolen. Rather violently, admitted, but that's all you did. Why do you have to know anything about ... him? Let it go. Move on.'

It wasn't me who couldn't say his name. Why was I the one who needed to move on?

'If there is a hearing or an enquiry or whatever,' I tried gently, 'won't it sound strange that I didn't know you'd been married

12

before? I mean, I'd look a right div.'

She seemed to think this over.

'Wouldn't be a first,' she said.

It had been a month since it had happened, but time just flies when you're answering police enquiries.

I had been involved in an archaeological dig in Suffolk – well, not so much involved as *supervising*, actually – though I'm not really an archaeologist, I just know how to look like one. I drive a delicensed black Austin Fairway cab, but it doesn't mean I'm a London taxi driver who has done The Knowledge, which just goes to prove that appearances can be deceptive. At least I hope they are.

The weird thing was not me wielding a trowel in anger for the first time since I was a student – or the other off-the-wall things going on at the dig – but the fact that Amy had insisted on coming with me. What I hadn't known at the time, though I should have suspected, was that Amy wanted to get out of London for a while. That alone should have set off car alarms in Dulwich. Amy never left London except to go to Paris or Milan or wherever the next fashion show was. Amy never left Zone 1 unless one of her customers was having a crisis and there was need for a rapid response fashion adviser. She was not the sort of woman – she was the last woman on earth – you could imagine exchanging a designer frock for breathable Goretex combat trousers in Desert Storm camouflage and forsaking her Jimmy Choo shoes for steel-capped rigger boots. (Actually, she took the Jimmys along just in case.) But there she was, digging with the best of them, hardly noticing there wasn't any Room Service.

Of course, as I discovered, she'd been hiding and, to be honest, an archaeological dig in East Anglia is a pretty good place to hide. Martin Bormann could have been digging in the next ditch and nobody would have thought to ask.

She was hiding from a man who had been out of prison for just a month but had used the time wisely to track down his ex-wife at her Oxford Street office, find out where we lived, break into our (Amy's) house, steal our (Amy's) new BMW, buy a gun, discover we were in Suffolk and decide to abduct Amy.

The only thing Anthony Keith Flowers hadn't bargained for was what happens when a bulldozer meets a BMW at right angles.

What I hadn't bargained for was that there was an Anthony Keith Flowers *at all*.

Life's just full of surprises.

I hate surprises.

Amy and I had been an item for about three years. No, at least three years, as I distinctly remember missing three anniversaries.

When we met, Amy was the leading player in a creative trio breaking into the High Street fashion market with a well-designed, well-researched and well-affordable multi-purpose blouse known as a TALtop after the triumvirate's initials of Thalia, Amy and Lyn. Within a few weeks, Amy was the sole player in the partnership thanks to a combination of criminal proceedings and an unfortunate traffic accident down the Columbia Road Sunday flower market in Hackney. Within a year, she had franchised the TALtop and herself to a national chain of clothing shops, become seriously rich and moved her manufacturing base from a sweatshop off Brick Lane to the side streets off the Via Monte Napoleone in Milan. It seemed a good time to move into her house in Hampstead, as my one-bedroomed flat in Hackney wouldn't have cut the mustard if *OK!* magazine ever came calling – as they did.

There was also the small matter that my flat at Number 9 Stuart Street wasn't big enough for three of us, for I had a sitting tenant in the shape of an irritable black cat called Springsteen. I use the term 'irritable' in its broadest sense: homicidal, sociopathic and possessed have all been bandied about in the past, and Stuart Street was declared a No Go area by the RSPCA many years ago. It just wouldn't have been fair to uproot a cat with an established territory and move him across London to upmarket Hampstead where the natural game reserves weren't enough to support his lifestyle. And anyway, I valued my skin too much to be the one to break the news to him. So I compromised and kept the flat on. The rent was a peppercorn thanks to an understanding I had with the landlord of the house and I'd invested in a catflap and the other residents regarded him as better than a Neighbourhood Watch, burglar alarms and a minefield when it came to deterring intruders. So everybody was happy and, as an added bonus, I had a crash pad I could use in case of emergency. And let's face it, there always are emergencies when it comes to relationships. So many, that I'm beginning to think the two things are mystically connected. Maybe I was just getting old.

Flat 3 at Number 9 Stuart Street also, I felt, kept me in touch with my people. Not 'my people' in any sort of religious or political sense; nor, for that matter, in any sense of class, intellectual, educational, occupational, sociological, sexual or genetic compatibility. In fact, thinking about it, I didn't really know why I liked them, but I did. It was probably because they didn't *bother* me.

In the flat above mine were Inverness Doogie and his girlfriend Miranda. He was a budding chef who was destined to have his own restaurant and probably TV series one day if only he could find the right gimmick, preferably one that did not involve fighting on the terraces at football matches, the third real love of his life after cooking and Miranda. Actually, as the terraces in football stadia had gone all-seater, most of the fun of starting a ruck with visiting fans had gone too so Doogie was in danger of calming down. Maybe it was Miranda who was softening his natural tendency to exuberant outbursts of violence. She was Welsh, which meant she knew that all silver linings had clouds, Rome wasn't burned in a day and these days the Good Samaritan would get mugged for his mobile phone. She had a powerful dampening effect on any free spirit, even Doogie's, and he had inherited his from a family tree which stretched back to the time when painted Pictish warriors head-butted Hadrian's Wall just for the hell of it.

In Flat 2 lived Fenella and Lisabeth, who were just about the longest-together couple I knew. But then, they didn't get out much. I could always rely on Fenella to put food out for Springsteen (as long as it didn't look too much like meat), make sure he could get in and out, pass on the rent money and take messages and deliveries for me. Lisabeth I could rely on to be Lisabeth and even though she now referred to herself as a

Woman Of Size and couldn't move as fast as she once could, she was still my first choice for the person I'd want to walk in front down a dark alley.

On the ground floor was the unassuming Mr Goodson, whom we saw rarely and who was something in local government but no one knew quite what, though he must surely be approaching retirement from it. Then again, he could be one of those men who were born at the age of 42 and spend their lives growing into the part. He kept himself to himself, put up with a lot and seemed happy to have the camouflage of the rest of the house around him, the house in its turn being camouflaged by the rest of Hackney – one of London's best-kept secrets.

Despite its history of extremist politics, its reputation for lousy educational achievement, pockets of severe poverty and the fact that nobody ever admits to coming from there, it is not that bad a place to live. People are always willing to talk to you there, in any of seventeen languages, even while stealing your car. In Hampstead, as I had found, hearing a neighbour's car alarm going off felt like you were intruding on their privacy. In Hampstead no one can be bothered to hear you scream. In Hackney they at least tell you to put a sock in it.

'So you feel there is a part of Amy's life

which she has denied you access?'

'Well, yes, obviously,' I said.

'Yet you live in different worlds, so there must be areas which you keep apart.'

'I wouldn't say that. We rub along quite nicely.'

'Despite the fact that she earns so much more than you?'

'Trust me, that's not a problem,' I said truthfully. 'It's not for her and it certainly isn't for me.'

'It must have come as a shock, though – finding out she'd been married before.'

'Bit of a stunner but, fair play, I'd never asked.'

'So you took her on trust and now you're thinking that trust's been broken?'

'That's a bit sexist, isn't it?' I argued. 'I mean it sounds as if I inspected the goods but didn't find anything wrong until I got her home from the shop. What was I supposed to do? Demand a warranty? Relationships don't come with warranties in my experience.'

'It doesn't sound as if her ex-husband's did. Didn't she know what he was like?'

'She must have. You can't live with some-body, sleep with somebody, and not get to know them at least, you know, in passing.'

'You seem to have managed it.'

'Hey – that's out of order. We're talking an entirely different scenario here.'

'Convince me.'

I was determined not to lose my temper. I clasped my hands together behind my head and leaned back to stretch out on the black leather upholstery.

'Whether she knew he was a villain before he was arrested, I don't know. Once he went inside, she divorced him. Far as she was concerned, end of story, new chapter, new life.'

'But not for him.'

''Course not. Bit of a bummer being slammed up in the first place, then to get the Dear John letter from her solicitor – could push anyone over the edge.'

'So he sits and festers in prison and then when he gets out, he – he does what?'

'He finds Amy – finds where she works, where she lives. He stalks her in fact.'

'And she knew about this?'

'Er ... yes,' I said slowly, knowing what was coming.

'And still she didn't mention him?'

Now that had worried me. I had discovered, almost by accident, that Amy had taken out a Restraining Order on Keith Flowers, supposedly to keep him away from where she worked and where we lived. It hadn't been a success.

'No, she didn't.'

'So she could have warned you but didn't. Is that it?'

'I wouldn't put it like that.'

'I would. So would most people. You feel – what? Betrayed?'

I said nothing to that.

'Then he turns up at this archaeology dig thing you're on and he pulls a gun. Did he say why?'

'We didn't exactly have time to chat,' I snorted. I'd been too busy trying to run him over with a bulldozer.

'But what was he going to do? Abduct Amy and drive off into the sunset?'

'It was the middle of the night.'

'Whatever. What was his plan?'

'I don't know.'

'Does Amy?'

'I don't know. If she does, she hasn't said.'

'No wonder you feel threatened.'

'Who said I felt threatened?'

'You must do. She's obviously holding back, keeping you out of the loop. Well, isn't she?'

'I suppose so, yes.'

'And that doesn't worry you?'

'Of course it bleedin' worries me. That's why I'm telling you all this.'

Something dawned on me.

I slid off the leather seat, put my feet on the garage floor and ducked out of the back of the BMW.

'Duncan, you're a fucking car mechanic. Why *am* I telling you all this?'

Chapter Two

Duncan the Drunken probably was the best car mechanic in the world, but as a psychiatrist he was pants. He had charged me £150 (cash) to go to a police pound in Suffolk with a flatback and bring Amy's BMW home to his lock-up garage and workshop in Hackney. He hadn't charged me anything for psychiatric advice but I knew it would cost me in the long run.

The car was encrusted with mud, had cracks in most of the windows, enough scratches down the near-side to make you think Freddy Kruger had been trying to break into it, a bulldozer-blade imprint on the off-side and two buckled frames where the paramedics had popped the doors in order to remove the unconscious Keith Flowers. I suspected that the petrol tank was ruptured and the engine had seized when the exhaust filled with dirt. (You had to be there.)

Duncan walked around it three or four times, hands in pockets, sucking in air over his teeth and shaking his head. After the fifth circuit, he puffed his cheeks and exhaled loudly.

'Insurance job?' he asked.

'Probably not,' I said carefully. 'Amy doesn't want it back. She thinks it's going for scrap.'

His eyebrows shot up at that, so high he almost had a hairline again.

'Bad associations, huh? So she just casts off the past and leaves you wondering...'

'Duncan, shut it. Can you fix it?'

'Sure I can, but it'll cost you lots of squids.'

'Work out an estimate and let me know. A proper one as well, not the usual back-of-a-fag-packet job.'

He pretended to look hurt at that but I headed for the garage doors.

'I thought we might patch it up, flog it and split the take,' I said over my shoulder.

'Nice one, Angel,' Duncan said to my back. 'That's more like the Angel I know. See, therapy does work.'

'Just fix the fucking car, Duncan.'

As I was in the neighbourhood – though if you drive a black Austin Fairway cab, anywhere in London is in the neighbourhood – I decided to call round to Stuart Street and see if anyone was home who fancied a chat rather than psychotherapy. Not that I have anything against psychiatrists *per se*. I have always held to the maxim that a problem shared is two people losing sleep, which is good because

23

you no longer feel alone, but there's a time and a place for everything. I was in Hackney. That wasn't the place. And as I had a full tank of diesel in Armstrong II, no job to go to, didn't have to wear a tie and the pubs would be opening in five minutes, this wasn't the time.

It was, however, the perfect time for me to arrive, if not in the nick of time, then right on cue to sort out the horror and chaos that had engulfed Number 9 Stuart Street that morning. Not that the place was a smoking ruin, or had fallen into a fissure in the earth, or had been drowned in a giant chemical spill or anything. It was worse than that.

As soon as I turned Armstrong II into the road, I was transfixed – hypnotized – by the sight that greeted me. There on the pavement outside the open door of Number 9 was my downstairs neighbour Fenella, arms aloft, jumping frantically into the air as if trying to block an invisible and considerably taller attacking basketball player. The sight was arresting because she was wearing pyjamas – knee-length shorts and top patterned with large green frog designs – under a belted pink satin dressing gown which she was having trouble keeping closed. On her feet were furry slippers in the shape of panda heads and on her back was a small bag made out of a furry monkey toy with long arms to form the straps. A vampire monkey, from the way the head was pressing into the back of her neck. To top it all she wore a hat, a battered brown canvas hat with embroidered flowers; a hat that people wore at Glastonbury Festivals when they were making an ironic post-modernist comment about the proceedings (or maybe just taking the piss); a hat Paddington Bear would have shunned as uncool.

As all my attempts at lip-reading have ended in disappointment, or a slap in the face, I couldn't tell what she was shouting over the throb of Armstrong's engine. But shouting she was and getting very agitated about something. Dressed the way she was, it was a sight which would have frightened the horses had there been any around and it seemed to have cleared the street of innocent civilians. It was a sight which would have made even someone as courageous as the late, great Queen Mum think twice about visiting the East End.

I drew up to the kerb in front of her and killed the engine. At last I could hear her, even without opening the windows.

'Help! Help!' she was yelling. Then, clocking Armstrong II: 'Taxi!'

'Fenella, it's me!' I shouted from inside the cab.

'Well, it's about time!' she screamed as soon as she focused on me.

Whatever was wrong, nick of time wasn't

25

going to cut it for Fenella this morning. I hear she has the same problem with Superman as well.

'What's happening, dudette?' I asked cheerfully, stepping out on to the pavement until Fenella slippered her way up to me and her panda feet were nose to toe with my trainers. I tried not to look down at them but they were hypnotic.

'Didn't you get my message?' she said in a voice which could have opened the prosecution at Nuremburg.

'What message?'

'The one I left on your mobile phone, the one you said was for emergencies only.'

Ah. The mobile phone which was switched off and locked in Armstrong's glove compartment.

'No, I didn't. You must've dialled the wrong number.'

'Well, when you didn't call back,' she said huffily, hands on hips, 'I dialed 999 but *they* wouldn't come either.'

'Who wouldn't?'

'The ambulance people.'

'Is somebody hurt?'

A frenetic split-screen of images fast-forwarded across my brain. Lisabeth slipping in the shower and unable to get up. Inverness Doogie drunk and running amok with a meat cleaver. Miranda, late for work, going arse over elbow down the stairs from

Flat 4. Mr Goodson, his secret life as a bank robber finally revealed, gunshot and bloodied, holed up in his room waiting for the final assault from Armed Police. Lisabeth in the shower again.

'Isn't it obvious?'

'No, Fenella, actually it isn't. What happened?'

'I phoned for an ambulance but they wouldn't come. So I came out here to try and grab a taxi.'

'I think I'm up to speed on that bit. Why wouldn't they send an ambulance?'

'They said they don't send them for cats.'

I hit the front door with my shoulder and took the stairs three at a time.

'He ... was ... eating ... something ... and ... it ... disagreed with him,' panted Fenella as she caught up with me on the landing which lead to Flat 3 – my flat.

'Food poisoning?' I scoffed. 'That's not possible. That cat's got a 5-Alarm Chilli stomach. His digestive juices could cut through metal. In fact, I think that's where they got the idea for the *Alien* monster.'

'No, I meant he was eating some*thing*. Something which was still alive and I think it was fighting back. It hurt him.'

I pinned Fenella to the wall by her shoulders but my hands slipped on the satin of her dressing gown and there was a moment there when it could have been embarrassing for me and probably a first for her. I clasped my hands as if in prayer, if only to keep them out of mischief.

'Look, Fenella, sweetie, just please tell me what you think you saw,' I pleaded.

'He was howling, that's what woke me the second time. It wasn't his usual "Let me in" or "Let me out" howl. It wasn't his usual "I've killed wildlife come and see" howl. I know those. This one was really sad, a piteous, tragic sort of a howl. And really, really loud. So I came out to see what was the matter and he was here.'

'Where?'

'Here on the landing, walking backwards in a funny way and howling, all the time howling.'

'Yes, yes, I got the howling bit.'

'And then I realized he was limping and he was dragging something in his teeth, shaking his head as if he was trying to kill it and then he went through the catflap. Backwards. I've never seen him do that before. It was horrible. The thing he was biting. It was long and brown... I thought it might be a fox. Are there foxes in Hackney?'

That would be just typical of Hackney. With the Government trying to ban hunting with hounds they must have thought they were safe here. Nobody had said anything about cats. But it was a moot point. There probably were more foxes in London now than there were in the countryside, where they didn't have to hunt – and be hunted – just help themselves to the rubbish bins. And whilst I fancied Springsteen's chances against most things, his motto being 'Four legs – potential snack; two legs – open target', even a soft townie fox wouldn't go down without a fight.

'I don't think it was a fox, Fenella,' I said reassuringly, having checked there was neither blood nor fur on the wall she was leaning against. 'How did he get in this morning?'

'I left your kitchen window open as usual,' she insisted. 'He must have used that as he didn't come in the front door.'

'Well, he wouldn't have come through there with a fox in his teeth,' I said confidently.

'I don't know how he gets in and out of that window anyway,' Fenella said, almost to herself. 'It's two floors straight down to the garden. At his age.'

'What do you mean by that?' I snapped, then immediately raised my hands in apology. 'Sorry, I know you're only trying to help. So where is he now?'

'Under your bed,' she said, drawing her dressing gown tighter. 'Growling. He's still got that thing in between his teeth and he won't come out.'

'Did you ring the vet, the one on Homerton High Street? I left you the number.'

Fenella flushed as pink as her satin dressing gown.

'They've banned me from going round there any more.'

I wasn't surprised. I knew they had warned her several times about taking dead, half-chewed birds and rodents round there in the hope that they could revive them after Springsteen had finished with them.

'That's why I rang for an ambulance,' she said sheepishly. 'I couldn't think of anything else to do. He's obviously in pain and the only thing I've got is aspirin and even if I could get one into him I remembered what you said.'

'Well done. Never give a cat aspirin, they just can't handle it. It kills them,' I said, though I wasn't too worried. Springsteen would have had her hand off before he'd take an aspirin from it. 'I'll go and see how he is. You go into the kitchen and get the bottle of brandy that's on top of the fridge.'

She rankled a bit at that.

'So aspirins can be fatal, but you don't mind pouring brandy down his throat?'

'Who said anything about *his* throat?'

Springsteen wasn't going to come out so I had to push the bed away from over him. His growling dropped a half-tone to a sort of sinister hiss and his eyes burned into me like a chestnut vendor's coals whilst his tail did that slow-time flick from side to side which tells you the clock's ticking. It was nice to be recognized.

'It's not a fox,' I said over my shoulder.

'Well, it looked like one,' said Fenella from the kitchen. 'Is this it? It says something ending in *Romana*. Is that brandy?'

'It'll do.'

Springsteen did indeed have something long and brown hanging from his jaw. Something long and limp, like a pelt – until you got close, that is. In my case I was still a good six feet away from where he lay on his side, which was quite close enough even though I could see that his right front leg was twisted at an unnatural angle.

The brown pelt was soaked with drool near his mouth and trailed off like a flattened snakeskin to his side, about four inches wide and some fifteen inches long. I guessed it had stuck over his teeth and without the use of his right paw he couldn't dislodge it.

I felt a gentle tap on my right temple. It was Fenella, knocking a bottle against my skull. I relieved her of it, took a swig and handed it back. Although Springsteen, concentrating his stare on me, wasn't moving or looking likely to move suddenly, she had positioned herself strategically behind me. She was learning.

'That's gross,' she said. 'Whatever it is. Whatever it was. What is it?'

'Well, from this distance, without forensic examination, I'd say "Mist" or maybe "American Tan" or possibly "Chiffon" and probably about 60 denier.'

She leaned forward to get a better look.

'You mean that's a nylon stocking?' she said as she focused, oblivious to Springsteen's malevolent stare swinging full-beam on to her.

'Or one half of a pair of tights,' I said reasonably.

Fenella straightened up as if she had a spring in her.

'You mean *he's eaten a whole girl?*'

'That's my boy,' I said. It seemed to soothe him, as he stopped growling at me.

I put my head back so I could whisper into Fenella's ear.

'Go and get me a couple of towels out of the airing cupboard.'

'You haven't got an airing cupboard,' she hissed back.

'Your airing cupboard. Big fluffy ones. They don't have to be new ones. In fact old ones that you wouldn't mind not seeing again might be an idea. When you come back, hang them over your shoulder, like you were going to have a shower. You know, casual. Give them to me quick when I say.'

'Right.'

She made to go, then leaned in so she could whisper in my ear.

'Why my towels?'

'Because Doogie and Miranda are at work and I can't ask Mr Goodson, can I?' I argued, putting some urgency into my whispering. Gibberish though it was, it was enough.

'Oh, I see. Sure, fine. On my way.'

As she backed out of the room, I moved carefully closer to Springsteen, crouching down until I was on my knees an arm's length away from him. The growls were coming in short bursts now as if his heart (if he had one) wasn't quite in it. The tail lashing became more pronounced and I could feel the thump as each beat hit the floorboards. It sounded to be in 9/8 time. Dave Brubeck can play in that too. At least his ears weren't flexed back. If you ever see that happen head-on, you're too close to the cat and with a cat like Springsteen, it could just be the last thing you ever see.

'You been in the wars, old son?' I said soothingly, tipping the bottle of Italian brandy so that the liquid soaked the finger tips of my left hand. Then I took a swig for myself before putting the bottle down on the floor.

I held my fingers out towards his nose and got them close enough so that his nose went into full wrinkle and his head went on one side and his mouth drooped open.

'You really should pick on someone your own size, you know. I mean, it's not that you're getting too old for a bit of playful homicide, but you've got to learn to pace yourself a bit more. Ripping women's tights off with your teeth is a young man's game; take my word for it.'

The brandy and the inane chat distracted him enough for me to get my right hand on the length of material hanging from his mouth. Keeping well away from his right side and the injured leg, I worked the nylon up and over his back teeth until I felt it go slack and could gently pull it out, trying to be as delicate as a surgeon operating on a private patient.

'That's *Chiffon*,' said Fenella behind me, making me flinch.

Springsteen, who hadn't indicated in any way that she was padding up behind me – pretending to be befuddled by the brandy fumes – took the opportunity, now I was distracted, to lash out with his left paw and rake me across the back of my hand. It wasn't a severe clawing; he couldn't get the angle right from the way he was lying to protect his right leg. There were only two tracks of blood.

'Oooh, did that hurt?'

I looked up at her and bit my tongue.

'I'm going to hang a bell on you if you insist on wearing those slippers,' I growled.

'I was only saying you were right,' she said, all innocence. 'That shade of tights is called Chiffon. Lisabeth has some airing in the bathroom.'

Now there was an image I didn't want to dwell upon.

With my back to Springsteen I zipped up my leather jacket to the collar then said: 'Just throw me the towels.'

At least she'd remembered them and had at least three large fluffy beach size ones draped around her neck. One was the official *Star Wars Phantom Menace* souvenir beach towel. I didn't ask; life's too short.

'Now?'

'Now.'

She bent her head and flipped the towels off her neck. I caught them and in one fluid movement, because I knew I wouldn't get a second chance, turned and flung them over Springsteen, rolling him into them as if I was trying to smother a fire. I grabbed the bundle, hugged it to my chest and got to my feet.

'Now what?' Fenella asked, a look of absolute horror at what I had just done on her face, which had gone a whiter shade of grey.

'Run!'

It was all that needed saying.

We thundered out of the flat and down the stairs, making so much noise I could hardly hear the Satanic growling coming from inside the bundle of towels I clutched to my chest.

'Get the door!' I panted, allowing Fenella to overtake me and jump the last few steps, her Panda slippers skidding on the fake wooden flooring.

Somewhat ungainly, she righted herself in time to whip the door open so I could barrel my way by her, yelling 'Car keys!' as I did.

'Where are they?'

'Trouser pocket,' I said, halting at Armstrong's side.

Her hand plunged into my trouser pocket and groped for the keys. There wasn't time for this. My bundle of towels was shapeshifting alarmingly, the growling was definitely getting louder and I distinctly heard the ripping of material.

'No, Fenella,' I said reluctantly. 'They're in the other pocket.'

I let Springsteen have the whole of the back of the cab to himself. It wouldn't have been fair to let Fenella ride locked in there with him, so I told her to get the bus round to Homerton High Street and meet me at the vet's surgery. I also suggested she might put some clothes on.

Getting him out of Armstrong actually

went smoother than I could have hoped. I parked on double yellow lines outside the surgery's front door and for a second considered writing a note to stick in the windscreen which said 'Vet On Call' – which never fails with policemen and parking wardens. Then I remembered I was a black London cab and thought to hell with it, I can park anywhere.

In Armstrong's boot I found an old pair of oil-stained black leather gloves and pulled them on. I could have done with the gauntlets they use to handle nuclear fuel rods, but these would have to do. Then I made a point of appearing in the offside passenger window before sinking down out of sight and crab-walking like a demented Cossack round the back of the cab to get to the nearside door as quietly as I could. At least a dozen good citizens of Hackney passed me on the pavement. Not one said anything or even gave me a second glance. That's why I love the place.

Then it was take a deep breath, whip the door open and play the roll-the-cat-in the towel game again, although one of the towels I noticed was now in two pieces, keeping low and turning my face away just in case.

A rising howl of primeval pain split the air, but nobody came to my aid.

I think it was that which made Springsteen

relax for a second, thinking he had scored a vital hit. That was all the time I needed to mummify him in towelling, for I was past caring about the blood. I was just grateful he'd missed my left eyeball.

Then I was kicking the door shut and running towards the surgery with my bundle clutched to my leather jacket, yelling: 'Coming through! Gangway! Emergency! Clear a path! Trauma case!'

An elderly lady with an ancient Jack Russell was just leaving the surgery as I charged up to the door. Both of them looked as if they could have done with hip replacements, but both were nimble enough to get out of my way and she even held the door open for me, a startled expression on her face.

I shouted 'Thanks' over my shoulder and burst into the waiting room where all eyes turned towards me. For a moment I thought they were going to dare me to jump the queue but nobody said anything. There must have been twenty people in there and at least the same number of animals, which made about thirty-nine eyes, allowing for the parrot in a cage with one eye bandaged up. The parrot looked pretty depressed, probably sick of pirate jokes from other parrots, but if he had any sense he would keep his beak shut as I simply wasn't in the mood.

I had to walk between two rows of chairs, knees and animals to get to the reception desk, where a buxom young blonde was making notes, a phone clamped to her right ear. She looked up and stared at me as well, disturbed by the fact that the surgery had gone totally silent. Well, silent apart from a constant one bass-note growling which was coming from my chest area. I think that, plus the fact that I could feel blood running down the side of my face, gave the impression that perhaps I did deserve to jump the queue after all.

A middle-aged woman with long curly red hair, wearing a Barbour and green wellies (in Hackney?) gave me a limp smile and reigned in a long-haired golden Labrador so I could squeeze by. A couple of cats in plastic carrying boxes with wire grills for doors scuttered as far back into them as they could get. A ten-year-old girl with two small, gerbil-sized boxes with air holes and the words 'Sparky' and 'Millie' crayoned on them, bunched up her knees and covered them protectively with her arms. A shaven-headed man with tattoos on his neck and knuckles tightened his grip on the lead of a Pit Bull as the dog shrank backwards under his chair. 'Steady, Laydee, steady,' he said, a look of doubt on his face.

I reached the reception desk and rested my towel bundle, still keeping a firm grip.

'I need a vet,' I said, deadly serious.

The young blonde put down the phone and gave me a killer smile. The name tag on her starched white medical smock said 'Amber' and I didn't need contact lenses to read it. I was close enough to feel the static.

'I bet you do,' she said with an Australian twang. 'But animals come first here.'

Before I could come up with the obvious reply, which would probably have earned me a fist in the face, Springsteen took matters into his own paws. One of his back ones actually, which burst out of his towelling shroud and lashed at Amber, missing her arm but sending the white plastic phone crashing on to the floor.

Amber kept on smiling, not a tooth out of place, not an eyelid batted.

'The vet will see you straight away. And the name is?'

'Springsteen,' I said, leaning on him in a vain attempt to muffle his growls.

'Like the old rock star?'

'I prefer legendary.'

'My mum really liked him,' she smiled.

'Er ... the vet. Can we see him?'

'Oh, sure. It's a cat, right?'

'Right.'

Just to prove it, Springsteen produced the sort of smell only nervous cats can. The towels were no substitute for a gas mask and personal oxygen supply.

40

'Any idea of the problem?' Amber said, her nose wrinkling but the smile still cemented in place.

'A totally meat diet plus a metabolism designed in the seventh circle of Hell, if you mean the smell,' I said helpfully. 'In more general terms, a psychotic personality which has not mellowed with age. Specifically, a broken leg which, if it's not treated soon, will bring that metabolism and that personality into play full whack, in which case I would fear for everything you hold dear and every living thing in this room.'

In the waiting room behind me, you could have heard a pin drop. Then I heard the big bald guy whispering to his pit bull: 'Come on, Laydee, we'll come back later.'

Amber still held me in her gaze and I couldn't help but stare at her smile. Under fluorescent lighting, I would have needed sunglasses.

'Will you be paying cash, Mr Springsteen?' she said.

'Absolutely.'

'Then let's go through, shall we?'

When we finally emerged, the waiting room was empty apart from Fenella, sitting there good as gold, changed out of her pyjamas, knees together, reading a copy of *Hello!* magazine.

I wasn't surprised she was alone. Once

Amber had lead me into the surgery, the vet's shout of, 'Oh, fuck, not that cat!' must have disconcerted some of the waiting patients.

The following cries of, 'Amber, lock the door!' and 'Just bloody believe me, this one *can* do door handles, it's happened before!' and particularly 'For the love of God, don't let go,' were also probably upsetting if you heard them in isolation coming from somebody, obviously hysterical, to whom you were about to entrust the health and well-being of your pet.

Of course I kept calm throughout – I think blood loss does that to you – and I warned him that trying to inject the anaesthetic through the towels was at best a hit and miss affair. But he had it his way and it wasn't my fault that Springsteen only pretended to be knocked out until the vet was in range.

Fortunately, I hadn't totally let go of him so we managed to isolate part of his rump and the vet got a needle into him. He did get off one parting shot before he went under, though, which meant that Amber refused to speak to me ever again. She would also need a new white smock and probably six or seven showers before she got her squeaky clean confidence back.

The vet, who seemed to have aged rapidly over half-an-hour, took my credit card and swiped it himself – probably twice, to pay for the cleaning bill. Then he gave me my instructions and a cardboard carrying basket for the unconscious Springsteen, which I lined with the few strips of unstained shredded towel I could find. Reluctantly, the vet agreed that I would have to come back to have the plaster caste removed.

'Try an evening surgery,' he said. 'Tuesdays or Thursdays are nice and quiet.'

'Your nights off?' I suggested and he blushed deeply.

Fenella wanted to know why I had asked her to come and meet us.

'To sit with him in the back of Armstrong to reassure him if he comes round,' I told her as we walked out of the surgery.

I didn't like to point out that the carrying basket was made of cardboard and that wouldn't hold him for ten seconds if he did wake up with a headache and a leg in plaster in the back of a cab. At least Fenella might buffer some of the initial impact.

As it was, he was still out when we got back to Stuart Street. Not even Fenella's constant coo-ing and 'poor boy' lullaby woke him up, which was just as well.

I didn't say much on the journey. I was too busy thinking about what the vet had said about the X-rays and how somebody had probably kicked him first and then stamped down on his leg.

I was going to find them, and find them I

would. There couldn't be *that* many women who wore heavy, probably steel-capped, boots and chiffon-coloured tights. Even in Hackney.

From what Springsteen had kept as a trophy, I could narrow it down even further to a woman wearing only half a pair of tights.

Who had a limp.

Chapter Three

'So what woke you the first time?' I asked.

'What? Who? Why? Please, Angel, I'm trying to cook.'

We had set up our observation post in the doorway of Fenella's flat, having decided that it was better to let Springsteen come round in his own good time and when he did, not have the distraction of human targets. I had opened the folding lid of the cat transporter and turned it on its side so he could simply roll out. There was food and fresh water for him and I had put anything breakable out of harm's way, so he had Flat 3 all to himself.

I had borrowed one of Fenella's chairs and parked myself in her doorway so I had an unrestricted view of the landing and the catflap in my door. After five minutes I searched her flat for something to read which wouldn't improve my spiritual being or teach me to be a better vegan and settled on the latest *Harry Potter*. Then I borrowed a large scallop shell from the kitchen (and how was I to know it wasn't an ashtray?) while Fenella nipped round to Mrs Patel's off-licence for a couple of bottles of Cahors, having ascertained that she had nothing in her flat worth drinking that didn't contain elderflower.

At least she offered to make lunch: smoked tofu on toast. I had helpfully suggested that she add red pesto, sliced tomatoes dusted with white pepper, fresh basil and Worcestershire sauce, but she just looked at me like she was the only one who had worked up an appetite that morning and she was going to do it her way. Pah! Call that cheese on toast?

'You said Springsteen's howling had woken you up *the second time*,' I explained. 'When I arrived, that's what you said. What woke you up the *first* time?'

She paused to think, one hand on the grill pan handle, oblivious to the wisps of blue smoke curling around her lobster-shaped oven glove.

'That would have been Mr Nassim,' she said; then she nodded to herself to confirm it.

'Toast's burning,' I said.

I refilled my glass and resumed my seat in the doorway, reassuring myself that there was no way he could get out of the catflap, across the landing and down the stairs before I could seal myself back in Fenella's flat. Not on three legs he couldn't. Surely not.

'So what did Nassim want?' I shouted kitchenwards.

Nassim Nassim is our esteemed landlord and it's not that he has a name so nice you have to say it twice, it's just that no one can pronounce his family name. When he first introduced himself, he knew it would be a problem and said 'Just call me Nassim Nassim', so we did.

'I'm not sure. Lisabeth talked to him just before she went to work but I don't think she got much sense out of him,' Fenella called back over a clattering of plates. 'You know what Nassim's like.'

'Indeed I do and I won't have a word said against him.'

I meant it. The old boy might be getting on nowadays and suffering from more than his fair share of 'senior moments' inbetween power naps, but he'd always done right by me. After a small favour I had done for his great-niece years ago, he had pegged the rent on my flat and turned one blind eye on my incorporation of a catflap and another on the No Pets rule. After all those years I was paying maybe a fifth of the rent he could realistically get these days and which the other tenants were undoubtedly paying. He was Top Man was Nassim Nassim.

'He had somebody with him from the Council,' Fenella was saying, 'from the Rating Office. Is that right? A Rating Evaluation Officer or something. Does that sound right?'

'The senile old fart!' I shouted. 'Doesn't he know better than to let a Valuation Officer in here?'

'I don't know about that.' Fenella handed me a plate boasting two blackened squares with white circles on them. They looked like sides of a dice. 'Lisabeth said she was really really nice.'

'*She?*'

'There's no need to shout.'

In a fit of pique she made to take the plate back. I should have let her.

'Did she go in my flat?'

'I don't know, I never saw her. Look, Angel, just *hear my lips*: I never saw the person. I never saw Mr Nassim. I was in bed, trying to sleep.'

I kept a straight face at the 'hear my lips' – just as she had – and pretended I was enjoying the mildly flavoured rubber charcoal she had served up.

'Working late nights again?'

She nodded.

'Don't those Chat Line phone calls wake Lisabeth?'

I knew that Fenella and her posh voice had progressed from cold caller to call centre sub-station, to chat line hostess without actually realizing what was going on. She just thought it faintly surprising that she got paid for talking to complete strangers about her school days and especially what she wore for PE lessons. She didn't seem to have noticed anything odd about most of the calls coming late at night after the pubs had chucked out either. I had seen three mobiles on recharging stands in the living room. Business must be good.

'Oh, no, I set the phones to silent ringing,' she said calmly, pleased that I was taking an interest in her career. 'And anyway, it's all text these days.'

'Text?' I said warily.

'Text messages. I'm in three different TCRs – Text Chat Rooms – a night now. My job is to keep the text flowing, though honestly, some of the spelling! And they use numbers for words, you know. Like four – the number four – stands for "for" as in f-o-r. And the number two is "to". It takes a bit of puzzling out sometimes.'

'Have six and nine come up in any combination?'

'Several times, now you mention it, but this is just an experiment. If it proves popular I could get a computer and go on line as they say.'

'Has anyone suggested using a webcam on you?'

'What's a webcam?'

'Never mind. Great tofu by the way,' I lied, not realizing you could actually spoil tofu. 'So you didn't see this Valuation Officer, then?'

'No, I told you. Lisabeth dealt with her. Why don't you ask Mr Nassim? He was the one showing her around.'

'Good idea. Well done that girl.'

'You can stay here if you like and use one of the phones. I've got to do the shopping but Lisabeth'll be home soon. If you want to stay until Springsteen wakes up. I think it's sort of sweet of you.'

It was, now I thought of it, but I couldn't face explaining my presence to Lisabeth.

'Thanks, but I'll wait on the stairs so I can be nearer to him in case he needs me. Pass the rest of the wine, would you?'

I was halfway through the second bottle of Cahors and had finally remembered how to sprawl comfortably on stairs (how quickly one forgets one's youth), when Inverness Doogie showed up.

I heard him long before I saw him as he must have had eight or nine attempts at putting his key in the lock of the front door. Then the door swung inwards and he stood there swaying, trying to get the key out of the lock. I wasn't sure this was a good idea as it seemed to be the only thing holding him upright. He had a leather jacket over his white chef's coat and chequerboard trousers and in his left hand he clutched a bottle of The Macallan by the neck. From his waist dangled a striped tea towel the way chefs wear them through their belt to wipe things with. Doogie's was noticeable as it appeared to have caught fire quite recently.

He succeeded in yanking out his key, rocked back on his heels then weaved two steps into the house and leaned on the payphone on the wall for support, his eyes widening as he focused on me lying on the stairs, wine glass in one hand, book in the other.

'Honey, I'm home!' he slurred loudly. 'What the feck are you doing here? Amy come to her senses an' thrown you out then?'

'No, she hasn't,' I said snottily. 'Though I haven't seen her since breakfast so she might have. How's yourself, Doogie? Hard day at the office?'

He climbed the stairs carefully and sat down a couple of steps below me, proffering the bottle of Macallan.

'I have curtailed my shift for the day,' he said haughtily, 'due to an industrial accident. This evening's diners will simply have to get by on whatever scraps my understudies can gather together.'

'Been cooking one of your specials again?'

'Aye. American guy. Comes in with his missus, eyeballs the place and demands to meet the chef, so they wheel me out front of house. The Yank hears my accent and says "You're Scotch" like I'd be fookin' surprised.

51

Then he asks if I can do him a genuine Aberdeen Angus steak, a big, thick one just like him. An' I says 'course I can and I can leave the horns on but would he like it the *reel* Scottish way?'

'Let me guess – that involves buying a whole bottle of single malt, right?'

'Ab-so-fucking-lutely, which puts it on the wee-bit pricey side. But money's nay object to this chuckleheed an' he puts doon his Gold Amex card and says to bring it on.'

'And this would be a steak flamed in malt whisky, something like that?'

He wagged the bottle at me like an admonishing finger.

'A steak *marinated* in malt whisky, broiled in malt whisky then served at the table *into*, and this is the clever bit, a plate of burning malt whisky. I think I'll call it Steak Sea Of Fire when I get ma own restaurant.'

'Check your insurance policy first,' I advised. 'And to drink with it...?'

'Malt whisky,' we both said together.

'But,' said Doogie, smiling, 'the really clever bit was keeping his missus happy while he was tucking in.'

'You got her drunk as well?'

'Nay, no. She was on the mineral water. I intoxicated her simply with the force of ma personality, a free run at the sweet trolley and a few tales of the Highland Clearances and life back in Bonnie Scotland. Naturally, she was "Scotch-Irish" so she lapped it up. Did you know there were more Caledonian societies in North Carolina than there are in Caledonia?'

He raised the arm holding the bottle to make his point and lost his grip on the stair carpet, bumping down three steps on his elbow but managing to keep the bottle upright.

'So how was your day?' he asked from below, straining to crawl up until he was level with me, putting more effort into doing so than the average mountaineer topping out K2.

'Been down the vet's. Somebody kicked the shit out of Springsteen.'

What little natural colour there was under the alcohol glow drained from his face.

'Shite-on-a-fookin'-stick, yer kidding me?'

'No way, Braveheart. He's in the flat coming out from under the anaesthetic. I thought it safer to stay out here until he's regained his sunny disposition.'

Doogie shook his head slowly at the awfulness of the world and began to open the bottle of malt as I emptied my glass of wine.

'What did you do with the body?'

'I just told you. He's in the flat, coming round.'

'No,' he said seriously, 'I meant the other feller.'

We were on the last of the whisky.

'Oh, there will be pain, Doogie. When I find whoever did this, I can assure you there will be pain. Not the nice spanking sort of pain but the sharp metal objects inserted and then twisted sort of pain...'

'Save me a piece of the scumbag, though, won't you?'

'I didn't know you cared,' I said, then added: 'About Springsteen.'

'Och, I dinna care aboot him personally.'

'You just don't like cruelty to animals as a whole. Is that it?'

I suspected my words were slurring now, but I wasn't really listening.

'Ahm a chef, yer bampot!' Doogie roared as if it was the funniest thing he'd ever said. 'I kill and cook anything that moves. It's ma job.'

'I've seen you deep-fry Mars bars in batter,' I said because it seemed like an important debating point. 'And Maltesers too. What harm did they ever do you?'

'The skill is in knowing when to pick them ... that point of pure ripeness. Actually, now you mention it, I'm trying out a new dessert at the moment. It's quick-fried Mars bar ice-creams. That'll get the food critics sitting up and taking notice.'

'You're not wrong there, Doogie. But I've had fried icecream ... in a Mexican restaurant.'

'They've pinched ma idea already? Where was this?'

'In Mexico.'

'Oh.'

There was a lull in the conversation whilst I tried to remember what it was about.

'So why are you so upset about Springsteen if you don't really like him?'

Doogie took a deep breath.

'It's another legend broken on the wheel of bitter experience,' he said, shaking his head. 'Who'd have thought that wee furry ball of malevolence would get bested in a scrap? It's the unthinkable but it's happened. Another wee spark of magic has gone out of the world.'

'Doogie, that's almost poetic.'

'Aye, I think I'm getting to the poetic stage. Shall I get another bottle?'

'I think you'd better, before I begin to believe that this new you really is you. If you see what I mean.'

'Whisssht! Listen!'

He put a finger to his lips with a surprising degree of accuracy and we both bent our heads and stretched our necks to look along the landing towards the door of Flat 3. From inside, beyond the catflap, came the sound of tearing cardboard. Then silence.

'He's out!' I hissed and instinctively we both lowered ourselves down the stairs in a reverse commando crawl until only our eyes were level with the landing.

It was at that point the front door opened and from below and behind us a voice growled:

'Just what are you two playing at?'

'Hello, Lisabeth,' I said, turning my head so I could flash my best smile at her. 'Had a good day at the ... wherever?'

She was wearing a green short-sleeved sweatshirt and green knee-length canvas shorts with turn-ups and huge cargo pockets bulging with unidentifiable stuff, giving her thighs a stereo effect which would have had most women screaming for a long frock or liposuction. She had lime green socks and khaki desert boots on the ends of her thick ankles.

'How yer doin', hen?' Doogie grinned inanely.

'Well?'

Lisabeth put her hands on her hips – they didn't have far to travel – and stared us out. Obviously, those self-assertiveness classes were paying off.

'We're caring for sick animals,' I said. 'Ask Fenella if you don't believe us.'

'I don't, but unfortunately Fenella always has,' she said testily as she clumped her way up the stairs to her flat door. 'Are you two just going to lie there and make the place untidy all evening?'

As she put her key in the lock she turned

her shoulder towards us and we both craned our necks to see what was printed on the back of her sweatshirt. It was a slogan in white saying: AROMATHERAPY – THE FINAL FRONTIER.

Doogie and I looked at each other and choked back the giggles.

'I hope Miranda doesn't come home and catch you like that,' Lisabeth was saying, turning back to us. 'You know how 'Randa's always saying your behaviour has improved so much since Angel moved out...'

'She says *what?*' I mouthed at Doogie, who had the good grace to blush.

'...and you hardly ever play music after midnight any more, not to mention...'

She trailed off suddenly, her gaze fixed on something above us and to the right of the stairs.

Springsteen was emerging from the catflap, fluffed-up tail and rear-end first, scrabbling against the door with his back legs so he could haul his plastered front leg over the lip of the flap. Slowly the injured leg appeared and he took a tentative step backwards and arched his back as if he could shake off the offending tube of plaster. Of course he couldn't, but he found he couldn't turn either – or some sixth sense told him he would overbalance if he did – so he continued backwards along the landing, the plastered leg held up and in front of him at an angle of forty-five degrees.

Doogie and I cowered below the top step as he approached, the tail three times its normal size, swishing silently from side to side. When he was level with us he swivelled around and sat down within inches of our foreheads. Then he howled at each of us in turn, so close we could smell his breath and I knew he had found the tin of salmon I had made Fenella open for him.

Then it seemed he caught sight of Lisabeth for the first time and he fixed her with a stare and let out a long, low growl of pure menace.

'You've trained him to do that!' squealed Lisabeth behind us and then we heard her flat door slam.

Springsteen looked down imperiously, the plaster cast on his front leg still jutting up and out at forty-five degrees.

'*What?*' I said helplessly, shrugging my shoulders at Doogie.

He just started giggling and tried to stand up.

'Look at him,' he spluttered, pointing at Springsteen. 'He's giving her a *Seig Heil!*'

Doogie flung his arm up in a return salute, slipped off the edge of the stair he was on and stumbled down three more before he grabbed the banister, collapsing against it in hysterics.

Springsteen held my gaze for a few

seconds more then lifted himself up and began to walk backwards on his three good legs until his arse hit the catflap and he pulled himself through it with as much dignity as he good muster, the plastered paw being the last thing to disappear.

Only when the catflap flapped behind him did I dare laugh.

Doogie said it would be fine to go to his flat for a while. It would give Springsteen time to settle down to having only three working legs, we could have a bite to eat and a drink or two and I could call a cab from there as I certainly wasn't driving mine home in my condition, was I? And no way would Miranda mind if she came home and found me there. *Me casa, su casa* ... old and distinguished friend ... matter of life and death ... sick animals in crisis ... anyway, who wore the *troosers* in this flat?

'Oh, my God, what's he doing here?'

'He's not stopping, luv, just a flying visit.'

Thanks, Doogie.

'My, but you're looking fit, Miranda. You've lost a bit of weight, haven't you? Don't you dare tell me you haven't. I notice these things,' I said, trying to rescue the situation.

'You lookin' at my bird?' Doogie growled automatically.

'You bet I am; every chance I get. She

59

never gives me the time of day though.'

All this nonsense kept both of them happy, though in fact I was looking at Miranda as she smoothed her hands over her hips as if searching for the missing pounds I had implied she had lost. She was wearing what I suspected was her one and only two-piece suit in a grey and charcoal check – which meant she had been somewhere official today – black patent low-heeled shoes and tan-coloured tights. They weren't ripped and when she kicked off her shoes in Doogie's general direction, I noticed she wasn't limping either.

'So why are you home in time to cook dinner, then?' she asked Doogie as she collapsed into a creaking wicker armchair.

(Their taste in furniture was eclectic to say the least and I suspected Doogie acquired a lot of their pieces from bankrupt restaurant sales.)

'Actually, ma sweet, we've eaten but I'll gladly whip something up for you.'

Doogie said all this whilst holding his breath so that the words came out roughly in the right order and the whisky fumes didn't strip the paint off the walls, and he exhaled slowly all the way to the kitchen. Miranda watched him go, her brown eyes no more than slits, then she turned to me with her head on one side.

'And what *are* you doing here, Angel? Has

Amy finally thrown you out?'

'No, she hasn't! Why does everyone assume that?'

'Do they? That's interesting. Why do you suppose that is?'

'Oh per-leese!' I said in a tone which meant she wouldn't argue as I helped myself to some more of Doogie's whisky. 'Do you want to hear my story of how we had to rush Springsteen to Cat Casualty or not?'

By the time I had told her, Doogie had presented her with a glass of white wine and a perfect smoked salmon souffle. She put the wine on the floor and balanced her plate on her knee, waiting regally for Doogie to give her a fork (which he polished with a white cloth) and to crack black pepper for her through a large wooden mill.

'I got beans on toast,' I said.

'You don't have to sleep with him,' said Miranda.

That seemed fair, and anyway, Doogie had said that beans on toast was what all professional chefs ate when they got home and put their feet up.

'So you suspect this Valuation Officer who came round with Mr Nassim this morning?' she said between mouthfuls.

'Had to be somebody in the house,' I said, 'as he couldn't have got back inside the flat with that injury, probably couldn't have got up the stairs, so more than likely it happened in the flat. You haven't been in the flat, the naked chef here hasn't. Mr Goodson downstairs just wouldn't. Fenella was the one who found him. Who else is there?'

'Lisabeth?'

Doogie and I exchanged looks.

'No way, pet,' Doogie said. 'She'd defenestrate Angel soon as look at him, but not a dumb animal.'

'Easy enough mistake to make,' she muttered under her breath. 'But I think you're right, Angel.'

'I am?'

'Right to be suspicious. I mean, where do you think I've been all day, dressed like this?'

I bit back the smart remark that it couldn't have been hanging around Shepherd's Market, even on a slow day.

'Been for a job interview?'

Miranda worked for a local newspaper which was part of a larger group and was always on the look-out for promotion to the bigger circulation titles.

'No, guess again.'

'You've been in court?'

The idea of Miranda as a court reporter was pretty scary. I would have 'fessed up to anything if I'd seen her glaring into the dock at me from the press benches.

'No such fun. Think really, really *dull*.'

'Annual General Meeting of the Hackney

and Islington Civil War Re-Enactment Society?'

'Now you're being silly. I was covering the Council.'

Doogie tried to look proud of her. I must have just looked blank.

'And...?'

'I'm the local council specialist and a stringer for Greater London-related matters,' she said.

Doogie still tried to look smug but I knew he couldn't keep it up for long.

'Which means...?' I offered.

'Which means I know about rates and precepts and business rates and exemptions and all that shit,' she snapped. 'And I can tell you there's no rating revaluation going on in Hackney at the moment. Too many votes at stake to tell people they have to pay more taxes. So your phantom Valuation Officer was...'

'Totally bogus,' I completed.

Doogie waved his glass at me.

'Och, yer wee dipstick. Has she not been trying to tell you that for the last five minutes?'

Miranda insisted that Doogie made me a pot of coffee and I agreed to drink it only if she would go downstairs and ask Lisabeth about our suspicious visitor. As soon as she was gone I laced my Golden Jubilee souvenir mug with more of Doogie's Scotch. Doogie didn't mind. He held the same view that I do: coffee doesn't sober you up, it just makes you a more awake drunk.

When she returned I asked her if she'd thought to look in on Springsteen on her way back upstairs. She gave me a killer look and said no, she hadn't – but Fenella had.

'And she's OK?' I asked, genuinely concerned.

'She got out alive, if that's what you mean,' said Miranda, 'and that unwholesome beast of yours is resting comfortably, so she says.'

I secretly thought Fenella was getting into this caring business and with a bit of training could be pinning daily bulletins to the front door.

'And what did Lisabeth have to say?'

'Not much. She said she only ran into the woman on the stairs as Mr Nassim was bringing her in. About my height, mousy blonde shoulder-length hair pulled back off the face with a wide purple scrunchy band, very light blonde eyebrows, blue eyes, hardly any make-up but bright red fingernails. No rings. Wore a Burberry raincoat over a short skirt and a polo-neck ribbed sweater. As Lisabeth said, she only got a glimpse. Hardly noticed her at all.'

'Did she get her dress size?'

'Twelve,' said Miranda without batting an eyelid.

Doogie let out a low, quiet whistle. He was impressed.

'But did she get a name?'

'Give the girl a break, we're talking complete strangers here, passing on the stairs for maybe a few seconds.'

Doogie and I stared at her all innocent, though I knew Doogie wouldn't have the nerve to say it, so I had to.

'And your point there is ... what?'

'Isn't it time we got you a cab?' she said through gritted teeth.

'He's already got one!' Doogie giggled.

'I'll deal with you later,' Miranda said to him and he cowered in his chair.

This, the man who listed 'football hooliganism' on his CV – the man whose favourite line at parties when someone was between him and the bar was 'Pick a window, you're leaving' – actually cowered.

Miranda suddenly had a mobile phone in her hand, as if she'd had it up her sleeve like a derringer on a spring clip.

'Any preference in mini-cab companies?' she asked, waving the phone at me so I knew what it was. I might have trouble focusing but I knew a Nokia at six feet when it was pointed at me.

'Wait a minute, you've got to ring Mr Nassim first,' I said reasonably.

'I have?'

'To ask him if this Phantom Menace had a

name or any credentials,' I explained patiently.

'Why me?' she argued.

'Because you're holding the phone, you're a valued tenant of his, you have the Power of the Press behind you, it's your job to ask questions and you'd like to know if the Council is up to something you don't know about, you'd like to know if he showed her into this flat while you were both out, and if you do it I'll get out of your hair.'

'The last one's the clincher,' she said.

It was the nearest I'd ever heard her get to a joke.

Of course I had to stand at her shoulder and listen in just to make sure she asked the right questions, though she deliberately turned her head away from me and preferred to repeat Nassim's answers out loud.

'So you *didn't* show her into our flat, I see,' she said loudly, giving a thumbs up to Doogie, who tried to look suitably relieved though I don't know what those two were worried about. They didn't have a cat.

'Just Flat 3? That was the only one she wanted to get into. I see.'

Well, I don't, I pantomimed, standing in front of her. *Why?*

'Because you might be eligible for a reduced rate rebate on rented property not occupied throughout the year? Oh, yes, of course.'

As she said this she put a finger to the side of her head and made a turning, crazy-man motion. I put a hand down below my waist and made the sort of gesture monkeys do whenever you take your parents to the zoo. Miranda looked away, pretending not to know what I meant. Then again, she was Welsh so she might not know.

'And she definitely did come from the Council? Oh, I see, she had a card. Yes please.'

She covered the phone with her hand.

'He's gone to get her business card. A rate *rebate?* From *this* Council? Is Nassim dopey?'

'I think the word is *bhudu* – it means "slow" – but don't call him that to his face,' I said, just to show that I could insult people in several languages.

Then she was back in listening mode.

'Alison George, I see. And is there a phone number? Yes, that's the number of the Council. No, I was just curious. We've been doing a series in the paper on fake gas meter readers and the like, conning their way into people's houses... No, of course nothing like that happened here...'

Ask if he left her alone at any time, I mouthed, pointing at the phone.

'And anyway,' she went on fluently, 'you

were with her all the time, weren't you? I bet you never let her out of your sight, did you? Not even for a few seconds...'

Miranda made eye contact with me.

'Except when the phone rang downstairs? I see. Yes, wrong numbers are a pain, aren't they?'

I shook my head and drew a finger across my throat to end it.

'Actually, I don't think we really need that house phone any more. We all have mobiles these days, even Mr Goodson in Flat One. It only gets used when somebody has to take a message for Angel and he's never here these days... No, of course I will... I'll give him your love next time I see him... Very well, then, not your love, just your best wishes... OK, I'll just wave to him. 'Bye.'

If I hadn't known better I would have said she had enjoyed that. And she had another surprise for me.

'Alison George, my arse,' she said as she closed her phone.

'What?' I pleaded.

'There is an Alison George works for the Council, I know her. She happens to be the Tourist Development Officer and she's on six months' maternity leave just at the moment. You know what that means.'

I slumped into a chair and the blood must have drained from my face such was Miranda's look of near concern.

68

'Angel? Are you all right?'

'Yes, I suppose so,' I said quietly, humbly holding out my glass towards Doogie's Scotch. 'It's just a bit of a shock, that's all.'

'I know,' she said soothingly. 'It's an invasion of your private space. An intrusion. It's like finding out that...'

'No, no,' I said, aiming the now full again glass to my lips. 'It's finding out that Hackney has a Tourist Development Officer. Bloody hell, what will they think of next?'

Chapter Four

'Of course I'm not paranoid! I've every right to be suspicious!'

If it hadn't been for the muscle-relaxant qualities of alcohol, I could have got quite worked up about the suggestion.

'An unidentified, totally bogus female wangles her way into our house by conning the landlord – who must have been enjoying what they call "a senior moment" these days to fall for it – and once in, doesn't nick anything, just makes sure she's alone in *my* flat and then kicks seven kinds of crap out of my flat-mate. Cause for concern or what? I think at least a severe furrowing of the brow is called for here.'

'Was he badly hurt, your flat-mate?'

'You should see the bill from the vet.'

'The vet?'

'Well, he is a cat. But the point is my personal space has been invaded and with malice aforethought. She only looked at my flat – wasn't interested in any of the others. And she put a bit of thought into it. Once in, courtesy of our senile landlord, she waits for him to trek downstairs to answer the phone and so she'd be all alone in there...'

'How did she know the phone would ring right on cue?'

'Easy-peezey. She's got her mobile in her pocket with the number programmed in and she just presses the Call button. Keeps it ringing until he gets to the phone then hangs up as he answers. She's left on her own.'

'She wouldn't have long, though, would she?'

'Well, no,' I admitted. 'But long enough.'

'Long enough to do what?'

Now that, unfortunately, was a good question.

'To snoop, to pry, to invade my privacy. She'd gone to a fair bit of trouble to get into my flat, if only for a few minutes.'

'How did she know the phone was downstairs?'

'What?'

'How did she know,' he said patiently, 'the phone was a flight of stairs away?'

'Fucked if I know, point is she did.'

Damn. Another good question.

'Sounds a bit thin.'

'A bit *thin?* Is that all you've got to say?'

'No, mate, I can say we're 'ere and that'll be fourteen pounds, please.'

'Fourteen quid?'

'Hackney to Hampstead, this time of night, guv... A black cab would have cost you more.'

But the advice would have been better.

I hoped none of the neighbours saw me arrive home by minicab.

I couldn't have cared less if they saw me weaving towards the house swaying, ever so slightly, in the breeze which strangely did not seem to be affecting the trees or flowers in the local gardens. But a mini-cab: that was letting the side down. When I first started parking Armstrong in the driveway, some of the neighbours probably tried to get a rate rebate. Not that I gave a hoot. I didn't know any of them and was happy to avoid the rota of Christmas parties we were no longer invited to. Well, not since that first one.

It was odds-on I hadn't been seen anyway. It would take a bomb going off in the street to arouse any interest once they had settled down behind their burglar alarms and closed circuit TV cameras for the evening, even though all the latest surveys showed that good street lighting was more of a deterrent to people on the naughty than CCTV. In fact in some boroughs, street crime had gone *up* when CCTV was installed.

Which thankfully made me remember our burglar alarm, which had been repaired at vast expense after Anthony Keith Flowers – the ex-Mr Amy – had nobbled it with ridiculous ease when he broke into the house and garage and made off with Amy's BMW. (I was having as much success with the house's insurance company about that as I was about the car, my first claim form having been returned as 'frivolous'. Bloody cheek.)

Whilst one part of my brain was trying to remember the combination as I struggled with the door, another part – the part which was prone to wandering to a land where the sun and women were warm but the beer and the music stayed cool and all were free – was thinking that Amy wouldn't have set the alarm if she was home and I wasn't. Especially not given my track record of setting the thing off by accident.

Therefore, I was home first which meant I didn't have to be quiet or creep into one of the spare bedrooms and maybe there was time for a nightcap or I could get into bed and pretend I'd had an early night after a pretty stressful day.

It never occurred to me that Amy had come home and gone out again.

Not until the next morning.

And it looked as if she'd gone for a while.

I didn't twig that right away, of course. It was only when I checked the shoe racks at the bottom of Amy's wardrobe and I realized that her Manolo Blahnik flat red sandals, her Sigerson Merrison green high heels and the lime green strappy sandals by Gina, along with her favourite Jimmy Choo's had all gone, that I knew something strange was going on.

Even later, I checked the garage to discover the Freelander had gone which sort of confirmed things. I suppose I should have looked there first, but I've never been hot on garages. You don't have to be if you drive a London cab, the kerb is your garage.

A month before, when Anthony Keith Flowers had burgled the house he had also helped himself to Amy's new BMW and I hadn't thought to check the garage then, so I didn't actually get to report it stolen until I had hit it with a bulldozer. Over such technicalities lawyers can argue for years.

Once I had the immediate priorities out of the way – orange juice, coffee, shower, breakfast and a couple of games of Free Cell on the computer with some downloaded Ry Cooder on the speakers – I began to wonder where Amy was.

I could have phoned her, of course, though that would have put me on the back foot immediately.

Where were you last night?

Where were you all day yesterday when I was trying to get hold of you to tell you I had to fly to Tierra del Fuego at really short notice?

I was ministering to an injured cat.

Yeah, right.

No. Too weak.

So I did what any caring, sharing partner would do: I hacked into her computer. Or, rather, took a deep breath and tried to.

I've seen computer boffs who carry cans of compressed air in specially made holsters on their belt and when all else fails, they will do a quick draw and shoot a couple of blasts into the keyboard. In my opinion, that's simply not punishment enough – in fact I think the computers quite like it. My instinct, when I lose my temper, is to go for a fast southpaw combination of feint then slap to the monitor followed by the heel of the hand on the processor bit which goes beep when you turn it on.

Actually, I have learned that one beep when you switch on is good. Three rapid beeps means trouble ahead, something's about to go wrong. When that has happened in the past it hasn't been unknown for a pint of Guinness to end up in the keyboard. But I hadn't lost my temper just yet and so I stuck to my Rule of Life Number 106: never let machinery know you're in a hurry.

Up came the screen saver, a favourite download of Amy's of the Mr Burns character from *The Simpsons* saying 'Excellent', and then the icon thingies started to appear to the theme from *Mission Impossible*.

And then it stopped burping and bleeping

and just hummed at me, daring me to make the next move.

I stared back at it. I knew what some of the icons meant – the one for the internet, the one for emails and the most important one, for GAMES – but what the hell was a WinZip? Who needed an acrobatic reader or a comet cursor and why was there a picture of Harry Potter made out of Lego building bricks? Of the others, at least twenty, most were art or design programmes but I suspected the really interesting ones were the ones that looked like briefcases and they would be password-protected, wouldn't they? Even the one marked DIARY in big flashing letters.

I clicked on it and it opened immediately.

This computer-hacking business was very over-rated.

There was only one entry for today, Wednesday, in Amy's spread-sheet diary. In fact it was the only entry for the whole week and it simply said: WELFASH FINALS – CARD U.

I was no wiser. It meant absolutely nothing to me, I couldn't remember Amy having said anything which remotely resembled it and no matter how long I stared at the screen, it wouldn't tell me anything else.

There was something it could tell me, though.

I shrank the Diary window and inserted a floppy disk. I know, I know, I was just working out how to use them as they became obsolete, but I firmly believe that they will make a comeback, like vinyl did, or eight-track car stereos or Betamax videos. Well, OK, not those last two.

On the disk I opened up a new spreadsheet, called it DIARY and typed in a couple of boxes of gobbledygook then tried to transfer it to Amy's version. The usual window came up asking if I wanted my DIARY to replace the version last modified...

The day before at 11:32:08, just about the time I was talking to Duncan the Drunken, give or take eight seconds, and I thought she was at her office.

Of course I couldn't be sure that was when she'd put in the reference for today, though the computer would probably tell me if I asked it the right way. Approached in the right way, anyone will tell you anything and it will usually be true. (Rule of Life Number 83.) But that only applies to people. You can't make eye contact with – or buy a drink – for a computer, so that put me at a disadvantage.

(The only other thing I know about computers is to put a fake address in your email address book, say: a.aardvark @ story-ofo.com. You are never going to use it but if some kind person sends you a virus developed by some smartarse in a California computer school, then you'll know you've got it when your server flashes up the address as undeliverable.)

So if I couldn't get any joy out of one robotic, mechanical, soulless entity, then I would have to try another and ring her secretary.

Amazingly I had never actually met Debbie Diamond, even though she had worked for Amy for over two years. Then again, I rarely get into Amy's office above a flash shopping piazza on Oxford Street. In fact I had never been *in* it, come to think of it. I was usually restricted to the sitting outside in Armstrong with the engine running role, waiting to ferry her home or to the City airport or to a fashion bash somewhere. I didn't mind that. Me and offices have never got on; for a start they're open really weird hours, like all day – as if you didn't have other stuff to do.

I had spoken to the Dreaded Debbie many a time, on the phone or over the intercom from the Security Desk downstairs which served both the shops in the Piazza and the office suites above them, and all I had heard backed up the mental picture Amy had painted of her. Tough, bulldog stubborn, fiercely loyal, lived with her invalid mother in Plumstead and she wore cardigans. Not

78

only that, but she wore cardigans with tissues pushed up the sleeve. Amy had repeatedly said she was lucky to have found Debbie D. as they didn't make them like her any more.

I knew the type and I knew I wouldn't get anything out of her over the phone. I decided on a plan: I would call in and see her. A social call. Surprise her, maybe with some flowers. That would even get me past Security as no one questions a taxi driver delivering flowers to a lady in an office.

Yes, that was a plan.

All I had to do now was remember where I'd left my taxi.

I tubed it via the Northern Line to The Angel and then hopped on a number 48 bus into Hackney and it seemed to take nearly forever, but I wasn't going to pay for another minicab. It's not the quids, it's the principle.

I lurked around the corner of Stuart Street debating with myself as to whether I should pop in to number Nine and see how Springsteen was doing. If Fenella was there, she'd have a go at me for not bringing him some smoked salmon or grapes or something. Miranda would have a go at me for leading Doogie astray yesterday; Doogie would offer me the hair of the dog; Lisabeth would just have a go at me because that was what she did best. The voices in my head decided by a clear 5–2 majority to make a run for it.

By the time I had rescued Armstrong and got up to the West End, pausing only to buy an impressive bouquet of roses at wholesale prices from a corner shop florists I knew near King's Cross and a cheap one-trip snappy camera from the chemist's next door, it was after four o'clock. I hardly knew where the day had gone.

On Oxford Street I parked confidently on the double yellow lines outside the shopping piazza so the guys in the Security booth could get a clear view of me. Since Oxford Street is supposedly a no-go area for civilian drivers – in theory only buses and taxis allowed during the day – I wasn't too worried about traffic wardens, but it was the summer and that meant zillions of tourists who didn't know the rules and it wasn't uncommon to see lost Belgian-registered cars or don't-care-anyway Italian ones chugging along behind the buses at an average speed of about seven miles per hour, which is slower than the Hansom Cabs did it in Sherlock Holmes' day.

Unless it was a really slow day the wardens didn't bother with taxis and I was confident I looked the part. Not only did I have an authentic black London cab, but I had found an old leather waistcoat, smelling accurately of old diesel, in Armstrong's boot and had slipped it over my crisp white T-shirt, the one with the legend: *My Other T-Shirt's A Paul Smith*.

Armed with the bunch of roses and the camera I marched into the piazza straight up to the Security office and rapped on the Enquiries window with my knuckles. An elderly white guy with tinted glasses and a fast-food belly hauled himself out of a swivel chair and wheezed his way over to pull the window up about six inches. The effort seemed to drain him.

'Yes?'

'Flowers for a Miss D. Diamond, second floor,' I said, trying to outdo him in sounding bored.

'Pass 'em through.'

'Personal delivery.'

'Is she expecting them?'

'Do I look psychic?'

'Then give them over. I'll see she gets them.'

'Got to take your picture, then,' I said, holding up the snappy camera.

'You pullin' my plonker?'

'You wish. Listen, mate, I get the flowers and the camera given to me by a punter with more money than sense. Take the flowers, take a picture of happy lady getting nice surprise. Take camera back to punter, get return fare. That plus the tip'll do me for the last job of the day. I am well sick of fucking tourists who 'ave no idea where they've just been let alone where they want to go and then they bitch about the fare, though the fuckin' meter's right in front of them, then they try an' pay in fucking Euros like I look like a bank in Strasbourg...'

That was enough.

'Yeah, yeah, tell me about it. Like I've not had to get a fuckin' interpreter in because some Japanese newspaper's said Stella McCartney's opening a boutique in 'ere today. You should've seen the bleedin' queues this lunchtime. Anyway, I don't give a shit, I'm off in half-an-hour. Second floor, mate, lift at the top of the escalator then ask at Reception.'

Sometimes it was a shame to take the money, I thought as I stood on the escalator. I really would have to have a word with Amy about how easy it was to get into her office building even though I knew she'd say you just couldn't get the staff these days.

All I had to do now, I thought as I got in the lift and pressed 2, was worm my way into the confidence of the Dreaded Debbie: the only pit bull known to do Tee-line shorthand and audio-typing according to Amy.

As it turned out, that proved quite easy as well.

The lift doors hissed open and I had taken

no more than two steps out on to the carpeted floor when a female voice said:

'It is you, Angel, isn't it? Thank God you're here.'

I needn't have wasted the money on the flowers.

I drove Debbie Diamond round to the Portman Hotel for afternoon tea. I knew the hotel from the days when it did Sunday brunch with live jazz and had even played there a couple of times. But that was a while back. Surely they wouldn't still remember the incident with the vintage claret.

I resolved to have a serious word with Amy – when I found out where she was – about her deliberately misleading me every which way about Debbie. She didn't strike me in any way as a battleaxe, a Rottweiler, a frump, a career spinster ('So afraid of marriage we call her The Ring Wraith'), someone for whom nightlife meant a long chat with a timeshare salesman from a call centre, or indeed a woman who had to wear a bra designed by Fisher-Price. She wasn't even halfway to her mid-forties and I call five-foot-one petite, not dwarfish. I quite liked the big round glasses and didn't think they made her look like a constipated owl at all and I saw no reason to call the fashion police over the stonewashed denim jacket she was wearing with the very short suede skirt which showed an awful lot (pro-portionately speaking) of very shapely, well tanned bare leg which ended in multi-coloured high heeled Cacharel sandals with white flowers on the straps.

On reflection, maybe I wouldn't go into so much detail for Amy.

'Yesterday it was the police, first thing in the morning when I turned up for work, as if that wasn't bad enough,' she started after her first sip of tea.

I nodded sympathetically, hiding my smug expression behind a bone china teacup.

Well, I mean: a few roses, a free ride in a taxi, a comfy armchair in nice surroundings and a cup of Orange Pekoe and she was answering questions I hadn't even asked yet. God knew what would happen when the Madeira cake arrived – she'd probably 'fess up to one or all of the recent Heathrow robberies.

'They were in with Amy for hours. *Taking statements*, they said.'

'And this would, of course, be about...'

I didn't make it a question, just trailed off with a wave of the teacup and quite a bit of sage nodding.

'Yes, you're right,' she said, nodding with me. 'Keith Flowers – what an awful person to stalk Amy like that. And you had no idea, did you?'

She put down her cup and saucer and

reached a hand out, placing it on my knee. I saw no reason to do anything but let it stay there but out of the corner of my eye I saw a pair of waiters talking together out of the sides of their mouths whilst staring at Debbie. They were probably betting how long it would be before I asked if they rented rooms by the hour. I was going to disappoint them. I knew already that they didn't.

'It did come as something of a shock,' I said with just the right touch of pathos.

'She was only trying to protect you, I think.' She gave a shudder and her grip on my knee tightened. 'God, what an odious human being. He kept after her even though she took out that Restraining Order. How on earth did a creep like that ever get to meet Amy?'

Probably at their wedding, I thought but I said nothing. It was clear to me that Debbie didn't know that the odious Mr Flowers was in fact the first Mr Amy May. Debbie had to know about the Restraining Order Amy took out because it covered the office, but she hadn't told Debbie everything. Still, she'd told her more than she'd told me.

A plate of cakes arrived and Debbie's eyes lit up.

'I shouldn't,' she said demurely as I offered.

'Nut allergies?' I suggested, straightfaced.

'I was thinking of my figure,' she said automatically, eyes on the plate.

'So are half the males in this room,' I said, gesturing grandly around the large open plan foyer. 'You've nothing to worry about.'

'Thank you, kind sir,' she grinned and helped herself but there were spots of blusher on her cheeks which hadn't been put there with a brush.

'The police. You were saying,' I promoted.

'Oh, yes. They were only doing their job, I suppose, but it did seem to take *ages* and afterwards Amy was on the phone for about an hour even though she knew one of the buyers was waiting to see her and it was making her late for the ten-thirty.'

'The ten-thirty what?' I tried.

'The ten-thirty management meeting. She never did make it. I had to cover for her. When she came off the phone she just grabbed her bag and shot off. The Security Desk said they saw her hailing a cab on Oxford Street.'

Which would give her enough time to get home and modify the diary on her computer at 11:38:08.

'Has she said what spooked her? I presume she was upset by something that had been said.'

'Well, as upset as Amy ever is. You know what she's like. But didn't she tell you about it?'

86

'I didn't actually see her last night and this morning she was up and gone before I was – awake.'

I almost said 'conscious'.

'Gone where?' asked Debbie, putting down her cake plate and staring at me from behind those round glasses which actually did make her eyes look bigger.

'Something called Welfash, according to her diary. I was hoping you knew what it meant,' I said as casually as I could.

'It means Welsh Fashion Week. It was a secret.'

'Fashion – in *Wales?* That is a bloody well-kept secret.'

'No, I meant Amy going there was a secret. She was headhunting one of the student designers who's supposed to be the next big thing. But it was supposed to be secret in case the competition got wind of it.'

'What do you mean, "was"?' I asked.

'Welsh Fashion Week was last week. Amy went down there on the train and back the same day. Last Wednesday, I think. She didn't mention it?'

'That she'd been to Wales? It's not the sort of thing you brag about, is it?'

I realized that came out snappier than I had intended.

'So where is she today?' I said calmly.

'I've no idea. She didn't come into the

87

office this morning and her mobile is switched off. I thought you were coming to tell me what was going on.'

Dream on, Debbie, dream on.

'Look, I've probably just misread her computer diary,' I said, trying to recover. 'I'm useless with computers, I probably just got the wrong week.'

'It doesn't explain where she is today, though,' Debbie said rather primly and I noticed that the hand had gone from my knee.

'No, it doesn't, so we've got to try and work it out. You haven't seen her since the police called at the office yesterday, right?'

'Yes,' she drawled it, rolling her eyes like I was being deliberately slow on the uptake. 'I said, didn't I?'

'OK, now can you remember the name of any of the policemen?'

'Of course I can, I'm Amy's PA.'

If there had been a high horse clopping by she would have mounted it with a single leap.

'And...?'

'Well, the main one was Detective Inspector Hood of...'

'West Hampstead nick,' I completed. 'He's the CID man in charge of the burglary Keith Flowers did on Amy's house.'

Not that Keith Flowers had stolen

anything other than some information about my flat in Stuart Street and Amy's BMW which we got back quickly enough albeit after I'd wrecked it. But as Keith Flowers had only been out of prison for a month when he turned us over, he had no doubt moved up the Prisoner Category and the law was going to sling everything it could at him this time. They don't like it when the system is shown to fail. They much prefer former prisoners to give it at least *two* months before booking a return stay at one of Her Majesty's Windsor Hotels.

'You know him?' Debbie cheered up slightly as if this was a straw within clutching range.

'Not really,' I said, though I had impersonated him once on the phone. 'But I can ask him what he said to Amy to get her so spooked she took off like that. Did she have any appointments for today?'

'Dozens, but none I couldn't handle or bluff my way through.' She considered this for a moment. 'I don't like lying, though. I don't think I'm very good at it.'

'Me neither,' I lied. 'When's the next big thing she really, really can't afford to miss or wouldn't miss even if she had to crawl in from her sickbed?'

'You think she's ill somewhere?'

'No, just surmising.'

People don't not go home just because they're feeling bad, unless they've been drinking with Inverness Doogie, that is.

'Friday, I suppose. Big meeting with the chain stores in the City followed by lunch in one of the Guild Halls – Ironmongers, that's it.'

That was typical of the City. No one knew what an ironmonger was any more, or where to find one, yet they did slap-up catering functions with so much antique silverware on the table you had to wear polaroids.

'So there's a good chance she'll turn up for that?'

'Oh, yes, that's a seriously large lunch.'

I liked that expression, though I suspect my definition and Debbie Diamond's definition were somewhat different.

'Has she ever gone missing before?' I asked her.

'You mean you've never noticed?' she gasped, pulling back well out of knee-clutching range.

'I mean missing from big business affairs, meetings, lunches, dinners, cocktail parties, that sort of thing. The sort of thing she never invites me to.' I saw Debbie's eyes narrowing so I softened that. 'Because she just knows how embarrassed I get being in the public eye. I think she tries to protect me from that side of things.'

'Hmmm,' said Debbie, not convinced.

'Short answer is no way has she missed anything that important, in fact she doesn't miss anything if she can help it. If she's likely to be five minutes late for something, she'll get me to phone ahead with her apologies. This really isn't like her.'

That wasn't like the Amy I knew but I didn't want to go into that.

'So the stuff she missed today wasn't important?'

'Nothing I couldn't handle and normally I probably would have dealt with, except for the mad woman who said she had an appointment, but I don't believe she had for a minute.'

'And this would be...'

'This afternoon. She turned up about an hour before you did. In fact, I only got rid of her about ten minutes before you arrived.'

'Not when, *who?*'

'She said she was from the Probation Office in Romford.'

'Romford?'

As far as I knew neither Amy or I had any connection with Romford. It's a place you tend to go through – quickly, because of an unenviable reputation for the speed with which parked cars are stolen – not have dealings with.

'The Probation Office there covers Chadwell Heath, or so she said.'

It took a full minute for the penny to drop

and I suspected that Debbie Diamond would have waited patiently for several more rather than help me out.

'Keith Flowers,' I said and she just nodded, almost approvingly.

By sheer dumb luck I had discovered that Keith Flowers had spent his initial month out of prison at a halfway house in Chadwell Heath. I hadn't been looking for him, he'd been looking for me and had rung the Stuart Street number and talked to Fenella, who had, naturally, grassed me up a treat and told him where I was. Thanks to the magic of 1471 last number recall (and why the cops on TV shows don't use it more often beggars me) I had got through to something called St Chad's hostel in Chadwell Heath and a very chatty Warden there, whose name I couldn't quite recall but he was a very helpful guy and it wasn't my fault that he somehow got the impression that I was Detective Inspector Hood of West Hampstead. Well, not entirely.

'She said she was the case officer for that Flowers person and that she had an appointment with Amy, but there was nothing in the diary and Amy had certainly never mentioned anything to me.' Debbie took a deep breath. 'When I told her Amy wasn't here, she said *then I would just have to do* and started asking all those questions.'

'About what?'

92

I was genuinely confused. I didn't think Debbie had even seen Keith Flowers, unless he'd been picked up by one of the security firm's CCTV cameras.

'About how many times Flowers had visited the office, had he met with Amy, where had they gone, that sort of thing.'

'Did he? Did they?'

'No, not to my knowledge. Amy came in one day and said there was a guy following her and she'd talked to her solicitor and he'd advised a Restraining Order. I had to screen all her calls of course, but if anyone rang I didn't know I'd ask for a name and if they wouldn't give one, they got snipped.'

She made a scissors movement with two fingers as if cutting a phone cord. At least I hoped that's what she meant.

'So he tried to get through?'

'I don't know if he tried, I just know he didn't get through me. I'm good at my job and we get a lot of rogue journalists trying it on all the time, not to mention models who are getting career-desperate and agents who are just desperate. If he called, he didn't get past me. But the bloody woman just kept on and on about him.'

'Did she say why?'

'Because Amy wasn't around. I said she had better talk to Amy as she was the one with the complaint against the guy, but I couldn't tell her where Amy was, could I? It made it sound as we were covering something up.'

'No,' I said gently, 'why was she asking about Keith Flowers?'

'It's her job, I suppose. She said she had to put together a complete picture – case file she called it – of what he did from the day he left prison to the day he was rearrested. I guess it's something to do with his trial.'

'Nobody's asked me,' I said sulkily. After all, it was me who put him back in prison. Well, hospital actually, then prison.

'Maybe you weren't around when she called,' said Debbie through gritted teeth.

'But you'd have thought the police would have given me a bell at least, even if this Probation Officer person hadn't got round to it... What did you say her name was?'

'I didn't, but she left me a card. It was Alison George.'

'Let's go,' I said, snapping to my feet and waving a hand in the air for the bill.

A white-coated waiter swung towards me like a homing pigeon. I've always found that in posh hotels. My bill is ready the minute I call for it, almost as if they were waiting for me to leave. Odd, really.

'Where are we going?' squealed Debbie, between gulps of tea.

'Back to the office to check the security tapes on your CCTV for this afternoon.'

'Why?' she asked, but she was not looking at me, she was hypnotized by a final slab of

94

marble cake on the plate in front of her.

I pointed to it as I slapped cash down on to the waiter's tray and said: 'To go.' Debbie scooped it up like a croupier.

'I want to get a good look at this Alison George,' I said.

'She's not your type,' she said automatically.

'How do you know that?' I said, caught off guard.

'If Amy's your type, she's not. Anyway, she's far too young for you.'

Now it was my turn to glare at her through slitted eyes.

'I don't want to ogle her,' I said haughtily. 'I just want to see if she limps.'

If Debbie Diamond thought I was suspect before, I had just gone off the scale of her weirdometer.

Oxford Street was thick with buses and I got honked by a 7, a 10 and a 159 – London buses being the only thing on earth brave enough to honk a London taxi – for illegally parking outside the piazza again, though I couldn't see what business it was of theirs. Perhaps it was something to do with the fact that I was near a bus stop but that was just silly. During rush hour the punters stepped on and off the still-moving buses as if they were little more than a bright red horizontal escalator.

At the Security Office I made Debbie get them to open up and demand the tapes for the time the mysterious Alison George – part-time probation officer, part-time rating revaluer and occasional cat-kicker – entered and left the piazza. Debbie was quite specific about her arrival and departure times and one of the guards reckoned her appearances would be on one tape but of course we couldn't see it there and then as his VCRs were recording and he didn't have one for playback.

'Hasn't Amy got one in her office?' I asked casually, not knowing whether or not she had a desk or a chair in her office.

'Good thinking,' said Debbie.

Amy's office had not one but two VCRs, a DVD player, a wide screen digital TV, a hi-fi with twin turntables and shiny steel speakers shaped like bullets and a glass fronted fridge stocked with Rolling Rock beer and fancy mineral waters. No wonder I'd never been allowed in there before.

'You could do some serious mixing with this gear,' I said as Debbie turned things on and inserted the security tape.

'Some of the designers do,' she said casually. 'They find it difficult to create without the right ambiance. Fashion is a mood, you know.'

'Absolutely,' I agreed, opening the fridge.

She stopped fiddling with the tape and

looked at me over the top of her big round glasses. My hand moved away from the beer section and chose a bottle of mineral water. The bottle was moulded plastic twisted to look like a corkscrew and quite stylish. The water was Ty Nant, a natural spring water from Wales of all places. Just my luck, but I opened it and took a swig as if I was really looking forward to it. I suppose it tasted better than London tap water, but then, how would I know?

The security tape was even less help than I feared. The quality was, as always, uniformly grey, grainy and crap. Why firms go to the expense of installing CCTV and then don't spend the extra penny providing enough tapes to stop constant over-taping or, even cheaper, a head-cleaner tape, never ceased to amaze me. Also, as I pointed out to Debbie and she actually made a note of it, the piazza's cameras were so geared towards spotting shoplifters legging it from the boutiques that they didn't actually have a camera covering the Security Office itself. Therefore the best view we would get of the mysterious Alison George would be walking away from the office towards the lifts.

Debbie zapped the tape fast forward using one of half a dozen remotes, one eye on the time clock counter in the corner of the screen. Then she stopped the tape and rewound.

'I'm *sure* this is the right area,' she said, pressing PLAY again. 'In fact I know it is because I'd just had to cancel a conference call with New York and I'd waited until... There she is, the cow! Look at that.'

'Look at what?'

I could see a grainy figure, or rather the back of one, hurrying towards the lift. Until I got my eye in and noticed the hips, I wasn't even sure I could tell which sex it was but in the few seconds she was on screen I took in some sort of plastic showerproof jacket (though it hadn't rained for days), a baseball cap and the fact that she was carrying a large square bag of the sort that have wooden handles and look as if they've been made out of Inca rugs.

The figure got into the lift and studiously kept her head down whilst pressing the buttons. No sooner had the lift doors closed then Debbie was fast-forwarding the tape, muttering 'Bitch, bitch, bitch' under her breath.

'Hey, chill out there, Debs. What's your problem?'

'Don't you see?' she hissed, her eyes fixed to the flickering screen. 'She deliberately deceived me. When she got out of the lift there was no see-through rain coat and no baseball hat. She had her hair bunched underneath it for the cameras and I bet they went in that bag she was lugging.'

'Maybe she just wanted to look smart for her meeting with Amy – with you,' I tried.

Debbie stopped the tape. Eagle-eyed, she had freeze-framed on the lift doors opening as 'Alison George' emerged, complete with rain coat and baseball hat pulled down over her eyes. She kept looking at the floor as she walked quickly out into the piazza and out of shot.

'Now tell me that's not suspicious behaviour,' said Debbie. 'That's an act for the cameras.'

'You could be jumping to conclusions,' I said, screwing up my eyes but still not able to be sure. 'Did you notice what shoes she was wearing?'

After half a minute of silence I turned to find Debbie staring at me, her eyes large behind the round glasses.

'Just what the fuck are you jumping to?'

Chapter Five

I was lucky to find Detective Inspector Hood still at his desk in West Hampstead police station, just catching up on some paperwork on unpaid overtime. Or so he said.

When I said who I was and I wanted to talk about Keith Flowers he couldn't have been nicer. He asked if this was off the record – as if policemen know the meaning of the words – and would I prefer to meet somewhere other than the police station, a pub, say? Despite my own Rule of Life No. 38A (you know you're getting old when the policemen appear helpful), I agreed and stifled a laugh when he named a pub on Shoot Up Hill which was as well-known for drugs deals as it was for after-hours CID parties.

I left Debbie Diamond in her office, putting the flowers I had brought into a glass vase which looked as if it had been designed for medical samples. She said she didn't need a lift anywhere as she could walk to Oxford Street tube, which was just as well as I hadn't offered. Well, she'd never said thank you for the flowers.

The traffic thinned out at Regent's Park and I was sure I would make the pub before Hood did but I was wrong. He was there already, leaning on the bar drinking a bottle of Budweiser by the neck. He looked just about old enough to be doing so legally.

We had met once before when he had taken a statement from me about Keith Flowers' burglary but what had happened subsequently in Suffolk was out of his patch. I had assumed that the more serious charges Flowers now faced in Suffolk would have meant that Hood's interest in him had diminished, so I was keen to know why he had been visiting Amy at her office.

'Mr Angel,' he said, tipping his bottle at me.

'Mr Hood,' I answered, neither offering to shake hands or say his rank out loud, thus observing pub/copper etiquette. 'Can I get you another?'

'Sure, thanks.'

A barman who didn't seem to speak English very well – well, it was London and it was the summer – produced another Budweiser and a orange juice for me and relieved me of a fiver. There was no change. What else did I expect from a pub where the idea of classy decor was shelf after shelf of Readers' Digest condensed books bought job lot by the yard?

We found an unoccupied table, made level

by a folded beer mat under one leg, and two chairs which almost matched.

'You've got something for me then?' he asked, sucking on his bottle.

'Actually, I was hoping you could tell me a couple of things,' I said, hiding my surprise. I'd never offered to tell him anything.

He didn't attempt to hide it. His eyebrows went up and his lips made a 'Prrft' noise.

'About what?'

'About Keith Flowers, the guy who burgled my house, stalked my wi– ... my partner ... and then pulled a gun on us.'

'That was out in Suffolk,' he said.

I noticed the 'out in' rather than 'down in' or 'up in' or even just 'in'. Suffolk was out *there*; beyond the M25; bandit country; duelling-banjoes land; mangel-wurzels and Tractor Boys. What did I expect? Like the vast majority of CID detectives in the Met he wasn't from London – I suspected Bolton or maybe Salford from his accent – but now he was here, nothing outside of London existed. Or nothing worth talking about.

'I know, I was there,' I said but I flashed my best smile to show I wasn't being lippy. 'I was just wondering where we were with the case.'

'Against Flowers? Fuck knows, I don't. That's down to the local force and the Crown Prosecution Service and even they

102

couldn't screw this one up. Only a matter of procedure now, going through the motions and a mountain of paperwork. I don't even think it'll make a full trial.'

'What? You mean Flowers could walk?'

I drained my glass almost as a reflex and realized that orange juice did absolutely nothing for my blood pressure.

'No way, Mr A.' He liked that. I think he'd been rehearsing that since I phoned him. 'Flowers is down and out, maybe for good. They might even section him.'

'You mean as in "Under the Mental Health Act" or whatever it's called these days?'

Hood nodded.

'He's mad?'

'Do normal sane people follow you around and pull guns on you, Mr Angel?'

If that was a serious question I was going to campaign for a Fifth Amendment, even though I wasn't quite sure to what. Thankfully, Hood didn't want an answer.

'What he did out in Suffolk was enough to get him a return trip to the jug without passing GO and certainly not collecting £200, but now his credit rating's shot up from Category D to B, which is enough to depress anybody. So naturally he's thrown a wobbler and gone into clinical depression. Tried to top himself twice, word is. The psychiatrists will be all over him for months yet. I really don't think we'll be pressing the burglary charges. No point.'

I knew what Hood meant by a prisoner's credit rating. Category A prisoners are top of the tree, a serious danger to the public – or an embarrassment to the government of the day. Category B were the dangerous sods – bank robbers, anyone using guns. Category C were prisoners whose escape should be prevented – if possible; and Category D were Open Prison fodder – company directors, ex-MPs, writers, people like that.

Every prisoner except the lifers or the totally bonkers would have a Release Plan with the aim of downgrading their status from A to D over a period of time. I guessed that the last stages of Keith Flowers' plan had been to Category D and the month he'd spent in the hostel in Chadwell Heath. Pulling a gun on us had jerked him back up the serious list to Category B and his Release Plan had gone out the window.

'What was he in for originally?' I asked. I had asked Amy that and never got a straight answer.

'I don't honestly remember, though it'll be on the computer somewhere. I suppose I could look up his record but I'd need a good reason to do so as it's not technically our case any more.'

He pushed his empty beer bottle to one

side and interlocked his fingers. He was after something but it wasn't another drink.

'For peace of mind, Amy and I would like to know and if you could see your way to helping us we'd certainly cooperate with any other enquiries you might have,' I said slowly, thinking it through as I spoke, checking for loopholes.

'Funnily enough, there is an enquiry you can help me with, a personal one.' Here we go, I thought. 'Your SOH, she's the Amy May as in the TALtop thing, that blouse thing, isn't she?'

When I worked out that SOH meant Significant Other Half, I said: 'Yes, that's her.'

'Well, the girlfriend tells me there's this new design with, like, silver stitching or something, but can I find one in the shops? Like gold dust they are and, you see, there's a birthday coming up...'

'What size?' I asked with a smile.

'Twelve.'

'I'll get her a ten. Don't worry, it'll fit and she'll be flattered.'

'Hey, that'd be really good of you.'

He opened his arms, palms out to me. Big mistake.

'And what size is the wife?'

His face froze as he realized it was too late to hide his wedding ring again. Fair play to him, he brazened it out.

'Fourteen.'

'I'll get her a twelve. She'll be chuffed, you get the double whammy.'

'Decent of you,' he said.

'I know. Just let me get one thing straight, though. You went to see Amy yesterday in her office, right?'

'Yes,' he said carefully. He thought I was going to ask him why he hadn't tapped her up for a free sample direct, but then he'd had another policeman with him and that wouldn't have been kosher.

'And that was to tell her about Keith Flowers going all depressive, right?'

'No, wrong.' He shook his head. 'It had nothing to do with Keith Flowers.'

'It didn't?'

'Well, only that Flowers came to our attention when Ms May – by the by, does she use the name Amy Angel?'

'No, never. I think she'd rather have hot needles jammed into her eyes or be forced to wear Spandex. You were saying…'

'We first became aware of Flowers when he was reported as a stalker and Amy – Ms May – took out the Restraining Order. It was just a flagging-up operation as far as we were concerned, but the computer remembered it.'

'Remembered what?'

The guy was driving me nuts. God knows what he would have been like if I hadn't already agreed on a bribe.

'The whole stalker scenario. When it happened again, the computer flagged it up again.'

'What's happened *again?*'

Hood took a deep breath.

'She hasn't told you, has she?'

'I haven't seen her since yesterday morning,' I snapped, then added: 'She's away on business, ordering some more of those silver-thread TALtops.'

'Oh, right, I get it. Look, Mr Angel, the reason we went to see her yesterday was because of the report we'd had from Ivan Dunmore.'

'Who the fuck is Ivan Dunmore?'

'Your neighbour.'

'He is?'

'From across the street or so I'm told. He's reported a suspicious person hanging around outside your house on two occasions now. Says he's seen her every morning for about a week and she follows Amy when she leaves the house.'

'*She?*'

'Yeah. Don't worry, it's not an ex-husband this time, it's a young blonde girl.'

As soon as I got home I was on the phone and got an instant result. My pizza would be with me in twenty minutes. Good. I was starving.

I cracked open a bottle of Leffe Brun beer
– supposedly brewed by Trappist monks in
Belgium and after a couple you could
understand the vow of silence bit – while I
waited.

Then I thought I had better check the
house just to make sure Amy wasn't back,
but there was no sign of her and her shoes
were still missing. I checked for emails on
the computer but there were none for me
(there never were as I never tell anyone my
email address) and the ones for Amy
seemed standard business ones, all from
names in her address book. There was one
message on the answerphone in the
bedroom but it was from Duncan the
Drunken telling me to call him regarding
Amy's BMW as he'd had some quotes for
the bodywork.

While I was in the bedroom and in
detective mode, I rifled through the drawer
where Amy kept her stockings and tights,
most pairs still in their packets as she
regarded hosiery as mostly disposable,
though there was a pair of neatly folded
pure silk stockings with seams which
brought back fond memories at least for me.

I was actually looking to see if her passport
was there, which it was. Or rather both of
them were. She has two, which is not
unusual, so do I. But Amy had got both hers
legitimately as a businesswoman of some

standing who might have to travel at short notice, so she has one with visas for America and Israel and one for countries which might take exception to that.

So wherever it was she'd travelled to at short notice this time, it wasn't abroad, which was comforting and I began to convince myself that I was worrying unnecessarily. If I could only think hard and straight, I was sure I could come up with a logical explanation.

The doorbell rang. It was my pizza and when I had paid the spotty moped-riding delivery boy (he'd taken 21 minutes and 15 seconds, so no tip) I opened another beer and flipped on the TV.

I never could think hard and straight on an empty stomach.

I heard the chirping of an electronic lock and then the sound of a key being cranked and finally not one but two deadbolts being drawn, and all the time I showed my best smile to the peep-hole as I stood there under the halogen security light. The door opened inwards but no more than twenty degrees.

'Mr Dunmore? Good evening. I'm Roy Angel, your neighbour from across the street.'

'I know you are.'

The voice was used to giving orders. It was

middle-aged, still had a suit and tie on in the house at nine-thirty in the evening and owned the new Mercedes parked in the drive. There was probably a second, smaller one in the garage.

'You do?'

'This is the third house you've tried, isn't it? The Cohens and the Elringtons rang me. We're all in the Neighbourhood Watch.'

He wasn't wrong, it had been trial and error on my part but it was their own fault. No one who is anyone is in the phone book these days – just think of the population of London and then look at the size of the Residential directory. And in Hampstead, everyone thought they were somebody.

'I believe you reported a suspicious character lurking around our house?' I said, keeping it friendly, hoping he wouldn't notice I wasn't wearing a suit and hold it against me.

'If you'd been a member of the Neighbourhood Watch, you'd have found out three days ago,' he said snootily.

'I wouldn't join any Neighbourhood Watch which would have me as a member,' I quipped before I could bite my tongue.

Ivan Dunmore looked as if he just had bitten his tongue.

'But seriously, I came to say thank you for being so vigilant,' I pressed on. 'We're trying to be careful. You know we were burgled about a month ago?'

'The police did mention it,' he said cautiously.

That was one up to the Neighbourhood Watch, wasn't it?

'So I was wondering if there was anything you could tell me about the person who was hanging around the other day?'

He shrugged his shoulders as if it didn't matter. He'd done his bit, after all, telling the cops. Why should he have to give a repeat performance for me? Because I was standing at his front door making his driveway look untidy and giving the rest of the Neighbourhood Watch something to watch.

'She was young, about twenty I'd guess. Blonde, quite long hair. I suppose you could say pretty if we're still allowed to say that without being a sexist pig.'

There was something in the way he said that which made me think a nerve had been struck and I really didn't want to go there.

'How was she dressed?' I said, to change tack but that only made him look down at me as if I was a pervert.

'The same way all girls of that age dress – in things which look as if they come from Oxfam and they only wear once even though they actually cost a small fortune.'

Whoops, I think he had a history here. I hoped he didn't know what Amy did for a living.

'Oh, the usual. White T-shirt with something written on it and those tight blue jeans with flares and the faded stripes up the legs and over the arse cheeks where there should be back pockets.'

On reflection, a Neighbourhood Watch this observant might just be worth joining.

'Can you remember what was on the T-shirt?'

'Yes I can, actually. It was "Fuck" but the letters were jumbled up.'

He meant FCUK, or I hoped he did. I knew several taxi drivers who had had T-shirts made up with FUCK OFF printed backwards so that drivers who cut them up could read it in their mirror and be afraid.

'She had a bag as well, a big shoulder bag thing which looked as if it could carry the kitchen sink.'

'And you noticed her when?'

'First thing in the morning three days ago. She was hanging around behind some parked cars watching your house as I was going to work. Then I saw her that evening as I came home. Miss May was unloading some things from her Land Rover and there was the girl again, just down the street, watching her. She was there the next morning, according to Mrs Cohen two properties to the west.'

I liked the 'two properties to the west' bit. Normal people would have said 'two doors down' but this was Hampstead.

'So you know Amy, do you?' I said with a smile.

'Not really, no. We did ask her to join the Watch when she first moved in here.' Then he added: 'When she was living alone.'

'What did she say when you asked her to join the Watch?'

'She laughed.'

That's my girl.

'Was this young woman acting at all suspiciously? I mean did she do anything that would be a cause for concern?'

Other than just be on a piece of pavement which you claim by divine right, I thought, but didn't say.

'Mrs Cohen is quite firm about the fact that she saw the girl taking photographs of Miss May as she was leaving for work the other morning.'

He let the implication hang in the warm night air. Amy got up and went to work; I didn't.

'Did she follow Amy, when Amy went to work?'

'I have no idea where she went, but she left the area shortly after, in a taxi.'

'She could be a journalist,' I said reasonably and I could see that the prospect of that worried him more than a bus load of burglars or somebody organizing a street party for the gay, black, disabled homeless.

'That's for the police – or you – to sort out. Now if you'll excuse me, I have some paperwork to finish.'

'One last thing. Did you notice what sort of shoes she was wearing?'

He stared silently at me for a full minute before he closed the door in my face.

I scoped the street before I went back into the house, hoping to spot a trenchcoated figure under one of the streetlights, a cigarette cupped in a curled hand, trilby brim snapped down over their eyes. But there wasn't a living soul in sight, not even a cat. They had probably all been rounded up by the Animal Branch of the Neighbourhood Watch. I had been right not to inflict a move here on Springsteen.

Which reminded me that I ought to check up on him.

Back indoors I cracked another Leffe and phoned Stuart Street, knowing that Fenella would be the one sent to answer the house phone.

She said she had to be quick as she had three separate text chats going at the same time and she'd broken two nails already that evening. Springsteen was still growling and moving about in reverse but he was eating well and drinking a lot of water. I said that was a good sign, though I had no idea if it was or not, and that she should try him with some lean minced beef or lamb. Fenella made the 'eeeuuu' sound only teenage girls can really make and said that handling meat was going a bit far. I told her not to worry, just buy a pack at the supermarket and throw it in the flat. Springsteen could easily unwrap it himself as long as it wasn't frozen – which just took longer. She said OK, if she really had to and, by the way, that car mechanic friend of mine had called round on the off-chance I would go to a pub with him and his wife but I wasn't to worry as he'd give me a ring.

I didn't bother to ask if 'Alison George' had paid a return visit, assuming that to be highly unlikely. Nor did I ask if Amy had rung as that would have sounded a bit weak and surely Fenella would have mentioned it.

Duncan the Drunken calling round to take me for a drink, now that could be serious. It probably meant the estimate for the BMW's repairs was going to be horrendous.

I dialled his home number, not really expecting him to be in and, sure enough, got the start of his recorded voice message.

This is Duncan. Me and the wife Doreen have gone down the pub and we're probably shit-faced by now so you can either come and buy us a drink or...

There was a click as the receiver was picked up and Duncan's Yorkshire accent cut across the message.

'Talk to me.'

'Duncan, it's Angel. Why aren't you down the pub?'

'Bit of a cock up, there, mate. We thought we'd try the karaoke down The Whalebone in Barking but it seems we're barred from there.'

'You forgot you'd been banned from the pub?'

'Not me,' he said haughtily. 'Doreen.'

'Oh. Fair enough. You have some bad news for me, then?'

'Aye, about the chassis on that Beamer. Could be up to three grand to sort it out before we start on the systems checks and then there's the bodywork.'

'All right, Duncan, don't sweat it. Let's cost the whole job like we said and see if it's worth getting it back on the road and maybe selling it on.'

'Just thought you'd like to know, now the insurance company's got it on the agenda.'

What insurance company? I hadn't even sent in the claim form.

'What insurance company, Dunc?'

'I don't think she said the name of it.'

'*She?*'

'The blonde bint who came sniffing round here this afternoon. I wouldn't mind having her on my case, I can tell you. Long as Doreen didn't find out, of course.'

116

'Would her name have been Alison George by any chance?'

'Aye, that's it. But she said I could call her Georgie if I wanted to.'

'I've got a few other names for her,' I said.

The next morning I awoke with a plan. I knew exactly what I was going to do.

But first, I reached over and patted the other side of the bed. It was empty, which was a relief.

It would have been a shame to waste such a good plan and, anyway, Amy would have killed me if she'd been there, what with all those empty beer bottles scattered over the duvet.

Chapter Six

It wasn't about me, or Amy, it was about Keith Flowers.

Whoever this Alison George character was, she was tracing Keith Flowers' movements in the month he spent out of prison. Flowers had stalked Amy in and around the Oxford Street office, so Alison George had been there only to give Debbie Diamond an earful when she found Amy had done a runner, having being warned by the cops that someone had her under surveillance.

She had hung around the house in Hampstead, the house Keith Flowers burgled, and she'd even been to Duncan the Drunken's garage to see the car he'd stolen. She would have known where to go from the Suffolk cops as Duncan would have signed for the wrecked BMW when he picked it up and he would have used a kosher name and address if there was a chance of a legitimate insurance payout. The one thing I couldn't figure out was why she visited the flat in Stuart Street. Keith Flowers had never been there – he'd phoned there when he tracked me and Amy to Suffolk (thanks, Fenella blab-mouth). But how would Alison George know that?

There was one other place where I knew Keith Flowers had been during his one moon cycle of freedom and that was St Chad's Hostel in Chadwell Heath, which I assumed was some sort of halfway house for ex-prisoners waiting to jump from the rock of confinement on to the hard place of life on the outside. I had no idea where it was or how it worked, but I had spoken to the warden on the phone a month ago. I would go and see him and ask for ... well, anything he could tell me. That was my plan, carefully thought-out, immaculately researched.

About halfway round the North Circular Road I remembered the warden's name – Roberts – and felt a lot more confident.

At the ridiculously named Charlie Brown's Roundabout (good grief!), I cut off under the M11 towards Gant's Hill and Eastern Avenue, then pulled in to a post office near the old Goodmayes Hospital, leaving Armstrong right outside with the engine running. The postmaster, a Sikh, took great delight in meeting a London taxi driver who didn't know everything and had to ask directions. After a couple of minutes of smirking he told me that St Chad's Hostel was in Sydney Gardens on the other side of St Chad's Park.

Back in Armstrong I consulted a battered A–Z once I was out of sight of the postmaster and worked my way through the suburban back streets parallel to Eastern Avenue and round the northern end of the park until I hit an enclave of streets named after either Australian cities (Adelaide, Melbourne, Sydney) or trees (Yew and Cedar) for no apparent reason. Who knew what had possessed the local town planners? And why did these Australian 'Gardens' all run in to Whalebone Lane, which crossed Eastern Avenue at the *Moby Dick* Roundabout? I swear you could make up any ridiculous street name you liked and Londoners would believe you. Don't try it on a real black cab driver, though.

St Chad's Hostel had a rusted metal plate on one of its gateposts saying just 'St Chad's'. It was just like any of the other detached houses on Sydney Gardens: two brick gateposts, though no gate, either side of a yard-wide concrete path which ran all of ten feet across a Kleenex-sized garden to a porched front door. The house was detached from its next door neighbours by a gap you could see but not squeeze through. Unlike its neighbours, St Chad's paintwork was bright and fresh. Indeed, there was a white haired old geezer wearing blue overalls halfway up a ladder painting a window frame as I arrived.

He nodded to me as I walked up to the front door and tried to draw on a thin hand rolled cigarette as he did so. The coughing spasm almost shook him off the ladder and I felt there ought to be something in the Health and Safety legislation about people like him being allowed to work more than three feet off the ground, or even with chunky heels.

''Mornin',' I nodded back. 'St Chad's?'

'So they tell me,' said the old man, concentrating on his painting again.

I pressed the doorbell and a single chime sounded somewhere inside.

The inner door opened and I saw a blurred figure through the frosted glass reach for the lock on the outer door, and then up above to a deadbolt and then bend over and lean down for another bolt. The door opened six inches – on a chain.

'Yes?'

The voice came from behind the moustache of a man in late middle age, balding and with that stiff upright posture that means either ex-serviceman or fallen arches or perhaps both.

'I'm looking for Warden Roberts,' I said politely.

The chain came off and the door opened. He wore dark heavyweight trousers with creases which could have sliced bread, shined black shoes I could see my reflection in and a white shirt and dark blue tie with a logo I didn't recognize. His one concession to informality was a green cardigan buttoned up the front which failed to hide the key chain running into his trouser pocket. I had the feeling he had so many keys on the end of that chain that he clanked when he walked.

'You've found him,' he said. Then, slightly louder: 'Hasn't he, Spider?'

'If you say so, Mr Roberts,' said the old man on the ladder, exhaling smoke and hot ash and tobacco shreds as he did so.

'So what's your business here?' he turned back on me.

'Detective Inspector Hood of West Hamp–'

'You're not DI Hood!' Roberts snapped and I saw him think about reaching for the door.

'Of course I'm not,' I said smoothly. Damn. It had been worth a shot. 'Inspector Hood of West Hampstead is investigating a burglary about a month ago at my house...'

'It wasn't me, guv,' said the old man on the ladder. 'I was securely elsewhere at the time, whenever it was.'

'Shut up, Spider. I'm sorry if you lost any valuables, sir, but whatever you think your grounds are, it is highly improper to bring them here. Now please leave before I call the police.'

It suddenly dawned on me why they had so many locks on the inside of the door here: to keep angry civilians out.

'I wish you would,' I lied, 'but they can't help. Inspector Hood and I spoke last night. He's unlikely to be able to follow up the burglary because the ... the ... er ... perpetrator faces more serious charges elsewhere. It's likely that the burglary charge and the theft of a very expensive car are going to be dropped. Meanwhile, I'm in the middle of a very complicated insurance claim.'

It was a bit thin but not bad for being made up on the spot. I only wish we had the charge of Grand Theft Auto like they do in America (rumoured to carry the death penalty in some States still). It sounds so much more impressive than 'TWOC' – Taking Without Consent.

'And what has this got to do with St Chad's, if anything?' Roberts growled, but he must have known what was coming.

'The car thief was Anthony Keith Flowers and he was living here at the time of the crime.'

'*If* this person was one of our residents at the time in question, and I'm not saying he was, I cannot possibly think what I could, or should tell you, Mr...? I didn't catch your name.'

'Angel,' I said, not seeing any percentage in lying about it, 'and really all I'm after is some idea of what Keith Flowers did during his stay here. It was a month, wasn't it? I just need to know anything about his movements...'

'I'm sorry, Mr Angel, if that really is your name, but that sort of information is none of your concern and, without instructions from an officer of a court, none of your business. I am certainly not prepared to help you on the doorstep, out of the blue like this. If there is any ongoing legal action then the proper authorities will have all the facts. I suggest you consult your solicitor. Good day.'

I was left looking at the door and hearing the slam of deadbolts and the snick of the chain going back on, still thunderstruck by his advice.

See a solicitor? Things couldn't be that bad, could they?

I could still see Warden Roberts' distorted figure through the frosted glass when a voice from above me – though not very far above me – whispered:

'End of the road; five minutes.'

'Got anything to smoke, then?' asked Spider, leaning into Armstrong through the nearside front window.

'Only tobacco,' I said.

'Factory or roll-up?'

'Ready made.' I pointed to the glove compartment. 'In there.'

124

His hands shot out as if on springs from his arms and he had the compartment open and was helping himself to one of my emergency Benson & Hedges which he lit with a disposable lighter. A hand shot out again – I thought to put the packet back – and retrieved my emergency half bottle of vodka (mostly full), which quickly disappeared into one of the large flapped pockets of his paint stained overalls.

'Hey, you're having a laugh now, aren't you?' I said but made no move to take it back. I noticed the cigarette packet had vanished too.

'Can't help it, mate,' he said, drawing on the cigarette. 'I'm a thief, in' I? A persistent offender, a *ree-sid-ivist*. Or so they tell me. You shouldn't give people like me the time of day.'

I resisted the urge to check that my watch was still on my wrist.

'That's probably the only useful thing you're going to tell me, isn't it?'

'How do you know that? I ain't said nothing yet.'

I put both hands on the steering wheel and began to tap out a little rhythm with my fingers, looking straight ahead and whistling *Take the A Train* loudly, but in the wrong key. That was usually good for sending Amy ballistic within two minutes.

Spider didn't last that long.

'You wanna hear what I've got to say, then?'

'Sure. Whenever you're ready. Take your time. But preferably while I'm still in my thirties.'

Spider hissed something which could have been 'chopsy little git' as he took another drag on the cigarette. He held it in between two fingers, but backwards, pointing into the palm of his hand. I bet he could nip the end out in an instant, with thumb and little finger if he had to. He was sixty if he was a day and he'd been smoking like that for a long time.

'There's somebody wants to see you.'

I stopped whistling. 'There is? Why would somebody you know want to see me?'

''Cos you're that Angel guy that's shacked up with that clothes designer Amy May.'

I kept a blank face.

'And you got this where? *Cosmo* or maybe *Vanity Fair*? I don't remember *Hello!* magazine coming round.'

Actually they had, but I had made sure I had a darts match to go to and Amy hadn't minded. In fact she'd seemed quite relieved.

'Got it from the 'orse's mouth – her husband hisself. OK then, ex-husband, but he talked about her all the time.'

'You know Keith Flowers?' I tried to keep my voice down but I wasn't sure I managed it.

'Yeah, I do. Did. No, I do. He's not dead, is he?'

'Not for the want of trying.'

'Ooooh! Now you're scaring me,' Spider shrilled.

'Look, you old toe-rag, where's this going? And how much is it gonna cost me?'

'Nuffing. I'm taken care of. I get paid to deliver the message. No concern o'mine what happens after that.'

I looked into his pale, wrinkled face. Another year and he could model for garden gnomes.

'Let me get this straight: you had a message for me and I just happen to turn up on your doorstep?'

'Being up that ladder and thereby able to earwig your every word was a bit of a bonus, I admit,' he said, nodding sagely to himself, 'otherwise I'd have had to come looking for you.'

'To deliver this message?'

'Yep.'

'That somebody wants to see me?'

'Yer getting there.'

'And who exactly is it wants to see me?'

'Mr Creosote.'

I burst out laughing as I couldn't avoid the image of the Monsieur Creosote in *Monty Python's The Meaning of Life*, the gargantuan vomiting character who eats so much he finally explodes after being tempted by one last 'waffer thin mint'.

Spider was clearly hurt that I wasn't taking this seriously enough.

'Don't tell me,' I sobbed, trying to get my breath back, 'he wants to meet me in his favourite restaurant!'

Deadpan, Spider said:

'Oh, no, *you* have to go see *him*. The law's very insistent about that.'

'No, don't interrupt,' I said, 'let me tell you what's happened as I see it because that'll give me a chance to get it straight in my mind as, frankly, it's starting to do my head in.

'It's clear to me that this Alison George is not the sharpest blade in the knife drawer. I mean, she goes to all the trouble of setting up her computer to print off business cards for phoney professions and yet she uses the same name all the time. What's all that about? If her IQ gets to 50 she should sell.

'She's interested in what Keith Flowers did in his month of semi-freedom, when he was out of jail but hadn't passed GO and certainly hadn't collected £200 anywhere that I know of. But he had made a nuisance of himself at Amy's office, so this Alison George goes there. He turned over our house, so Alison George is hanging around there, almost like visiting the scene of the crime.

'It wouldn't surprise me to find out she'd been up to Suffolk, or maybe she just called the cops up there, but she knew about Keith Flowers' nasty accident with Amy's BMW and she turned up at Duncan's garage just to see it for herself. It's as if she's trying to retrace his steps.

'I know, I know,' I held up a hand to stifle the questioning looks. 'Flowers never came to Stuart Street but he did ring here. Now how she knew about that is interesting, but there was never anything here to find that connected to Flowers. It's like she's trying to get a *feel* for things somehow.'

I lit up a cigarette – just to help me concentrate – despite the audible sniffs and glaring eyes.

'I know, I know,' I admitted, 'but I need it.

'So I figured the next logical place for her to go would be St Chad's, if she really was walking back the cat.

'No, that's just an expression which spies used. Don't ask me how I know. "Walking back the cat" means following a trail backwards not to find where somebody's going but where they started from.

'Now I can't think of a way this Alison George would know about St Chad's, I mean it's only dumb luck I did. And even if she knew about it, I don't know how she would find it and anyway, I shouldn't think the cops or the Prison Service would release details like that and if she did go there, they wouldn't talk to her. But lo and behold, there was somebody there waiting to talk to me!

'Would you believe a Mr Creosote? I mean this just gets better and better. And according to his ageing messenger boy, who looks like he was the Artful Dodger's understudy, to see him *I have to go and visit him in prison.*

'Well, I suppose the authorities might look a bit askance at him nipping out for lunch down Soho for a couple of hours, though if you've been, say, a Cabinet Minister, you seem to get away with it.

'So now I've got two problems: a rogue female dogging me wherever I go and a hardened criminal in Belmarsh high security prison snooping by remote control. And as far as I can see, both of them are trying to track not me, but Keith-soddin'-Flowers and find out what he did on his brief holiday from Her Majesty's Prisons.

'What I don't know is *why*.

'Why are people suddenly interested in Keith Flowers when all the time he was inside nobody mentioned his bloody name? He comes out and now he's going back inside for attempted maiming and mayhem on his ex-wife. Mostly. Plus being certifiable; I suppose that helps.

'So why the sudden interest in the month

he was out? Why has it spooked Amy into doing a runner? It's not like her to just disappear for days on end. That's what *I* do. I know, I just thought I'd say it before you did.

'But what does it all *mean?* Gimme a break here, *think of something.*'

Springsteen raised his splinted paw at me in a mock salute – if he'd had fingers, the middle one would have been upright – and limped backwards into the kitchen with as much dignity as he could muster.

Fat lot of use he'd been.

As I left the Stuart Street flat, I thought that the day just couldn't get any weirder, which was a dumb thing to do because as soon as you think that – it does.

But even I couldn't have guessed that I was about to be kidnapped and then beaten up in full view of eleven million Londoners.

Maybe it's to do with getting older, but I'm really beginning to hate surprises.

One of them piled into the back of Armstrong almost as soon as I had the driver's door open. [Mental note: It was a daft idea to install central locking.] The other one had climbed out of a white Rover 600 and rapidly crossed the street on the diagonal, only coming into the corner of my eye when it was too late to do anything about it.

My first impression was that they were calm and professional, which was worrying. My second impression was that they were both Welsh, which was frightening.

'Jubilee Gardens, please, down near Waterloo,' said the one who had climbed in the back, his voice modulated with the unmistakable Celtic lilt.

'Sorry, mate, this isn't a licensed cab, it's a private vehicle and not for hire,' I said, almost on autopilot as I had done a thousand times before when unsuspecting punters had jumped in the back at traffic lights or in pub car parks. 'I couldn't take your money even if I wanted to.'

'No one said anything about money, did they, Huw?'

I became aware that something was preventing me from closing the driver's door: a pair of hands gripping the top of the door frame. Huw, I presumed.

'Wouldn't count on a tip either,' said Huw.

They were both mid to late twenties, clean shaven and with short hair. They could have been Mormons but the fact that they were the only two people wearing blue, beltless gabardine raincoats in London on a warm August afternoon singled them out as Welsh.

'Anytime you're ready,' said the one in the back, still polite and cheerful. 'You've got about thirty-five minutes.'

'Where are we going?' I asked him casually, making no move to start the engine, like I was interested.

'I've told you once. Jubilee Gardens near Waterloo. You've got thirty-five minutes.'

He stared me out with a faint smile, head slightly on one side as if he forgave me for not hearing him the first time.

'What I really meant,' I tried, 'was *why* do you want to go to Jubilee Gardens?'

'Now that's a good question, isn't it, Huw?'

'Certainly is, Barry,' said Huw over my head. 'Can't say I want to go and you could probably think of better things to do, but we don't have much choice in the matter really, do we?'

'None at all in the matter,' said Barry philosophically. 'And all this chit-chat and gay banter means you now have about thirty-three minutes.'

Barry on the back seat had been sitting with his hands resting on his lap on the folds of his unbuttoned raincoat. Now he pulled back the coat slowly and delicately, like a stripper revealing a flash of stocking top. Across his knees lay a big, ugly silvery revolver.

'I think you'd better start your engines, but try not to make it a bumpy flight, eh?'

I had no idea what he was talking about but Huw did as he started to giggle, still hanging on Armstrong's door.

'Not two in one day, eh, Barry?'

'Did you bring the sick bags, Huw?' Barry replied with a laugh.

I looked from the gun to Barry and then turned my head to Huw, who was reaching inside his raincoat for something.

I started Armstrong up as quickly as I could, not fancying the idea of a gun in each ear one bit. But Huw didn't have a gun, or if he did he didn't draw it. His hand came out of the folds of his coat with a pair of handcuffs and before I could react he had caught my right wrist and snapped one bracelet on. The other half of the cuffs he clicked on to the rim of the steering wheel.

'I'll be right behind you,' he said into my face, 'but don't go too fast if you wouldn't mind, 'cos I'm not used to driving in the big city.'

'Don't dawdle, though, Huw,' said Barry. In my mirror I could see him folding his coat back over his lap and smoothing it down. I didn't know whether to be more frightened of his gun or his fashion sense. 'We don't want to miss our flight.'

Huw chuckled some more then slammed the door on me and stalked across the road to the white Rover, shaking his head as he went.

'He hates flying, that's his problem,' said Barry.

We were almost at Liverpool Street, the white Rover right behind us, before I realized we were going for a ride on the London Eye.

Barry-in-the-back wasn't giving anything away, even when I used my most subtle approach.

'Want to tell me what's going on, then?'

'No, I don't think I will. You'll find out soon enough. Patience is a virtue and everything comes to him who waits.'

He deserved a slap as much for the platitudes as the sing-song accent in which he delivered them, not that I was in a position to give anyone except myself a slap, anchored to the steering wheel as I was.

'We'll be going over Tower Bridge, then, will we?' Barry asked.

I arched my back and strained my buttocks so that I was taller in the driving seat and could get a better angle in the driving mirror. Barry had a paperback-sized London A–Z open on his knee, the bastard. For a real London cabby, that was more threatening than the gun he'd shown me earlier.

'Can do,' I said, trying to keep my voice level, 'but we'll lose the Taffy in the Rover. Once you... Ow!'

Barry had jumped forward and swatted me on the left ear with the A–Z. It didn't hurt much as a smack; the pain came from the indignity and the humiliation of wincing away in case another blow came. It was only later that I considered the farcical nature of my situation. To an innocent observing Londoner, it must have looked like a fantasy come true or a set-up from a 'reality television' show. The scenario: a black cab driver handcuffed to his own steering wheel, being beaten about the head with an A–Z guide by an irate passenger fed up with being taken the long way round.

'He's not called Taffy. Nobody's called Taffy these days,' Barry was saying. Even though my ear was ringing I could tell his voice was calm and reasonable. 'Now why aren't we going across Tower Bridge?'

'We can if you want but on the other side we'll probably lose your friend in the Rover in the traffic system.' I chose my next words carefully. 'Unless you know where you're going, you can end up halfway to Kent before you can turn round.'

'Fair enough but it's a pity. I was looking forward to seeing the Tower,' he said with a note of genuine disappointment.

I was tempted to tell him that if he tried what he was doing to me on one of the real fraternity of London cabbies then he might find himself *inside* the Tower as there was bound to be a law still on the books to cover such outrages.

'I'm going through the City and across Southwark Bridge, if that's OK,' I said instead.

Barry flicked a page in his A–Z.

'That looks acceptable. You've got about twenty minutes before flight time.'

That was when it clicked.

'You're going on the London Eye, aren't you?'

'We all are,' said Barry and his smile filled my mirror. 'Should make a nice day out, shouldn't it.'

It wasn't a question but I risked another burning ear by answering it.

'So it's a day out for you guys, is it? I didn't know there was any rugby on this week-end.'

You don't actually have to know anything about Rugby Union to know when they're playing the Six Nations championship and the games are in London, you just have to hang around the pubs. All London publicans – and customers – love it when the Irish fans are in town because it guarantees a party; they don't mind the Scots because they keep to themselves and get on with the serious drinking; the French pop in for some pub grub before hitting Marks & Spencer's, so they aren't really any trouble; and the Italians – well, nobody is quite sure what they do as they've never been seen. But when the Welsh hit town on the Friday before a Saturday match, publicans give their best staff the night off and only employ those who don't mind the constant whining about London prices, the fact that there are no public bars any more (where the beer is traditionally a penny cheaper), or that no one sells mild ale (cheaper) in London nowadays.

It didn't seem a good idea to share any of this with Barry-in-the-back-with-a-gun.

'No, there's no rugby on,' he said chattily. 'We're here on business. The sightseeing is just a perk of the job, you might say. Travel broadens the mind and all that.'

I hoped he had lots of Air Miles stacked up.

'Can I ask what business you're in?'

'Oh, I don't think you'd want to know that and if the boss wants to tell you, he'll tell you.'

'The boss?' I asked, but he didn't reply.

Trying to psych me out with a menacing silence is quite a good tactic and it always works for Amy, but Barry was Welsh and just couldn't stand the pressure of not hearing his own voice.

'You'll be meeting the boss. He's waiting for us and we'd better not be late. He's been looking forward to his trip on the big Ferris wheel for ages. He's just a big kid at heart, but don't tell him I said that, will you?'

'Gets upset easily, does he? This boss of

yours?' I tried, pushing it.

'Best hope you don't find out,' said Barry.

I parked the Armstrong in the shadow of the archway which carries the rail line over Hungerford Bridge and the white Rover pulled up behind me.

Barry got out and stood there looking at the few passenger capsules you could see from this angle, suspended up in the air and rotating so slowly it didn't look as if they were moving at all. I didn't join him because I couldn't. I had to wait for Huw to climb out of the Rover, lock it with an electronic remote and take his own sweet time approaching my door and opening it.

He looked down at me and at my wrist still cuffed to the wheel.

'Tut-tut,' he scolded, 'and they said you big city boys were smart.'

He reached in and grasped the cuff on the wheel with two fingers and it sprang open immediately, falling off the wheel and dangling from the one still on my wrist.

I held my wrist up and examined the bracelet still intact. If you looked carefully you could see that what was supposed to be a keyhole was actually a raised button in the metal. I pressed it and that half fell away with a ratchety click.

Huw held out his hand for the cuffs.

'Just toys, really,' he said. 'Get them in the

local sex shop, we do.'

'Sex shops in Wales?' I said before I could stop myself. 'I thought they were called farms.'

I remember being impressed as to how strong he was for a man of his size and how he must work out down at the gym, maybe doing the weights. That was as I was being lifted out of the Armstrong by the ears and slammed against the bodywork. It was only when I'd got my breath back from the three punches he put into my stomach – pausing only to reflect on the fact that he'd been so quick he'd had time to slip the steel hand-cuffs over his right fist as a knuckleduster – that I realized he must be a boxer. There were other telltale signs – like the way he had positioned his feet and balanced his weight and not wasted effort, taking short distance jabs rather than wild swings – but mostly it was the pain that convinced me.

He put a hand on my shoulder to keep me from sinking to my knees while I frantically tried to remember how to breathe. To passers-by heading to and from Waterloo Station just across the road, it must have looked like we were having a friendly chat about the current programme at the National Film Theatre.

Barry appeared from behind the Armstrong, or rather the bottom half of him did for I could only register his shoes, trousers and the bottom half of his raincoat without raising my head and that seemed just too damned difficult.

'Oh, dear me,' said Barry. 'You didn't mention sheep-shagging, did you? The Welsh national sport. Something like that? Huw doesn't like that. None of us like that, now I think about it. 'Specially not Mr Turner. He definitely doesn't like such talk. Better keep it to yourself for now, eh? Come on, he'll be waiting and raring to go. It's this way, is it?'

I staggered after him as he strode across Jubilee Gardens, mostly propelled by Huw's hand in the small of my back. If I'd been able to think, I would have remembered I had left the Armstrong unlocked and the key in the ignition.

If I'd been able to speak I would have asked who the fuck Mr Turner was.

Chapter Seven

It's London's fourth-tallest structure at 450 feet, has thirty-two ovoid capsules carrying twenty-five people each, it takes thirty minutes to rotate through 360 degrees and on a clear day can offer views of up to thirty miles out as far as Windsor Castle and Heathrow. What else did I know about the London Eye? It was the only worthwhile remnant of the Millennium beanfeast – the famous wobbly footbridge down by the Tate Modern had already been forgotten and everyone pretended that the Dome had never happened at all. It had been interrupted twice, once when a WWII unexploded bomb had been dredged up by Hungerford Bridge and once when the River Police had to fish out a 'floater', and when it opened to the public the Ministry of Defence building in Whitehall directly across the river issued instructions to its staff to keep the windows closed and the office curtains pulled in case the Eye carried coach parties of spies with binoculars.

The other thing I knew was that even though the novelty had worn off, you could still queue for an hour or more to get on at quiet times in the winter. Now was summer and London was tourist central, which should have given me plenty of time to find out a bit more about the mysterious Mr Turner by quizzing Barry and Huw when I got my breath back.

No chance.

With Barry and Huw so close to either side of me that I could have slipped under their raincoats in the event of a sudden shower, we marched straight up the switchback concrete ramp to the head of the queue – and then beyond it.

I was about to protest, or rather get the people in the queue to protest but most of them were Japanese and far too polite to cause a fuss, but then we were over the yellow line and through the gates with the attendants waving us through to the curved landing platform.

'Come on, lovely boys, you're just in time. This one's ours.'

Up that close you can't help but feel dominated by the Eye as it towers above you and especially when one of the capsules inches in along the loading platform. You automatically look straight up to the capsule over 400 feet directly above at the top of the arc and you think that in fifteen minutes you'll be up there hanging in the air with people down here staring up your trouser leg through the transparent capsule walls.

The big difference between the Eye and the amusement park rides called 'Terminator' or 'Scream Machine' is that *they* don't give you time to think.

I tried to spot where the voice had come from and through a melee of disembarking passengers (all chattering happily and none of them even the slightest bit green) and bustling attendants, I saw its owner.

He was a small man, no more than five foot four, stocky but not particularly fat and balding, the skin on the top of his head glowing pink where he'd caught the sun though not enough to persuade him to take off his raincoat. He was at least pensionable age and he had a hearing aid plugged into his right ear. He waved an arm to hurry us on and almost did a jig with excitement. I bet his eyes twinkled when he smiled and he was somebody's favourite grandad.

Immediately behind him, hands clasped together near his groin in classic bouncer posture, was a much taller, younger version of the old man. This one was somewhere around the mid-forties, built like a rugby prop-forward and his eyes scanned the crowd like an American Secret Serviceman guarding a president. He wasn't wearing a raincoat, just a denim blouson jacket, he was that hard.

Even as I was hustled towards them I noticed the family resemblance. The

144

middle-aged bouncer was almost certainly the son of the old man and, after a quick look left then right, was probably the father of Barry and Huw. That made the old man their favourite grandad.

Up close, the old man beamed at me and when he spoke he leaned slightly to his left so he could catch what I said in his hearing aid ear.

'Ah, Mr Angel, so glad you could join us. I've been looking forward to this.'

I put on my best bemused expression, somewhere between a drunk after ten pints of snakebite and a rabbit caught in headlights.

'I'm sorry? Who did you say?'

It was worth a shot. After all, neither Barry nor Huw had actually asked me who I was.

It fooled Grandad for about two seconds.

'Oh, very good, Mr Angel. You did that with a straight face.' He pointed a finger at me, then wagged it. 'You could have had me going there, but you see I know who you are. Now come for a ride on this wonderful contraption with us.'

'I'm scared of heights,' I tried.

'Don't be, Mr Angel,' smiled Grandad, taking me by the arm. 'There are plenty of other things you ought to be frightened of before you worry about heights. But do bear in mind, Mr Angel, that just because I'm up in the big city for the day, it doesn't mean there's a village somewhere that's deprived of an idiot. You with me?'

'Absolutely,' I said. 'Don't we need a ticket?'

'All done and dusted,' he said proudly, steering me to the platform edge where a capsule had seemingly come to rest, though they never actually do. 'Private Capsule Hire, that's the name of the game, though I wish they'd called them carriages. Capsules sounds like a suppository, don't you think?'

Once the last of the passengers was out of the capsule, two attendants dived in armed with short sticks or wands with mirrors on the end. They homed in on the central light fitting of the capsule and held up the mirrors along either side, checking in case the previous occupants had left a bomb.

'I think the security's a bit amateur–' the old man said in a stage whisper, pronouncing it 'ammerchewer' '–if you ask me.'

I agreed silently with the old man, thinking about the gun Barry had shown me in Armstrong.

Then I was distracted by another attendant who clambered on board the slowly moving capsule with a small metal trolley loaded with trays covered with white cloths, ice buckets, glasses and three bottles of champagne.

'Thought a snack might be called for whilst we chat,' said Grandad. 'It's only £155 plus VAT on top of the three hundred for the private hire, but if you're going to do things you might as well do them right, mightn't you?'

'You really have hired this?'

'Oh, yes. Private hire and you can take up to ten people with the buffet. Funnily enough, they do a thing called "Cupid's Capsule" which costs fifty pounds more but you and a lady friend get the whole thing to yourselves. Goodness knows what people get up to on those trips. I bet those mirror-on-a-stick boys find plenty of unpleasantness after one of them. Come on, climb aboard.'

I stopped automatically as my feet reached the edge of the platform. I wasn't consciously trying to resist – there didn't seem much point as I could feel Barry and Huw and the other one right behind me, shepherding me into the nine-tonne transparent egg-shaped cell.

Grandad tightened his grip on my arm and looked up into my face. There was no expression of concern on his.

'Who are you?' I asked.

The question seemed to surprise him.

'I'm Len Turner. Haven't you heard of me?'

'No, can't say I have,' I said apologetically.

'Well, that's probably been for the best for you. Up until now of course.'

I stepped in and we went up.

It had been a bit of a miscalculation on my part that nothing untoward would happen to me in a see-through cage rotating ever-so-slowly through 360 degrees in full view of eleven million Londoners. Correction, eleven million people, which is reckoned to be the day-time population during the tourist season though not all of them are Londoners. And not all Londoners can actually *see* the Eye – surprisingly few of them actually – as though it dominates the skyline, the natural inclination is to live nearer the earth and then the buildings tend to get in the way. And even if a fair proportion of the, say, eight million residents were actually looking in the right direction and upward to a point about three hundred feet in the air and did in fact catch a glimpse of me having my face smashed against the inside of the plexiglass capsule, would they give a shit? Probably not.

It all started innocently enough.

Our private capsule inched its way into the air and Len Turner – whatever and whoever he was – made a fair fist of being the genial host. He even introduced the big bouncer type as his son Ron, who was indeed the 'Da' of Barry and Huw, who I'd already met, hadn't I? Boxers all three of them, they were, he'd told me proudly and I'd said yes, I'd noticed.

'Now that down there, that'd be Westminster Bridge, wouldn't it? I recognize that one from the telly.' He pointed just like a tourist would. 'And that's the Houses of Parliament, or the English Parliament as we have to say these days. So what's that one?'

It seemed to be up to me to do the guided tour bit as our London Eye attendant was busying himself with his trolley, laying out aluminium plates of canapés and sandwiches on the wooden bench which ran down the middle of the capsule.

'That's Lambeth Bridge,' I said cautiously just in case it was a slap-earning trick question, 'and the next one down is Vauxhall Bridge.'

'And the other way?' He turned and pointed down river.

'That's Hungerford Bridge right there, or rather Bridges: the railway one and the new footbridge. Then it goes Waterloo, Blackfriars, Southwark, London, Tower and eventually the Thames Flood Barrier but I don't know if we'll see that.'

'Tower Bridge. That was the one the youngsters wanted to see.'

He thought for a moment then added: 'And who forgot to bring the binoculars out of the car?'

There was a silence and then a shot rang out and my heart stopped. What kind of man would shoot his grandsons for forgetting the binoculars?

'At last, lunch is served,' he boomed.

My heart started going again as a glass was thrust into my hand and our 'Flight Attendant' began to share out the champagne from the bottle he'd just popped.

'Let's drink to London,' said Len Turner raising his glass. 'London all around us but, most importantly, below us.'

Why not? I thought. I had to get through the next twenty-five minutes somehow and the Thames looked an awful long way down already.

'Look at it, boys, all laid out below you.'

The diminutive Len Turner was waxing lyrical, taking a dramatic turn so that his initially friendly gnome-like face was morphing into evil-troll. If we'd been in a pub I would have started to back towards the door. But once you're on the Eye, there's nowhere to run.

'All below us, the result of two thousand years of invasion, feudalism, civil war, social evils, plague, fire, imperialism, political turmoil and corruption and what does it produce? Chaucer, Shakespeare, parliamentary democracy, Christopher Wren, the Great Exhibition, Karl Marx, Churchill, the Trades Union Congress, the British Museum and the *Carry On* films.'

He flung out a hand in no particular direction but as it held an empty glass the flight attendant filled it and started work opening another bottle.

'And somewhere over there: Switzerland.' He paused for dramatic effect, but wisely not for too long. 'Four hundred years of peace and brotherly love and what does *it* produce? Cuckoo clocks.'

His chest inflated as he reached his conclusion and he beamed at his family and at me.

'And Toblerones,' said Huw.

I bit my tongue.

'And watches, good watches,' said Barry.

'And bob sleighs, like at the Winter Olympics,' added Barry.

I started to chew the lining of my cheeks.

'I was *paraphrasing*,' stormed Len. 'I was quoting from a famous film, you morons! *The Thin Man*. A very famous film. Haven't you lot ever seen a film in black and white? No, you wouldn't have, would you? Beneath you, it would be.'

I was beginning to see where the idea for the voice of Yoda in *Star Wars* came from but I couldn't trust myself to say anything.

'Know who wrote that?' Len rounded on his grandkids. ''Course you don't. It was Graham Greene. A bloody fine writer for an Englishman. And a Catholic at that.'

Len drained his glass and handed it to his son Ron.

'Get us a refill, Ron, and you two, you might as well get stuck into the grub. It's paid for.'

Barry and Huw didn't need a second telling. They sat down on the central bench and began to hoover up small triangular sandwiches three at a time. Nobody offered me anything and as I put my glass down on the floor I could feel the champagne refermenting in my empty stomach.

'Better take care of the Trolley Dolly whilst you're at it, Ron.'

Ron grunted as he handed over his dad's refill, then stepped towards Barry and held out his hand for something. Barry dug into the flaps of his raincoat and for one awful moment I thought he was going to produce the revolver he'd shown me earlier and Big Ron was going to take care of our flight attendant permanently. But whatever it was he did pass over fitted easily into the palm of Ron's large paw.

I don't know what Ron said to the flight attendant and I couldn't see his expression as he was hidden by Ron's shoulders, but I could see two twenty-pound notes being slipped into the attendant's jacket pocket. And then the attendant had turned around to face the glass at the far end of the capsule and was busy screwing in a set of earplugs.

I watched fascinated by the unreality of it all as more of London unfolded beneath us, the human figures rapidly turning into ants and not one of them concerned with what was happening up here. With our personal Trolley Dolly now bribed, deaf and effectively blind, I was on my own with three generations of inbred Welsh nastiness.

'We could do with one of these in Cardiff, you know,' said the elder Turner, squinting towards the west as if to check you really could see Heathrow on a clear day should you want to. 'Put it somewhere down Queen Alexandra docks and you could see up to the valleys and Caerphilly or across the Channel, maybe as far as Bristol.'

That sounded cruel to me, like the prisoners on Alcatraz being able to see the lights and night-life of San Francisco without being able to touch it.

'You got the Millennium Stadium, we got the Eye,' I said.

'That's true,' he agreed, 'and the English football teams have to come cap in hand to play their big matches there, not that they're grateful, mind you.'

The little old man moved to my side so he could place his hands on the rail which ran around the inside of the capsule and stare out to the north-west.

'You haven't asked me how I know you,' he said, gazing into space. 'You haven't asked why I wanted this little chat. In fact you haven't asked anything, Mr Angel. Cat got your tongue?'

I knew a cat who'd have his once he was

feeling better.

'I think you're going to tell me, Mr Turner,' I said, turning round so that I was in the same position and gripping the rail like he was. The main difference was that my knuckles had already gone white with the strain. 'Sometime in the next twenty minutes or so,' I ventured.

He made a show of consulting his watch.

'Yes, you don't get long on this thing, do you? Still, the view's worth it. So let's get the ugly business part over with and we can enjoy the rest of our flight.'

If he made a signal to Ron behind me I didn't see it. Maybe Ron had been waiting for a raised eyebrow or something, reflected in the perspex. Whatever. The next thing I knew my right leg had given way and my chin was bouncing off the rail between my two hands, rattling my teeth. Then Ron grabbed a handful of my hair, pulled my head back and slammed it against the capsule wall.

Nothing else happened for a while after that. I realized I was on my knees, still holding the rail like someone taking communion, trying to focus on a trickle of blood on the plexiglass. I turned my head slightly to see if it hurt. It did and more blood spotted my shirt front.

'Ron was always getting into trouble at school, giving the other boys the dead leg.

Some of the girls, too,' Len Turner was saying but now I had to look up to him. 'He's quite good at it.'

'What was that for?' I managed, resisting the urge to burst into tears.

'For not answering my questions.'

'You haven't asked any, have you?'

I tucked my head into my shoulder in case there was another blow. It was all I could do as I had no feeling in my right leg at all. Still, where was there to run?

'No,' he said reasonably, 'but I'm about to and it was you yourself who pointed out we don't have any time to mess about, so I thought it best if Ron showed you we mean business beforehand. Ready, then?'

'Anything, anything,' I mumbled, thinking it best to go for the defeated, totally servile approach. It wasn't a hard act and I think I was pretty convincing.

'Keith Flowers. There's a name you'll know.'

'Yes, yes, I do,' I said quickly.

'A guest at one of the better Windsor Hotels – Her Majesty's Prison Belmarsh to you – until a month or so ago. Now he's in a padded cell at Rampton – a maximum security looney bin – and totally unapproachable, which is why I'm having to ask you these questions and not him.'

'I know nothing about the guy,' I said, trying to make it sound as if I was pleading for mercy – and doing a good job of it.

'You knew him well enough to put him in hospital,' Len said, still taking in the view. 'And you know his wife very well from what I hear.'

'Ex-wife,' I said automatically.

'Don't tell me she never mentioned him? Or the divorce?' He looked down at me for the first time and smiled. 'No, she didn't, did she? Well I can't blame her. She naturally would want to put all that behind her now she's so successful. Anyway, its her "ex" I'm interested in, not her. I want to know what Keith Flowers was up to between coming out of one prison and you putting him back in another, which, as I understand it, involved a fair proportion of violence with a bulldozer. Sounds like you're not a man to cross, Mr Angel. At least not on a building site.'

He allowed himself a chuckle at that, while I wondered how the hell he knew it.

'Look, he came out of the night at us. He was trying to abduct Amy. She didn't want to go with him. He took a shot at me. I stopped him.'

'That sounds a fair summary of what...' Len started but he was interrupted by Barry – or it could have been Huw – from somewhere behind me.

'What sort of a gun did he have?'

For a split second there was fire in old

156

Len's eyes, his face the troll rather than the garden gnome again as he glared at whoever had spoken out of turn. I averted my eyes before he could see I'd noticed.

'I don't know, it was dark,' I mumbled. 'The police took it. I'd never seen the guy before that night but I'll tell you something for nothing, you're not the only people interested in what he was doing while he was on the loose.'

Now it wasn't strictly true to say I'd never seen Keith Flowers before that night, but in high-stress confrontational situations I've found it helps relieve the pressure if you can offer something as a diversion. Normally it's called lying.

'What makes you say that?'

At least it hadn't resulted in any more pain. I risked shaking my head to clear it and noticed that we were almost at the top of the Eye's axis. Immediately below us were all the other capsules filled with happy-go-lucky sightseers and not one of the bastards looking my way.

'Because somebody's been following me – and not just me, but anyone who could possibly have had anything to do with Flowers while he was out on licence or whatever it's called.'

'Really?' said Len Turner, mildly interested. 'Could it be the police?'

'They're not interested. As far as they're

concerned they have enough to hang Flowers with already. Anyway, he was arrested in Suffolk and I'm saying somebody's interested in his movements here in London.'

Old Len, the grandad from hell, reached out his right fist and took my nose between the knuckles of his first and middle fingers and twisted.

I can't remember if I screamed but I certainly fainted – one of those narcoleptic rushes you get when you're dreaming sometimes and you wake up thinking you've just stepped off the edge of a cliff or a platform on the Jubilee Line. (Why is it always the Jubilee Line?)

The faint lasted just long enough for me to topple sideways and come to just as the back of my head bounced off the floor of the capsule and now I was looking up at all of them. The entire Turner clan with not an expression between them and our flight attendant at the far end of the capsule, his back to us, his hands clasped behind his back, oblivious, but forty quid better off.

Barry and Huw made to get up off the bench but Ron, their dad, didn't need them to pick me up and lean me against the hand rail. I could feel something in my right leg now but not a lot. Everywhere else just hurt, especially my nose.

'It's not broken,' said Len, wiping his hands on a handkerchief. 'Or if it is, it's nothing serious. It'll heal. So when did you notice our little detective?'

'What?'

For a moment I thought my hearing had been affected and it was me who should have had the hearing aid, but maybe I just had brain damage.

'The private detective I've had looking in to things – at great expense I might add.'

'What?' I said again.

'The ... other ... people ... interested ... in ... Flowers,' he said slowly, so I could take it in. 'There aren't any, it was me all the time. I hired myself a detective to find out who Flowers saw and where he went. Thought it best to call in a London firm, you know, us not being used to the big city that is. And would you know it, but it all seemed to come back to you, Mr Angel.'

He reached inside his raincoat pocket and I flinched, expecting a gun or a cosh or a set of thumbscrews. His hand came out with a yellow envelope, the sort you get photographs back in from the Kwiksnap/Fotoflash/Expresspix type of franchise on most street corners in the West End.

'Take it. Have a look.'

I took the envelope as if it contained anthrax. It had FASTFLASH and 1-Hour Service printed on the front and an address in Shepherd's Bush and it contained photographs but no strips of negatives. I was so relieved my hands hardly shook at all as I flicked through them.

The prints were standard six-by-four inch holiday snap size and hardly works of art, but a couple of them did show my good side. There was me going in to Duncan the Drunken's garage, me coming out of same garage and saying something over my shoulder. There was me talking to Fenella on Stuart Street then one of the back of me running into the house followed by one of me running out of the house with a towel-wrapped bundle in my arms. There were several of me and Debbie Diamond, on Oxford Street and leaving the hotel on Portman Square, all good shots and the very stuff of divorce cases in years gone by before the 'Oh let's just call it a fucking day' solution came in. There was even a very fuzzy one of me standing in a doorway, lit only by a security lamp and the nearby streetlight. It took me a while to work out that was me talking to my neighbour Mr Dunmore. It seemed like years ago.

The ones that really interested me, though I tried not to show it, were half a dozen shots of Amy. Three showed her leaving the office, three showed her leaving the Hampstead house with her Gucci overnight bag and getting in to the Freelander parked in the driveway. She was wearing a light blue two-piece suit I couldn't remember ever seeing before and the last shot was of her sitting sideways on the driver's seat, taking off her red Jimmy Choo heels so she could drive in her stockinged feet, as she always did on long journeys.

'Very nice,' I said, handing back the envelope. 'And to answer your question, I didn't spot your pet snooper. The local Neighbourhood Watch did and they reported her to the cops.'

Len pocketed the photographs.

'Well, that doesn't matter now, but I'll bear it in mind if I ever need their services again. You have to admit, though, that you take a good picture. You could offer me a penny for my thoughts and I'd have to give you change if I didn't think there was some connection.'

'Connection with what?' I realized my voice was getting shrill so I tried to chill it and took another tack.

'Look, Mr Turner, you're a reasonable man...'

'What makes you think that?' he said with a look of such innocence I almost believed he was interested in an answer, so I chanced one.

'Because there's four of you, one of me and we're still three hundred feet off the ground. I don't want to get off this thing before the people six capsules in front of us do.'

Ron took a deep breath and probably clenched his fists. I didn't see him do it, just felt it, as I was keeping eye contact with old Len.

'Go on, then,' Len said, not flinching.

'So think this through. Keith Flowers – and I'd never heard of the bastard until a month ago – has caused me nothing but grief. He comes out of the nick to find his ex-wife is hitched up with someone else and he throws a wobbler. All I did was get in his way. I'm the one he shoots at. It's my car he trashes. It's me who has to answer questions from the cops. You think I want this in my life? Christ, it'd be bad enough finding out there was a stamp-collecting, civil servant of an ex-husband, let alone a psycho with form and a gun.'

Len tilted his head and there was something close to pity on his face.

'You really didn't know about Keith and young Amy?'

'No, I didn't,' I said but I was thinking: *how does he?*

'You poor bugger. I suggest you have a long talk with that woman of yours.'

Yeah, right. If I could find her.

'But where does that leave us, Mr Angel? It doesn't solve my particular problem.'

'And I don't know what that is, Mr Turner. If you've got some sort of candle burning for Keith Flowers, then I'm sorry for what happened to him but he brought it all on himself.'

Len Turner smiled and his teeth reminded me of tombstones.

'If I lit a candle for Keith Flowers, it would only be to jam it up his arse, flame first. Maybe you can't help me after all.'

'Why not try telling me what your problem with Flowers is? If it puts him deeper in the shit, I'm up for it.'

'I think he's just about as deep in the shit as it's possible to be and still be breathing without a snorkel,' said Len Turner, looking out at the view again, downriver this time. 'My information is that he genuinely has gone mental, you know. It's not an act. But even if you did act your way into Rampton, you can't act your way out of that place. Trouble is, I can't get in to ask the little scumbag where my money is.'

I blinked. I know I did for it hurt my forehead and more blood dripped on to my shirt.

'Money?'

'Ah, got your interest now, have I?'

He had mistaken my wincing for interest.

'I'm always interested in money,' I said, glancing down to my left and seeing the Thames and the concrete landing pad getting nearer.

'Well, let me say this,' he said pompously. 'I gave Keith Flowers a deposit on a certain transaction we were engaged in and – partly thanks to you, no, mostly thanks to you – he never managed to complete the deal. He's in no position to do so now, so I'd like my deposit back. It's not so much the money, it's the principle. You with me?'

'I think so. You can't get to Flowers so you're tracking whoever he might have seen or had contact with in his month out of Belmarsh.'

'You are with me. Good. Huw, get one of those cloths and wrap some ice in it. Mr Angel seems to have a nosebleed.'

'I told you I was scared of heights,' I said.

'So you did. They must disagree with you. But I think this little trip has been useful. I mean, we've seen the sights and I've learned something very useful.'

'What's that?' I said warily, taking the makeshift icepack from young Huw.

'That you know fuck all. Oh, and that London detective agencies are a waste of money.' He sucked on his bottom lip. 'I suppose you were a long shot anyway, but I had to be sure. You see, the only people Keith Flowers had contact with on his brief holiday from custody were you and your Amy. Now, Amy takes out a Restraining Order on him, doesn't she? That doesn't sound too friendly, even if it's understandable. So that left you and you were unknown. You weren't one of the old gang so I had to be sure you weren't his silent partner. I'm sure now that you're not, because you're basically a little innocent at large, aren't you, Mr Angel? I'm a good judge of character and you'd be out of your depth in a puddle in a pub car park.'

'You're not wrong there,' I said very quietly, no more than a whisper, from behind the cloth stuffed with ice.

'No, I'm not, am I?' he answered, proving that his hearing aid was either state of the art and capable of picking up a mouse fart on Saturn or it was just for show. 'Come here a minute.'

He pulled my hand so that my icepack came away from my face and he studied my nose.

'How many fingers am I holding up?'

'None,' I said, bemused.

'Correct,' he said and he straight-fingered me in the stomach with his right hand.

It didn't hurt that much; hardly enough to take my mind off the throbbing in my nose or the dull ache in my leg, but enough to keep my attention.

We were coming into land now, the capsule below us already disgorging cheery passengers. In a few minutes we would be at head-height of those in the front of the queue.

Old Len took the cloth with the ice and, using a damp corner, cleaned half a dozen spots of blood – my blood, already dried in the sunshine – from the inside of the perspex where I had come into contact with it.

'See to our Trolley Dolly Huw, and compensate him for the tea towel. Oh, and bring that other bottle of bubbly. It's paid for.'

He handed back my icepack and I folded it as small as a large handkerchief so as not to upset the tourists. I zipped up my jacket so the red spots on my shirt couldn't be seen either.

Turner watched me closely.

'Good thinking,' he said. 'Don't draw attention to yourself. It might be best if you get off first.'

'But when the doors open, right?'

He actually smiled at that, though maybe it was the way my voice sounded as if I had the mother of all head colds and it probably came out as: 'Dut ben de doors dopuh, drite?'

'Sure, sure. No hard feelings, eh?'

I glanced around. We were almost at the landing platform and our flight attendant was gathering up the glasses and plates of canapés, studiously avoiding catching my eye. Outside on the concrete, two more staff with mirrors-on-sticks were poised to do their security sweep. As if anyone dare plant a bomb in Len Turner's presence.

'Oh yes, I'm afraid so, Mr Turner,' I said quickly and quietly so that only he could hear me. 'Lots of hard feelings, but not against you. I'm saving them all for Keith Flowers. I blame him for getting me into this and the cops are going to want to talk to me again.'

He mulled this over and even ran a hand over his bald pate but there wasn't time for subtlety now. We would either land and I'd walk away or he'd hit me again.

'I could find out what *they* know,' I said. 'I mean, he shot a gun at me. I'm a victim in all this so I have some rights, don't I? I can ask questions. See if they know who Flowers came into contact with. Would you be interested?'

'I might, Mr Angel, I might just be. But this would cost me, wouldn't it?'

'Naturally.'

Number One son Ron moved closer to us, wondering what the whispering was about. Behind me I heard the capsule doors start to slide open.

Old Len shot a hand inside his raincoat and it came out holding a wallet. Instead of money though, he produced a white business card and held it up in front of my eyes so I could read it. There were two lines of print – *Haydn Rees, LLB* and underneath, *Solicitor* – and then a phone number starting 02920.

'You can contact me through my solicitors, with tact and discretion,' Len said as I took the card and thrust it into my jeans pocket.

The doors were opening fully now and I was tempted to say I thought that With, Tact and Discretion was a funny name for a firm of solicitors, but I didn't. It wasn't the time or the place. With Len Turner I somehow didn't think there ever would be a time or a place.

So I just nodded to him, even though that stung my sinuses and misted my eyes, and stepped backwards off the eye and kept my head down as I pushed through the crowds.

I found the Armstrong unlocked and the keys in, exactly where I had left him.

As I climbed in I noticed that the white Rover which Huw and Barry had driven had a number plate which said the supplier of the car was www.expolicecars.com. I also noticed that it had been issued with a parking ticket and the Armstrong had not.

So, there was *some* justice in the world after all.

Chapter Eight

I needed to think. I needed pen and paper to write things down before I forgot them. I needed a drink. I probably needed a doctor. I needed food. I needed to put the river and some distance between me and the Welsh Mafia. I needed to go somewhere where black cabs could go but white Rovers with parking tickets (ex-police cars or not) driven by grockles thumbing through the A–Z couldn't.

I did a dog-leg around Waterloo and zipped over Westminster Bridge only marginally over the speed limit, though everyone knows that doesn't really apply to taxis. There was nothing in my mirror – or at least nothing white and Welsh – but I did two circuits of Parliament Square just to be sure, then cut across the traffic into Parliament Street alongside the Treasury. Using a number 88 bus as cover, I hung a right and shot down the side street on the corner of the Red Lion pub and which lead to Cannon Row police station and, in days gone by, the former New Scotland Yard.

Well, if you were going to park illegally and drink and drive, you might as well do it with style.

With my head down and a damp, pink tea-towel over my nose, I bypassed the entrance to the downstairs bar and went for the main door on the corner. Once inside you can nip up the stairs to the toilets without having to enter the bar – one of the few pubs left in London where you can do that.

In front of the mirror in the Gents I cleaned up as best I could. The bleeding had stopped but I had a blue-green-black bruise forming nicely across the bridge of my nose. I had lifted my fake Raybans from the glove compartment of Armstrong and they hurt like hell but covered the worst of it. All I had to do now was negotiate the steep staircase down to the bar and hoped they gave priority to a blind man.

The main bar was busy as it usually is, but with tourists rather than with MPs who listen out for the Division Bell when Parliament is in session just across the Square. Parliament was on holiday and so was most of Europe by the accents of the thronging customers but as always happens when a pub is full, nobody noticed a scruffy, wet-haired (to remove the dried blood) oik wearing sunglasses limp his way to the bar and order a large vodka and the last brie and bacon baguette in the place. The Australian barman didn't bat an eyelid when the vodka disappeared before the sandwich arrived, or say anything when I grabbed a thick wodge of paper napkins, took the baguette and handed back the plate. What the hell, for half the year his customers were mostly MPs. He must have seen worse.

Back in the Armstrong, who I had turned around to face Parliament Street in case I needed a direct line of escape, I used two of the napkins to hold the baguette and the rest I formed into a neat pile on my thigh where the numbness had subsided into a dull tingling sensation.

Behind the driver's sun visor, which like real cabbies I only use as a filing cabinet, was a battered, well-out-of-date A–Z and a felt tip pen which still worked. As I ate I composed my thoughts: one per napkin in big letters as I still didn't trust my eyes to focus properly.

1: LEN TURNER

I wrote on the first one, the felt-tip blurring and smudging the ink as it ran on the tissue paper. Then again, that might have been my eyesight.

2: IS NOT MR CREOSOTE

He couldn't be. That ageing toe-rag Spider had only told me of a 'Mr Creosote' an hour or so before the Chuckle Brothers had picked me up at Stuart Street, and any way, 'Mr Creosote' was unavoidably detained at Her Majesty's pleasure. Which meant there *was* another party interested in

Keith Flowers, apart from Turner and his private detective.

3: BUY MORE CIGS

That toe-rag Spider had palmed my emergency packet.

4: PRIVATE EYE

So my mysterious stalker – and almost certainly Springsteen's assailant – was a private eye and probably a cheapskate one who had surveillance pictures developed like holiday snaps at – where was it? – 'Fastflash' in Shepherd's Bush. As it happened, I knew a real firm of private detectives who worked out of Shepherd's Bush. Maybe I could hire a stalker to stalk the stalker.

5: TURNER KNEW ABOUT AMY

Or at least he sounded as if he did. He was Welsh and Amy was supposed to have gone – maybe had – to Welsh Fashion Week. As a connection, was that tenuous or what? He'd also said something about me not being one of the 'old gang'. Did that mean Amy was? I supposed I could ask her.

6: FIND AMY

I'd better do that too.

7: FLOWERS

How did Turner know about Keith Flowers' arrest? And the Restraining Order Amy put on him? And that he was now in Rampton and that he trollied big time in the mental department? Could a private eye have dug all that up for him?

8: SILENT PARTNER

Turner was sure I wasn't Flowers' 'silent partner' – so who was? And in what?

9: GUN

One of the younger Turners had asked what sort of gun Keith Flowers had used on me and while that wasn't in any way an unusual question for people who actually carried them and may have been no more than professional interest, old grandad Len had skewered him with a filthy look, effectively telling him not to go there. Was it important? What did it all mean? Was there anything else I'd forgotten?

10: AMY...

I ran out of napkins.

But at least I had a plan.

There were people I had to talk to. One was this Mr Creosote character, and that was out of my hands but in hand, or so I'd been told. Another was DI Hood of West Hampstead, who ought to know something and if he didn't then he ought to know a man who did.

Above all, there was Amy. Where the hell was she and why hadn't she called?

Maybe she had. I should get to a phone.

I had a phone.

If my nose and forehead hadn't hurt so much I would have gladly banged it against the nearest wall or maybe just slapped them

173

and gone 'Doh!'. Instead I dug into the glove compartment for the mobile phone she'd bought me, hoping the battery still had juice in it. She was always complaining that I never turned it on and I bet she'd left hundreds of messages on it just to wind me up.

The battery had held up and there were three Missed Calls and three Messages, all from Amy's office number.

All from Debbie Diamond, each voice message more obscene than the last but the gist was that I really ought to try and find the time to ring her if it was at all convenient. Oh, and that I was a minging pillock.

Minging? Charming.

Her mood hadn't improved between the messages and my voice.

'Where have you *been* all day?' she snarled, like today of all days she could intimidate me.

'Sightseeing,' I snapped back. 'Any word from Amy?'

'No, there sodding well isn't – and just where does that leave Madrid?'

That floored me for a minute.

'Somewhere in central Spain?' I tried.

'Oh, sweet Sister Fidelma, will you grow up? Amy's supposed to be in Madrid next week, flying out there on Monday afternoon. Or had you forgotten that as well?'

'No, I hadn't forgotten.' How could I have? I didn't know about it. 'I'm sure she'll be in touch. Somehow.'

I hoped that didn't sound as if I mean with the aid of a psychic.

'By the way, has anybody called Turner phoned, or tried to get into the office?' I said casually so as not to alarm her, though I wouldn't give the office security men more than half a minute up against Ron, Barry and Huw.

'No, nobody called Turner but there's a woman been after you all day. Well, it seems like all day and I'm pretty sure she's mad.'

With the women I knew, that didn't narrow it down but I put my money on it being Fenella.

'What does she want now?' I asked, resigned.

'She wants to invite you to a party, in fact more than that, she sort of insisted you went. Said it was important. Vital, actually.'

That didn't sound like Fenella.

'And she must be mad, because she said the party started this afternoon, at 3 p.m. sharp,' Debbie went on. 'Which is a bloody funny time to hold a hen night if you ask me.'

A hen night?

'This wasn't Fenella, was it?' I said confidently.

'Who's Fenella? I'm talking about Stella,

175

not Fenella.'

I didn't believe it.

'I don't believe it,' I said.

'Well, it is a bit odd, but she was very insistent.'

'We are talking about Estelle – Stella – Rudgard, right?' I said, just to be sure.

'That's her. That's the name. Spelled it out for me like I was a right div. Said she was getting married tomorrow and simply had to talk to you today and that you knew her number but if you couldn't ring by three o'clock, you had to go along to her hen night at somewhere called Gerry's in Soho. She said you knew it. I mean, what sort of a person holds their hen night in a Soho club at three o'clock on a Friday afternoon?'

'Stella Rudgard would,' I said.

'I mean, can you really believe that?'

'No, Debbie. Like I said, I just don't believe it.'

But what I didn't believe was the awful coincidence.

Somewhere on the floor of the Armstrong where I'd dropped them was a paper napkin with 'Private Eye' written on it to remind me to use the one real private eye firm I knew of to check out who Len Turner had hired to follow me.

The detective firm in question: R & B Confidential Investigations.

As in (Stella) Rudgard & (Veronica)

Blugden Confidential Investigations.
Of Shepherd's Bush.

Long before I ever met Amy, I knew Stella Rudgard and had a healthy respect for her exhaustive dedication to sex as a cross between aerobics and training for the Olympics heptathalon. I suspected that her enthusiasm for sex was the one thing which kept her borderline sane, but it still made her dangerous to know. But then, I only knew her briefly. Very briefly; and it was long, long before I met Amy. Several years in fact.

Veronica Blugden was another kettle of fish entirely. From school reports which had said things like 'this young lady has delusions of adequacy' she had graduated to dead-end jobs and annual staff appraisals ranging from 'she has set low personal standards and consistently failed to achieve them' to 'this employee should go far and the sooner she starts the better', which is what she did. Moving to London with only the vaguest of ideas about being a private detective – in fact, all her ideas were vague – she found herself working for a one-man enquiry agency run by an ex-Met copper called Albert Block. Her first case, almost by accident, involved finding Stella Rudgard, even though Stella didn't actually want to be found and was working her own agenda. Anyhow, Albert Block retired and Veronica inherited the agency, such as it was, and Stella – in a bizarre variation on the Stockholm Syndrome, where the kidnappee goes over to the kidnapper's side – had joined forces to form R & B Investigations. They had done well. I had read a couple of magazine articles about how they only employed female operatives, which had probably been good for business, with no mention of their policy of occasionally employing unlicensed male cab-drivers with more time on their hands than sense – and then quibbling about their expenses.

I reckoned R & B Investigations owed me a favour and maybe Stella wanted to repay me or – if she really was getting married tomorrow – maybe she wanted to buy my silence. Unless she'd had a character transplant since I'd last seen her, I could guess that hubby-to-be would be (a) rich, (b) posh and (c) connected. Definitely not the sort to be impressed by stories of Stella's raucous past. That could give me an edge.

I could imagine what sort of friend Stella would invite to her hen night and what sort of hen would go to a party at Gerry's Club at three in the afternoon. I would need an edge, but then, an invite was an invite.

I looked in the mirror to check I was presentable enough. With the fake Raybans on I reckoned I wouldn't be the scariest thing in Soho that afternoon, and Gerry's was dimly lit so the spots of blood on my shirt probably wouldn't show. I could have gone home and cleaned up but then again it was already 3.30 p.m. and I was missing the party.

Plus, there were two uniformed policeman strolling up the lane towards the rear of the Armstrong.

I started the engine and pulled out, signalling right towards Whitehall.

Party on.

The traffic was snarled in Trafalgar Square and it took ages to find a place to park in one of the alleys behind Frith Street. That plus stopping off to buy a wedding present (a bottle of rice wine in a set with a transparently thin china flask and two matching bowls on special offer in a Chinatown supermarket) meant I was well late for the hen night, if it had started on time.

On Dean Street, I pressed the intercom on the wall at the door of Gerry's and said 'Rudgard party'. The response was incomprehensible due to the background mix of music and high pitched screaming, but the door lock clicked open anyway.

Gerry's is a discreet subterranean drinking club, founded for actors and theatre people. Most of the clientèle of the flashier Groucho

Club, virtually next door, stumble by the front door without even noticing it, for which most of Gerry's members are eternally grateful.

The stairs go down to a blank wall and then they turn almost back on themselves and take you down into the club proper. The noise washed over me before I turned the corner and could see into the club proper. It's not a big place, but usually you can find a spare seat or at least see a square inch of floor space. Not today. I was looking down at a sea of women, all standing, all talking, some singing along to a piano being played in the far corner, the piano and pianist taking up about twenty per cent of the floor space. Some seemed to be trying to dance or perhaps they were just swaying in the tide. Most of them were smoking, holding their cigarettes up at eye level because they couldn't lower their arms without making a pass at someone, such was the crush.

Behind the bar, besieged like a scene out of *Zulu*, Michael the owner and two T-shirted blondes who could have been twins (but the light was bad and I was wearing shades) were handing out bottles of wine and champagne like their lives depended on it. They probably did. Some were passed, as if floating, over the heads of the revellers, others just sank into the mass and disappeared without trace.

I elbowed my way to the end of the bar, being twice bounced against the cigarette machine by soft but unyielding female flesh.

'Angel, my dear chap,' said Michael, proffering his hand over the bar when I got within range. 'Sorry about the crush, but all the regular members were told there was a private do on.'

Even with a hundred thirsty women waiting to be served, Michael couldn't resist the dig, but he did it with a twinkle in his eye and a grin thinly hidden by his blonde beard.

'Sorry I haven't been in much lately,' I said loudly, above the chatter, 'but I'm invited to this one.'

'You're not the stripper they ordered, are you?' Michael asked with a look of genuine horror.

One of the blonde barmaids said something to him and he listened, nodded, then turned back to me relieved.

'It seems he's been and gone,' he said. 'Lasted about thirty seconds, I'm told. Usual?'

I nodded and he stretched out to hand me a bottle of Becks with the top off.

'Sorry it's warm. Fridge is full of champagne.'

I shrugged philosophically. There I was in a small room with dozens of women clad in their scantiest summer clothes, many of them already the worse for drink with some already eyeing me up, and the piano player was making a decent fist of Bonnie Tyler's *It's A Heartache*, though few of the party-goers looked old enough to remember Bonnie Tyler, and yet the beer was warm. It was as if the gods had decided there had to be one thing to stop it being perfect.

'I'm looking for Stella Rudgard,' I said, hoping Michael could lip read.

'Table by the piano,' said Michael, pointing with an empty champagne bottle.

I turned but couldn't see where he meant even though the piano wasn't more than fifteen feet away. There was nothing for it but to push through the wall of female flesh, beer in one hand present in the other, saying 'Excuse me, coming through' as I went. I was fondled once and groped twice, which, given the distance travelled and the factor by which I was outnumbered, was probably a fair average.

And then I was at the piano, my knees no more than an inch from the stool the pianist was sitting on and I still couldn't see Stella. So instead I tried to look as if I was enjoying the music, just swaying in time with everyone else.

The pianist was good and well worth a second glance, even from behind.

Especially from behind.

She was another blonde – long, straight

hair flipped back over her ears – and she wore a tight, short-cut white top and tight, low-cut jeans. Between the bottom of the top and the top of the jeans, she had a breaching dolphin tattooed right in the small of her back. As she bent forward over the keys of the ancient stand-up piano, which was almost in tune, the dolphin seemed to fly even further out of the water. As she straightened her back, it dived into the beltless rim of her Wranglers.

'Angel! You made it!'

I heard that above the music and the background noise and turned to see Stella sitting at a table no more than a yard away. She had only seen me because two women had decided to change positions, probably to avoid cramp. I pushed between them to get at Stella and one of them said 'Oooh!' and flashed me a killer smile, but then Stella's arm was round the back of my neck and she drew me in until my knees hit the table to kiss me full on the lips. I had a beer in one hand and her present in the other. I was powerless to resist.

'That was nice,' she shouted in my ear. 'I'd forgotten just how nice. What have you done to your face?'

'*I* didn't do anything to it,' I shouted back as the pianist pounded out the opening bars of *Satin Doll*. 'Are you really getting married?'

She nodded, her face about an inch from

mine. 'Tomorrow morning at eleven, down in Sussex. Very posh do, not allowed to misbehave. No smoking, no drugs, no boozing, so, naturally, you couldn't be invited, but I wanted one last night on the town. What d'yer think?'

She shooed away the two women sitting at the table with her, then she pushed the table away so that it almost collided with the pianist's stool. She didn't seen to notice; she had her head down (dolphin rising) concentrating on the high register chorus and making a good job of it.

I squeezed in to the space Stella had made and examined her as she stood, hands on hips, her left leg bent slightly at the knee.

Stella was taller than me barefooted and in heels she towered above me. She was dressed almost entirely in black: a black chiffon tie shirt over a black lace-panel corset top, and a narrow black hook-and-eye skirt which ended at the knee, but a slit up the left side showed a lot of leg and the lacy top of her hold-up stockings plus a glimpse of white flesh. The only splash of colour was in her shoes, three-inch heeled pink sandals trimmed with black lace from Kurt Geiger which cost £159. Amy had a pair of them.

'You on the pull, then?' I said, leaning in to her hair which she'd had cut almost boyishly short since I'd last seen her.

'No, just the tease.' I should have known.

184

Stella had a PhD in Tease. 'That's why I'm not wearing my engagement ring.'

'I noticed that,' I said. Well, I would have eventually.

'Not that the insurance company would let me,' she said casually. Then she put her hands gently on my face and pulled me in for another kiss and when she broke for air she said: 'We could hock it and disappear somewhere.'

'But I haven't finished my beer,' I said, 'and you haven't opened your wedding present.'

I handed over the box I was carrying.

'Pressy!' shouted Stella and ripped off the gift wrapping the girl in the Chinese supermarket had slaved over in one deft movement.

'Oh, sweet!' Stella said, then placed the box on the table and pulled the small bottle of rice wine out of its holding slot. Stella tapped the bottle on the shoulder of a small redhead in a green satin dress. 'Ask Michael for some glasses and some ice for this, would you, Randy?'

'Randy' cut her through a pair of rimless octagonal glasses.

'Certainly, miss. Will there be anything else, miss? What did your last slave die of, miss?'

'Oh, shut up you old tart,' said Stella with a grin.

'Slag.'

'Slapper.'

'Hag.'

'Bitch.'

'Minger.'

'Er ... it's supposed to be served warm,' I said.

'Then tell Michael to stick it in the microwave,' said Stella.

'I don't think he's got a microwave,' said Randy, blowing cigarette smoke at us.

'Then stick it down the front of his trousers for five minutes,' said Stella, like it was the most obvious thing in the world.

Randy cheered up at that, took the bottle and headed for the bar.

'You just can't get the staff these days,' Stella said, moving closer into me than was strictly necessary.

I took a pull on my beer and reached for the pack of cigarettes Stella had left on the table. It meant I had to lean into her but she didn't seem to mind.

'Randy is staff?' I said, fumbling with the cigarette packet and trying to ignore Stella's left knee as it nudged its way between my legs. I was in danger of being assaulted in front of witnesses twice in one day. That would be a record even for me.

'We have lots of staff now, we've expanded,' Stella said, so close to me now she didn't have to shout.

The pressure of her knee increased and I drew heavily on the cigarette I had finally managed to light. Stella caught my hand and directed the cigarette to her own lips, tilting her head to do so, but her eyes never leaving my face. If she got any closer she'd be behind me. I had to break the spell.

'Is Veronica here?'

'No, she's on a job on a cruise ship in the Baltic trying to spot which of the crew are diddling the passengers.'

Her knee moved back a fraction and suddenly I felt a lot cooler. Talking about Veronica obviously had the same dampener effect on both of us.

'So she'll be missing the wedding?'

'Yes,' Stella smiled. 'But then she's not really a wedding person.'

'I didn't think you were.'

'I was sure *you* weren't, but, hey, what do I know?'

'You must know something. You called me.'

She edged backwards, leaving enough room for cigarette smoke to drift between us, and then came to a decision.

'Yes, you're right, I did. We need to talk before I get totally trollied. Come on.'

She grabbed my hand and began to push through the crowd, smiling, talking, air-kissing as she went, ignoring the suggestions and nudge-nudge, wink-wink accusations thrown at her from virtually everyone in the room. At one point she responded with, 'It's my party I can do who I like,' and she also managed to liberate an almost full bottle of champagne from someone. I had just time to grab her cigarettes and lighter from the table before she dragged me in her wake.

The pianist had started a very slow version of *I Wish I Knew How It Felt To Be Free*. She was good even if, with my back to her now, I couldn't see what the dolphin tattoo was doing. Some of the guests were swaying (as much as was possible) and humming along and I caught snippets of conversation as they tried to remember which TV show it had been used as a theme for, which film it had featured in and who had done last year's grim cover version. None of them would have ever heard of Nina Simone, but the pianist probably had. She was good.

'Back in a few minutes. You enjoy yourselves. Get more drink. Call of nature, that's all,' Stella was saying to all and sundry.

As we came level with the end of the bar I saw Michael tangling with Randy, who had managed to get behind the bar and was tugging at the belt of his trousers, waving the small bottle of rice wine in front of his face. He caught my eye at the same time he realized what Randy was suggesting, shrugged his shoulders and with a smile, let

188

her work the bottle down the front of his trousers, making lots of over the top faces and giving me the thumbs up sign with his right hand.

I realized that Stella was dragging me towards the toilets and when Michael saw that, his grin broadened, and he put both thumbs up in the air.

Chapter Nine

There were catcalls and wolf whistles loud enough to drown out the pianist as Stella dragged me through the door to the toilets. There would have been more if they'd seen her carry straight on into the Gents, slam the door behind us and then lean on it.

'Tobacco me,' she commanded, crossing her legs so that the skirt fell open again and putting the champagne bottle to her lips. When I had lit a cigarette from the stub of the one I had, we swopped.

'You're really getting married tomorrow?' I asked between sips.

''Fraid so. Missed your chance there.'

'Just naturally lucky, I guess. You going to be in any fit state?'

'Fuck it, I'm not going into that church sober!' she laughed. 'But don't worry about me, Angel, I've planned ahead. Everybody gets shit-faced here, then we move round to the Rasa Sayang for some Malaysian nibbles about seven, then I disappear in a pre-ordered limo. Anyone still standing gets to go on to a club – whatever. I'm on my way to a five star hotel near Gatwick where my future mother-in-law is imposing maximum security.'

'Hey, dropping out of your own hen night, that's impressive. You must be serious about the guy.'

'Not as serious as he is about me.'

As she said it, she licked a finger and drew it up her left leg from the knee to the stocking top, making a 'sssss' noise as if quenching a flame.

I handed back the champagne.

'Down, girl, down. Exactly how rich is this guy?'

She licked her finger and made the hissing noise again.

'I get the picture,' I said. I handed the champagne back to her and lit myself another cigarette. For some strange reason I needed one. I was sure it was absolutely nothing to do with the way she was leaning against the door.

'We'll be going on our honeymoon tomorrow night,' Stella was saying, 'so we'll be away for a couple of months.'

'As you do,' I said casually.

'So when I found out what was going on, which was, like, just this morning, I swear it, I had to get hold of you.' At that point she giggled, then said: 'Well, you know what I mean.'

'You've been following me,' I prompted.

'Not personally!' she protested.

'Of course not,' I reached out and stroked

her cheek slowly with the back of my hand, then relieved her of the champagne bottle. 'I would have noticed *you*.'

When she opened her eyes she said: 'You don't fancy a quickie, do you? I mean, they all think that's what we're doing anyway.'

'You were saying?'

God, I could be strict.

'OK, I really did only find out this morning, right?' I nodded and had another drink. 'Good, because if I'd known it was you I would have told you, you know I would have...'

'Get on with it.'

'Right. I was away from the office and Veronica was setting up the cruise ship job I told you about, when a client registers with us wanting some info on a guy called Keith Flowers.' She paused, did some serious smoking for a minute, then narrowed her eyes. 'You don't seem surprised by any of this so far.'

I took off my Raybans and for the first time she saw (and I saw in the mirror above the sink) the mottled bruising above my nose.

'I'm ahead of you, I think,' I said. 'But carry on.'

'OK, but just remember I wasn't there. I only found out about this this morning when I saw the weekly timesheets.'

She held out a hand for the bottle and

took a long swig.

'I didn't know we'd agreed to do a background check on this Keith Flowers. Honestly, I didn't. It was one of the new girls – I said we'd taken on new staff, didn't I? Anyway, it all seemed above board and anyway, I had other things on my mind. Whatever, it wasn't until one of our operatives started to ask about Amy May – just casually like, around the coffee machine, nothing formal – and I mentioned you and how I knew you – had known you – before, like … and even then I didn't put two and two together until I saw a copy of her initial report and I realized she'd been dogging you.

'Now, I don't know what's going on,' she said between slurps on the bottle, 'but what I read about this guy Flowers didn't sound like he should get my vote in a Citizen of the Year poll. And when I realized that he was your Amy's ex, I thought uh-oh, maybe I should give you the heads-up that somebody was interested in your sordid little life. For old times' sake if nothing else.'

'Pity you didn't do it sooner,' I said.

'Give me a break. I only saw the report this morning.'

'When did the client see it?'

'Yesterday, maybe,' she said quietly. 'Is that important?'

'Not now,' I said, moving over to the

mirror above the sink and making a point of examining my bruises. 'But I don't think your client was completely satisfied with the report he got. Had to come and ask a few more in-depth questions.'

'Hey, babe, don't lay that one at my door.'

'So who's your client?'

'I can't tell you that, babe, I'd lose my licence.'

I took the bottle back from her.

'Bullshit. You don't have a licence. The only licences for private detectives in this country are Office of Fair Trading ones authorising people to do credit checks. Oh, sure, they've now set up the Private Security Industry Authority and they're *going* to be issuing licences, but they haven't yet. I bet you haven't even got an application form filled in.'

'You need a form?' she started, then stopped herself. 'You're good, babe, you know that? You fancy working for us full time?'

'I thought you only employed females.'

'We could cook the books.'

'Just tell me who hired you – who hired the firm.'

'I shouldn't really,' she said, going all coy, squirming against the door to make her skirt ride up.

'And I probably shouldn't turn up in Horsham tomorrow – around eleven

194

o'clock, say?'

'Come on, Angel,' she said, straightening up, 'we're talking client confidentiality here. I've already told you more than I needed to.'

I had to admit that was true, so I lit two cigarettes and passed one to her.

'Then let's do it this way. I'll say a name and you just tell me if I'm wrong. You don't have to say it's right, just if it's wrong. OK?'

'So I don't have to say "yes", I just get to say "no" if I want to?'

She pretended to mull this over.

'Sounds like my kinda party game. Go ahead.'

'Your client was a psychotic Welsh git called Len Turner,' I said, drawing smugly on my cigarette.

Stella blanked me – she was good, she was very good – and timed it just right before making a noise like the klaxon on a U-Boat going into an emergency dive and shouting: 'Wrong!'

She wasn't the only one who could put on an act, though.

'But he said he was. He told me about you, showed me the photographs developed at that place just round the corner from your office in Shepherd's Bush. Then he hit me because he thought I knew something ... and then the others hit me as well and I thought...'

'Hey, here, babe.'

Her arms went around me and her corseted breasts seemed to be everywhere.

'I've never heard of anybody called Len Turner, honest. The guy who hired us was straight-arrow respectable. He's a solicitor, for Christ's sake. Mind you, he was Welsh...'

I let her hold me for perhaps a minute longer than was necessary. Or maybe five minutes. Then I groped in my pocket and produced a crumpled business card.

'Name of Haydn Rees by any chance?'

Stella's head shot back from the clinch but I pushed her up against the door again.

'I'm saying nothing,' she said, then made a zipper movement across her lips.

'Right,' I said, remembering the rules of engagement. 'But there's something else I've got to know.'

'Me too,' she said huskily, squirming against me.

'What?' I asked, distracted.

'Is that the champagne bottle or are you really, really pleased to see me again?'

I lifted the bottle clear of where it had somehow got trapped between our thighs.

'Bit of both, probably,' I said. 'Sorry.'

She took a drink from the bottle and then held it to my lips. I had somehow forgotten to move away from her.

'What was it you wanted to know?'

She looked at the bottle, realized I had emptied it and held it out at arm's length before letting it drop. It didn't break, it bounced and then rolled across the floor and under the door of the cubicle opposite the urinal.

'Shit!' somebody exclaimed.

Stella and I looked at each other, then at the cubicle.

'Just who the hell is that? Are you some sort of *perv?*' she shouted. 'All I have to do is scream and my friends will be in here like a shot.'

'No, Christ, no, don't do that,' said the voice. 'You just made me jump that was all.'

'We did sort of barge in here,' I whispered in Stella's ear. 'I mean, the guy was probably having a quiet dump and...'

She wagged a finger in front of my face and shushed me, then winked.

'It's the male stripper. I wondered where he'd gone,' she whispered. 'Another mystery solved. That's why I'm the detective here.'

'It's OK, you can come out now,' she said towards the cubicle. 'Just go straight up the stairs and out, don't look back, don't stop for anything and don't expect a tip. I'll keep them off your back until you're clear.'

The lock on the cubicle clicked back and the door opened inwards. The young lad who stepped out barefooted was wearing a policeman's helmet, a torn white shirt covering an impressively worked-out torso and dark blue trousers which he had to keep up by bunching the material in his hands around his crotch. Obviously they didn't make velcro like they used to.

'You got taxi fare?' Stella asked him and he nodded sheepishly.

'Good. Go quickly – and consider another line of work. I really don't think this one fits your pistol.'

She opened the door and stepped out into the little corridor, then opened the door to the club. I could hear the piano giving out a ragtime version of *New York, New York* and thinking yet again that dolphin girl was really good.

Then Stella was flapping her arm, waving the stripper on and he actually said 'Excuse me' as he ran by me. Stella held up her hand to stop him, stuck her head out of the door, then waved him on again.

The poor sod hadn't made the first step of the stairs before she yelled 'Stripper!' at the top of her voice and then there was this primeval, deep-throated roar.

I never saw what happened to him because Stella let the outer toilet door swing back and returned to the Gents, closing that door behind her as well.

'Now, where were we?' she asked.

'What I wanted to know was...'

'No. Where *were* we?'

She put her arms around my neck, leaned back on the door and pulled me into her.

'That's better. And it wasn't all champagne bottle after all, was it? Now, what were you saying, babe?'

It took me a minute to remember.

'Oh, yes. It wasn't you following me around, I would have noticed you. And it couldn't have been Veronica. Spy satellites would have noticed her. So who was on my case?'

'Now let me think.'

She nuzzled into me until I could feel her breath warm on my neck. So close and so warm it made me shiver, which she must have taken for encouragement as her pelvis began to grind into me.

'I'd really like to know, because I didn't spot anybody at all,' I said but my voice, oddly, didn't sound like mine.

'It was Steffi, one of our new girls. Sorry, *operatives*.'

She murmured into my ear and then bit the lobe gently. I hoped to God she wasn't going to do the tongue trick.

'Steffi?' I croaked.

'Steffi Innocent. No, that really is her name. Been with us about a month. An absolute natural. Lot to learn, but keen as mustard. She'll go far that one. Very talented.'

'Well, she fooled me. I never thought any-one could tail me around London without me spotting them.'

'I told you she was good. I would have put

her on your case – if I'd known you were involved, which I didn't...'

'I get the point. You're innocent by nature and she's just Innocent by name.'

'Good one,' she breathed, nipping my ear lobe again.

It occurred to me that perhaps I should be struggling more. Or at least some.

'I'd like to meet her,' I said, for the want of something to say.

'I thought you had,' Stella purred. 'You've been looking at that dolphin on her arse ever since you got here.'

She did the tongue trick before I could stop her.

We slipped back into the party with hardly anyone noticing us apart from the five or six women nearest the toilet entrance who shouted 'Go, girl' and applauded Stella as she swept regally by, and Michael behind the bar who made a big show of pulling back a cuff to look at his watch, tugging his beard and nodding slowly as if deeply impressed.

Steffi Innocent, dolphin submerged, was doing *Georgia On My Mind* and playing it well though I reckoned few if any of Stella's guests recognized it.

Stella was holding my hand and leading me to another bottle of champagne which had been left unguarded on a chair. I tugged her into me and said 'She's good.'

'Yes she is. And she can play piano.'

'I want to talk to her,' I persisted.

Stella looked at her watch – a sparkling rectangle with slightly fewer diamonds than, say, Amsterdam – and drank from the bottle before answering.

'Half an hour here, then we're round to the restaurant. We'll lose a few on the way so it should calm down a bit. You can talk there. Have a few drinks. Steffi will run you home, she knows where you live and she doesn't drink.'

I knew there was another reason I didn't like her.

'I'd better make a call,' I said, fishing for the mobile I had miraculously remembered to bring with me.

'They don't work down here. That's why you're a member,' she said, and she was right on both counts. 'Come and meet some of my old school friends. Haven't seen them for years. Tell them you're a ... pornographer. How about that? Tell them you've just finished editing *The Illustrated Guide to Lesbian Bondage*. Good, huh?'

'Good? It's selling hand over fist.'

By the time Stella organized the move to the restaurant, I had convinced various friends of hers that I was (a) indeed a pornographer, (b) a film producer who had had an artistic disagreement with a script-writer and (c) the official bouncer for

Gerry's, though not a very good one, hence the battered face. What was scary was that all three of these scenarios seemed to them not only believable, but appealing. When I forced my way to the bar to get another bottle of something, my butt was nipped and tweaked all the way there and back as if by an army of crows pecking at some juicy piece of roadkill. Four different hands – and the same one at least twice – groped the inside of my thighs under the table; one of them actually came on to me with the line 'Chicks dig scars, you know' and looked affronted when I laughed, three of them wrote their mobile numbers on the back of my hand, and one seriously wanted to star in my next movie – and that was when I was being the pornographer.

It must have been something to do with it being a warm evening, a dark club, too much booze and a hen night. If I'd met any of them out on the street, even wearing a suit and tie and tipping my hat and holding doors open for them, they would have reached for the pepper spray.

Steffi Innocent had stopped playing the piano and had disappeared into the throng drinking from a bottle of mineral water. I tried to spot her but failed as Stella began to herd her noisy flock up the stairs and out on to an unsuspecting Dean Street.

'Are you really taking all this lot for a

meal?' I asked when I got next to her.

'Some of them will drop out because they're pissed, some 'cos it's Friday night and they have to go out with their man, some will go out looking for drugs and then there's those who think they've got a nut allergy and all that Satay sauce may not be a good idea.'

'Good thinking, if you're worried about the bill.'

'I'm not, I'm not paying. My darling soon-to-be-husband is.'

'So he is rich, is he?' I asked, realizing in an instant what a daft question that was where Stella was concerned.

'For the moment,' she said with a grin of pure evil.

I think twenty-eight of us made it to the Rasa Sayang, but it was difficult to tell. The staff met us with plates of their speciality – cubed orange chicken on wooden skewers with peanut satay dip sauce – and growing looks of apprehension on their faces as the cream of the Home Counties in their best designer party frocks swarmed in like fire ants.

I had already made up my mind that the Armstrong was just going to have to take his chances in Soho overnight and I would get home somehow, making a mental note to add 'Get home' to my to-do list. Having decided this, I ordered a Tiger beer at the reception bar and by the time I turned around to follow the ladies, all the orange chicken had gone and one of the younger waiters was standing with his knees together and was biting his lower lip in agony.

'They must have gone that way,' I said to him, but he didn't respond, so I just followed the perfume trail downstairs.

The restaurant had laid out a long table and curtained it with bamboo screens which were nowhere near strong enough to contain this lot, or protect the other customers. Stella took control from one end and announced that the seating plan would be 'Girl, girl, girl, girl, girl, girl, me, BOY, girl, girl, girl, yada-yada.' Despite the catcalls and booing and shouts of 'She'll be nipping to the loo again soon' she also announced that her 'associate' Randy was settling the bill, the banquet was on its way – she had ordered everything on the menu at least once but anyone with a serious nut allergy was going to die – and she would get round all of them personally before she sneaked off for an early night.

I took the chair next to Stella's although she stayed on her feet, waving the waiters with open bottles of wine forward. Most of them just put the bottles on the table and legged it. Down the table I spotted Steffi Innocent, who was either very good at avoiding eye contact or simply hadn't registered me, negotiating with a fleeing waiter for a bottle of mineral water.

I felt a hand on my left arm. Its owner was a small redhead in her early twenties. She was wearing a sleeveless peach-coloured satin material dress with Chinese or Japanese calligraphy strokes down the front, which showed off the freckles on her arm. Her hair was long and frizzy, parted in the middle to frame sparkling blue eyes (though you can do that with contact lenses) and apart from a pale orange lipstick she was fresh-faced and obviously proud of her complexion. She would have been on anyone's shortlist for a 'Miss English Rose' calendar were it not for her prominent, not to say large, not to say hugely out of proportion to the rest of her, breasts which strained the satin dress to its limits. I couldn't have missed her in Gerry's, it would have been physically impossible.

Now, I'm not one to gawp but it took a few seconds for me to realize she was speaking to me.

'I just *loved* that book you did on lesbian fetishism and now I hear you're making the film of it,' she said in an accent which would have got her into the Royal Enclosure at Ascot. 'Are you auditioning actors yourself or do you have somebody who does that for you? I mean, I'm not really a professional –

205

I don't have an Equity card yet or anything – but I'm not averse to a little girl-on-girl hot action as I believe it's known.'

There was a time when I would have drawn up a contract on the back of a menu and got her to sign it on the spot. I must be getting old, as before I could even think of something to say which didn't involve a lot of drooling, Stella came to my rescue and pulled me towards her.

'Butt-out, Charlotte, I need his full attention,' she told the redhead.

'Oh, strewth, I was only trying to get a rise out of him,' said Charlotte and her accent was suddenly Australian, or perhaps New Zealander, as she turned away and started to talk to the girl next to her.

'She's very good,' I whispered to Stella.

'She's a stand-up comedienne and she could do you and the Hackney Empire with one hand tied behind her back, so don't mess with her. Now listen up.'

Stella talked fast in my ear as I liberated a bottle of wine and filled glasses for both of us. Food came and went in front of us and I got busy even if Stella abstained. I had meals to catch up on and a blood count to rectify. She only had to fit into a wedding dress.

'I'm going to do the rounds and thank everybody for coming and then piss off, OK? I'll get Steffi to come and sit here and you can ask her anything you like and I wasn't kidding, she really will drive you home.

'Now I've told her to come clean and tell you anything you want to know. She's not keen on the idea, says it breaches client confidentiality, it's probably unethical and unprofessional. And this is from a chick who takes her work seriously. Her dad is a copper, her brother's a copper. She would have joined the Met herself but I think she's too right-wing for them. Whatever, I've overruled her. Management decision, the buck stops here, I'm the boss. If it involves old and distinguished friends, then I intervene. That's one of my principles. I don't have many, but that's definitely one of them.'

Yes, Stella, especially friends who could tell a few tales out of school. Maybe make a speech at your wedding...

'Mm ... mm,' I said with my mouth full. Stella took it as a sign of encouragement.

'Now I really, really didn't know about this case until this morning.'

'You've said that. I believe you.'

'Good. What happened was I was away and Veronica was distracted so Steffi took the call from this guy Rees who said he was a solicitor, up in town for the day, and needed an enquiry agent to do some leg work in London. Steffi met him, took the brief and Veronica drew up a standard contract to fax to this Rees guy's office in Cardiff.'

'Did you check him out?' I asked, testing a meatball dipped in plum sauce.

'Check him out? He's a fucking solicitor. We get fifty per cent of our work from solicitors.'

I shrugged and drew a plate of spare ribs closer.

'Our retainer comes in the post next day, so Steffi starts work having assured Veronica that, although she's new, she's up to the task and frankly, I wouldn't have queried that because that gal went up the learning curve on a skateboard. Plus, the job was tracking this Keith Flowers jerk. There was no mention of you, or the famous Amy May.' She paused at that but I didn't respond. 'At least not then. Now, fair play, she did ask me – just like in passing – about Amy and I said I didn't know Amy personally, but I knew *Mr* Amy and that we'd had a few laughs in the past.'

'And you mentioned the flat in Hackney,' I said, real casual, still chewing.

'I might have done, but point is I didn't put two and two together until I saw her report this morning, and she'd already faxed it to the client. But, honest, there was nothing in there that could have dropped you in it.'

'There was enough, but don't worry, I'm not blaming you.'

'As if you could,' she said, wide-eyed. 'Now wipe that rib sauce off your mouth. Give Stella a big kiss and wish her luck as she abandons her old life and embarks, whatever the hardships ahead, on a new one.'

I did as I was told.

'So what exactly will you be giving up?' I asked as she stood up.

'Overdrafts,' she said.

Chapter Ten

Steffi Innocent took the chair Stella had abandoned, pulled it away from the edge of the table and turned it at an angle so it faced me, sat down and crossed her legs at the knee. She used her thumbs to hook her straight blonde hair back from its central parting and pin the strands behind both ears, then she leaned forward, clasped her hands around her knees and looked me straight in the face. She could have been a student waiting for a tutor to discuss her essay. I was glad I wasn't the tutor having to break the news that she had got less than a B+, so I smiled at her and carried on eating.

Her nerve gave way first. Maybe she wasn't that tough.

'Stella says I've got to tell you whatever you want to know,' she said at last. There was a faint hint of Scots in her voice, but she had it under control.

I spooned some noodles on to my plate.

'Tomorrow night's Lotto numbers?'

Her expression didn't change.

'I'm not apologizing. I was just doing my job. I've got nothing to apologize for.'

I filled my glass as a bottle of white wine

seemed to levitate in front of me. I took a long drink, put the glass down and then took off my sunglasses before looking at her.

'Your client has,' I said.

'My client is a respectable solicitor,' she said without emotion.

'There's no such thing!' I snorted. She didn't twitch a muscle.

'You think I didn't check him out? I'm a professional. If you have personal issues with him, that's your problem.'

'Issues? Damn right I've got issues. I've been sightseeing with a family of Welsh psychopaths, thanks to your client.'

Her small face still remained impassive.

'I know nothing about what happened to you today. I'm talking about personal issues between you and Haydn Rees.'

'I'd never heard of Haydn-fucking-Rees until this afternoon.'

'Yeah, right.'

She looked down to her left and shot her eyebrows up as she said it. I was so shocked that her face had cracked, I put down my glass.

'It's true,' I said.

To my left, Charlotte the comedienne cracked the joke about the woman in the queue at the sperm bank and half the table screamed at the punchline, so I missed what Steffi muttered.

'What?'

'Like you didn't know Haydn Rees was involved in Amy May's divorce?'

I picked up my glass again to buy myself thinking time.

'We need to talk. Let's go somewhere for a quiet drink,' I said.

'I don't drink,' she said primly.

'I don't care.'

Finding somewhere quiet for a drink in the Dean Street area on a warm summer's evening was no more difficult than DIY dentistry without a mirror, but it gave me a chance to look at Steffi Innocent in what remained of the daylight and think of the things I needed to ask her.

One question she had already answered as soon as she had sat down beside me and crossed her legs. Ankle-high olive green hiking boots, made from waterproof Gore-Tex with about thirty unnecessary metal loops for their 150centimetre laces and called things like 'Explorer' or 'Challenger', were not exactly the height of Bo-Ho chic this season but they were just as comfortable pounding the mean streets of London as they were hiking up peak in the Peak District or doing whatever it is you do up a Munro in Scotland. They also had steel toe-caps which put them way ahead of trainers in the kicking-your-way-out-of-trouble stakes.

The other burning issue was how the hell

she had dogged me around town without me noticing her. She'd actually got close enough to photograph me in different locations, which meant a vehicle but even if I'd missed a telephoto lens as long as a musket I would have spotted the same car turning up time and time again, wouldn't I?

The rest I felt confident I could piece together. I was confident, partly because of my alcohol intake but partly because I knew of another piece in the jigsaw which I was pretty sure she did not.

We settled on the *Nellie Dean*, or rather I did. Steffi just shrugged her shoulders and stomped through the open doors, zeroing in on a corner table which had two empty stools near it as most of the customers were outside, leaning on the windowsills and making Dean Street look untidy. There was a time when the *Nellie* had been the almost exclusive haunt of film technicians – cameramen, sound men, lighting techs, electricians – who worked on industrial films for big business or Government information films or recruiting shorts for the Army or Navy. Nowadays, video or digital camcording and computer enhancement could produce broadcast quality material for half the price of a five-man unit out on location, so the pub now let just anybody in.

I got to the bar and bought a glass of mineral water with ice and lemon and a pint of lager. There seemed to be no change from a fiver but I knew better than to argue with a barman in Soho on a Friday night.

I put the drinks down on the table and straddled the stool, so close to her that the tips of my trainers and her steel toecaps actually touched briefly. I took a drink, smiled my best smile and decided that a charm offensive would be the best way to get her to loosen up.

I never got the chance.

'So Stella's going to fire me, is she? Just for showing a bit of initiative. Typical. Well, I should've known. Hard work, initiative and honesty – no match for sex, is it? Never was, never will be.'

I took another drink. Quite a long one, quite quickly.

'Don't go away,' I said and dived back to the bar where I bought a box of matches with another five-pound note and had just enough change to get a pack of cigarettes out of the machine in the corner.

By the time I got back on my stool and lit up, Steffi had managed to bring herself to pick up her glass of water and moisten her lips. If she carried on enjoying herself like that I might have to sedate her.

'Right, let's try again,' I said. 'What the hell are you talking about?'

'You know well enough,' she said petulantly.

I was confused. The dolphin tattoo (and no attempt to hide it) and the ability to play really smooth soulful jazz in public just didn't sit with the straight-arrow, work ethic persona. Maybe she was just very, very young. Maybe I was looking at the Conservative party of the future.

'No, I really don't,' I said. 'Explain.'

'I do a job, a job I took on from first client meeting up to final report, and I do it well. But because it involves someone who has a history with the boss and is not adverse to a quickie in the toilets, then the whole thing will get sat upon. Instead of "job well done" it'll be a P45 as soon as Stella gets back in the office, just for daring to mention one of her many ex-boyfriends in my report.'

'Now hold on a minute.' I waved a finger at her. It didn't seem to scare her. 'For a start, Stella will have forgotten about this by–' I made a point of looking at my watch and counting down three seconds '–about now, I'd say. For another thing, what is there to get sat upon? You just said you'd handed in your final report. What can she do now, even if she wanted to?'

I didn't bother to add that if Stella had kept a tighter rein on her staff and noticed me being put in the frame even a couple of days earlier, it could have saved me a good kicking. But then, I'd never have got to ride the London Eye.

Steffi nodded and pursed her lips, which I took to be a sign that she was with me so far.

'Now I'm not saying Stella doesn't feel guilty about you spying on me, and...'

'I don't like "spying",' she said. 'I had you under surveillance and you'd never have known if she hadn't told you.'

'Actually, you're wrong there. The Neighbourhood Watch in Hampstead spotted you – you were wearing an FCUK top, which you should have known would have got you noticed up there. They reported you to the cops, I'm afraid, not me.'

She looked crestfallen at that and, if it was possible, even younger and almost waif-like. I decided not to tell her that there was a lesbian in Hackney who had her down to her dress size, a video tape of her in disguise on Oxford Street and a car mechanic in Barking who would examine her big end for free.

'Anyway, like I said, even if Stella does feel guilty about you having me under surveillance, that's business, isn't it? And what's done is done. All I need now, and Stella said you'd help, is to know what this client of your knows so I can deal with anything that comes up in the future.'

'So it is about you and Haydn Rees.'

She said it smugly to herself, reaching for her glass of water, not expecting an answer.

I finished my beer and stood up to get

216

another. It was less hassle than causing a scene by strangling her there and then.

'Look, I've told you, I'd never heard of this Rees character until this afternoon. All I know about him is he's a solicitor who represents some very dodgy people and he's probably Welsh with a name like that. Now there's at least two bloody good reasons for not knowing him or wanting to know him.'

'So it's not about Keith and Amy Flowers' divorce? I mean, like it's not personal at all?' She looked up at me with mild, but only mild, curiosity.

'Why should it be? There was a divorce. One of them needed a solicitor, so what?'

I lit up another cigarette in case there was a wait at the bar.

'No, I think you misunderstood what I said. Haydn Rees was *involved* in the Flowers' divorce, he wasn't their solicitor. He was the co-respondent when Keith divorced Amy for adultery.'

I realized that if I didn't go to the bar now, right this second, I would just stand there swaying and looking foolish.

I dropped the pack of cigarettes into the lap of her Wranglers.

'I don't smoke,' she said.

'You will.'

So, OK, she had more or less ambushed this Haydn Rees character when he'd turned up at R & B Confidential (hah!) Investigations office on Shepherd's Bush Green without an appointment, on a day when the senior partners were otherwise engaged. But then, he was a solicitor and what he wanted seemed absolutely kosher, so why shouldn't she pick up the ball and run with it? Veronica had been perfectly happy to issue a standard no-fault contract on the basis of one week's retainer, which had duly arrived by bank credit the next morning. Steffi had assured her she could handle it, after all it seemed like no more than an extended background check, and was allowed to do the leg work.

Rees' brief had been simple but vague, which in my opinion should have set off Steffi's alarm bells as solicitors are usually incredibly *complicated* and vague. But then I was beginning to suspect that Steffi didn't have an inbuilt alarm system.

He represented – or at least gave the impression that he represented – someone called Keith Flowers, who was in custody in a 'secure medical facility' in Nottingham-shire, pending several serious charges. The mental state of his 'client' (though he never actually used the word, now she thought of it) was such that there was little issue over whether he was guilty or not. There was a chance, however, that mitigating circum-stances could be entered in his defence if it was possible to track his movements in London during the month he spent preparing for his return to society.

Flowers, Rees had said, had served four years of an eight-year sentence, which was the norm these days, and had been a model prisoner. The fact that his last spell inside had been in HMP Belmarsh was entirely due to him wishing to be in the London area prior to release and nothing to do with Belmarsh's status as a high security containment facility. In fact, the High Security prison at Belmarsh is actually *inside* the normal Belmarsh prison, which gets used as a transit station as well as a local nick for the Old Bailey.

What had he been put away for? Naturally, Steffi had asked that right up front as she was, after all, a professional and an eight-year stretch was definitely something more serious than non-payment of parking fines or having to take the rap for your offspring playing truant from school.

The gist of it seemed to be a fraud, the embezzlement or misappropriation or just downright theft, of a substantial amount of grant aid money from the EEC (now known as the EC or just 'Europe') for the regeneration of an underdeveloped area (known as Wales), coupled with a stubborn reluctance to say where the cash had gone. Pressure from the Inland Revenue was enough to make sure that the book would be thrown at

Flowers, who was – surprise, surprise – a qualified accountant, let alone the fact that the whole thing had come to light when he assaulted with an office stapler two Cardiff VAT inspectors on a routine visit. (An assault so severe that both inspectors had taken early retirement and counselling, but would probably never enter a branch of Office World again.) The plea that he had been under pressure during a particularly acrimonious divorce didn't seem to butter any parsnips as far as the judge at Cardiff Crown Court had been concerned.

To get Flowers out of his current predicament, some more mitigating circumstances were necessary: anything which would explain why a model prisoner suddenly went off the rails like that.

Here, Rees had an idea. Flowers was on semi-release in London. Amy May, his ex-wife, lived in London. Amy had taken out a Restraining Order on him, so we knew he had at least tried to see her. Maybe that was too much for him and he'd cracked under the strain of being restrained. So a logical place to start would be with Amy and, by extension, the person who had replaced Flowers in her bed.

Steffi had set to with dogged determination. Police and court records in Suffolk confirmed the details of Flowers' re-arrest and Suffolk Traffic Police had gladly given her details of how the wrecked BMW Flowers had stolen had been taken away at my request by an idiot car mechanic from Barking. A chance word with Stella about the famous Amy May (and, yes, she admitted she'd been trying it on here, but she had heard rumours) revealed that Stella knew me and where I had lived. Steffi had to check it out, though she had no particular idea what she was looking for, but it would prove to her client that she'd covered all the bases.

She made no attempt to hide the fact that she had more or less broken into my flat in Stuart Street. In fact she became almost animated at the thought of it.

'There was a cat there and it attacked me!' she had said.

'No! Really?'

'Yes, it did. Me – who loves cats...'

But she hadn't found anything worth reporting to her client, so it had hardly been worth the effort.

So what had she reported to her client?

Very little.

She could prove that Keith Flowers had had contact, or attempted contact, with Amy at her office and with me (albeit briefly) but that was about it. Yes, she had photographed everything she could and express delivered a set of prints, but it had all seemed a bit thin.

The gaping hole in the enquiry had been that she had not been able to find out where Flowers had been living during his month of pre-release. The Suffolk police didn't know or wouldn't tell her; the Prison Service certainly wouldn't tell her and her own sources had drawn a blank.

'You just wouldn't believe how out of date the Police National Computer is,' she had said.

I had said I believed it and was probably grateful for the fact, but how did she know? Who were these 'sources' she had?

For the first time she had avoided eye contact, gazed at the floor and murmured: 'My dad.'

An ex-policeman by any chance? Of course. Retired early and now a Risk Management Assessor, whatever that was. And why shouldn't she use his old network of contacts? That was how she'd checked out Haydn Rees, with the help of one of daddy's old mates now on the South Wales Crime Squad who knew a bloke on the *Western Morning Post* who had a whole file of cuttings on him. And yes, he was a solicitor, one of the brightest and best in Cardiff, with his own practice in the regenerated docks. More of a company law man than anything else, highly thought of in the Rotary Club, prize-winning trout fisherman, supporter of Welsh rugby club football, schoolboy air pistol champion, charity worker, trustee of Cardiff prison library and once named as South Wales' most eligible bachelor.

But, there was black mark, or at least a question mark, against him. He had been Keith Flowers' solicitor when Flowers was arrested the first time. No sooner had Flowers gone down for the count than Rees had been named in his divorce petition. That sort of thing made you think, didn't it?

Too right it did. It would have made me think that the sod wasn't trying very hard to get me off, so he could get off with the wife. But then I have a suspicious mind.

And that was it, really. I was welcome to a copy of the report even though it went against all her ethics of client/detective relationships, because Stella had told her to give me it. It seemed that old friendships meant more than ethics or principles.

Well, I bleeding well hope so, I had said.

'But that's just not *right*,' she said as if a door had slammed on her high-minded future.

'It is when your client is actually covering for a bunch of hoods willing to beat the crap out of me,' I said, pointing to my face, which I have to admit I hadn't looked at in a mirror since Gerry's Club and had stopped hurting about five drinks ago.

'Stella didn't know about that when she

called you,' she said, which was a fair point.

'But her instincts were right on the button,' I said primly.

'That comes with age, does it?'

I let that one go.

'One last thing, then you can drive me home. Did this Haydn Rees at any time mention anyone called Turner? Len Turner? Ron Turner? Anyone called Barry or Huw?'

'No, never.'

'Did he give you any indication that he was representing somebody else?'

'Not at all. If anything he gave me the impression he was representing Keith Flowers. You mean he wasn't?'

She gave me another one of her limited range of facial expressions: the dumb one.

'I would think that extremely unlikely. For a start, Flowers' solicitor would have access to his pre-release details, so he would know where he'd lived and how often he'd checked in. Then there's the awful co-incidence of you sending your report, mentioning me, with photographs, featuring me, down to Rees in Cardiff – when?'

'Yesterday lunchtime.'

'And lo and behold, I get sorted by a Welsh gangster this afternoon – a Welsh gangster who has the pictures you took and, call it a coincidence if you like, who has a solicitor called Haydn Rees.'

'The bastard! He used me.'

'Of course he did. He hired you. Hello? Isn't that what you're in business for? Private dick for hire?'

I thought that funnier than it was and realized my glass was empty.

'So what did he want, this Len Turner?'

And there she was again, staring expressionless into my face. It wasn't a come-on, it was a curious puppy, but without the endearing cuddly factor.

'Oh, I couldn't say what transpired between us. That would be breaching client confidentiality,' I said, waving my empty glass under her nose. 'But buy me another pint and I might reconsider.'

It took her a good ten seconds to pull a purse out the back pocket of her jeans and then she grabbed my glass and was at the bar in a flash. As she strained on steel-tipped toes to attract the barman, I noticed that the dolphin was breaching again. Though I wouldn't swear to it, as my eyes were having trouble focusing (no doubt due to sinus trouble), the dolphin had a distinctly depressed look about him.

'So what was this Turner after?' she asked, all keen, almost panting. If she'd had a tail she would have wagged it.

'More or less the same thing your client Rees was after,' I said, tucking into my pint.

'So what did you tell him?'

'Same as I'm telling you,' I said, opening

the pack of cigarettes. 'Absolutely nothing. Smoke?'

She sat back on her stool, rocking it slightly.

'When you've finished that, I'll drive you home, but only because Stella said I had to.'

I toasted her with my glass.

'You can drop me off and get back here for the rest of the party, it's still early.'

And by God it was. It was still daylight outside, although only just. Or maybe the contrast control on my eyesight was going.

'No thanks. Going clubbing with two dozen pissed-up girlies dressed like tarts isn't my idea of fun on a Friday night,' she said.

'What's it like to be a minority?'

But she wasn't going to rise to the bait this time and she sat in silence until I had strung out my beer as long as I could. Then I said I had to visit the toilet – for the purpose for which it was intended, this time – and that might take a while as it was down a steep flight of stairs and was known locally as the Eiger of toilets.

She didn't even smile and when I returned safe and very much more sound, she was standing by the door, arms folded, face blank.

Without a word I followed her out into the street and noticed that it finally was starting to get dark. Quite a few other pedestrians noticed this as they were stumbling along the pavements too, but most, like me, took it in good humour. In fact Steffi was probably the only person in Soho without a big grin on their face.

I followed her without really looking where we were going, except that we'd cut through to Wardour Street and were walking in the road against the flow of traffic, which thankfully no longer included those idiot student types on bicycle rickshaws.

Steffi wasn't making any attempt to talk to me and I thought of one thing that would cheer her up.

I hadn't noticed her tailing me – and I would have said that was impossible – so I would give her credit where credit was due and ask her how she'd managed it.

Before I got a chance to, she had turned into a small courtyard and was reaching into the pocket of her Wranglers for a set of keys.

Even in the fading light and in the condition I was, the full horror of what was lying in wait there struck home and I knew instantly how she had managed to dog me around London without me spotting her.

The bitch owned a taxi.

It was only a TX1 but it still qualified as a black London cab.

When they had first appeared, about five years ago, the TX1 had been hailed as the black cab for the Millennium. It was, to be fair, the first new design in black cabs since the Fairway (like Armstrong II) about forty years before, but it just didn't *look* right. It has a rounded shape to the point of snub-nose which gives the illusion that it's smaller than a Fairway although it is actually taller and a little bit longer. The 2.7 litre Nissan diesel engine is more than decent enough and was supposed to be top-notch on emission control and fuel consumption, especially on the automatic version, which was unusual, and it had been fairly priced at around £27,000 when new. Most real taxi drivers I knew couldn't quite put their finger on why they didn't like them. They would admit, begrudgingly, that the front cabin had more room for the driver and seat adjustment, comfort and all-round visibility were excellent, but even so... One particular one, a musher of the old school, came up with the theory that they would never catch on because the seats in the back were upholstered with fabric instead of black vinyl. 'You try hosing that down after the Friday night drunks had thrown up in there,' he'd confided. Whether he was right, or it was just that his concern was shared by the rest of the brotherhood, the TX1 (sometimes referred to as the 'Tixilix') never caught on in big numbers whereas the other new cab design of the 1990s, the

Metrocab, did and it's those you see most of in London these days.

Steffi saw me gawping at the cab as she unlocked it, misreading my jaw-dropping expression for approval.

'These delicensed cabs are really very good for getting around London, aren't they? Nobody notices you in them. I bought it through LondonCabMart.co.'

If I didn't have enough reasons to hate her before, I did now.

I remembered that my idiot neighbour Ivan Dunmore had said 'she'd left in a cab' but seemingly failed to notice she was driving it! Surely the Neighbourhood Watch should have points deducted or something for missing that. Perhaps he was just being snotty about it. I'd get him too one day. He was on the list.

Steffi climbed in the driver's seat and started the engine. She made no move to open the rear door for me so I had to do it myself and climb in.

I knew she was watching me in the mirror so I made a show of stroking the upholstery on the seat next to me, then pulling down the rumble seat in front of me and doing the same.

'Nice material,' I said, slurring my words – something which came to me remarkably easily. 'Bet it's a bugger to get clean when somebody spews on it.'

She didn't answer, just jammed the automatic stick into DRIVE.

Maybe because I didn't criticize her driving (which I could have) or the route she picked (Tottenham Court Road at this time of night!), she seemed to become more relaxed on the journey home. Perhaps it was because she was at the wheel and I was a centrally locked captive in the back behind a toughened plastic screen, which put her clearly in control.

I knocked on the dividing panel and she slid it open an inch or so with some difficulty. She wasn't used to passengers.

I pressed my hands and face against the plexiglass, a bit like Hannibal Lecter on visiting days.

'So what was this Haydn Rees like then?' I asked and in the mirror I saw her nose wrinkle. There must have been diesel fumes in the cab.

'What do you mean, what was he like?' she said. I noticed she drove with the tip of her tongue protruding from her lips, concentrating too hard. I bet she ground her teeth when she got stressed.

'You're the detective,' I said reasonably. 'Detectives are supposed to observe, aren't they? So what did you observe about him?'

'Early thirties, you know, younger than you–'

Cheeky cow. She was so going down for that.

'–and smart but not flash. Good suit, but M&S, not Hugo Boss. Supposed to be top flight provincial solicitor who didn't seem out of his depth in London. Could be he's happy being the big fish in the smaller pond.'

The trouble with big fish in small ponds was they always got caught by somebody outside the pond, using a rod or a net or a hand grenade.

'Sort of local hero, then, down in the valleys?'

'Not really. Valley boy made good, I suppose, but a bit squeaky clean. I mean, a grown man with all those toys.'

'Toys? What toys?'

'Didn't I mention it? He's won loads of prizes for making models.'

'I didn't know they gave prizes for...'

'Model aircraft, model boats, radio-controlled helicopters, even steam trains. Real ones. Well, not full size, but ones that go round on rails and you can sit on. Gives rides to kids at village fetes and charity events. He's had his picture in just about every local rag in South Wales. Model engineer, that's what he is. Writes a column in *Model Engineering Monthly* or whatever it's called. He was even on *Blue Peter* once.'

'Bloody hell.'

'The only black mark on Mr Clean is this business with Amy May's divorce. I mean it's odd the papers never got hold of that, as Amy May's quite a well-known name in the fashion business, isn't she?'

Given the way she dressed I was amazed she'd even heard of Amy and I didn't like the way she was referring to her in the abstract.

'How did your sources find out about the divorce?'

'Public knowledge, well, public record. Keith Flowers was from Cardiff and that's where he filed. Just ring the right bit of the Magistrates Court and they tell you all the gory details.'

I sat back in the seat and fumbled for a cigarette.

'I don't like smoking in my car,' she said.

Good. I flicked ash on to the floor and pretended I couldn't work out how to open the window. By the time I had, I'd finished the cigarette and there were at least two burn holes in her upholstery.

I needed the nicotine as it had come as quite a shock to learn that Amy had been married to a Welshman. Still, it had all happened a long time ago in a small country far away.

'Can your sources down in Taffy land come up with anything else on this Rees?' I asked, smearing my face against the sliding panel again.

'Such as?'

'Where he lives, who his clients are and any connection with a family called Turner.'

'Who are these Turner people you keep on about? He never mentioned them.'

'Having met them, I don't blame him, but he was the go-between. They were the ones you were really working for.'

'I could check them out. My dad... I've got good contacts down there.'

'Do it from a distance.'

'Can do, but does this mean you're hiring me? I mean the firm.'

'Not in a financial way,' I said in measured tones. 'Let's just say my credit with Stella is good for a while yet. So yes, go ahead, see what you can dig up. And I'd like a copy of the report you sent to Rees and a set of the photographs you took. And the negatives.'

'That's not possible.' She shook her head as she said it and almost clipped a passing Mazda.

'I think Stella will go along with it. You can ring her tomorrow morning, about eleven, if you want to check.'

I could tell she was fuming. It felt good to make her fume. It was a start.

'When Rees briefed you,' I went on, 'did he mention any names other than me and Amy?'

'No.'

'Not at all? He didn't give you any other leads?'

'No, he didn't, and he was really apologetic that he couldn't give me more to go on.'

'Not even an address for Flowers?'

'No. He didn't have one. It was the one thing I couldn't find out.'

I allowed myself a smile because I knew that and she didn't. But then I realized that if she'd still been on the case this morning she could have followed me out to St Chad's in this damned Tixilix and I probably wouldn't have noticed.

It also confirmed that Rees certainly wasn't representing Keith Flowers now, even if he had in the past. A defending solicitor would have access to his prison files, not to mention access to the prisoner himself, even if he was in a padded cell and wearing a paper suit.

'You're sure he mentioned no other names?'

'Yes, of course I'm sure.' She sounded irritated.

Irritated was good as well, but still not enough.

So did that mean that Rees didn't know – and therefore the Turners didn't – about 'Mr Creosote', as Spider had called him? Then again, what the hell did I know about him?

The circle was coming round to Keith Flowers again, except there was a big gap where, somehow, Amy fitted it in. But where was Amy? And why had I left my to-do list on the floor of the Armstrong back in Soho?

Steffi was indicating right and I realized I was back on home turf in Hampstead. Right outside the house in fact.

The house which had a Freelander parked outside.

'Looks like Amy's home,' said Steffi.

Chapter Eleven

I was quite prepared to shout 'Honey, I'm home!' but as the rest of the house was dead quiet, I could hear her in the upstairs shower.

At the foot of the stairs, just where I could have fallen over them had I been sober and not wearing sunglasses indoors, were her laptop and a big black document case with a shoulder strap. There was white printing on the flap of the bag, which was the standard freebie you get at conferences these days, but when I tried to read it, I realized my eyesight had been irreparably damaged either by alcohol or by close contact with a capsule wall on the London Eye.

It just didn't make any sense. It was probably upside down.

I took my glasses off and bent down to get a closer look, almost overbalancing in the process.

Wythnos Ffasiwn Cymru.

What the hell was that? It wasn't English, unless it was a gimmick and you had to hold it up to a mirror to read it. Or was that Swedish?

Then I noticed the circular sticky-backed badge which somebody had slapped on the fabric. That showed a smiling woolly sheep and had the legend: 'Cool Cymru: The Welsh Aren't Sheepish!'

That gave me a much needed clue and I so I read the second line of printing.

Welsh Fashion Week.

It looked like all roads, not just the M4, were leading to Wales.

I climbed the stairs making as much noise as possible so as not to give Amy a *Psycho* moment in the shower. I needn't have bothered as she had locked the bathroom door, which was unusual.

'Have you eaten?' she yelled, turning the power shower down but not off when I announced my presence outside the door.

'I grabbed a snack on the way home,' I said slowly, framing each word carefully in advance.

'Good, so did I. I'm knackered and I'm hitting the hay pronto. You OK?'

'Yeah, fine,' I said. 'I could do with a shower myself.'

It was true. In fact I could do with a complete range of Stain Devils, judging by my clothes. On my shirt alone I could identify beer, peanut sauce and blood and I probably reeked of smoke, stale perfume and Stella. (Not that we'd managed anything really naughty, it was just that Amy would *know* I'd thought about it.)

She hadn't answered me or rushed to

open the door so I shouted:

'Tell you what, I'll go and clean up downstairs. See you in a bit.'

'Right. Good thinking,' she said and if she said anything else, it was lost in the blast of the shower.

I congratulated myself on a lucky escape. I had forgotten about my bruised and blackened face, which even Amy might have noticed, so the least I could do was try and reduce the swelling.

I dived into our bedroom to retrieve the towelling robe hanging behind the door, the one she's always reminding me I've forgotten to put on, and kick off my trainers. Amy's Gucci overnight bag was lying on the bed, the front panel unzipped. A few pieces of paper had fallen out on to the duvet cover. I didn't touch them, but I did lean in close enough, almost falling over in the process, to see what they were. The bits of paper were till receipts from a bar in the St David's Hotel and one was a ticket stub from the Health Spa at St David's. There was also a plastic coated badge on a neck ribbon saying it was a 'V.I.P. Pass' for Wythnos Ffasiwn Cymru, but there was no personalized name or photo ID on it.

I sneaked downstairs as quietly as I could and turned the TV on, flipping the channels until I found an imported US sitcom with a loud laughter track. It wasn't difficult, it was

Friday night. Then I went to the ground-floor bathroom, turned the shower on full and stripped off my clothes.

The shirt would have to go. I was in no fit state to even try and get the stains out of it, so I scrunched it up between my hands and nipped into the kitchen, pretty sure that there was enough background noise to cover me even if she turned off her shower.

From the cupboard under the sink I took a black bin liner and stuffed the shirt to the bottom then looked around for rubbish to throw on top. There was nothing to find except some pizza cartons, an empty carton of orange juice, some egg shells, a carton of milk I'd forgotten to put back in the fridge two days ago, a pile of junk mail, two empty wine bottles, the contents of three full ashtrays and four used coffee filters. It was like nobody had lived here for days.

I tied a knot in the top of the bag and opened the back door quietly (that is to say, checking I hadn't set off the alarms). The small rectangle of lawn outside the back is what passes for our garden but in fact provides a sheltered living space for our dustbins. Neither Amy nor I had ever found any other good reason to go out there. Both plastic bins, typically, were full but that was probably because I hadn't put them out for collection whenever it is the bin men come to empty them. And there was another plastic bag, just like the one I was holding, tied at the neck with a twisted-over rubber band crammed behind the bins.

I knew I hadn't put it there and I hadn't noticed it before, though that wasn't saying much as I rarely ran security checks on our garbage, unlike most of the neighbours.

The lights were still on in the upstairs bathroom and I could hear water trickling down the outside pipes. She was certainly having a good hose down and hopefully it would last while I opened up the bag by undoing the several dozen twists she'd put in the rubber band.

The bag contained only one thing or, rather, two. A light blue wool two-piece suit that I'd never seen before and would have sworn in court wasn't part of Amy's wardrobe.

Had it not been for the fact that kindly old Len Turner had shown me a picture of her wearing it as she climbed into the Freelander.

I rubbered up the bag again and kicked it behind the bins. She was probably putting it out for recycling or to give to Oxfam, that was it. Nothing sinister.

'And if you believe that, sunshine,' I said quietly to myself, 'you've had far too much to drink.'

Which was, of course, true so I spent the next twenty minutes trying to shower the alcohol out of my pores and then another twenty minutes holding a pack of frozen peas from the freezer over the bridge of my nose whilst watching anxiously in the downstairs bathroom mirror to see if the swelling would go down or the bruises paled back to flesh colour.

Neither happened so I crunched on a couple of Paracetamol, turned off the TV in the lounge (even though it was now on to the Friday night soft porn movie) and crept up the stairs to bed, fingers crossed, numerous explanations at the ready.

My luck held. Amy was already in bed and the light was off.

I pulled the hood of the bathrobe up over my head like a boxer and slipped under the duvet alongside her but so we were back-to-back. She was breathing deeply and rhythmically, but you can never be sure with women as feigning deep sleep is a natural talent for them. I slipped over an exploratory hand and discovered she was wearing a night shirt of some sort, though I wasn't aware she possessed one. It was a long one too, well below the knees. Which was unusual.

Now was not the time. Explanations could wait until the morning.

The best ones usually can.

Saturday started as it usually did but once I had remembered where I was, I swung into action.

First thing was to check where Amy was and an exploratory hand minesweeping down the far side of the bed confirmed she was up and about. Second thing was to check how I looked. So far, a fairly normal Saturday.

The bedroom mirror was kind to me for once.

There was an egg-shaped brown, green and blue bruise arcing from the bridge of my nose over my right eyebrow but fortunately it was only the size of a wren's egg. In a strange way I felt rather disappointed as it had hurt a lot more than it looked, but at least my nose didn't click or bend out of shape when I wiggled it.

I could pass muster, or at least think of some good excuses. A wet shave and some clean clothes and Amy would never know the difference.

But I never got the shave because Amy was in the shower.

Again.

I made do with a battery-operated shaver after taking four more Paracetamol with some orange juice to counteract the noise it made. The shave wasn't perfect but at least I didn't draw any more blood. Once I'd brushed my teeth I felt almost presentable.

Amy was in the kitchen making coffee. She was wearing a long black shirt over wide white trousers – the sort Marlene Dietrich had been fond of. I could smell the shower gel on her even over the warm, damp coffee grounds in the cone filter but her hair was dry and brushed so she must have tied it up in the shower.

She had the radio on so she didn't hear me immediately and then as she glided to the fridge for milk, I noticed that she wasn't quite limping, but she was definitely not putting all her weight on her right leg.

'What happened to your face?' she said, still with her back to me.

Then I realized she could see me reflected in the chrome of the giant toaster we have but never use. (American friends have always laughed at us for putting toast under the grill instead of using the toaster, but how the hell else do you stop the cheese falling off?)

'I was born with it,' I said with a stage sigh. 'What happened to your leg?'

She straightened up but for a moment, I thought she was stopping herself from rubbing her right knee. It was just an impression and maybe I imagined it.

'Cramp, arthritis, rheumatism, I don't know. Just driving all that way with the pedal to the metal. I must be getting old.'

'Take the weight off, deary. You should look after yourself at your age,' I said, pulling one of the high stools (which are really naff) from under the 'breakfast bar' (even naffer) which had come with the house, or so Amy had said, and which we'd never had the opportunity to throw away or even at somebody.

Amy kicked the stool out of her way and if we'd been in a Western, the shooting would have started then. Instead she came up to me and gently put her fingers on my forehead.

'Did somebody hit you?' she asked, examining the bruise. Like she was a doctor!

'No,' I said honestly. After all, I had hit some*thing*. Pointing out that it had been one of London's premier tourist attractions might have broken the spell.

'Tell me who did this and I'll rip her liver out. How's that for a deal?'

'I was at a hen party...'

She flicked her fingers dismissively in front of my eyes and turned away to finish making the coffee.

'Then you're on your own there, son.'

I came up behind her and put my arms around her waist and I have to admit that while I had dismissed her jibes about getting old, I had the treasonable thought that maybe she was getting, well, a bit plump. But then, only a bit. And maybe I was suddenly remembering Stella, who, whatever else had happened in her life, was still the same dress size as when I'd first met her.

'Would you believe I was hit by a toilet door in Gerry's Club? A door thrown open by a paranoid, naked male stripper who'd been hiding in there to get away from Stella Rudgard's hen night guests who had allowed his act to last a full fifteen seconds? And all this by 3.30 on a Friday afternoon?'

She considered this for a full minute, then started to pour coffee into mugs.

'Sounds reasonable,' she said, and handed me a mug. 'So who's Stella Rudgard?'

She looked me in the eyes when she said it and I was sure it was a genuine question. I mean, she's good, but then so am I.

'Stella Rudgard as in Rudgard and Blugden, confidential enquiries. Our local private eyes, well, Shepherd's Bush anyway. You know them. I did a job for them once.'

'Oh, yes, right, got it now. Did I ever meet her?'

'Probably not. You'd remember if you had.'

'She's not the dumpy one with the glasses who could get away with it if she wore lots of black and loose, at least a size bigger than she is instead of squeezing into a size smaller than she is? And lower heels.'

'No, that's be Veronica, her partner.'

'So who's this Stella getting married to then?'

Just when you think you're getting away with it, in comes the trick question.

'Er ... I'm not sure. I sort of forgot to ask, but it's bound to be in the papers today or tomorrow. He'll be rich if not famous.'

And if he was marrying Stella he would be famous, whether he wanted to be or not.

'So you've been having a good time, then?'

'So-so. How about you?'

'Productive, you might say. I think I've got a steal on the Next Big Thing in terms of designers. He's hooked, lined and almost signed up for some exclusive work. Drawback, of course, is he's Welsh, but he's young and innocent and that's how I like them.'

'The hit of Welsh Fashion Week, was he?' I said in what I thought was a passable singsong Welsh accent.

'Christ, no. That was the whole point of me going down there. I'd been tipped off about this kid – his name's Gwyn, by the way, 21 and bent as a nine-bob note – and when I saw his portfolio I persuaded him to pull half his collection from the show.'

'The good half, I presume, so that the opposition overlooked his potential,' I said.

'Hey you're good. You should be the detective, not this Stella person.'

Then she kissed the first and middle fingers of her right hand and placed them gently on my forehead, just above the bruise.

'Poor baby. Did you miss me?'

'Hardly noticed you were gone. I mean, I've been the only man at a hen night in Soho, I've had a few drinks with Duncan the Drunken and some old friends up in

Barking and I even popped over to Hackney to see how Springsteen was doing.'

She didn't flinch at the mention of Springsteen.

'Still spitting bile, invective and feathers in equal proportions, I trust?' she said.

'Oh, yes. And funnily enough, Duncan reckons that the BMW is repairable as long as we don't mind him welding the back half on to the front half of a Vauxhall Vectra and selling it to Latvia.'

She held up a hand in the Stop! sign.

'I've told you, don't go there. The car's history, just let it go. Now what about Madrid?'

I did a double take at this jump in logic.

'Madrid? As in Spain, right?'

She reached for the coffee pot to pour us a refill. I hear Starbucks do the same.

'I *did* tell you,' she said in her not-to-be-messed-with voice. 'I'm flying to Madrid on Monday afternoon, be there all week, back Friday night or Saturday morning, depending on how it pans out. It's a business trip but everybody knows the Spaniards don't do serious business after about one in the afternoon, so – lots of free time. Why don't you come along?'

'Me? Won't I cramp your style?'

'Not if you stay in bed until one o'clock. That shouldn't be a problem, should it?'

'I suppose ... if I set my mind to it ... with

severe mental discipline... Oh shit!'

I slapped myself on the forehead, forgetting it was still a sensitive area, so the 'Oh, shit' really was genuine.

'I've promised Dod – you remember Dod? He plays drums, trad jazz stuff, I've played with him before. He's a mate of Duncan's from Barking way. He's asked me to stand in for a few nights whilst his regular trumpet player goes in for a vasectomy or something. A few nights next week. Starting Monday.'

It was thin, I know, but the best I could do on the spur of the moment.

'I could tell him to find a sub, of course, but then I was his first choice and it was kinda flattering in a way as I haven't done much recently.'

'You haven't played for ages!' she exclaimed, though I don't know why she was surprised. She was the one who'd banned me from rehearsing in Hampstead.

'I know that; you know that. Dod doesn't. Anyway, I was, like I said, flattered. Couldn't say no. I mean, this could be my big comeback.'

'Come back to *what?* You have to have *been* somewhere before you can make a comeback.'

'Not necessarily, think of... Anyway, jazz never dies.'

'Your sort did, about 1930.'

'Hey, that's not fair. There's nothing so

potent as cheap live music, especially if the alternative is some spotty yoof giving himself carpal tunnel syndrome twisting two decks with vinyl on in opposite...'

The doorbell rang. Twice. It had to be the postman.

'Let me get that,' I said with a smile.

Amy went shopping for the rest of the day. What is it they say about when the going gets tough?

Not that it had – got tough, that is. Oh yes, she ranted about there not being a damned thing in the house to eat and so she was going to the nearest Sainsbury's (once I'd given her directions) to stock up on decent stuff and she was definitely, quite definitely, going to make an effort to cook proper meals at regular times from now on. Well, just as soon as she got back from Madrid, that was. And when, two hours later, she'd returned and I'd helped her unload the Freelander and put things away, including fresh vegetables in a special rack that I found in one of the kitchen units, she grabbed a high-energy muesli bar for lunch and announced that she just had to go up the West End and buy a few essentials for her trip to Madrid. And had Armstrong been parked in the drive all morning?

I had lied about that and told her a friend had driven him home from Gerry's Club, whereas in fact I'd called a mini-cab as soon as she'd left for Sainsbury's and tooled it down to Soho to rescue him.

Armstrong was back and in pride of place outside the house, annoying the neighbours.

Amy was back and out shopping.

All seemed right with the world.

She got back about six, loaded down with bags which read like a phone book of designers. Naturally, despite her best intentions, she was too shattered to actually start the new regime of wholesome cooking right now, so I did the decent thing and offered to nip out for a take-away Indian.

I picked up a couple of packs of Kingfisher lager and rented a video on the way back.

It turned out to be an almost perfect Saturday night, especially when Amy suggested we make it an early one, which we did, although she turned the lights off and insisted they stay off as soon as we got to the bedroom.

Which was unusual for her.

I'd had plenty of solo time (as we're supposed to call it these days) while she was shopping to open what the postman had brought, recorded delivery, for me and which I had manage to keep out of Amy's sightline.

It was an official visiting order allowing me, nay, inviting me, to attend HM Prison Belmarsh to visit with prisoner Malcolm Fisher at times which were convenient to the said prison.

Spider had told me to expect one but I was impressed how quickly it had arrived. Now all I had to do was check in with Spider and then wait for the phone call.

From prisoner Malcolm Fisher.

Mr Creosote.

I still hadn't a clue who he was, but I had a nasty feeling he might be Welsh.

I had phoned St Chad's whilst Amy was out shopping. If Warden Roberts had answered I was supposed to say I was Spider's nephew and put a handkerchief over the mouthpiece to disguise my voice. Thankfully that didn't have to happen as whoever picked up the phone just grunted then yelled 'Spider!' so loud I could hear the echoes down the line.

When he came on, I had told Spider that the visiting order had arrived and he'd said I was to meet him Sunday morning at 11 a.m. in St Chad's Park. He would be walking Warden Roberts' dog along the footpath by the playground near the north entrance.

Before I could ask whether he'd be wearing a wire or whether I should check the trees for snipers, he had hung up on me.

Part of my grand plan seemed to be coming together at last. Problem was I couldn't really remember what the plan was and then I remembered my notes, which were still on the floor of the Armstrong.

While Amy was out it seemed a good idea to get my filing system collated, or at least out of sight, as even Amy might wonder why the front of the cab was littered with inky napkins. As it happened, the first one I picked up was the sheet which said 'GUN' and I had an idea that I might be able to do something about that, even on a Saturday afternoon.

I didn't think much of my chances of getting hold of DI Hood, unless the Met really was dishing out the overtime, but Keith Flowers had been arrested in Suffolk and the police there might just have more time on their hands.

I got lucky. A very nice receptionist at the Suffolk Police headquarters at Martlesham near Ispwich put me through to CID without any hassle and the phone was picked up by a female Detective Constable with a broad Suffolk accent called Priestley.

I gave her my name and said I was ringing in connection with a car insurance claim, citing the reference number the cops had given me for that very purpose, resulting from a crime incident. I told her I knew that charges were pending against a certain Keith Flowers and no doubt it would all come out in court, but what I needed, or rather the nit-picking insurance company needed (and she knew exactly how annoying they could be), were details of the weapon used by Flowers.

What sort of details? Well, I didn't rightly know. I supposed they wanted to be sure I wasn't just embellishing my claim, or just checking that it was a real gun not a toy, something like that. They hadn't been terribly clear, but then insurance companies were never clear when it came to paying out, only when collecting their premiums. That, she'd said, was something I could say again.

She left me hanging on for five minutes then came back to tell me that the case file had gone to the Crown Prosecution Service but all the evidence bags were in their secure evidence room, which was routine where a firearm was involved. She would go down and have a look and ring me back. I told her she was very, very kind, and only if she could spare the time. She probably could, she'd said. It was fairly quiet in Suffolk.

In case she rang back when I was out I rehearsed what I would say if Amy took the call or heard a recorded message. No problem, I was filling in an insurance form, sensibly this time. She hadn't shown any interest in the wrecked BMW so far and would probably blank it again.

I couldn't think why one of the younger Turners had asked me what sort of gun Keith Flowers had used. At the time, in the dark, being shot at, I wasn't paying much attention. My first impression had been that it was big and shiny and perhaps an automatic, but I wasn't sure then and I certainly wasn't now. I hadn't seen it close up as I'd had no intention of getting up close and afterwards the police had kept us well away whilst Flowers was cut out of the BMW and then taken Flowers, the gun and the wreck into custody.

I had Radio 5 on for the football results when DC Priestley rang back.

'You're in luck, Mr Angel,' she said.

'I'd like to think I was,' I said. 'Any particular reason why?'

'Your weapon is quite famous.'

'Thank you.'

I could almost hear her blush down the phone.

'I'm sorry... I mean the weapon in your case... I mean the case against Flowers... It was quite unusual. First one we've had in Suffolk.'

'First one what?'

'It was a Brocock,' she said proudly.

'Really? I'd never have guessed. That's quite interesting.'

I toned down the sarcasm. It was never a good move with policemen.

'Can I ask what the devil a Brocock is?'

'It's an air pistol,' she said.

Chapter Twelve

'You're up early,' said Amy. 'What you looking for?'

I clicked the mouse and moved on to another window before she got near enough to see the screen.

'Band parts,' I said, smiling at her.

'Excuse me?'

'For Dod's band. I'm trying to make this thing do some basic arrangements of some of the old standards, for trumpet, piano and sax and print them out so we've got something to rehearse with.'

'We have a programme that does that?' she asked innocently.

'As a matter of fact we do. It's called *Sibelius II* but I'm buggered if I can get it to work. Dod's lot probably can't read music anyway, so we'll wing it.'

'I thought that was what you were supposed to do with jazz.'

'Yeah, well, I ain't winging anything unless I put in some serious lip practice. I don't suppose...'

'Oh, no,' she said quickly. 'You know the rules. No trumpet playing here, it'll annoy the neighbours.'

'This is a detached house,' I pointed out.

'I've heard you play,' she said, like it was a threat.

'Then I'll just have to go over to Hackney and annoy the neighbours there.'

'Yes, I'm afraid you will,' she flounced, turning on her heel.

It had worked like a charm.

I got out of the Sibelius programme, which I had been using for cover, then logged into three or four more sites on the Internet connection just in case Amy checked the History file to see what I'd been surfing. Buried among them would be the search I put out for 'Brocock' which may or may not mean anything to her.

It certainly meant more to me now.

I had another cup of coffee while Amy was in the shower – again. What was wrong with her? Then I grabbed my jacket and Armstrong's keys and yelled that I was going.

'I'll look in on Springsteen while I'm there,' I added. 'Give Fenella some money for cat food.'

'Whatever you're paying her isn't enough!' she yelled back from the bathroom.

'Why? What's he done to you lately?'

I listened carefully for her response. I knew she hadn't seen Springsteen for months, or so I thought. But then she did have a limp...

'Nothing to me,' she answered innocently. 'But he is on the RSPCA's Most Wanted list.'

'Ha, ha, very funny.'

I shook my head at my own stupidity for ever suspecting her. I *knew* who had kicked seven bells out Springsteen and, just to be perverse, Springsteen actually liked Amy and had never attacked her, even in fun. Plus, there was no way Amy would ever wear a shade of tights called Chiffon and especially not if Lisabeth did.

Having worked all that out I was feeling quite pleased with myself and I was nearly at the door when I heard her yell:

'If you won't come with me to Madrid can you at least give me a lift to Heathrow tomorrow lunchtime?'

'Yeah, sure. No problemo,' I shouted back. Idiot.

In St Chad's Park I wore sunglasses for the purpose for which Raybans had intended for once, as it was a beautiful bright sunny morning. So did Spider. In fact his aviator-style shades were probably real Raybans, but they didn't do much for him. They would have looked cooler on Warden Roberts' ancient golden labrador, who wheezed along behind Spider at the end of an extendible lead.

'You got it then?' Spider whispered,

glancing furtively around. Apart from half a dozen kids in the nearby playground, there was nobody for miles.

'The visiting order?' I said loudly and he automatically flapped his hands to shush me, jerking the dog lead and the dog as he did so. 'Don't spread it around, they'll all want one. Come on, let's walk. Got to keep old Fang here moving 'til he vacates his bowels. We sit down somewhere he'll nod off and not do the business, but if that daft old sod Roberts thinks I'm using the pooper-scooper, he's got another think coming. Nobody followed you, did they?'

I put my hand over my glasses and swivelled my head, pretending to scan the horizon.

'Did you say St Chad's Park or Gorky Park? Who would've followed me?'

'You tell me. I'm just being careful, like I was told to be. Pays to be careful where Mr Creosote is concerned.'

He yanked on the lead and the dog started off down the footpath. Spider gave him about ten feet of lead then we followed.

'So who is this Malcolm Fisher, then?'

Spider's head snapped round.

'How did...? It was on the VO, right?'

'Oh, no,' I sneered. 'The visiting order said I could go and visit Mr Creosote and then Captain Blood, Frank "the Enforcer" Nitti, Hannibal the Cannibal, Ming the Merciless,

Slasher Carmichael, Minnesota Fats, Deptford Eddy, Barking Brian, Mad Dog Cockfosters Colin...'

'You know Slasher Carmichael?' he asked, then it dawned that I was winding him up.

Or maybe he was winding *me* up.

'Come on, Spider, why the meet? If it's got nothing to do with Prisoner 8281 Fisher, M. then I'm not really interested and there's an elsewhere I could be.'

'Hey, I'm here 'cos I was told to be. Got to run through things with you.'

'Such as?'

'The procedures, the ett-ee-ket, how not to get on the tits of the screws, that sort of stuff.'

'I'm sure that'll be useful, but I really would like to know who the hell it is I'm going to see before I get the rough guide to prison visiting.'

'Fair enough,' said Spider. 'Got a smoke?'

'No.'

It was true. My throat still rasped from Friday night. Spider sighed loudly and dug out a packet of Dunhill from his trouser pocket, followed by what looked suspiciously like a gold-plated Dunhill lighter. Automatically, I checked to see if my watch was still on my wrist.

'So you've never heard of Malcolm Fisher, right?' he said through a cloud of smoke.

'Never.'

'Then I suppose you've been lucky so far.'

Somebody else had said something very similar lately.

'Let me take a wild guess. He's a mate of Keith Flowers and – shot in the dark here – he's Welsh.'

'Right twice, Sherlock. He's a Taffy from Cardiff and that's where he did some business with Flowers in the past. Fast-forward to last year and he ends up sharing a cell in Belmarsh with Flowers. Luck of the draw. Malcolm's waiting for a transfer to Maidstone, Flowers is relocated to London to start his downscaling to release day.'

'How come they got put together?' I asked during a temporary halt whilst Fang thought about the state of his bowels.

'Pure chance. Flowers had asked for a move to London to see out the arse-end of his sentence.'

So he could be nearer Amy, I thought.

'Malcolm was moved from Cardiff because of certain things what happened down there and they reckoned Maidstone was far enough away, but you know, Maidstone's really popular with the old London lags, who've all got family down in Kent, so, like, there's a waiting list. Malcolm was still waiting when Flowers turned up. He's still waiting as it happens.'

'So they had a reunion and talked about the good old days in Cardiff. So what?

Where the fuck do I come into this picture?'

'That's for Mr Cre... Fisher to tell you. I don't know any more and I don't want to know any more. All I have to do is make sure you get there for two o'clock tomorrow. I tell you, this being outside is doing my head in. I'll be chucked out of St Chad's in a month's time and what does the future hold for me, eh? Know any *Big Issue* pitches going spare?'

'You done a lot of ... time ... bird?'

I wasn't sure what the correct term was.

'Made a career of it. Used to it now. Tell the truth, I'm not looking forward to Christmas on the outside one bit. It's warm inside, the food's free and I'm too old to appeal to anybody in the showers now, so that's not a problem. I reckon, come October, I'll be looking for a nice bit of burglary. No violence, nothing like that, just enough to pull a six-month over Christmas. Do me fine.'

In a heartbeat he stopped being philosophical and turned on me.

'And don't try and be clever when you're in Belmarsh. Don't use words like "bird" unless you know exactly what they mean. That's what gets the bacon into trouble.'

'Bacon?'

'Bacon is what they call the new intake. First-time prisoners they reckon are "vulnerable" – that's the word. Mostly they're put in

Fraggle Rock for a coupla weeks to see if they can handle prison life.'

'Fraggle Rock?' I asked, happy to admit I was out of my depth here.

'The hospital wing. Daft really, 'cos nobody's sick in there. Place is full of bacon to keep them out the way of the old lags, but they're mixing with the real nutters from maximum security who are not only ill, but sick, sick, sick and that lot are all on three-man lock-downs.'

I decided that now wasn't the time for a translation, but Spider was ahead of me.

'Anyway, don't you worry, 'cos I'm coming with you, for the ride anyway.'

'You are?'

'Oh, yes. I got an excuse to be there, showing you the way. I'm on Mr Cre... Fisher's list. His phone list.'

'Phone list?'

'Since they did away with phone cards – pity, really, 'cos they was like currency inside – anyways, since they went you get your own personal PIN number. You know, Personal Identification Number.' I nodded as if I was being shown a You-Are-Here map to the Holy Grail. 'Well, you put all the numbers you're likely to want to ring on a list, right? And you get your wages, such as they are, and any bits of dosh that come in from outside – it's only pennies, like – and you make your phone calls during Association on your PIN number and they, like, discredit your account, but only if the numbers are on the list.'

'I think I get that. What's "Association"?'

'That's when they open the doors and you can go out on the wing or the block, wherever, and mix with the other lags. That's when you do your Canteen.' He titled his sunglasses on one side. 'Your sort probably know it as the Tuck Shop or something posh. It's when you put your order in for life's little luxuries.'

His voice tailed off towards the end, as if he was remembering something he really missed.

'All this is fascinating, Spider, but what's the point?'

'Just giving you a bit of background, that's all.' He walked on, pulling a reluctant Fang behind him. 'Serious part of the briefing is as follows.

'One: do not draw attention to yourself. Two: do not talk to anyone except a prison officer and only if they talk to you first. Three: do not be cheeky, or pretend to know what you're talking about. So you do not say "porridge", "banged up", "screw" or anything like that.'

'You did.'

'I'm allowed. I'm a known face, that's why I'll just be taking you as far as the Visitor Centre, show you the ropes. After that you're on your own. That's why you've got to remember Rule One.'

'Which was?'

'Don't draw attention to yourself!' Then he realized he was shouting and lowered his voice. 'Anyway. Number four: make sure you've got some genuine ID with you, with a photo for preference. Five: don't take more than six quid in with you. That's all that's allowed, but you'll need it to buy tea or coffee and you can leave the change in Malcolm's account. Six: do not take anything to write with. No paper, no pens. Prisoners aren't allowed to write anything or sign anything during visiting. And for Christ's sake don't go in there with a mobile phone. That's asking for it. Seven: don't bother taking any fags in there, they're trying to make it a healthier environment. And eight: do not carry any sort of drugs in with you and, to be safe, don't wear any clothes that have been near any drugs lately. Don't laugh, those sniffer dogs are good and if they pick you out, the next sound you hear is the smack of a rubber glove and it's bend over and spread 'em for the anal search. If you're lucky, they'll remember the Vaseline.'

'I'm rapidly going off this whole idea,' I said. 'I mean, I'm still no clearer as to why I'm visiting this guy Fisher anyway.'

'Bit late to start worrying about that, inn'it? You pick me up outside the hostel at twelve, eh? That should do it. Be a nice run round by Dartford in that taxi of yours. Don't forget some cash for the toll bridge, though.'

'Now wait a minute.'

I caught his arm and pulled him up short. Fang took the unscheduled stop to squat down and finally do what he was supposed to do, right in the middle of the footpath.

'You haven't given me one good reason why I should take up this Mr Fisher's nice offer of an afternoon in one of Her Majesty's prisons. What if I just don't show?'

'That's up to you, son.' Spider looked around him, anywhere but at me. Just an old man waiting for his dog to finish fouling the walkway.

'But I'd always bear it in the back of my mind as to how Mr Creosote got that name.'

'Do you know, I've been meaning to ask that.'

'Well put it this way, the last person who crossed him – it was down in Cardiff and when he was in Cardiff nick – the next day, they comes home to find their living room had been creosoted. You know what I'm talking about? Creosote. The stuff like tar, that you use outside on your roof or on your garden shed that you just don't ever, ever, get on your clothes? Imagine coming home to find your walls, the carpet, the three-piece suite from Ikea, the television, even your fucking dog, all done out in creosote. And not just a bucket of it thrown slapdash like some young hooligan would, but a proper job. Three men in there for most of the day, applying two coats and not a drop spilt on the front doorstep to tell you they'd called.

'He can make that happen from inside his cell. That's why he got the name.'

'And that's why you're scared of him?'

'That's why *you* should be scared of him. You've got a fucking living room, I haven't.'

I called in at the Stuart Street flat on my way back to Hampstead to collect my old B-flat trumpet to bolster my alibi.

I told Springsteen he was looking well and it wouldn't be long before the plaster came off. Then I made a chain saw sound and he lashed out at me, but he was slow, far too slow.

For a moment I seriously considered joining Amy on that flight to Madrid but the prospect of coming home to a weatherproof lounge worried me.

Then I realized I was picking Spider up for the jaunt to Belmarsh at roughly the same time I had agreed to take Amy to Heathrow, and that worried me as well.

On my way out I stopped at Flat 2 and gave Fenella some dosh for Springsteen's food and nursing. I also told her that if three men in overalls turned up with tins of what looked like paint, she was *on no account* to let them in. They had not been hired to repaint my flat, it was all a cruel practical joke, but the guys in overalls wouldn't know that and they might turn ugly if they thought they were losing a job.

If they turned violent, there was only one thing Fenella could and should do.

Shout for Lisabeth.

In an odd sort of way I was curious to see if Mr Creosote could top that.

'How long are you going for?' I almost added: *this time.*

'Back on Friday. Plane lands at eight fifteen – that's p.m., so don't panic. You could pick me up from Heathrow if you like.'

Amy concentrated on packing yet another dress into an already straining suitcase.

'And you want me to drop you there tomorrow as well?' I said, as if I'd just remembered it.

'If it's not too much trouble.'

'Well, actually, I've been volunteered to pick up one of the band over in Chadwell Heath about twelve. We've got the offer of a warm-up session at a pub down Canary Wharf.'

'On a Monday lunchtime?'

'They don't get much entertainment down Canary Wharf.'

'Well, OK, I'll take the Freelander and stick it in the Long Stay car park.'

'No, that's always a hassle, don't bother with that.'

I had a vague feeling I might need the Freelander. Far too many people had seen me in the Armstrong lately: Spider, the Turners and even Steffi Innocent.

Now there was an idea.

'I promise you there'll be a cab here on the dot of twelve,' I said confidently. 'On me. You won't even have to fiddle your expenses. And I'll pick you up on Friday night. That's a guarantee. What about tickets and stuff?'

'I'll email Debbie at the office and she can bike them round first thing. All the paperwork can be downloaded from the office computer into my laptop. I don't have to go in.'

She stood back from her suitcase which covered most of the bed and glared at it, willing the pile of clothes to shrink.

'Why this sudden concern for my welfare?' she asked suspiciously.

Typical.

'Welfare? Whose welfare? I want to make sure you don't miss your plane. That way I get you out of the way for five days and I get to go and revisit my misspent youth, touring with the boys in the band, making good music, staying up late, getting drunk and taking drugs and fighting off the groupies.'

She screwed her eyes up and waited for the moment.

'Damn, you must have a long memory,' she said.

First thing on Monday morning, I rang Rudgard & Blugden Confidential Investigations. Steffi Innocent picked up the phone. I'd just known she would be the first one in the office, at her desk by 8.30.

I told her I had a job for her, an important job. She asked if I was hiring her and I said no, giving her a chance to pay off her debt to me. Before she could ask what debt, I said there had been a *development* in the case she'd got me involved in and I needed her and her Tixilix taxi at twelve noon sharp. Before she could ask what case, I told her she had to pretend to be a regular taxi – prepaid and ordered by me – and to pick up Amy and drive her to Heathrow. She was not to reveal who she was or anything about her following me and Amy around last week, or mention Haydn Rees or Keith Flowers, in fact just talk normal taxi driver/passenger stuff. In fact, just pretend she was a real taxi driver.

'It sounds as if you just want me to give her a lift to the airport,' she moaned.

As if, I'd said. Didn't she realize I needed a trained observer to check whether or not Amy *was being followed?* Not to do anything if she was, mind, just take notes and check in back with me later.

Was somebody following her? That was for her to find out, wasn't it? After all, she was the detective.

By the time she hung up she was quite enthusiastic about the whole thing and I felt fairly pleased with myself as well.

I'd just saved thirty quid, with tip.

I actually parked at the end of the road just to check that Steffi turned up on time, but of course Miss Perfect Professional was fifteen minutes early. Which was fine by me as I was only slightly late getting over to St Chad's to find Spider hopping from one foot to the other outside the hostel.

'Cutting it a bit fine, aren't you?' he growled as he piled in the back.

'Can wait to get back inside, can you?' I said, a tad cruelly.

'The warden's gone to the cash 'n carry but he'll be back soon and it don't look good if he sees me getting into a cab, does it? I mean, he'll begin to think I've got a source of income. And anyway, I'm not going inside – well, not today. You are.'

He sank down in the back so he couldn't be seen clearly until we were well on to

Eastern Avenue. Only as we were circling Romford did he move on to the rumble seat behind me and start chattering in my ear. I was tempted to slide the partition into place; not from what he was saying but because of his breath, which stank as if he'd been stealing Fang's dinner. I wished I had a cigarette to give him.

'You got your VO?'

'Yes.'

'You got some photo ID?'

'Yes.'

'You got any drugs on you?'

'No.'

'You carried any hard drugs on you in the last week?'

'No.'

'You smoked any dope in the last thirty days?'

'No,' I said, surprised. 'Why thirty days?'

'They reckon that's how long it stays in your system. Or, least, that's what they say when they do MDTs on you.'

'In English, please,' I said.

'What?' he snapped back.

'What does MDT mean?'

'Mandatory Drugs Testing – piss tests to you and me. It's what they do inside. Your name comes up on their computer and you get to pee in the bottle. Ten to 14 days on your sentence for cannabis, 21 to 36 for opiates. You don't take the test, they add on

36 days anyway. How much money you got on you?'

'Five pounds 99p.'

'Correct. But that's just what you can take in. I hope you got some stashed away somewhere so you can buy me a pint on the way home.'

'I thought this was your way home.'

He threw himself off the rumble and on to the back seat, snorting in disgust.

'Easy thing for you to say, but you've got no poxy idea what it's like inside. I can handle it, you couldn't. They won't need to do an MDT on you, you'll piss yourself with fright in the visiting room.'

I supposed I deserved that. I just hoped he wasn't right.

We joined the M25 off the Southend Arterial and thanks to a clear run we were on the Dartford Bridge within a few minutes. We were halfway across before Spider spoke again.

'It's the views you miss, you know.'

I checked him in the mirror. He was gazing out over the Thames at its widest, greyest and most industrial, a view rarely seen on postcards.

'And it's the views that do your head in as well. In Belmarsh some of the local lags on remand can see their own flats over in Thamesmead West or Plumstead. "I live there, third balcony down," they yell, just like big kids. Then there's the City Airport just across the river and you can see the planes come in and go out all bloody day and night. Fucking cruel it is, sometimes.'

I knew about the Alcatraz syndrome where the real punishment for the prisoners there came not from the incarceration itself so much as being able to look across the bay and see the waterfront lights of San Francisco and actually hear the music and sometimes the voices of the revellers on Fisherman's Wharf. I'd never thought a view of a council tower block in Plumstead or a short take-off stumpy plane full of irritated businessmen or bored civil servants heading for yet another showdown in Brussels could match the delights of Frisco. But then, each to his own, especially when the alternative is thirty-foot high redstone walls.

'I thought you quite fancied the idea of going back inside,' I said over my shoulder as I flipped coins into one of the automatic tolls.

'I have to admit I do,' said Spider mournfully.

'And why's that?'

'My age? My circumstances? Trust me, it's more of a prison on the outside.'

I put my foot down and zipped the Armstrong into the correct lane for Dartford and the strangely-named Erith, cutting up a couple of trucks and several families of holidaymakers on their way to

Dover and the continent. No one minded. Even returning Belgian motorists knew better than to honk a London taxi.

It was only when we were on Bronze Age Way, which is in fact a brand new dual carriageway, that Spider spoke again.

'You know this was all marshes once,' he said wistfully. 'Erith Marshes and Thamesmead Marshes.'

'I'll believe you,' I said though the modern road had been cut and banked so there wasn't a view, which was probably a good thing as I knew that a huge sewage works lay between us and the river.

'It's true. That's why Belmarsh is technically a floating prison, 'cos it's built on marshland. Funny really, as back in Dickens' day they used to moor their prison hulks here. You know, similar to them in *Great Expectations*. Funny how nothing much changes, inn'it?'

'Makes it a sod to tunnel out of, I guess.'

'Don't think anybody's tried that. Wouldn't go over the wall either if I was you,' he said like he was giving me good advice.

'I was planning on using the front door,' I said. 'Both ways. In *and* out.'

'I was speaking figuratively in a metaphor,' he said grandly. 'What I meant was the top stones and the cornice of the wall aren't cemented in, they're just loose, lying there. So if you put a grappling hook or a rope ladder up there, fucking great lumps of stuff come down and land on your head. Nobody'll try that. Again.'

'Shouldn't we be nearly there?' I asked him, uneasy because I hadn't seen any signs to or sign of a prison, just trees along the roadside and the occasional slip road into light industrial trading estates.

'They don't believe in advertising much,' said Spider. 'They call it London's best kept secret. Keep going down here then just before the roundabout there's a sharp left turn down to the Magistrates' Court. Take that and follow the signs for Visitor Centre, it don't go anywhere else.'

Belmarsh is three things: a court, a jail and a high-security prison. The high-security prison is separate but within the prison confines though the first thing you see, off to your right between the trees, is a side road to the court block with a lifting barrier and its own security men. The court works as both a magistrates court and a crown court and most everyone knows there is a tunnel from there into the jail. I say most everyone, but perhaps that should be everyone who ever drank in a pub in Plumstead or Woolwich when they were building the place back in the 'Eighties, where disgruntled contractors and builders would try and flog you a set of the plans for twenty quid. It still catches out the younger, embarrassingly keen press photographers and TV cameramen who wait vainly for the shot of a well-known accused being put in the Black Maria or driven off to prison. If they're up before the beak in Belmarsh, they disappear down the tunnel without a grand exit. Never have the words 'take him down' been used so literally in a courtroom.

I followed the signs saying Visitor Centre as the one-way road curved round to the left and away from the Court building. There were single-storey buildings here in among the trees and, suddenly, a large car park. The whole scene was reminiscent of the entrance to, say, a National Park in America and I almost expected to see camper vans and backpackers pulling on hiking boots.

But there was nowhere to hike to because the eyeline was irresistibly pulled towards the large stone wall which seemed to run east—west forever, so big so suddenly did you see it that it just didn't seem real. It was almost as if it was a facade; a prop for a movie set near the Great Wall of China, or maybe a reworking of *Gormenghast*. For some reason the walls didn't look real. Somehow they just weren't in the right place. It was almost as if they were a long way away in the distance and only seemed to be here and up close. The scale of things was deceiving and there was probably a local legend that no matter how hard you threw, you could never get a stone or a cricket ball to reach them.

And once I'd parked and killed the Armstrong's engine, it was so quiet it was unnerving. Somewhere on the other side of that wall were – on a bad day – maybe a thousand prisoners plus several hundred staff, secured by hundreds if not thousands of doors and thousands if not millions of keys.

'You coming or what?'

Spider rapped on Armstrong's window with his knuckles and then opened the door for me.

I got out, patting my jacket pockets to make sure I had everything I needed and didn't have anything forbidden.

'Don't forget to lock the cab,' said Spider. 'There's some dishonest folk about these days.'

Chapter Thirteen

Nice doggy, keep moving. There's a good dog. Don't sit here. Please don't sit here.

Spider was as good as his word and he steered me through the process in the Visitor Centre, where I presented the visiting order and my ID, had my photograph of my face taken with a Polaroid camera and a print of my right hand geometry taken with a machine which looked straight out of a science fiction movie.

I didn't need Spider to tell me that all this was to ensure that it was me who walked in and me who walked out again – the same principle behind the fact that I was told to leave all my ID in one of the lockers available. But it was useful to get the odd survival tip, such as to leave my car keys and any other metal in the locker as well. 'Anything that shows up suspicious on an X-ray or triggers off the metal detectors,' as Spider had said. 'Think what you have to go through at airports, then treble it.'

The most important piece of advice, though, I didn't fully appreciate at first. 'Do not, repeat not, start chatting up any of the other visitors. Keep your eyes on the ground. No smiling, no eye contact. Don't talk to the women or the kids. Specially not the women.' I had assumed this was to avoid confrontations of the *You looking at my bird/wife/kids?* kind once inside and it seemed like good advice, so I followed it. After all, there were potentially a thousand very frustrated husbands the other side of that wall, which was a pretty scary thought.

Over two-thirds of the other visitors were women and a few had small children with them which they clutched like security blankets whilst answering the questions of the prison officers registering their visits with sullen monosyllables. None were very old and two seemingly travelling together, one white, one black, wore PVC micro skirts, denim jackets with the sleeves cut off, day-glo yellow scrunchy hairbands around their wrists and ankle boots with spiky heels. They laughed loudly at just about anything, swore profusely and screeched when they answered questions, adding 'fuck' to emphasize just a-fucking-bout every fucking word.

'Diversion,' Spider had whispered in my ear. 'The two tarts will make a scene and get hauled off for a strip search and the Vaseline digit treatment.'

I had read, probably in some dubious

'Men's' magazine, that the record for a woman visiting a prison was 27 wraps of heroin smuggled 'internally'. I winced as I remembered that.

'They'll distract the POs while the carrier goes in,' Spider confided. 'The stuff'll be on one of the quiet ones. Or one of the kids.'

I tried to resist scanning the faces of the other women, remembering what Spider had said about eye contact. Apart from the two garishly dressed girl decoys, most had dulled vacant expressions which gave nothing away except the fact that they had all been here before.

'Some of them get two hours a month visiting,' my tour guide hissed out of the corner of his mouth. 'And it's an hour and a half too much.'

And then it had been time to leave Spider in the visitor centre and walk towards the main gates of steel and glass behind a bomb-proof outer door and there were white-shirted prison officers, male and female, and we were told to form a line and have our VOs checked. While we waited in line we all had plenty of time to read the big notice which warned us not to try and smuggle drugs into the prison and how there would be an amnesty for anyone who dumped their stash in one of the bins provided before we got inside.

The first door was an airlock system,

allowing two or three of us in there at a time, one door hissing closed behind us. Only when there were officers enough to deal with us on the other side did the second door open and men were directed one way and women another.

The search area was similar to the set-up at an airport in that there was a large metal detecting portal in the middle of the room which you obviously had to walk through and an X-ray machine like they have for hand luggage, but the actual procedure was a tad more thorough. After going through it I could understand why nobody had ever hijacked a prison.

I was told to take off my jacket and put it, along with anything from my trouser pockets, in a plastic tray to be slid through the X-ray. Then I was told to add my belt to the tray, which I hadn't expected and a 'first-timer' expression appeared on the faces of all the Prison Officers in the room.

Then I had to step through the detector door, tensing myself – as you do – for the inevitable buzzing sound as the nail file or the keys you'd forgotten about set it off. There was no buzz, although they made me stay in the detector frame whilst a burly male PO positioned himself about four feet in front of me and planted his feet apart, almost like an American football player waiting for a tackle. He signalled me forward with small 'come on' movements of his fingers and then asked me to spread my legs and stretch out my arms.

I think the proper expression is a 'fingertip' search but I'm sure there were a couple of knuckles in there somewhere as he patted me down, then asked me to turn round so he could do the same from behind. The hands didn't linger on my crotch, but they made sure there was nothing in there that shouldn't have been.

Then they asked me to stand over by the wall and take my shoes off. While the male officer who had patted me examined my best pair of Russell Bromley brogues (my only pair, actually), bending the soles, tugging at the laces, twisting the heels, a blonde female officer approached me, stretching on a pair of thin surgical gloves.

'Would you open your mouth for me, please?' she asked in a soft Scottish accent.

I was so relieved I almost made a witty remark, but remembered where I was just in time and did as I was told.

Her rubber fingers ran over my teeth and probed the roof of my mouth and down the sides of my tongue, then squeaked down the sides of my back teeth.

Her clear blue eyes met mine as she withdrew her hand and I thought for a moment she was going to compliment me on my teeth, which I do take care of, but she just said I could get my things and move into the waiting area.

Six of us congregated in a corridor while an officer locked one door behind us and then unlocked another with keys from a bunch chained to his belt. Through that door we were in an enclosed courtyard in the corner of which stood two more officers each holding Alsatian dogs on tight leads.

We were lead diagonally across the courtyard and were able to catch a glimpse of the upper floors of the cell wings and, beyond, the roof of the high-security prison-within-a-prison. We could also see the outer walls from the inside and the 'skyhawk' cameras on tall posts which offered somebody somewhere pinpoint closed circuit television pictures of us as we headed for another door bearing a sign saying Visitors.

The waiting area reminded me of a cinema foyer, though I couldn't think of a cinema I knew which had large signs asking customers to dump their drugs in the bins provided or announcements that the toilets were about to be locked. Being British, we formed an orderly queue leading to the double doors at the end. They had even painted a yellow line on the floor to show us where to stand and everyone was behaving themselves; even the two micro-skirted foulmouthed girls had reduced the number of 'fuckings' in their conversation by about a third.

It therefore seemed totally unfair when they set the dogs on us.

Keep moving, there's a good doggy. Move along, little doggy, move along. Just don't sit here...

So it wasn't exactly a slobbering, growling, flesh-ripping hound. In fact, I was tempted to say 'Frankly, Mr Baskerville, we expected something larger' but I kept my lip buttoned and hoped the damned dog did as well. In any other set of circumstances, I would have been tempted to bend down and stroke him or pat his head or find somewhere to hide him if Springsteen was in the vicinity. I've always had a soft spot for spaniels, though I was prepared to make an exception in this case.

Spider had warned me about the active and the passive sniffer dogs the prison used, tossing in at no extra charge that Belmarsh had the largest population of working dogs of any prison bar one in Northern Ireland, as if that was a comfort. The active sniffers, an unholy alliance of labradors and spaniels, were known as the Dogs From Hell, being bouncy, unstoppably enthusiastic and totally dedicated to finding hidden, abandoned or buried dumps of drugs. But it was the passive sniffers you had to wary of. They were mostly spaniels, trained from pups to sniff out drugs on a person. They didn't bark or slobber or whine or drag their handlers as if they were saying 'Come on, get a move on, it's over here...' The passives, all bright-eyed and bushy-tailed, just wandered casually in and out of people's legs so you wouldn't know they were there, until they found the scent they were sniffing for. Then they did an awful thing. They sat there and stared up at you with their big brown spaniel eyes. They sat there and no matter how hard you tried to send them a telepathic message to piss off, they just wouldn't move.

Come on, Fido, give us a break. Move along. Please. For God's sake, don't start getting comfortable.

The dog had been let off the lead by the door and had trotted along the length of the yellow line behind which we all stood, backs against a wall. Then the damned animal about turned, trotted back about halfway down the line to where I was and sat down, his front paws up against the other side of the yellow line, like a sprinter on the blocks.

I glanced to my left as surreptitiously as I could. Next in line was a young black guy, his shaven head pressed right back into the wall, his eyes staring straight out front, his face expressionless. He had totally ignored the dog's presence, and wasn't that a sheen of sweat on his head?

Now he looked guilty, or at least more guilty than me. I could see that, why couldn't the bloody dog? Why did it have to park its bum right in front of me?

But looking down, resisting the twin urges to say 'good doggy' and to kick the thing into touch, maybe the sniffing spaniel *wasn't* right in front of me. Come to think of it, he was halfway between me and the person to my right.

To avoid any sudden guilty moves, I turned my head slowly as if my shoulders had been nailed to the wall, and eyeballed the woman in front of me in the queue.

I honestly hadn't noticed her before. She was a short, overweight white woman, maybe thirty-five, which made her and me among the oldest there, wearing a crumpled and in parts threadbare grey pinstripe two-piece. She had large black-framed glasses, wore no make-up, had her hair scraped back in a stubby bun held by a pair of garish yellow hairbands (the only splash of colour on her) and she clutched a dog-eared paperback Bible to her chest.

Surely not?

Then, down the line I saw the two micro-skirted girls looking up the line towards me and the dog. Looking very anxiously.

'Come with us, please,' said a voice.

Two officers, one male, one female, stood in front of me. Or were they in front of the woman next to me? My mouth was dry and I couldn't think of a way to phrase the question. The damned dog wasn't helping, just gazing balefully upwards and actually wagging its tail whilst still sitting there, making a swishing sound on the polished floor.

I knew there was something to say, but I couldn't think what or how to say it. I couldn't think at all.

'Yes you, madam,' said the male officer. 'This way, please.'

I must have exhaled loudly or perhaps even giggled. I certainly felt as if I was in control of my bladder once more and however boorish my response to the misfortune of others, it was nothing to the reaction of the Bible-holding woman next in line.

'I've got my period!' she screamed. 'That's what your fucking dog can smell!'

'Please, madam—'

'Don't you fucking touch me, you twat!'

'Just come with us, my dear,' tried the female officer.

'I'll have you for assault, you fucking dyke cunt!'

They each grabbed an arm and pulled the woman between them down the line and towards the doors we had come in through. She tried a half-hearted kick at the dog as it watched her, mildly amused, as she was hauled away.

I winked at the dog.

'Good boy,' I said softly.

Down the line, Spider's two tart-decoys were staring openly now, their jaws sagging. The black one raised her arm and gave the finger to the backs of the officers and the white girl joined in and did the same.

'Let go of me, you twatting fucks!' the woman shouted and, naturally we all turned to watch.

Almost at the door, the woman wrenched herself free from the two officers (who had shown remarkable patience in not slugging her so far) and then, like a frisbee, she flung the Bible she had been clutching towards the big metal bin reserved for those who wanted to opt for the drugs amnesty.

Whilst the officers' attention was diverted and before they had a chance to get hold of her again, she had managed to put a hand up behind her head and flip off the two day-glo yellow scrunchy hairbands she had been wearing. The officers holding her didn't seem to notice what had happened, nor did anyone else in the queue, and once they had a fresh hold on the woman – who was still screaming and spitting in their faces – they began a determined march towards the doors.

It was only me who was looking not at the free show, but at the two yellow hairbands on the floor.

Me and the two girls in micro-skirts further down the line, who had worn them on their wrists when they were in the Visitor Centre.

Me, them, and the dog, who had quietly gone and sat right next to them, his tail wagging and his nose twitching.

There's a good doggy.

The Visits Room proper looked like the conference suite of a hotel or a polytechnic lecture room apart from the fact that the rows of plastic chairs were bolted to the floor. There were tables with individual chairs, all bolted to the floor, near the entrance, each with a number card on them and there were two desks, one by the door we were using and one on the other side of the room, serving an entrance we couldn't see. There were no more than six officers in the room, although if they were expecting a full house, I reckoned that around 200 visitors could be accommodated.

I waited in line for the desk and then my VO was checked, I signed in and one of the officers used a rubber stamp to ink a purple square on the back of my left hand. I guessed it would show up under ultra-violet light and could well have got me into any Friday night disco in Plumstead, but I didn't say anything as I suspected the officers may have heard that one before.

They told me I would be Table 7 and to take a seat on one of the row chairs until they called me. I picked an empty row and sat quietly, avoiding all the other visitors, especially the two micro-skirt girls who were sitting right at the back, eyes on the floor, dejected.

It gave me a chance to get my bearings, though, and to note that there were black dome CCTV cameras in the ceiling – the black plastic domes meant you couldn't see which way the cameras were pointing, but they could probably see you. There was also a small canteen where you could buy tea, coffee and jugs of fruit squash, although Spider had warned me that sales of orange squash were monitored closely. (An inordinate amount to drink during a visit would suggest the exchange and swallowing of smuggled wraps of drugs.)

It also became clear that the second desk across the room was where the prisoners entered and the first few had already done so without me noticing. They wore casual clothes and were only distinguished from the temporary visitors by the fact that they all wore fluorescent sashes across their chests, the sort cyclists wear after dark.

The man who was shown to Table 7 was wearing one. He was small, balding, aged anywhere between fifty and sixty and had a barrel chest which strained the neon sash to its limit. He didn't look like any cyclist I'd ever seen.

'Table 7,' said the prison officer at my side for the second or third time.

'Oh, yeah. Right. Thanks,' I said and got shakily to my feet, hoping my legs didn't give way before I got to the table.

Then again, I could have broken into a run and gone straight by Mr Creosote, heading for the doors at a rate of knots. But I didn't rate my chances.

They were probably used to people doing that in here.

'Roy! So good of you to come, boyo!'

For a moment I almost looked around to see if there was someone behind me.

'Mr Fisher. Good of you to see me.'

I took his outstretched hand and he squeezed it hard.

'Just keep smiling and sit the fuck down,' said Mr Creosote, the Welsh accent evaporating. 'We're on camera but they don't have sound, so we can talk.'

'They don't have sound mikes?' I said stupidly.

My immediate thought was that no one was going to hear me scream for help. It would also be impossible to prove what we had talked about, should I have to do so later.

'Some European Court of Justice shit,' he

291

said. 'They can't read our mail and they can't listen in on our conversations. So, no microphones, so we can have a nice chat. In a funny sort of way–' I noticed a Welsh lilt creeping back in '–we have complete privacy sitting here. There's not many places you can say that about, is there?'

He sat back and intertwined his fingers, resting his hands on the edge of the table. His face was circular and weatherbeaten although a white prison pallor was beginning to take effect. He was stocky, not large, and didn't exude menace but he wasn't the sort of guy you'd push out of the way to get to the bar.

'You're not chatting, Mr Angel,' he said.

'It was you wanted to see me,' I said, finding my voice.

'No, you don't understand. You've got to play their game. I told you they could see you – no, don't look up, you prat – but they couldn't hear you. But if *you* just sit there like a lemon and *I* do all the talking, then it looks on the cameras like I've called you in here for something and that'll make them suspicious.'

'But you did send for me. I don't really know why I'm here at all.'

'Keep talking for a bit,' he said without moving his lips.

'All right then, if you want to be a captive audience, that's fine with me. After all, you've had plenty of practice.'

Seeing that he wasn't taking offence, I leaned my elbows on the table and wagged a finger at him as if I was laying down the law. I hoped somebody in the control room was appreciating my performance.

'And I am the injured party here. I'd never heard of you until last week but as soon as I do hear about you, I start to hear a lot of other things as well. Things involving an ex-con called Keith Flowers, who served time in this very nick. Coincidence? I think not.' I was getting into my stride now. 'And then I run into a very nice family called Turner.'

I watched his face closely but he was giving nothing away.

'Tell the truth, they're not very nice but, interestingly, they're Welsh and so, I would hazard a guess, are you. And then there's another character who keeps cropping up. A solicitor called Haydn Rees and he's Welsh too. Is there a welcome in the valleys for me or what?'

I paused for a beat, but he came in.

'Don't lean too far forward, Mr Angel. They'll think you're trying to pass me something.'

I pulled back my elbows and resisted the temptation to look up to see if one of the cameras was watching me, not that there was any way I could have told. In doing so, I lost any initiative I might have had.

'Right then,' said Fisher/Creosote, 'let me

293

put you straight on a few things. First and foremost is that whatever dealings you've had with the Turner clan, I reckon they've been unpleasant. Am I right?'

'I don't want to repeat them,' I said, nodding for the cameras, as if he was asking me if Aunty Vera had recovered from the operation, or similar.

'Thought not, but bear in mind that even though they're out there and I'm in here, I'm the one you really should be frightened of.'

'Hey, look, I don't want my lounge creosoted.'

'Stop flapping your hands like that,' he said. 'It looks like I'm threatening you.'

He hadn't moved, his fingers still linked in front of him.

'I thought you were,' I said, stuffing my hands in my jacket pockets.

'Not yet, I'm not, just telling you what's what. You'll know when I'm threatening you.' He allowed himself a brief smile. 'You've heard about the creosote job, then?'

'Spider told me.'

'Thought he would. Sad case, that Spider. Anyway, we're here to talk about you, Mr Angel, so let's do that, shall we?'

'Me? What have I done?'

'What have you done? You've put my old and distinguished friend Keith Flowers in a mental hospital where even I can't get a message to him. Well, didn't you?'

'It was probably me,' I said reluctantly, 'but I didn't know he was your friend. He was your *friend*?'

'No, not really,' he said calmly. 'More a business associate.'

'That's funny. That's what Len Turner called him.'

I watched him closely for a reaction to that, and I got one; but not the one I expected.

'I know,' he said, grinning like a loon.

Malcolm Fisher summed it all up beautifully.

'Let me pose a question, Mr Angel. What interests do prisoners share?

'Think about it. You're banged up with people you'd normally cross the road to avoid but in here you can't avoid them. You eat with them, you shower with them, you shit with them, you share a cell with them so they fart in your face when you're asleep. What do you do to break the monotony? They've taken your wife away, your mates, your kids. You can't nip out for a pint or to put a bet on. They won't even let you buy a Lottery ticket.

'OK, so you can't vote and you don't get calls from double-glazing salesmen, but those are the *only* advantages of being inside.

'And it is so boring you could scream.

'Boredom is the one thing everybody in here has in common, so what do they do to kill the boredom? Do they swap stamp collections? Do they sit around discussing books they've just read or make model airplanes or do Open University degrees? Do they bollocks.

'They plot, that's what they do. They plot revenge on who put them inside because most of them firmly believe they're only in here because somebody stitched them up, or grassed them up or dropped them in it.

'Not the police, mind you – not unless a bent copper's involved. Mostly the cops are just doing their job.

'No, it has to be somebody they know who let them down. Somebody who deserves a good slapping when they get out and they while away the long nights and the even longer days by plotting exactly how they're going to give them that slapping.

'Biggest single leisure activity in prison is plotting. Sod learning a language or metal-working or sociology or creative writing classes. Revenge is the one and only self-improvement course they all sign up for.'

And that was what it was all about.

A chance assignment of cell space in the overcrowded prison system had thrown Keith Flowers and Malcolm Fisher together for six months. Six long months of plotting as it turned out.

For reasons I didn't need to know (and

certainly wasn't going to ask), Fisher had issues, bones to pick, topics to debate – whatever – with a rival 'businessman' called Len Turner. It had something to do with Turner being an upstart from Port Talbot and not fit to wipe the boots of the real hard men of Cardiff, but there are some things you are better off not knowing.

Keith Flowers probably felt the same, at first.

Then bells started ringing. Len Turner had a solicitor, didn't he? Bit of a wiseguy called Haydn Rees? And Flowers had issues/bones to pick/topics to debate and so forth, so fifth, with that very same Haydn Rees. Not only had Rees been spectacularly inefficient as a solicitor (Flowers was inside, after all, wasn't he?) but he'd been co-responding with Flowers' wife on the side.

If they could get at Len Turner *through* Rees, causing maximum grief to both, it would be a job well done. Two straw voodoo dolls and two sharp needles for the price of one. Buy one, get one free.

But how to set them both up? What was to be, as Hitchcock would have said, their McGuffin?

'When you put Keith in hospital,' Malcolm Fisher asked casually, 'had he pulled a gun on you?'

'Oh, yes,' I said, keen to tell him anything

he wanted to know. 'And he used it, several times. That's why I had to do what I did.'

As if even I would have had to trash a brand new BMW if he'd only been using harsh language.

'Any idea what sort of a gun he was using?' Fisher said vaguely, like he wasn't really interested.

'Oh, yes,' I said again, anxious to be of assistance. 'It was a Brocock.'

'Oh, fuck!'

A normal person would have kicked the cat, smashed their fist into the table, slapped their forehead and yelled, 'Doh!' Malcolm Fisher just sat in silence.

It was scary. If I had been a census taker I would have served him my own liver and opened a nice bottle of Chianti for him, right there and then.

He said nothing. Neither did I and I estimated that we wasted about five per cent of the allocated visiting time sitting in silence not looking at each other. Then again, looking around the room, everyone else seemed to have run out of conversation. Why should two complete strangers have any more to say than family members? I wasn't sure who I felt more sorry for, the prisoners or the visitors.

'So, you know what a Brocock is, then, do you?'

Fisher's voice, with the Welsh accent fully engaged again, snapped me out of my reverie.

'It's an air pistol,' I said, hoping he was right about there being cameras but no microphones, 'which fires a lead pellet but it uses a self-contained gas cylinder system, so your pellet comes in a mini gas cartridge, just like a bullet. In my day you had to compress the air by pushing the barrel against a brick or breaking a lever open to charge it. Of course, in my day – when I was a kid – air pistols looked like air pistols. Nowadays they look like proper guns.'

'Yeah, they do, don't they?'

He smiled at that, but it was a forced grimace and for some reason I thought of the story of the German General von Molkte who was said to have only smiled twice in his life – once when told his mother-in-law was dead and once when the Swedish Ambassador insisted that Stockholm was impregnable.

'But,' I started off hesitantly, knowing I was probably pushing it, 'with the revolver version – though you can't get them so easily now – if you chuck away the gas cylinder and pellet and you make a shell case that will fit the cylinder then you can put a real .22 bullet in there and fire it. Or so I'm told.'

Fisher narrowed his eyes at me. He looked

like a man desperate for a smoke. I knew I was. Who the hell had the idea to make a prison non-smoking? Somebody cruel, that's who.

'You are very well informed, Mr Angel,' he said. 'Who was it told you all this?'

'I got it off the Internet,' I said.

'Jesus fucking Christ, is nothing sacred?'

'Not on the Internet.'

He leaned forward over the table, but kept his hands palms down, non-aggressive, for the cameras.

'Do they tell you on the Internet that the beauty of the Brocock is that owning the gun isn't illegal – it's an air pistol, for Christ's sake. But owning the doctored ammunition to fit it, now that is a crime. Think about it. In every other case it's the other way round. You walk into a bank with shotgun *cartridges* about your person, no crime. Go in with a shotgun, even if it's not loaded, and it's next stop *Crimewatch*. And the other thing your Internet doesn't tell you is just how easy it is to make the shell casings, does it? Any idiot with a small light engineering workshop can do it.'

As he was speaking, things he was saying were triggering alarm bells. He was telling me things I already knew. Or should know for some reason. Things – bits and pieces – somebody else had said. Things which I should have seen coming but at the time...

At the time I hadn't paid much attention. Things that Steffi Innocent had told me, ironically in all innocence.

'Oh, fuck!' I said.

Well, it was my turn.

'Haydn Rees was an air pistol champion as a schoolboy and he makes models, light engineered type of models – trains, remote-controlled helicopters, that sort of shit. Even got a *Blue Peter* badge for it. It's him you're setting up, isn't it? With Brococks, and he's just the sort of nerd who would fall for it.'

'Keep your voice down,' said Malcolm Fisher. 'Just because there are no microphones it doesn't mean nobody's listening in here.'

'But that's it, isn't it? You and Keith Flowers...'

I knew now how that spaniel sniffer dog had felt back in the waiting area.

'We had the idea, but it seems as if you've managed to ruin it for us.'

He sat back in his plastic chair and folded his arms across his chest.

'Not necessarily,' I said.

Fisher stared at me for a full minute. As job interviews went, I'd had worse.

'You're up for this, aren't you?' he said at last.

'Depends on the plan,' I said, feeling more confident than at any time since I had got out of the Armstrong in the car park.

'Len Turner wants guns. He doesn't think his boys look tough enough unless they're tooled up and I don't mean just his idiot son Ron and his grandsons, I mean his crew. They've got interests all round the coast of South Wales, from Newport to Swansea, and he's trying to expand over into Bristol. He's got a problem there, because he's up against some of our darker-skinned bretheren who've got diddly-squat respect for an old git who made his name running tarts in Port Talbot. So he thinks a few shooters will impress them.'

'This wouldn't by any chance conflict with your business interests in that neck of the woods, would it?' I chanced.

Fisher shook his head slowly.

'Rule of Life number one, Mr Angel, you never, ever ask somebody what they're in here for.' Then he shrugged his shoulders. 'But there's nothing to say I can't tell you if I wanted to, though I don't really want to. Let's just say I'm a robber, I work alone and have been known to get carried away sometimes, so much do I love my work. That's more or less what it says on the charge sheet. What's between me and Len Turner is strictly personal, not business.'

'Fair enough. So the plan was to – what?'

302

'Build up a stock of Brococks, manufacture the shell casings to fit them, load 'em up with live .22 ammo, get Len Turner interested in buying a job lot, say a hundred, even get a down-payment off him. Then plant the guns and the ammo on Haydn Rees, call the cops and sit well back from the fan as the shit hits.'

I let him have half a minute of looking pleased with himself.

'You call that a plan?'

Fisher looked as if he'd been slapped. The last person who had questioned him like that was still sitting on a creosoted sofa watching a creosoted television. But he took it well, leaned in towards me and spoke quietly and quickly.

'It'll work because there'll be so much circumstantial against Rees. He's an air pistol nut and has a whole armoury of them, a lot of them Brococks. He also has his own workshop up at his country place in Tregaron, lathes, machines, the lot, where he builds his poxy toy models. He's well-known as Len Turner's brief and there's a fair few cops, even in South Wales, who know he's dirty but have never been able to prove anything. Even the cops think twice before fitting up a solicitor.'

'You're saying he's slipped out of things before, so why can't he talk his way out of this one?' I asked.

'Because Keith has stitched him up good and proper, using his special expertise. You do know what Keith was good at, don't you?'

'No I don't as a matter of fact.' And I wasn't sure I wanted to.

'Fraud, that was Keith's thing. He trained as an accountant – the best sort of accountant.'

'You mean a bent one,' I said.

'Exactly.'

'That doesn't narrow it down.'

Fisher smiled his General von Molkte smile.

'No, know how you feel. I don't like 'em either. Still, Keith had a good idea way back. That was his trouble, he was always having good ideas which went bad. Anyway, before he went down, he opened a bank account in Gloucester or somewhere in the name of Haydn Rees. He kept dribbling money into it, no big sums, mind you, and writing the odd cheque but never going overdrawn. Then he gets lifted and the account sits there earning a bit of interest but not attracting the attentions of the taxman. When he comes up with his master plan, he needs a bit of working capital – which is where I came in, having a few bank accounts of my own – but he has enough cash in this Haydn Rees account to get a credit card...'

'And buy Brococks over the Internet,' I finished for him.

'You're very sharp,' he said and I think he meant it.

'It's what I would have done. About the only place you can buy the Brocock revolvers now is from individuals who are selling second-hand. I spotted that when I surfed the web. Something called the National Crime Intelligence Squad is clamping down on official retailers. You can still get the automatics, but not the revolvers.'

I had been amazed at the deals the air pistol people had done with the arms industries so that a Walther or a Beretta air pistol now looked exactly like – and weighed the same as – the real thing.

'Very good,' nodded Fisher, 'but I bet you didn't check the wholesalers in Europe did you?'

I saw where he was going. Where Keith Flowers had gone.

'You wanted a job lot, so you bought in bulk. There would be paperwork, invoices, delivery notes; all with Haydn Rees' name on them.'

'You're getting there,' he breathed heavily.

'But how could Flowers set this up while he was inside?'

'He couldn't. I told you, they won't even let us buy a fucking lottery ticket in here.'

'He had to have a business partner, didn't he?' I jumped in, remembering Len Turner using the phrase. 'On the outside.'

'Correct,' Fisher said approvingly.

'Oh, my God,' I said before I could stop myself. *'Not Amy...'*

Fisher let out a short bark of a laugh.

'Fuck, no. She wouldn't even *talk* to Keith, from what I hear. I told him to leave it alone but no, he had to try and see her, didn't he? Should've known then that he was losing it, taking his eye off the ball.'

I wasn't really listening to him, even though he was confirming what was going through my head.

Amy had avoided Flowers like the plague when he started stalking her on his semi-release from Belmarsh. She'd taken out a Restraining Order. He'd come after her with a gun when he couldn't take the rejection any more. No, Amy couldn't have been his 'business partner'. Len Turner seemed to know about her anyway and yet it was me he took for a ride on the Eye, not her. So he didn't think, he knew she wasn't the silent partner. That was why he'd got Rees to hire Rudgard & Blugden and by sheer dumb luck he'd drawn their one operative who took the job seriously.

'Flowers had a mate,' Fisher was saying and it was time to listen up, 'a mate called Ion – John – Jones. Known him for years, bit

306

of a nutter, like Keith I suppose. *Mae'n off ei ben* as they'd say in Welsh – he's off his head – but he has this knack with machinery, light engineering stuff.'

'Bullets?' I suggested.

'It doesn't take a rocket scientist what Keith wanted doing, which is just as well as this Ion Jones, according to my sources, is a case of the gates are down and the lights are flashing, but the train isn't coming. But Keith trusted him to set things up.'

'You said "trusted".'

'So what?'

'As in past tense. Trust*ed*, not "we still trust him".'

'Ah, well, that would be because he's sort of disappeared off my radar. You see, he was Keith's man. Keith knew him, trusted him to do what he was told and set him up with the phoney Rees bank account to buy the shooters. Soon as he'd done his probationary month at St Chad's, Keith was going to pop down to Cardiff and do the nasty on our solicitor friend. Trouble is, he never made it, 'cos he ran into you, Mr Angel. And so, somewhere down in Wales there's this idiot with a hundred Brococks, enough doctored ammunition to start a small war and a downpayment from Len Turner who's expecting to buy them.'

He sat back in his chair, giving the impression that it was straining against the bolts holding it to the floor.

'So guess what I want you to do, Mr Angel.'

'Recommend a good private detective?' I tried.

'No, I want you to go and find Ion Jones and make sure our plan is still on track,' he said.

'That would have been my second guess.'

Our time was almost up.

'Tell me why – just one good reason – why I should do this,' I said to him.

So he did.

Chapter Fourteen

I signed out, had my ink stamp checked under ultra violet light and my hand geometry read by the palm print machine, went through a dozen doors and waited for them to be locked behind me and then, finally, I was in the air lock by the main gate, waiting for the pneumatic hiss which meant: outside.

I needed a drink, a pen and paper, a street map of Cardiff and then probably another drink in that order. I got Spider.

'You had your money's worth, didn't you? Thought they'd decided to keep you in there.'

I shuddered at the very idea.

'Your Mr Creosote had a lot to tell me,' I said after I had collected my things from the Visitor Centre locker and we were walking across the car park.

'Did he mention me?' Spider asked, snapping at my heels.

'Yeah, he told me to find a nice house you could burgle so you could be back inside for Christmas.'

'That was decent of him,' said Spider in all seriousness.

I stopped dead and he went on a stride before turning and seeing my expression.

'What?' he asked.

'You really want to go back into a place like that?'

'It's what you know, inn'it? Got a smoke?'

'No. Have you?'

'Yeah.'

He produced a pack of Marlboros this time, and what looked like a silver-plated Ronson and I took a cigarette and a light from him without asking any questions.

'Tell you what,' I said, 'let me buy you a pint on the way back to St Chad's and I'll give you a couple of addresses.'

As the rush hour traffic slowed me down, I called Debbie Diamond on the mobile.

And almost immediately regretted it.

After an earful about how I hadn't told her anything and what the hell was going on, she admitted that Amy did appear to be alive, well and back at work. Or at least back at work in Madrid, as she hadn't actually seen her in the flesh.

'That's OK,' I said cheerily, 'I have. Has she made it to Madrid?'

'Yes, she rang me half an hour ago. Her plane landed on time. That's why I was still in the office, waiting for Her Master's Voice to tell me what I had to do before I could go home. Now I've also talked to Her Master's

Voice's echo, I suppose I can get a life of my own.'

'Do I detect a note of dissatisfaction here, Debbie?'

'I'm a mushroom, that's what I am. Covered by shit and kept in the dark.'

'Chill out, Debs. What exactly is Amy doing in downtown Madrid?'

'Doesn't she talk to you either?' she said bitchily. 'It's her latest all-purpose present-ation; the four basic food groups of fashion. Uptown Girl, Screen Siren, Boho Chic and Glam Goth. Which will survive? Discuss. Use one side of the paper only. Have you any idea what I'm talking about?'

'Of course. Uptown Girl is the white or cream trouser suit with matching fedora whilst trying not to look like an extra from *Our Man In Havana*; a Screen Siren wears satin, backless gowns with spaghetti straps and only goes out at night; the Boho Chic chick shops at flea markets and goes for the mix'n'match look with a compulsory element of something South American – Inca or Andean llama-herder, that sort of thing; and the Glam Goth is the modern day femme fatale, not the gloomy teenager vampires with two tons of black make-up. How did I do?'

'You're weird,' she said and hung up.

I wasn't going to let her depress me. For the

first time in days – weeks – I had something definite to do and I was going to do it. If I did it right, Amy could stop hiding from her past, the lounge would remain un-creosoted and Len Turner wouldn't take me to any more tourist attractions. And, thinking about what he could do on the Eye, I would make a point of not going anywhere near the London Dungeons.

That was all assuming there would be no further complications, such as getting arrested in the process. Or, say, running across Steffi Innocent again.

There was a black London cab parked in the driveway of the Hampstead house and it wasn't the Armstrong. I was driving him. I parked next to it, giving it room to reverse, and giving Steffi Innocent room to get out and march round to confront me before I had switched off the engine.

'You conned me! There was nobody following Amy, she just needed a free ride to the airport, you bastard!'

'No, I needed a diversion,' I said, supremely confident, as I climbed out. If I could survive Mr Creosote in prison, handling Steffi would be a doddle.

'A diversion? What for?'

She almost stamped her foot in frustration. She'd probably missed lunch and had been waiting for hours. I was surprised the Neighbourhood Watch hadn't arrested her.

'So I could go and sort out the mess you've landed me in,' I said haughtily.

She stood there, hands on hips, cheeks inflating as she took deep breaths to keep her temper, whilst I took the two frozen pizzas I had stopped off and bought at the local 7/11 from the back seat.

'Mess? What mess? How *dare* you say that?'

I looked at my watch without saying anything, which is a good way of making anyone nervous. It was 6.30 and Cardiff was 150 miles away. I should be able to do that before the pubs shut, even in Wales. Just time to get a few things together and eat some pizza on the hoof.

'I asked you how you think I got you into...'

'Your client's a scuzzbag,' I said. 'Garlic chicken or pepperoni supreme?'

I showed her into the kitchen, pointed to the oven and the cupboard where the baking trays were kept and handed her the pizzas.

While she was still reading the instructions, I put my mobile on its charger and made a mental note to take the charger with me, then I packed a bag with the essentials I might need for a short summer break in Wales: thermal socks, a couple of fleeces, two sweaters and a shirt in case I went anywhere posh. I added a rubber torch and

313

a pair of leather gloves and then an unopened bottle of Italian brandy, just in case. I checked that I had cash and that the credit cards in my wallet were in my real name (Keith Flowers wasn't the first to think of that one) and while I was upstairs in the bedroom I used the phone to get Directory Enquiries.

I asked for the number for the St David's Hotel, Cardiff and for an extra 45p they connected me. What the hell, I wasn't counting pennies now. A very nice lady with a Welsh accent told me they only had executive doubles free and only one of them as they were very busy and I said that'll do nicely, told her to book me in for two nights and read her a credit card number.

I collected shaving gear and toothbrush from the bathroom and was back down in the kitchen before the pizza crust had burned.

Steffi was more or less where I had left her, leaning against the kitchen units. She'd been worrying and I could tell she'd been chewing her fingernails from the way she snapped her hands down to her jeans' pockets as I came in. Either that or she was hungrier than I was.

'Get the pizzas out, then, and let's eat. I'm afraid I've got to run.'

'What did you mean...'

'Plates,' I said, pointing to a cupboard as I

314

took a large knife out of a drawer and ran it through the wall-mounted sharpener a couple of times.

She didn't even flinch.

I got the pizzas out and on to a chopping board and cut both into four segments, ground some black pepper and sea salt over the pile and offered her first pick. She took two slices without hesitation.

'You said...'

'Haydn Rees is a scuzzbag,' I said as I ate. 'I have it on very good authority, trust me on that. He must be one of the dodgiest solicitors around and I don't say such things lightly because it doesn't narrow it down, but take it from me he has been involved in money laundering and fraud and just happens to represent one of the biggest hoods in South Wales. He also thinks nothing of stitching up former clients if the need arises and has, so I'm told, some personal habits which are probably still illegal in forty-plus states in America.'

She took a bite of pizza and waved the remains of the slice at me.

'You think he's gay, that's what it is!'

It was my turn to stand back in amazement.

'What?'

'Mid-thirties, bachelor, still lives with his mum. Of course that's what *you'd* think. And he's Welsh, so you've probably been making sheep-shagging jokes about him as well. Amy didn't think he was gay, though, did she?'

I did some serious chewing to keep my mouth occupied. God knows I had reason enough to hate this prickly little bitch, but now wasn't the time. She deserved something special.

'You've got it so wrong, Steffi. I don't for a minute think Haydn Rees is gay. Gay would be good, gay I could handle – well, you know what I mean.' Maybe she didn't. Oh, what the hell. 'The basic point is this guy is iffy, bent, a wrong 'un, a nasty piece of work, call him what you like. He's used you to gather information on me and on Amy and he's passed it straight on to a Welsh thug called Len Turner. You might try running that name by your contacts in the Leek Squad.'

'I can do that,' she said seriously.

'In the meantime you can tell me where this Rees character lives and works.'

'Most of the solicitors in Cardiff have offices in Park Place or the Boulevard de Nantes near the law courts, but Rees has gone all upmarket with a place down near the Bay. He has a house in Pontprennau which is where the young professionals live and his mother's installed there. His father died ten years ago, by the way.'

'Oh,' I said, like I cared.

'Then he's got a place in the country, somewhere called Tregaron, which he bought for the fishing rights.'

'Fishing rights? That would be on the coast, right?' I played dumb.

'No way, it's up in the hills somewhere. He's into trout fishing, or wild trout fishing I think they call it, big time.'

'A man of many hobbies,' I said, then added: 'If you include the model building, the charity work and the air pistol shooting.'

'So what's your point?' She picked out another two slices of pizza.

'Nothing. Listen, sorry to throw you out, but I've got to go.'

'You're going to Cardiff, aren't you?' she said, but not like it was a sudden revelation to her.

She'd been listening in on the downstairs extension. She really did deserve something very special in the revenge market.

'That's for me to know and you to wonder. Your job's finished.'

'No, it isn't,' she pouted.

'I thought you'd done your final report for Rees. Has he hired you to do extra stuff?'

'Well, no...'

'Has Stella asked you to ... oh, no, of course she hasn't. She would have told me, us being such good friends and her being your ... what's the word? Oh, yes – boss, that's it.'

'But if Rees hired me – us – the agency – for something illegal, and I've only your word for that, then it's up to me to find out what really is going on.'

'You don't want to do that.'

'When it's my reputation at stake I do!'

She tried to look angry but it didn't really come off with her holding a piece of pizza in each hand. I fought the urge to smirk.

'Did Rees pay for your services? The agency's, I mean?'

'Yes.'

'Did the cheque bounce?'

'No.'

'So your point is what? You're done, *finito*, out of it. Your conscience is clear.'

'But that's just not *right!*' she shouted.

I thought for a moment that she was going to throw the pizza slices down and storm out, but instead she checked herself, held on to the pizza and then stormed out towards the front door.

She was wearing a suede jacket with vents up the back, but cut long so I couldn't see what the dolphin tattoo was doing above her waistband. I sort of hoped it was drowning, though I've nothing against dolphins per se.

I did have a lot against her though. Driving a delicensed London black cab so nobody spotted you was sneaky enough. Taking photographs of you and listening in on private telephone calls was downright

318

naughty. Finding things out about your partner that you didn't know, and then making assumptions – that was well out of order. Accusing you of being homophobic and anti-Welsh (well, all right then, homophobic) – that was the pits.

But saying 'Me – who loves cats?' with a straight face after what she'd done to Springsteen.

That was serious.

I could wait.

I parked Armstrong in the garage and remembered to lock it, and the house, and set the alarms. I piled all my gear into Amy's Freelander and set off towards Golders Green to pick up the North Circular, then dropping down Hanger Lane to the Chiswick Roundabout and the M4 motorway heading west into the bright, slowly setting sun which was still so bright I had to fumble in my bag for my fake Raybans.

It wasn't until I stopped to fill up with petrol at the service station outside Reading that I was sure it was Steffi's TX1 following me. Even as far out as Reading you're not surprised to see a black London cab on the motorway. It's only really beyond Swindon that they become rare.

I paid for my petrol and bought a bottle of mineral water and a pack of cigarettes as emergency rations, though I was pretty sure they had such things in Wales by now, got back on the motorway and put my foot down.

There was no way the TX1 could keep up with me, but then she knew where I was going and she'd find me. After all, she was the detective and I had a feeling that she may have some small part yet to play in all this herself.

It had been a while since I had been to Wales, but some things never change. For instance, the spectacular toll bridges across the River Severn charge you to get *in* to Wales, but going *from* Wales into England is free, presumably on the basis that they think you've suffered enough.

The weather too was always reliable. Halfway across the bridge I took off my sunglasses and threw them on the passenger seat, reckoning I wouldn't need them again for a while. And before I reached the outskirts of Newport, I was fumbling for the windscreen wipers.

Cardiff itself was unrecognizable.

When I had known it, and then only vaguely from fleeting visits as a student earning cash during vacations by driving trucks, it was famous for Tiger Bay and the shipping docks, the redlight districts of Grangetown and Butetown, heavy drinking in a city centre pub called the Philharmonic, the Arms Park where once the Welsh ruled the world of rugby and the beers of S.A. Brain & Co., whose advertising slogan 'What you need is Brains' became the unofficial motto of the university.

Nowadays, more English fans flocked to the new Millennium Stadium to watch English teams play in football cup finals than there were Welsh rugby fans and they drank lager rather than Brain's famous S.A. bitter. In my day 'a pint of S.A.' meant the ale named after Sidney Arthur Brain. Today it stood for Stella Artois.

I remembered that Brain's had their 'new' brewery (dating from about 1920) in a grim, grey area called Splott, basically because you never forget a place called Splott if you've ever been there. Splott was now a desirable residential area being tarted up like mad and the 'new' brewery was long gone, as indeed was the 'old' brewery on St Mary's Street, though the Philharmonic was probably still there. The working girls and boys of Grangetown and Butetown were probably still there as well, or at least not very far away, but their customers had changed.

Grangetown now had its own mosque and a fair population of muslims and Butetown houses the Welsh Assembly now the country had a semblance of self-governance. But the main difference was that it was no longer a ships and docks town. The Queen Alexandra Dock was the only remaining one in working order and no one mentioned Tiger Bay any more. Cardiff Bay was now an in place to be and be seen, with most of the best restaurants and the poshest hotel and health spa. The old docks had been tamed and not so much gentrified as *media*-fied.

The 'media' was possibly Cardiff's main industry these days, not only home to studio complexes belonging to the BBC, HTV and the Welsh Channel 4 (SC4), but a positive rash of arty design companies, animation studios, web designers and so on. They cross-fertilized with probably the city's biggest employer, the University of Wales, who ran lots of media-based arts courses and were all constantly on the look-out for artistic funding, especially from Europe, claiming they were a third world country recently released from the English imperial yoke and they had a native culture and language to protect.

Which was odd, really, as Cardiff is probably the most *un*Welsh town in Wales and virtually nobody speaks Welsh there unless they were applying for a grant. And perhaps it was trying just a little too hard to be arty and cultural, with its public sculptures on roundabouts made out of rehashed road signs and trendy new bars – or 'media watering holes' as they are known

– such as the Ha!Ha! and the Cayo Arms and the new Union, the Welsh version of the Groucho Club.

But what did I care? After a long drive there was the St David's Hotel, Cardiff's 'most stylish landmark' with its glass-backed atrium offering every comfort for 'those connected with the mass of inward investment' into Wales, whatever that meant. (But it was on their website so it must be true.)

I parked the Freelander and grabbed my bag, hoping that they really had reserved me a junior suite (£220 a night as opposed to the £295 a night master suites).

I wished I'd remembered a raincoat, though.

I was one of the handful of diners left in the restaurant, enjoying a chunk of lamb shank (Welsh, of course) which had been slow-cooked in rosemary and perusing the Cardiff A–Z kindly supplied by the hotel concierge, when she slid into the empty chair opposite me, her hair plastered to her head and her suede jacket stained dark with the rain.

She didn't say anything at first, just looked enviously at my plate. I hoped she was a vegetarian and concentrated on the A-Z.

'Rees has a house in Pontprennau – a flash four-bedroomed executive home. Shares it with his mother,' she said at last.

'I know; you told me.'

'I could help you find it,' she offered, watching my fork as I cut the lamb with it, it being so tender a knife was irrelevant.

'I've found it,' I said. 'Well, the place if not the house. Came through it as I left the M4.'

'Oh.'

'You could find his office for me if you wanted to,' I threw her a crumb – of comfort if not of protein.

'It's in the Bay area somewhere,' she said looking around for a window. 'It can't be far from here. Just out there somewhere.' She gestured vaguely into the rainy night. 'I can find it.'

'How about Len Turner? Can you use your contacts to find him?'

Preferably before he found me.

'I've already had him checked out, after you mentioned him on Friday. He's got a posh house in a village called St Nicholas, out towards Cowbridge, wherever that is.'

Her face lit up. Surely she'd done enough for me to throw her a bone?

I finished the last of my succulent lamb and carefully placed my knife and fork across my empty plate.

'Thanks for that. Where are you staying?'

'They won't give me a room!' she wailed, then lowered her voice as she caught the eye of a waiter.

'Well, it is a very busy hotel,' I said, 'not to

324

mention rather exclusive.'

'It's because I don't have a credit card,' she hissed. 'I spent most of my cash on petrol following you down here and I can't get any more until the banks open in the morning.'

I tried to hide my surprise. I thought everybody had credit cards these days. Goodness knows, they were easy enough to get hold of, even legally.

'I've got a suite,' I said smugly, not letting on that it was 'junior' one. 'There's a sofa in there you could crash out on – as long as you promise to behave yourself.'

'Why shouldn't I?' she asked with an awful seriousness.

How did a plank like this play such good jazz piano?

'And there's a condition – that you stake out Haydn Rees' office for me tomorrow morning.'

'I can do that,' she said. 'Are you having a dessert?'

'No.'

'Can I use room service, then? I'm starving.'

'If you must,' I said with a sigh and a shake of the head.

She looked down at herself, examining her scoop top and her suede jacket, even tentatively sniffing at the shoulders.

'Is there a laundry service?'

'Don't push it.'

I let her order some sandwiches from room service and she helped herself to some Ty Nant mineral water from the mini-bar. I let her use the shower and the complimentary bathrobe and free shampoos and even gave her the loan of a pillow for the leather sofa.

In the morning, I only complained once about her snoring and took her to the breakfast buffet with me.

She asked me then what exactly I intended to do in Cardiff and I told her I had some private business to take care of which was none of hers. But whilst I was here, I just might take the opportunity to meet Mr Haydn Rees.

Convinced I wasn't going to do anything she might miss, Steffi pulled up the collar on her jacket as she walked by the registration desk and out of the hotel. She would find a bank, get some cash and then stake out Rees' office in the Bay, reporting back to me at the St David's at 5 p.m.

'You're not going after this Len Turner are you?' she had asked, and I had assured her I had no intention of doing so.

It was the last thing on my mind. I was more interested in avoiding the Turner clan than having them welcome me to Wales.

As soon as Steffi had left, and I followed and watched until the black TX1 had moved off, I asked the concierge for directions to

Tyndall Street.

'Did I know Roath or Adamsdown?' he asked me and I said not really.

How about the prison at Newtown? It was near there.

I could find that. I was good at prisons.

I slipped him a tenner and pocketed his A–Z, then asked for my bill, paid it and checked out.

Malcolm 'Creosote' Fisher had given me a name – Ion Jones – and the address of light engineering works called Pengam Moor Tooling on a small industrial estate of Tyndall Street, only a grappling hook's throw from Cardiff prison. That was my mission in Cardiff.

And from the start it was Mission Incredible.

It was the sort of place where you didn't want to leave the car unattended. To be honest I wasn't too sure about even slowing down, but I had to. The sign saying Pengam Moor Tooling swung from the one corner still attached by blue baling twine to a bent panel of Heras fencing. Underneath it was a hand-printed sign saying 'These Premissess Are Garded By Pit Bulls' but there was no sign of a dog anywhere. Maybe they'd been stolen. Or perhaps they meant a real bull that had worked down the mines and had only become a guard bull since the pits closed.

There were two vehicles in the yard – a dark blue Ford Escort that had seen better days and a dirty white Transit van that had probably never seen a good one. They were parked in front of an oblong brick shed with a flat roof and a shuttered door opened to head height to let fresh air in and the smell of hot oil and grease out. It also let out Radio 2 playing at full blast, which just about covered the whine of machinery.

I reversed the Freelander so I was facing the way out of the yard and locked it. Then checked I'd locked it, then turned my jacket collar up against the light drizzle and went and peered into the gloom of the shed and rapped on the shutters with my knuckles.

'Helloooo? Shop?'

A tall gangling youth wearing dark blue overalls and a pair of plastic protective goggles appeared out of the shadows.

'You'll be wanting the boss then, is it?' he shouted over the background radio noise.

'I'm looking for Ion Jones, is what I am,' I said, realizing immediately that I was doing a bad imitation of his singsong Welsh accent and hoping he wouldn't think I was taking the piss.

'Mr Jones!' he yelled over his shoulder. 'Visitor!'

A small, no more than five feet tall, middle-aged man with a goatee beard appeared from behind a work bench where he had been completely obscured by a new Super 7 lathe and a couple of cheap Taiwanese bench drills. My first thought was that he must have to stand on a box to use them. My second thought was: why was he advancing on me carrying a still-glowing red-hot soldering iron in one hand?

'Can I help you, young sir?' he said, giving me a big grin which flexed his goatee to make him look positively satanic. That and the red-hot stick he was holding towards me.

'I was looking for Ion Jones,' I said nervously, ready to jump backwards out of the shed if he came much closer.

'Oh, it's Ion you want, is it?' he said.

'Yes,' I said, thinking I seemed to be doing all the answering, or maybe the Welsh just naturally spoke in questions.

'Not *Gareth* Jones, then?'

'No.'

'Because that's me, you see.'

I couldn't tell if that was a question or not, so I didn't take my eyes off the soldering iron until he casually plucked a cigarette from behind his ear, stuck it in his mouth and applied the soldering iron to it. When it was lit he put the iron down on the concrete floor and stepped over it, to exhale smoke in my general direction.

I just breathed out.

The bearded dwarf stepped by me and out

into the yard, seemingly impervious to the drizzle.

'Ion's not with us any more. Was there anything we could do for you?'

He held his cigarette between forefinger and thumb and flicked ash off the end with his middle finger.

'I was told he worked here,' I said.

'So he did, didn't he? Up until about a month ago. Is there a problem with Ion?'

'I don't know,' I said honestly. 'I was told he'd be here, but... I know this might sound crazy, but you're not related to him, are you?'

'What, Ion?' he roared, still determined to answer a question with a question. 'no more than I am to Tom – or Catherine Zeta, more's the pity.'

'Of course,' I said, blushing. 'Jones is quite a ... er ... popular name here, isn't it?'

Now I was doing it.

'Popular? Dead common, I'd call it.'

'So would I, actually,' I said with a tentative grin, 'but I'm not from around these parts.'

'You're not?' he said deadpan. 'Get away with you, thought you were a native.'

'I guess I deserved that. Can you tell me what happened to Ion?'

'You know Ion, then?'

Damn him.

'Nope, never met him in my life, but I

330

have to follow up a bit of business he was involved in.'

'Would this be the model business, then?'

'Yes, it would.'

A straight answer seemed to stump him, but only for as long as it took him to draw on his cigarette.

'Great one for the model engineering was Ion. Caught him working late on one of the machines once. Said he was making a gas-turbine model locomotive, would you credit it? Him who needed help tying his boot laces, he's there building a jet engine the size of a can of Coca-Cola which could do 160,000 revs per minute. What rpm does that fine beast of car of yours there do?'

'About 6,500 rpm flat out,' I said, wondering if this was going anywhere.

'So was that what he was working on for you?'

I decided to play along.

'No, nothing so elaborate. I was looking for a model...' I thought quickly. '...A model traction engine and I was told Ion was the man to build one.'

'One that ran on Welsh coal, was it?'

'Naturally,' I said, as if I knew what he was talking about.

'You didn't give him any money up front, did you?' the other Jones asked and for the first time he avoided my eyes, making a big play of dropping his cigarette and crushing it out with semi-circular turns of his boot.

'Yes, I did, as a matter of fact,' I said, taking a chance. 'Was that a bad idea, you think?'

'It might have been. Ion's not a bad lad, but then again he's not the firmest slate in the chapel roof.'

It took me a second or two to realize he hadn't asked me a question and that I had cracked it. There was no point in trying to engage in conversation with the Welsh, what they wanted was *gossip*.

'You didn't have to let Ion go, like they say these days, did you?' I went on the question offensive.

'Oh, no, nothing like that. He was a good worker...'

'Well, I'd heard that,' I chipped in.

'But a bit of a dreamer and one day he said he wanted to branch out on his own, set up his own business.'

'Wouldn't have been fair to try and stop him, would it?'

I was getting good at this and quite prepared to throw in a few rhetorical ones just for effect.

'No, you can't take dreams away from a lad like Ion. And anyway, he had the money.'

'You *saw* it?' I said, lowering my voice and hoping I wasn't overdoing the awe.

Mr Jones leaned into me conspiratorially,

which meant I had to bend at the neck.

'Seven thousand of your English pounds,' he whispered. 'Saw it myself, I did. I hope it wasn't yours.'

I pushed my hands into my pockets and shuffled my feet.

'Not all of it...'

Gareth Jones looked triumphant. It was just as he'd thought. A daft Englishman with his fancy big car had been taken in by local boy Ion. But Gareth Jones wasn't one to gloat.

'Well, I'll say this, I never had cause to question Ion's honesty and if he said he'll make you one of his models, then I'm sure he will. He seemed to be serious when he gave his notice in. I mean, after all, he bought one of my old machines off me, though he got a fair price, mind you.'

'He bought a machine?'

'Oh yes, one of my Boxford lathes. It has a few miles on the clock, I don't deny, but he wouldn't have got one cheaper anywhere else.'

'So he bought a lathe to set himself up in his own business?'

'Yes, he did. Said he'd got some premises dirt cheap and might even get a grant from Europe if he employed anybody. And he certainly had a bit of start-up capital, like I told you.'

'And this was about a month ago?'

'That'd be right. It was what he'd always wanted to do. He was model-mad, that boy.'

I put on what I thought was a suitably anxious face.

'Look, Mr Jones, this model I was after...'

'The traction engine, was it?'

Was it?

'Yes, that one. It's not the money, it's just that this was going to be a present for someone and...'

'You don't have to tell me, I've got children of my own and in this day and age any son of mine who wanted a finely-tooled model traction engine instead of a Game Box or whatever they call them, well, that's to be admired, isn't it?'

I was so glad he'd swallowed that. I was still stuck with the image of explaining away a model traction engine as Amy's Christmas present.

'So would you know how I get hold of Ion, then?' I asked, throwing myself on his mercy.

'Derek in there can tell you exactly. He delivered the Boxford to Ion's premises in the van, didn't he?'

Mr Jones stepped back into the gloom of the workshop and shouted to make himself heard above the radio and the machinery.

'Derek! Where was that place in Tregaron you took the Boxford to?'

Chapter Fifteen

Gareth Jones (no relation) and the boy Derek (still wearing plastic goggles) described the route to Tregaron, which they said was about ninety miles away and would take me two hours at least, but I couldn't go wrong. It was between Lampeter and Aberystwyth, as if that meant anything to me.

At the first garage outside Cardiff I bought an Ordnance Survey Landranger map (No. 146) and wasn't much wiser. It was indeed between Lampeter – which I had heard of because it had a university which specialized in theoretical archaeology – and Aberystwyth – which I'd heard of because it had a university which specialized in Welsh.

Tregaron on the map seemed surrounded by green patches with conifer tree icons, which I took to be forests, and close circular brown curves which I knew were contour lines and indicated hills. To the north of the town was marked a wide blue marsh area astride the River Teifi which was labelled Cors Caron Nature Reserve and seemed to be some sort of swamp. To the south-west there was the site of a Roman fort and bathhouse, though no indication at all as to how you actually got near enough to see it. I might as well have been looking at one of the maps of Middle Earth in the back of *Lord of the Rings* for which anyone over the age of about ten needs a magnifying glass.

Fortunately, the first tranche of the journey was M4 motorway all the way; to the end in fact, by-passing Port Talbot and Swansea on the one side and ignoring the signs to the other which said things like Tonypandy, Treorchy, Pontypridd and Merthyr Tydfil, which brought back faint classroom memories of rugby, trades unionism, coal mining and male voice choirs, but could just as well have actually come from *Lord of the Rings*.

From then on I was following the map and driving with one hand, which became slightly hazardous, not just because of the rain, which seemed to have set in, but because the road started to rise then fall then twist as I followed signs for Llandeilo and then Llandovery and other places which started with a double 'L'. As if that wasn't bad enough, I then worked out that Llandovery was actually the same place as Llanymddyfri and by that time I was quite willing to stop and ask a passing hobbit for directions. Trouble was, they were all sensibly indoors keeping out of the rain and stoking up their coal fires, the smoke from the chimneys of the squat stone houses the only sign of life, and one that anyone from smoke-free London would notice straight away.

To be fair, as I crossed over the arse end of the Cambrian Mountains, I suspect the scenery would have been stunning on a day when it wasn't raining. The average tourist takes a gamble on finding that day and I hear that the National Lottery offers you better odds at 14,000,000 to 1.

I saw a sign saying Lampeter and followed it, heading north-west as the main road branched north-east. I had the windscreen wipers on slow so I could pick out the quaint stone village houses of Pumsaint, which I knew meant 'Five Saints', and the signs leading off the road to Dolauchti and to the gold mines – yes, gold mines – that had been there before the Romans arrived. In fact, they were one of the reasons the Romans came in the first place and they had literally moved mountains (using water sluices) to get at what little Welsh gold there ever was in one of the first acts of environmental vandalism ever recorded.

And then I was in Lampeter, or Llanbedr Pont Steffan as I was told to call it. The only university town in the United Kingdom without a McDonalds. But it did have a police car, the first one I'd seen in Wales, with 'Heddlu' painted on the doors and, backwards, on the bonnet. The biggest bonus though was it also had a signpost saying Tregaron.

I wasn't sure what to expect, but then I didn't really know where I was going. I was just dropping down from a country road into a small town nestling at the bottom of the River Teifi valley. Suddenly there were slate roofed houses and a school and a library and then a narrow street with cars – lots of cars – parked down both sides of the narrow roads and then there was a bridge and over that seemed to be the town centre: a bank, a post office, a garage, a butcher's shop, a Co-op store ('open til 10 every night'), a sign pointing to something called the Red Kite Centre and then a town square of sorts, with a statue of some politician or other (you could just tell), which doubled as a municipal car park. Or so I thought as I slowed down.

There seemed to be no other reason for all those cars parked there in such a haphazard way. It must be a car park, though in truth it seemed to be a road junction, a crossroads in fact.

Then I realized that I had automatically come to a stop – as had so many others – outside The Talbot Hotel, where all the lights were on, even though it wasn't dark. In fact it wasn't yet three o'clock in the afternoon, yet some cars – and not all of them Volvos – were driving on side lights.

A good time seemed to be being had by all, judging from the music coming from within. It seemed as good a place to start as anywhere.

I followed the local custom and didn't so much as park the Freelander as simply abandon it on the crossroads. In London I wouldn't have lasted twenty seconds without a ticket.

I pulled up the collar of my jacket against the rain but doing so only made me wish I'd brought an umbrella, and ran for the front door of the Talbot. As I got nearer the music seemed to get more familiar, but it came with singing, which didn't immediately register as quite right.

The music was easy, that was *When The Saints Go Marching In*, but the words weren't in English and the music wasn't ... well, wasn't the brass ensemble syncopated treatment you would expect. I could hear bagpipes for Christ's sake!

I stopped a yard short of the door and listened carefully, trying to work it out, get the sounds clear in my head.

Yes, there were bagpipes and yes, there was singing in two languages, English and – not Welsh, but *Breton*, as in Brittany in France.

Here I was in the middle of Wales, miles from the nearest *anything*, and here was a pub with a live bagpipe band playing traditional jazz.

Things were looking up.

The bar was heaving and there was only one large solid looking barman on duty, but he seemed perfectly able to deal with the crowd, serving drinks with a mechanical fluency without moving his feet and managing to speak three languages – Welsh, Breton and English in that order – without pausing for breath.

In a timbered alcove, three pipers – the authentic *binou* pipes – and a guitarist were segueing into *St James Infirmary* and from the audience came the hum of singing but whether they were singing the proper words or not – and in which language – I couldn't tell.

The barman told me the kitchen had closed, though it would reopen at six, and served me a pint of lager and a packet of roasted peanuts whilst pulling drinks for at least two other customers and he still had time to chat.

'This lot are a bit off the beaten track, aren't they?' I jerked my head towards the band and the singing, which was definitely in Breton. Or maybe Welsh.

'Come here every year for the arts festival, don't they?' he said.

'Arts Festival, is it?'

He gave me a quizzical look. I had to stop

doing the phoney Welsh inflections.

'Oh, yes, very popular. You've just missed it, really. Finished on Sunday night officially, this lot are going home to France tomorrow morning.'

'So there'll be a bit of a party tonight, will there?'

'It's party night every night this lot are here, but if it's a party you want, you should be here tomorrow night. That's when the Irish turn up.'

'The Irish?'

'They'll be here for the races. You couldn't keep them away.'

'Races?' I asked uncertain if this was a joke or not.

The barman pointed a finger, whilst holding a pint, at a poster stuck on the open bar flap. The barman did not lie. Tregaron, it seemed, was the trotting race equivalent of Ascot.

Trotting races, arts festivals, Breton bag-pipers and invading Irish gamblers (horses plus the Irish equals gambling)? What was going on?

'Have you thought of putting in for European City of Culture?' I asked.

'Do you get a grant?' he came back like a whip.

'I dunno, probably. I don't suppose you've got a room, have you, with all this going on?'

'No chance. Booked solid all this week.'

'Oh, that's a bummer. I didn't much like the look of Lampeter.'

'You've been to Lampeter?' The barman said it like he would say Samarkand or Timbuktu, but did so whilst handing over two glasses of wine and working the cash register and all of that in time to the music.

'Didn't take my coat off; wasn't stopping.'

'Sensible. You here for the kites, then?'

They had a kite flying festival as well? And then I remembered the sign I had seen.

'That's right, the Red Kites.'

'Famous for them we are. From endangered species to most successful reintroduction to the wild, no question. So successful, the farmers'll be complaining their taking the lambs soon, but you know what farmers are.'

I may be a stranger in these parts but I wasn't going to fall for that one.

'Hey, don't knock the farmers, man. Foot and mouth, the Common Agricultural Policy, the bloody supermarkets controlling the prices... I'm surprised you've got any farmers left. You should look after them before they become an endangered species.'

It wasn't that good a guess. I mean, this place was surrounded by hills and green stuff – there was nothing else for miles except countryside, which meant that the majority of his year-round customers in the bar, at least, were farmers.

I'd given the right answer.

The barman leaned forward and lowered his voice whilst pouring a pint of Guinness for someone.

'We really are booked solid but if you don't mind the home cooking, go and see Delith Williams just round the corner, house called "Nodfa". She does bed and breakfast. Say John the Beer sent you.'

'Thanks for the tip,' I said. Then I couldn't resist. 'John the Beer?'

'My name's John and I serve the beer,' he said.

The man could speak three languages, serve fifty customers in a crowded bar without spilling a drop and still he had to deal with idiots like me. The man deserved a pay rise.

'I don't normally do the bed and breakfast, Mr...?'

'Fitzroy.'

'But if John the Beer told you, then they must certainly be full at the Talbot and we'll just have to do what we can.'

'You're too kind, Mrs Williams, but only if you're sure it's convenient. If it's not I'll be out of your hair and try Lampeter, but only if I can have another piece of that ginger cake.'

Mrs Williams flapped at my protests with both hands and shushed away the very idea, then reached for the teapot again. The ginger cake wasn't half bad, but then I was starving.

'There'll be no need to go all that way to the big towns if all you need is a bed with clean sheets.'

All that way? Lampeter was about twelve miles and it wasn't exactly Gotham City.

'That'll do me. It's probably only the one night and only if you *promise* me it's not putting you out.'

It was going to be all right. I could tell from the way she sat back in her armchair and crossed her legs at the ankles.

'Not at all. We've got the space, you see,' she explained, 'now that my son has gone up to Jesus.'

That stopped my teacup half way between saucer and mouth.

'Oh, I'm so sorry, Mrs Williams.'

She looked at me as if, like John the Beer, Tregaron had been invaded by idiots.

'Jesus College, Cambridge. He's studying anthropology. Not at the moment, of course, he's on his summer holidays in Fiji. It's his room you're having.'

I grinned inanely.

'Must be a bright lad,' I said weakly, but I meant it. If he was studying anthropology, coming from Tregaron gave him a head start and he was in Fiji, I was in Tregaron. Which one of us was the prime candidate for natural deselection?

'Oh, he is and we're very proud of him. I'm sure he wouldn't mind if you had a read of some of his books and he's got his own television and video tape player in there too, so if you wanted to rent a video just pop along to John Video and tell him you're staying at Nodfa. He knows us.'

'John Video? That would be the chap who runs the local video rental shop, right?'

'Yes. Of course.'

'Who runs the garage?'

'John Petrol runs the shop side but if your want repairs...'

'John Repairs?'

'No, John Garage.'

'Of course. What's the local butcher called?'

'We've got two,' she said. Here it comes, I thought. 'There's Ernest Smith and Frank Spurgeon. Why do you ask?'

'Oh, it's just that I might need a bit of work on my car,' I fluffed, 'and I thought about taking some Welsh lamb home with me.'

I better had buy some meat now. She'd probably check.

'Well I'm sure we can make you comfortable whilst you're here. There is one thing I've got to ask you, though, Mr Fitzroy, before I show you the room.'

'Yes?'

'How do you get on with cats?'

'Excuse me?'

'Cats. How do you get on with them?'

Was this a trick question? Some ancient Welsh superstition? I knew that the word 'Welsh' came from the Saxons and it meant 'strangers'. Did they have some strange rituals involving...?

No, that was crazy. I obviously didn't have a cat with me so she was referring to one in the house and I know my reaction to people who say 'Oh, cats love me'. I knew Springsteen's reaction too.

'Fine and noble creatures,' I said, 'which show grace and beauty and bring comfort to a lot of people. But they're not like dogs. Don't try and tell them what to do, like dogs. Cats are independent; tell them to do something and they just think "Why should I?"'

I felt I was on firm ground there. After all, I knew a cat who would argue with a signpost.

'The reason I ask, Mr Fitzroy,' said Mrs Williams and she was actually wringing her hands, 'is that the room you'll be having is my son John's...'

That would be John Anthropologist.

'...and John has had this cat since he was a little boy. We call him Tom Sean Catty.' She waited for a response to that but I didn't get it.

'I know,' I said, 'the cat likes using John's

346

room when he's away at college. That's it isn't it?'

Mrs Williams looked truly pained, her face creased with anguish.

'Not so much uses... Mr Fitzroy, can I be blunt? Are you *frightened* of cats?'

'I don't think so. Should I be?'

'Of this one, yes. I know of grown men – big men – who are scared of Tom Sean, with good reason. You see, Tom Sean's a one-person cat. He likes – he loves – our John, always has. He's putty in John's hands, he is. But John's the only person in the world he likes. He absolutely hates everybody else in the world.'

So the cat liked one person, eh? I'd call that weakness. Maybe he wasn't that hard.

'I'll just pretend he's not there, that way he can't take me for a threat,' I reassured her.

'Well, if you're sure...'

'Trust me, Tom Sean Catty holds no terrors for me.'

'In that case, would you mind going upstairs first?'

I said I would but I needed to get my bag out of my car first, which wouldn't take me a second as it was parked in the official town car park across the road, which was no more than fifty feet from the back doors and beer garden of the Talbot. (The car park was nearly empty. The road junctions were double-parked. Go figure.)

While I was at the Freelander I took the pair of yellow leather gardening gloves which Amy keeps as part of her tool kit in case of a breakdown and slipped them inside my jacket. Actually, they were Amy's entire tool kit as she had pre-sprayed some oil on them and the plan was when the Automobile Association man (or whoever it was she phoned) turned up she'd be wearing them and would swear that she'd tried just about everything.

I had insisted that Mrs Williams let me go to the room alone. If he wasn't there, I would call her. Second door on the left at the top of the stairs. Yes, I think I could find that. I'd found Wales, hadn't I?

Going up the stairs I slipped on the gloves and unzipped my hold-all and rooted around until I found the T-shirt I'd worn yesterday, pulling it to the top of the bag so I could get at it. Then I opened the second door on the left and marched in.

He was lying on the bed and God, he was big.

'Are you all right, Mr Fitzroy?'

'Fine, Mrs Williams. Come in.'

She opened the door about two inches, checked, and then entered.

'I heard the growling,' she said.

That had been mostly me. Tom had been

mostly hissing.

'Was he…?'

'Tom's gone out,' I said, indicating the window which I had left open. Well, it wasn't cold and it wasn't raining that much.

'He didn't give you any trouble?'

'No, we just got to know each other. I don't think he liked me, so he went out.'

She looked.

'I'll make your bed up,' she said quickly, obviously hoping I hadn't noticed the fine covering of long ginger hair in a circular patch on the eiderdown.

'Oh, there's no need to do that now,' I said generously, gazing out of the window. Below me was their tiny back garden and down to the left, a metal coal bunker on which rested the remains of my shredded T-shirt. It hadn't been a favourite.

'I'll give you a key for tonight as I don't expect you to be staying in.' She said it like there was no choice in the matter. 'I have a meeting of the *Merched y Wawr* to go to.'

'I'm sorry?'

'Daughters of the Dawn – you'd call it a Women's Institute sort of thing.'

'And Mr Williams?'

'Oh, he doesn't go. He'll be in for his tea and then out himself. He's one of the stewards at the races, which start tomorrow and they'll be setting up the railway tonight.'

She was stripping the covers off the bed as

she spoke and I gave the bookshelves and her son's CD collection the once over. It was exactly what you would expect from a male first year student; he had left all his Harry Potter books, his Terry Pratchetts and a handful of serial-killer thrillers at home in case any thought him uncool, along with all his Manic Street Preachers CDs in case anyone thought him too Welsh. Surprisingly, given the spotless nature of the rest of the house, there was a thin film of dust on the shelves. Tom Sean Catty had obviously not wanted his large ginger-haired rump to be disturbed.

And, speaking of which, I suddenly noticed a slim volume on the top shelf of the bookcase, and one of the few books in what I presumed was Welsh, though it could have been Patagonian for all I knew. It was called *Twm Sion Cati*. I brandished it at Mrs Williams.

'Is this Tom Sean Catty?'

'Oh, yes. Of course the book is about the hero, not my John's cat. We just called him that because it was John's favourite when he was a boy. Very famous, Twm Sion Cati was, a bit of a Welsh Robin Hood, except he was a poet too. Something of a highwayman – there's lots of stories about him – who hid a cave in the hills until he was pardoned for his crimes by Queen Elizabeth. The first Queen Elizabeth, that would be.'

'Right ... naturally. Listen, Mrs Williams, I'll take that key because I want to have a look around whilst it's still light and I need to put petrol in the car.'

'Don't forget to ask for John Petrol, and tell him you're staying at Nodfa. He'll do you a good deal.'

'I don't think you can get discount on petrol, Mrs Williams,' I said perhaps just a little too patronizingly as I followed her down the stairs.

'Well, if you want to pay the price it says on the pumps, go ahead, but everybody here knows that's three pence higher this week because of the visitors coming in for the races.'

'Well, thanks for that, I'll certainly remember to mention your name.'

Maybe being in with the locals had some advantages after all.

'Did you say Mr Williams would be setting up a railway this evening?' I asked as she handed me a front door key on a key ring to which was attached a small ingot of slate.

'Oh, yes, very popular with the kiddies is the railway.'

'Let me guess, it's a steam train.'

'Of course, but a model one, not a real one. The driver sits on the tender to drive it, but it has a real fire and boiler and it runs on coal. You've seen them. They have carriages which are just back to back benches on wheels and it takes people once round the race course in between races. Become an annual attraction has the steam train. Ever since Mr Rees moved into the town.'

'Mr Rees?'

'The man who owns the model engine. Built it himself he did.'

This place was a detective's paradise; people told you anything sometimes without you asking the question. I suspected, though, that if you did ask questions, they would remember you forever.

So I was grateful that I didn't have to ask directions to Ion Jones' place. When Gareth Jones had got his lad Derek to tell me where he'd delivered Ion Jones' newly purchased lathe, I had made him draw me a map on the back of a piece of corrugated cardboard. It was pretty crude but with an Ordnance Survey 1:25 detailed map it should be easy enough to find Bryngwyn, which could be a house, a farm, a suburb of Tregaron or a mountain range. Young Derek hadn't been terribly clear, which was why I made him draw me a map and that was fine if I just wanted to pull up and knock on the front door. I would feel a lot happier if I knew where the back door was and who the neighbours were. I was in no doubt that Mrs Williams, or John the Beer, or John Petrol could have told me if I had asked, but they would have told everyone they knew that I had asked.

As it was, I got more than I bargained for at the garage when I went to fill up the Freelander.

The garage was near a bridge over a rain-swollen river in the middle of the town and the garage forecourt seemed to impinge on the road. Judging from the way people parked around here, a queue for the petrol pumps which actually blocked the main through road wouldn't attract any attention.

The pumps did indeed show a price at least 3p a litre higher than I was used to paying in London but when I plucked the nozzle of its hook, nothing happened.

'Let me do that, it's not self-service!' somebody shouted.

I turned to the garage, where a man was pulling on an anorak before venturing across the postage-stamp sized forecourt. John Petrol, I presumed.

'Right, sir,' he said as he took the pump from my hand, 'fill her up, is it?'

'Only if I get the right price.'

'And what's that, then?' he shot back, not waiting but inserting the nozzle and starting the pump.

'Whatever you'd charge Delith Williams.'

'Oh, you're staying at Nodfa, are you? You should have said.'

I thought I more or less had.

'Here for the races?'

'Well, I came to see the Red Kites, but now I've found out about the races, I might have a small flutter, if that's allowed.'

'Oh, I wouldn't know about that, sir,' he said with a big wink. 'But watch where the Irish money is going, that's always a good indicator.'

'Thanks for the advice. Do you sell local maps?'

'Oh, yes, we've got the big scale maps of most of the river and the bog. You know, Cors Caron, the Tregaron bog. Famous, it is.'

'Yes, it is. And the river's good for the trout, isn't it?'

I hoped that didn't come out in a Welsh accent.

'Mostly it's the tributaries up in the hills, but don't even think about it unless you've got a licence.'

'Don't worry, fishing's not my scene. How much do I owe you.'

'Come inside and I'll work out the discount.' He grinned conspiratorially. 'And I'll get you a map.'

As we walked the few feet to the garage office – in the window of which was a handwritten sign saying 'No cheques accepted from Morgan (W) and Harding (G)' – John Petrol looked back over his shoulder at the Freelander.

'Nice motor, that. You don't see many of them round here.'

'Really?'

'Though we had one in the town just like that, same colour and everything, only last week. 'Course I really remember it for the girl who was driving it. Dressed to the nines she was and a right cracker. Ooh yes, she'd be at the top of my cracker list. Wore these dead sexy red shoes. Real fuck-me shoes, I think you call them.'

He rang up a price on the cash register which was 2p a litre less than the price on the pump. I paid in cash.

'You get to chat her up?' I said, my mouth suddenly dry.

'Oh, she was too good for the likes of me. To be truthful, she's the type of woman that scares me a bit. No, she was just asking for directions to Haydn Rees' house.'

I pocketed my change and turned to go.

'Who's he, then?'

'Our famous local solicitor. They have all the luck, don't they?'

Not if Icould help it.

Chapter Sixteen

It hadn't actually stopped raining – I suspect it never did – but it had thinned to a faint mist, or maybe I just didn't notice it any more. I reparked the Freelander in the public car park near Nodfa and perused the map I had bought.

I used the Talbot to orientate myself as most roads seemed to start from there; one running north-west towards Aberystwyth, two running south-west towards Lampeter on either side of the Teif river valley and one running north-east to the Cors Caron nature reserve and somewhere called Pontrhydfendigaid which I didn't attempt to say out loud.

The road I was looking for, which the lad Derek had described, went nowhere. Literally. Well, technically it went up into the mountains to the east and then stopped dead in a conifer plantation. Single track, it followed what looked to be the ridge of another small valley through which ran the river Berwyn, a tributary of the Teifi. There were half a dozen farms or houses off the road on tracks marked with dotted lines and, sure enough, just as Derek had said,

356

there was one called Bryngwyn. It was less than a mile away up the same road Nodfa was on, to the left of the Talbot as you looked at it, but the road rose steeply up the mountains to about 1300 feet according to the map and the rain had brought the clouds down so I couldn't see anything from where I was.

I decided not to take the Freelander. It was a dead-end road going up a mountain and I preferred to go where I knew I had an exit. Plus, it was a vehicle which had already been seen and noted in the town and I didn't want to draw attention to myself. So I opted for a foot patrol and cursed myself for not bringing any hiking boots or waterproofs. There was something in the Freelander that could be useful, though. Amy always kept a pair of Praktica binoculars, with up to x40 zoom magnification and light enhancing lenses, in the glove compartment. She claimed she used them at large fashion shows to make sure she didn't miss a single pleat, cut or seam in a new item. A likely story, but they were perfect for the idiot birdwatcher walking in the rain. I put up the collar of my jacket against the drizzle and set off down the road, hoping my shoes would hold up to the damp and that I wouldn't meet an ornithologist coming out of the trees saying 'The name's Bond, James Bond' as had happened once to Ian Fleming.

The streets were narrow here, with front doors opening on to the road and though there was little traffic, what there was seemed to move at 90 m.p.h. and twice I had to take refuge in somebody's doorway to avoid being scraped along the walls.

Then suddenly the houses ended but the road continued to snake its way upward, flanked on one side by a two-strand barbed wire fence to stop traffic – or at least sheep – from going down the scree slope to the river. To my right, were a series of unmade roads leading off to individual farms or houses, some with their names on wooden arrows or carved into slate blocks: Ty Mawr Farm, Brynteg and Garth Villa and then, finally, Bryngwyn.

I was relieved because the cloud had come down, or I had gone up to meet it, and I could no longer see the town behind and below me. I was quite prepared to believe the scare stories about mountain walkers getting lost and dying of exposure, and I was less than a mile from an international centre of trot-racing, bagpipe-playing birdwatchers and I'd left my emergency bottle of brandy in my bag back with Mrs Williams.

Still, no need to panic yet. It wouldn't be dark officially for about another three and a half hours, though the visibility couldn't get much poorer, but it meant no one could see me leave the road and follow what was little more than a farm track towards whatever Bryngwyn was.

After about a quarter of a mile, the track dropped away to the right until I lost sight of the road. I reckoned I was heading back on myself around the slope of a hill and if I kept going down and in a circle, according to the map, I would eventually hit the back road to Lampeter, just the other side of the Talbot. I would have felt more confident if I'd had a compass.

Bryngwyn was a ghost house.

It was a low, black stone house with the obligatory slate roof, seemingly crouched down, burying itself into the hill, with a couple of ramshackle outbuildings at the side. There was no sign of life, no sign of a vehicle and although there were overhead electricity wires running in to the house, not a light showed anywhere.

I was pretty sure there was nobody about to see me, but for the benefit of any Red Kites floating above, I walked up to the front door and knocked loudly. There was no answer and judging by the amount of mould around the door frame I guessed this wasn't the most-used entrance anyway.

I wandered around the side of the house near one of the outbuildings which was a garage affair of corrugated iron sheets around a wooden frame. It had been so twisted by the damp that the whole thing leaned to one side as if a giant foot had squashed it. There was tongue-and-hasp lock on the door but instead of a padlock, it was held in place by a rusty six inch nail.

I reached out for the nail then paused. I had Amy's leather gloves in my back pocket and I put them on as something was telling me it was better to be safe than sorry. It was only as I pulled them tight that I noticed the dozens of Twm Sion Cati claw holes which had gone through the leather but not the thick furry lining.

The garage contained an old Kawasaki motorbike which had seen better days, with a helmet and a pair of gauntlets balanced on the seat. I sniffed the exhaust pipe and slipped off a glove to feel the cylinders with the back of my hand. That and the fact that a spider was busy weaving a cobweb over one of the wing mirrors, confirmed that it hadn't been run for at least a couple of days.

I continued round to the back of the house where a flimsy half-glass door, obviously not an original feature of the house, lead in to the kitchen.

I looked around nervously but from the back of the house could see only cloud-covered hills. There was no one watching me, not even a sheep. I turned the knob on the door and prepared to put my shoulder to it, but it opened without any undue pressure. Not locked. Well, they probably didn't get many burglars up here.

I stood there in the kitchen and only when I was sure I couldn't hear a thing, did I breathe out.

Somebody had been here until recently, judging from the dirty plates and cups in the sink and the pan on the Calor Gas stove which contained the desiccated remains of some tinned ravioli. No great detective work – the empty tin was on the side of the sink.

There was a parlour and two rooms at the front of the house. The first one I tried had a military issue camp-bed in the middle of the floor, complete with a pillow wrapped in cellophane and a sleeping bag. Apart from a radio cassette player, a copy of *Mayfair* and a magazine called *Big Ones*, which I'd never heard of, there was no other furniture in the room.

The other room was unusual as well. Not everybody has a Boxford lathe in their living room. They probably don't have a metal work bench with a vertical drill either, or a digital caliper gauge, or a tungsten carbide parting tool, or interchangeable drill bits on a speedloader clip; nor, for that matter, a stack of about twenty 12-inch mild steel bars by the skirting board in front of a blocked-off fireplace, probably removed and sold at an antiques market down the Portobello Road. These things are for sheds at the bottom of the garden.

The floor was a concrete one and uncarpeted and had been swept by a long-handled broom which was propped against one wall by a pile of dust and silver metal shavings. I poked around in the pile with a gloved finger until two solid objects surfaced. They were hollow cylinders which had been drilled out of a solid bar of mild steel, less than half an inch long with a rimmed end. They would have been drilled to a set depth and then reamed to the correct width. These two had been trial runs. They looked like newly ejected cartridge cases from a hand gun. Except these hadn't been ejected from a gun, they were meant to go in one.

I turned on the lathe and it whined into life. I turned it off again at the switch. That proved the house had electricity, nothing else. It didn't tell me when the lathe had last been used. Sherlock Holmes might have done a monograph on the oxidization rate of freshly cut metal slivers, but I hadn't.

I had a good idea what the lathe had been used for, though. If he was following the plan cooked up by Keith Flowers and Malcolm 'Creosote' Fisher, then Ion Jones would have been churning out casings which would fit the chambers of a Brocock air pistol, replacing their gas-and-pellet cartridge. Inside each of these casings he would have inserted a real .22 bullet and I remembered Fisher laughing when I asked if they were difficult to get hold of. I had picked up one thing off the Internet he hadn't known, that a micron out in the tooling could make the live rimfire .22 'inner' cartridge highly unstable. There were reports of the things going off when dropped during police confiscations, without a gun in sight.

I stared at the blue-metalled lathe some more but it didn't tell me anything. There was still no sound from inside or outside the house. That was the trouble with the countryside, it was so damn quiet it was like being in solitary confinement.

There was nothing for it but to check the upstairs and for that I risked turning on the lights. I made it to the top of the stairs without being attacked by a knife-wielding maniac and looked into the two bedrooms, both doors of which were open. They revealed nothing, absolutely nothing as they were empty of anything but dust. No furniture, no curtains, not even a light bulb in one.

Tell a lie, there was something, two sheets of printed paper on the floorboards. They were particulars from an estate agent and letting agency in Lampeter and told me that Bryngwyn was available for short-term lettings (unfurnished) until the end of September when the new owners would redevelop the property. (Estate agent code for second/holiday home bought by the English.) I noted that it was ideally situated for wild trout fishing (with permit) and the pony-trekking/wildlife centre that was Tregaron. The other room upstairs was a bathroom which was in use, with soap, a razor and a toothbrush on the sink. There was also a can of industrial grease-remover and a towel which had once been lime green but was now basically black with grey-green stains. There was an airing cupboard with some more towels and a couple of T-shirts hanging from one of the shelves. There was hot water in the tank for the central heating and the T-shirts had been there long enough to dry.

Lots of indications that Ion Jones had not gone far and there was nothing to say he wasn't coming back. He hadn't taken his motor-bike, for a start, so maybe he'd just nipped down the hill into town. Maybe he was drinking in the Talbot at this very minute.

I retraced my steps to the kitchen door and stepped outside. The rain had stopped and the sky was clearing, making it lighter than at any time since I'd arrived. It was just after six o'clock and the kitchen of the Talbot would be open. There was nothing like a walk in the fresh mountain air for working up an appetite. Come to think of it, the air did smell different up here. Apart from the ever-present scent of coal fires, there was a noticeable absence of petrol fumes, blocked drains and hot and sweaty humans. It must be all that rain.

I took another lungful and decided to celebrate with a cigarette, leaning on the metal coal-bunker which seemed to be issued by the local council like dustbins around here.

The plan for the evening was a giant steak at the Talbot – unless the Welsh lamb was compulsory – and keep a low profile. Thankfully I had hit the two weeks of the year when Tregaron was crawling with strangers.

I had quite a view now thanks to the clearing cloud and I remembered the binoculars so opted for a bit of bird-watching or at least mountain-watching as there didn't seem to be a living thing in sight. Unzipping the Prakticas, I dropped the fake leather case on the ground and immediately bent to pick it up before I forgot it, not wanting to leave any trace of my visit.

It had landed on a small pile of coal, leaking from the coal bunker's small trap door which you slide up and then insert your shovel or coal scuttle. Coal was something you don't often see in London these days.

Nor in a house, albeit in Wales, which has electric central heating.

And no fireplaces.

The lid of coal-bunker was about a yard square, weighed about half a ton and I had to use two hands to lift it and slide it back. Inside was: coal.

Or at least a thin sprinkling of small nuggets and a lot of coal dust resting on folded sacking. The sacking peeled back more easily than the tab on a carton of orange juice to reveal a cardboard box, the sort you used to get in supermarkets to carry your groceries (until some officious Health and Safety twit decided they were a fire hazard). This one had once contained loose Spanish Red Peppers grown and picked for Jose Suarez Ltd. of Almeria.

It now contained, give or take the odd one, twenty-five loaded revolvers.

Well, I couldn't say they were unexpected, could I?

It still unnerved me enough to slam the lid back on the coal bunker and to look furtively around in case anybody had seen me.

What if they had? Was coal-theft – because that's all it could have looked like really – a hanging offence in Wales? It probably was.

There was nobody to be seen with the naked eye. But then, I had binoculars and I used them to sweep the surrounding scenery.

There were no other houses visible from this side of Bryngwyn and the nearest properties off the road I had walked up were hidden by undulations in the hill. In front of me the ground sloped down and round to where I reckoned Tregaron was and, if I had read the map right, that was open country sloping gently down to the road near the Talbot and then up again into more mountain and the conifer plantations.

Nothing. Not even a sheep. I scanned the area twice and then noticed something to the right and down the hill in the direction of Tregaron. Because it hadn't moved, I had dismissed it at first as a patch of brown ferns or a patch of weathered topsoil, but using the Praktica's zoom facility I saw that it wasn't.

I had been right about there not being another living thing on the mountainside.

I don't know how tall Ion Jones had been in life, but he was about three-foot-six in death, kneeling as he was in soft boggy earth.

He had slumped down and forward on to his knees, still clutching a cardboard box just like the one I'd found in the coal bunker. A few inches from him was a rubber torch buried in the mud. The switch said it was still ON.

I circled him warily. From the front I

could see what had happened. He had stumbled, slipped – whatever – and one of the two dozen or so Brococks had gone off. Unluckily for him, it was one pointing his way. Right at his heart judging by the brown stain and scorch marks on his shirt.

Where had he been going? Obviously away from Brwyngwyn but if he was going into Tregaron this way at night, instead of by the road, carrying what he was carrying, he was an idiot. Well, obviously he was; he'd shot himself.

I straightened up and looked around me. Just hills – it was a sadist's definition of an open prison. I jogged up the slope, in the direction of the road, and almost immediately went into a crouch. I was in the back garden of another house, except this being the wild west Wales frontier, there were no garden fences or hedges or anything. The house ended, there were a few plants and a square of lawn and then the mountain began.

Because of the dip in the slope, no one from the house could have seen Ion Jones' body knelt in prayer like it was, not even from the upstairs windows. Not that the house, a bigger more imposing version of Bryngwyn, seemed to be inhabited.

The poor sod must have been there most of the night and all of the day and because he was so far off the beaten track, not even somebody walking their dog had found him.

The local foxes had though.

'You look as if you've had a good blow, Mr Fitzroy.'

'Pardon?'

'A good blow in the fresh air,' said Mrs Williams.

'Oh, yes, of course. Been for a walk, haven't I?' Damn, I was doing the accent again, but she seemed not to notice. 'Just popped back to get changed before I have dinner at the Talbot.'

'Ah, the Talbot. There'll be parties and whatnot every night this week,' she said disapprovingly, 'what with the Irish in town for the racing. They always make an unholy row after hours. Sometimes into the small hours.'

'Do you ever have to call the police?' I asked casually as I started upstairs.

'The police? Pah! The nearest station is Lampeter and it's supposed to take them eighteen minutes to get here. That's what they call their response time, but it's more like half an hour, that's if they bother answering the call in the first place. The town council's complained time and time again. Not that we're always having to call the police, mind you, it's the principle of the thing. Oops, there's my programme.'

She had been keeping one ear on the television set in the lounge. I guessed it must be time for *Pobol y Cwm*, of which even I had heard usually in the context of a pub trivia, as it is one of the longest-running TV soap operas in the UK (if not the world) and the only one not in English.

'You carry on, Mrs Williams, don't mind me.'

'Oh, by the way,' she said to my back, 'I put a key in the lock of your room. You might like to keep it locked; you know, to keep the cat out.'

'OK, thanks.'

Note that. Twm Sion Cati had to be locked out. Merely closing the door was not enough.

I took the key out of the lock and pocketed it, closing the door behind me and reaching for my bag, determined to do some damage to the bottle of Italian brandy.

I was sitting on the edge of the bed, the bottle to my lips when I felt the first rake of claws across the back of my ankle. Fortunately, Italian brandy is a good anesthetic and I was too busy drinking to cry out, so I just leaned back and lifted my feet off the floor. In completing this complicated manoeuvre I consumed more than I had intended and when I had finished spluttering and trying not to wipe the mud off my shoes with the Williams' eiderdown, I realized that I now had the upper paw, so to speak.

Twm Sion Cati was a big boy, I reckoned

twice the size of Springsteen even allowing for the longer hair, and it was probably a bit of a squeeze for him under the bed there. I took another belt of the brandy and put the cork in. Then I pulled off my shoes, threw them into my bag and got to my feet and started bouncing. I hoped Mrs Williams had the television on loud and that it was a particularly dramatic episode of *Pobol y Cwm*. If she had come in then and found me jumping on a bed waving a bottle of brandy – well, she wouldn't have been the first.

On the fourth or fifth bounce, Twm had had enough and emerged from under the frame with as much dignity as he could muster, despite having to bend his back until his stomach scraped the carpet in order to do so.

I bent my knees and came to a stop, toasting him with another drink whilst he strode over to the door, sat down and began to lick every piece of fur that been ignominiously displaced, quite determinedly ignoring my presence.

So I ignored him.

But neither of us really took an eye off each other; neither of us was stupid.

Keeping the bed between us, I pulled my bag towards me and fished out a clean shirt. As I took my T-shirt off he flashed both yellow eyes at me, like the headlights of an oncoming truck in the rain. I wasn't going to catch him with that one again. Very obviously, I put the T-shirt back in the bag. As it was, I couldn't spare another one.

My shoes weren't that bad, considering that I'd run down a mountainside without looking back; my socks were damp but they'd mostly dried out when I bounced on the bed. I'd blame Twm for that.

But I also had to thank him for taking my mind off things.

I put my jacket back on and zipped it up the front, then I took a step towards the door and waited, arms at my side. Eventually he stopped licking his fur and stared at me for a good minute. I guessed at him weighing in at over twelve pounds and with the long hair he could have been mistaken for a small pony at a distance. When he stood up, his paws looked the size of a puma's.

He took one tentative step towards the bed. I didn't move. Then another, and then he was on the bed in one fluid leap. When I still didn't make a move, he circled twice, not taking his eyes off me, plucking gently at the eiderdown. Then he wrinkled the skin down his back, a gesture of contempt which only cats have perfected, and lay down, curling his great brush of tail around him.

But he kept his head up and his eyes open until I'd left the room.

I went as planned to the Talbot and ordered

a pint of their local ale – which turned out to be keg Welsh Bitter – their largest steak and no fried onion rings. I got the onion rings anyway.

While I was waiting, the shakes started over what I knew was on the mountain less than half a mile from the cosy back bar, and through the french windows I watched the night fall on Ion Jones for a second night, or perhaps a third.

The bar was busy, with half the customers speaking Welsh and one of two groups speaking Breton, which I understood at least the gist of. A few said 'Hello' and 'Here for the races?' and I smiled politely but didn't get drawn into anything, even when the Breton band started up.

I ate my steak and drank my beer, and then another one just to be sociable. When most people's attention was on the band, I sneaked into the hotel side where there was a public phone in an oak-lined alcove, complete with a local telephone book.

It was a long shot, but it paid off. Something had to go right for me, I was long overdue.

I had expected a book full of Joneses, and possibly an entire appendix of Williamses with perhaps a separate chapter of Pughs. I hadn't expected so many Reeses, but it was worth ploughing through to find that he was listed, as *Haydn Rees, LLB.*

His address was: *Brynteg, Pentre, Tregaron.*

I had walked right by his house that afternoon, and then looked in at the back of it.

Ion Jones had been his next-but-one-door neighbour and had been headed towards Haydn Rees' house when he shot himself.

Well, at least that was the way the body was pointing.

I left the Talbot before the party got going, not trusting myself not to join in and went back to Nodfa. I don't think anybody noticed I'd gone.

Mrs Williams was out at her Daughters of the Dawn meeting and Mr Williams was watching the local news in Welsh on the television. It didn't take long. We said good evening and I said I was turning in now. He asked me, nervously, if I'd seen the cat recently and I told him not to worry, I had a key. He said: 'Use it 'cos that bugger can open the handle somehow, believe it or not.' I told him I believed, I believed.

Twm Sion Cati was asleep on the bed, or that's what he would have liked me to believe.

I ignored him, went to the bathroom, came back and turned a bedside light on.

He had left me just enough room if I thought I was hard enough.

I kept my underpants and shirt on and perused the Williams son and heir's bookshelves. His Terry Pratchett collection was mostly hardbacks. He was a serious fan. I picked one at random and with the bottle of brandy in the other hand, I slid under the covers.

I don't think Twm Sion Cati was impressed with my choice of bedtime reading, but he knew that a hardback hurt more than a paperback.

Thanks to the brandy I slept a dreamless sleep and was woken by Mrs Williams knocking on the bedroom door and telling me that breakfast would be in about ten minutes if that was OK and, by the way, had I seen the cat?

I answered in the affirmative to both questions and she scurried downstairs, unsure whether to cook the bacon or get the first aid kit out.

Twm Sion Cati was stretched out full length across the bottom of the bed and I slid out without disturbing him.

I drew the curtains and was greeted with a fine bright morning with hardly a cloud in the sky. A red letter day in Wales indeed.

From my window I could see across the road into the municipal car park and there was the Freelander safe and sound.

It couldn't last; and it didn't.

Parked next to the Freelander was a black London cab. A TX1.

Chapter Seventeen

Using the binoculars I discovered that the TX1 wasn't empty and that Steffi Innocent had spent the night in the back seat. She didn't seem to be stirring either, so I could sweet-talk Mrs Williams into making an extra mug of tea and take it out to her. But then I caught the smell of frying bacon coming up the stairs, and so did Twm Sion, who began to stretch so that both his front and back legs extended over the width of the bed. And I thought that if I dallied too long, he might claim the bacon before I did. Steffi could wait.

Over breakfast – which included fried bread, something that had been outlawed by the calorie police in London years ago – Mrs Williams told me that the racecourse was on farmland about two miles out of town to the north-west and that the jollities began about twelve o'clock when the beer tent opened. She added, for no good reason, that Mr Williams 'was a bit too fond of the pint pot sometimes' and I put on my best 'that must be terrible' face when asking if there was any more of her homemade marmalade.

The trotting went on all afternoon but there were plenty of stalls and sideshows for the kids – like the model railway – and maybe a traction engine or two, not to mention a cake stall womanned by the Daughters of the Dawn. I took the hint and asked her if she was contributing. She'd made a token offering, no more than a dozen chocolate eclairs, a cream sponge cake or three, two dozen brandy snaps, six apple pies and several kilos of homemade jam.

I reached for my wallet.

I rapped on the side window of the TX1 and she sat up like a reanimated corpse in a shoddy horror film.

'Breakfast,' I announced and showed her one of Mrs Williams' cream cakes and the carton of orange juice I had bought in the local Co-op. She didn't look impressed, but then women are always slow to wake up when you want them to. When you don't, they're like cats.

She opened the back door and rubbed her face with the back of her hand.

'You checked out of the hotel,' she said without looking at me, but she made a grab for the orange juice and ripped the tab off.

'Something came up,' I said and I had a mental flash of Ion Jones kneeling over a damp cardboard box of guns.

The orange juice triggered an instant reaction.

'I've got to take a piss,' she said climbing out. 'What the hell is that?'

'Cream cake. It's the traditional Tregaron breakfast.'

She wasn't amused and she surveyed the car park. I pointed to the whitewashed stone building which said 'W.C.', though for once there wasn't a sign in Welsh for it.

'Don't go away. I want a word with you.'

She stalked off across the car park, shaking the stiffness out of her legs.

I opened the rear of the Freelander and deposited my other purchases from the Co-op, a box of Belgian chocolates for Mrs Williams and two extra power torch batteries. Then I sat in the open hatch and treated myself to a cigarette.

She had splashed cold water on her face and dried herself with toilet paper, as there were white flecks of it in her hair. I offered her the cake, still in the bag Mrs Williams had put it in.

'Haven't you got a knife?'

I shook my head. She shrugged her shoulders, reached the bag and tore off a chunk, squirting cream and jam everywhere.

'I knew you'd come here,' she said, though her cheeks were stuffed like a hamster's. 'I sat outside Haydn Rees' bloody office all day and there was no sign of him, so I made a few enquiries and was told he was spending the week here.'

'I didn't come here to see Rees,' I said.

'Yeah, right.'

'I've never met the man and I don't want to. If he's in town, I haven't seen him. Wouldn't know what he looked like, anyway.'

'You expect me to believe that?'

'Suit yourself.'

'So what are you doing here?'

'Just a bit of birdwatching. It's a Red Kite reintroduction to the wild success story.'

'Yeah, and I'm Liza Minelli.'

'And what are you doing in Tregaron, Miss Minelli?'

She have me her second fiercest look – there had to be one more fierce than that.

'I want to know what's going on. I think I've been taken for an idiot by Rees – and by you. I don't like that. If Rees is working for a Cardiff gangster, he ought to be brought to account for it.'

'A noble objective, but what're you going to do about it? You're a righteous citizen, with right on your side and more moral high ground than there are hills round here with chapels on. But he's a solicitor.'

'I'll *shame* him somehow. They think the sun shines out of his arse. What if they knew he was consorting with criminals?'

'That's what solicitors do for a living,' I pointed out. 'Well, tell you what, you could keep an eye on him for me while I finish my business locally. I don't want to run into him, you see.'

She eyed me suspiciously.

'This isn't a set-up like in Cardiff?' she said.

'No way. I need you to identify him for me, and watch him for me. I know where he's going to be most of the day and if he sees you watching him, that's going to get him rattled a bit, isn't it? Induce a sense of paranoia?'

'I like that. What will you be doing?'

'Oh, I'll be up to no good.'

The first thing to do was check out of Nodfa so I crossed the street and let myself in.

Mrs Williams was putting her coat on. She was surrounded by enough freshly baked produce to supply a UN airlift.

'Mr Fitzroy, what are you doing back?'

'I've come for my things, Mrs Williams. I won't be staying tonight. You won't believe this but I've just met an old friend...'

'That would be the young lady in the car park?'

Didn't miss a trick.

'Er ... yes. Bit embarrassing, really.'

'Now there's no need for that. We in Tregaron can be as broadminded as people in the big cities.' I had a nasty feeling she meant Lampeter. 'Your young lady is welcome to stay the night.'

The old devil...

'No, it's not like that, Mrs Williams. I meant it was embarrassing because she followed me here all the way from London. There's just no telling her, she's so young, you see. Much too young for me. And anyway, even if there was something between us – and I've tried telling her there can't be – she doesn't get on with cats.'

Mrs Williams' expression went from fire to ice in an instant.

'That's the trouble with young girls these days, Mr Fitzroy, they can't say no and they won't take no for an answer. It's none of my business and I'm not being nosey, you know, but will she be all right about it?'

'I think I'll take her to the races and talk her into going home. Thanks for your concern, though.'

'Well, if you change your mind, you can always let yourself in round the back. Nobody locks the back door in Tregaron.'

That was nice to know.

'Thanks for the offer and for the use of your house,' I said, handing her the key to the front door. 'Now, I said I was staying a couple of nights, so I insist on paying for two. No arguments. I don't want us to part on a bad note.'

'Now, there's no need for that. You've been a lovely guest and you ... got on with everyone.'

She meant I was the first one ever not to complain about Twm Sion Cati, and probably the first not to run screaming from the house.

'I insist,' I said, reaching for my wallet again.

'Well, we'd normally charge forty pounds for the bed and breakfast...'

'And a good breakfast it was, I won't eat again today.'

'Oh, get on with you.'

I counted out eighty pounds in tens into her hand.

'There you are, two nights at forty pounds...'

She started to say that she'd meant forty pounds for the two nights, but she stopped herself just in time.

'I'll get my things. Do you want a lift somewhere with all those cakes?'

'No, no, don't trouble yourself. Mr Williams is coming for me in the van. They've been setting things up down at the races since dawn. I'll see you down there, will I?'

'Count on it.'

I got my bag from the bedroom and by the time I got downstairs she had the look of a woman who had just hidden a windfall forty quid somewhere an unsuspecting husband would never look.

We said goodbye and I glanced around but there was no sign of Twm Sion Cati.

Not in the house, that is. He was on the wall of the car park across the road, lying down with his front paws tucked under him, challenging me to a staring contest.

I didn't give him the satisfaction, just walked on by until I got to the Freelander and put my bag in the back.

The bag with three-quarters of a mangled cream cake lay there and I broke a chunk off and walked back to the entrance, keeping behind the wall so Mrs Williams couldn't spot me desecrating her cake. Near where Twm Sion lay, I put the chunk on the floor and opened it up so there was cream on both sides.

'There you go, boy, knock yourself out.'

Then I turned and walked away without looking back. When I got to the Freelander I angled the wing mirror to see him slink down off the wall and take an exploratory sniff of my offering.

I thought he might have flicked a tongue out for a taste of cream, but he didn't bother. He just stuck his face in and chewed up the lot; sponge cake, jam, the works.

I'd hate to see him tackle raw meat. No wonder the sheep round here stayed on the higher ground.

'What does *Dim Parcio* mean?' Steffi asked.

'No parking.' Even I had worked that one out.

'So why are all those cars parked there?'

'They're Welsh. It doesn't apply to them.'

'So why are the signs in Welsh?'

'You don't get a grant from Europe to put them in English.'

She furrowed her brow at that. It never occurred to her to laugh.

We were in her taxi. It wasn't exactly inconspicuous but then the whole point of the exercise was to let Haydn Rees see her. The Freelander, on the other hand, I had to assume he knew belonged to Amy. Admittedly, it had been parked in the municipal car park all night right next to the road leading to his house, but I wasn't too worried about that. The car park had been fairly full and who looks into a car park if they're not parking? Most people can't find their own cars in a supermarket car park, let alone someone else's.

We followed the homemade signs out of town to the racetrack which was basically a large flattish field with an oval track laid out with hay bales and the occasional traffic cone. A man wearing a yellow reflective, high visibility 'viz' vest pointed to a spot where we could park and I told Steffi to reverse into the space between two Land Rovers (neither of which had tax discs). When she asked why, as I knew she would, I said that way she was pointing the right way for a quick exit and she seemed to see this as the seriously good advice it was.

As she killed the engine and we sat there, her in the front, me in the back, we heard the whistle of a steam train.

'That'll be him,' I said.

'Rees?'

'He drives the model steam engine. Gives kids a ride on it. Made it himself.'

'Nice image. Local hero, good works for the community, yet takes money from gangsters.' She turned around and looked at me through the driver/passenger sliding panel. 'We're going to take him down, right?'

'If you say so.'

I had half a plan, but I was only going to tell her a quarter of it.

'I want you to make sure Rees sees you, but I want you to keep him at arm's length for as long as possible. Keep him wondering what you're doing here. Get him worried. As I understand it, he'll be tied up here most of the day. As soon as you've found him and we're sure he's busy, I want you to run me back into town. Now I've got things to do that it's better you don't know about.'

What had Stella said about her? Failed the police entrance test for being too right-wing? In such cases, ignorance was not only bliss, it was vital.

'I want you to come straight back here and watch Rees like a hawk. If he looks like he's leaving the race track for any reason at all, you're to ring me. You've got a mobile? Right, well, I want you to put my number in the memory. Have it on speed dial if you can. I must know if Rees looks as if he's leaving. OK? That's vital, absolutely vital. If I've finished what I'm doing, I'll ring you and we'll meet back at the car park.'

'And what will you be doing?'

'You don't want to know. Trust me.'

To my surprise she seemed to go along with it, or at least she didn't argue.

The trotting races consisted of one-horse, two-wheeled lightweight chariots careering round the track at high speed, seemingly glued together so that it was impossible to decide the winner unless you were in line with the finishing post. It was *Ben Hur* on a smaller scale without the whips, or the pod-racing sequence from *The Phantom Menace* without the engines, which was in fact *Ben Hur* without the acting. I'd seen the same thing before, but only in Kentucky at a State Fair, which was on a considerably larger scale.

There was no doubting the enthusiasm of the spectators, though, most of whom were Irish by the sound of it, probably fresh off the Rosslare-Fishguard and already making the beer tent bulge. The locals politely visited the stalls and sideshows first, before breaking for the bar or the bookies. There were cake stalls – from which I reckoned I had diplomatic immunity – a stall promoting the Countryside Alliance, one where you throw darts at playing cards to win a teddy bear, one promoting the Red Kite Society, face painting for kids and a stall promoting homeopathy. All were doing good business and there was already a fair crowd at the start line of the race circuit. It looked as if the whole town was there.

I hoped it was; I was relying on it.

We watched a race get underway and I tried to work out which language was coming over the public address tannoy. By the time I was convinced it wasn't Welsh, but strangled and distorted English, the race was over.

'Are you going to put a bet on?' Steffi asked me.

'No. I don't gamble. Well, not on horses.'

From somewhere not very far away, we heard the shrill scream of a engine whistle advertising rides between the races and we moved towards it, me hanging back until Steffi was a good yards in front.

There was already a queue, which we avoided by moving along a single rope barrier strung between iron pegs at knee height. The rope marked out the track, about two hundred yards of miniature railroad, the rails no more than five inches apart fixed to miniature sleepers.

Mingling with the crowd we looked down the track to where a green model locomotive was getting up steam. Two men in overalls and flat leather engineer's caps were standing over it with old-fashioned oil cans in their hands. The green locomotive shone in the sunlight and its brass fittings twinkled. Even at this distance I could smell the hot oil.

'It's Thomas the fucking Tank Engine,' hissed Steffi.

'No, it's an express, more like Henry the Green Engine which ran on Welsh coal,' I said.

'You remember steam trains, do you?'

'I remember reading the books.'

'There were books?'

I realized she had only seen the animated TV series narrated by Ringo Starr. I bet it would be another shock to find out that Ringo had a career before 'Thomas' but I wasn't going to be the one to break it to her.

The engine had a tender which carried the driver and it pulled two bogies which were little more than padded rectangular boxes on chassis, with a footplate, where the passengers would sit back-to-back.

Somebody shouted 'All aboard!' and the queue surged forward to thrust money into the hands of an old man dressed in the uniform of a Great Western Railway guard. He was old enough and the uniform fitted so well, he probably had been one and he could hardly wait to show that his whistle still worked. When the 'carriages' were full to the point of people clinging on – and a suspiciously large number of passengers were middle-aged men making their children wait their turn – he gave two good blasts.

'Grown men... Really,' Steffi said under her breath.

One of the men in overalls took off his cap and produced a pair of aviator goggles from a back pocket.

'That's *him!*' Steffi hissed.

'Stay near the track,' I said and I backed away from her through the thickening crowd.

With goggles in place and his cap back on, the driver straddled the tender and fiddled with the controls. The engine gave a double toot on its whistle and began to move off, heading towards us, to a small smattering of applause from the crowd.

In about five seconds the driver, his head at our waist height, was drawing level with Steffi and I watched his goggled face closely.

No reaction.

He didn't notice her.

He didn't notice her because he was looking at me.

I'd never seen Haydn Rees in my life, but he recognized me.

And then the engine went by me and I was looking at a slab of happy smiling passengers and, weakly, I waved back.

Before the train got to the end of the line and did the return journey in reverse, I had reached Steffi and grabbed her by the shoulders.

'It was those fucking photographs! Why didn't you remind me you'd showed him the photographs you'd taken? He recognized me!'

'So what does that mean?' she asked, dead cold.

I shook her some more just because it felt good.

'It means we've got to move now and fast.'

The TX1 roared back down the country road towards Tregaron. Fortunately, the only traffic on the road was going the other way towards the races and for once the town square in front of the Talbot was empty of illegally parked cars. There had been so many there when I had arrived yesterday – only yesterday? – they had completely obscured the *Dim Parcio* signs.

Steffi took the road to the left, passed the only public phone box I had seen, and swung into the car park. I jumped out of the back as soon as she stopped moving and the central locking came off.

'Now remember, make sure he sees you

390

and if he looks like leaving, ring me.' I illustrated the point by waving my mobile phone at her. 'If he does make a move, try and keep him talking.'

'What shall I say?'

'Ask him about Len Turner.'

'I know about Len Turner. It was me who told you...'

'I know that, but he doesn't. Oh, just make something up. I need an hour. Try and keep him there for an hour.'

'An *hour?* How am I supposed to do that?'

'You probably won't have to. He's busy playing with his train set, remember?'

'What will you be doing?'

'If you don't know, you can't lie about it. Now go.'

She swung the taxi in an arc and it turned in a circle smaller than the Freelander needed, then she was off and I was climbing into the Freelander. But where she had turned left out of the car park, back to the town square, I was turning right up the mountain road to Bryngwyn, the last place Ion Jones would ever rent.

Twm Sion Cati was sitting up on the wall of the car park, like one of those giant stone lions or jaguars outside a temple door in the depths of the jungle. I braked, hopped out and opened the boot. There was about half of Mrs Williams' cream cake left squashed in its paper bag. I tore the remains in half and laid one of the pieces on the ground.

Twm Sion watched me but didn't move until I had got back in the car and was moving off again. In the wing mirror I saw him drop like an eagle on its prey.

I hadn't intended taking the Freelander; I was going to walk up the hill like yesterday, only now there might not be enough time.

And it would just have to be a rainless, clear day, wouldn't it? Not exactly a clear blue sky, which would probably be classed as a heatwave in Wales, but fine and dry with visibility stretching for bloody miles.

In the mirror I could see Tregaron fall away behind me but I could still see it. But then the road curved around the hill and the town was hidden from view. So, therefore, was I, although I was relying on most of the good townsfolk being way over on the other side at the races.

I came to the offshoots of the road with the slate block signs and there was Brynteg. I kept on going and the next was Garth Villa and then Bryngwyn. I turned off the road on to the track to the house and slowed to engage the fourwheel drive. I didn't like the idea of doing this in broad daylight on a mountainside up a dead-end road, but at least if I had to make a run for it I could take the Freelander the short way down the slope I had stumbled down yesterday.

The track dipped so that I couldn't be seen from the road, but even so I pulled up between the side of the house and the shed where Ion Jones had kept his motorbike. That was still there, undisturbed except by spiders; the back door was still unlocked, the house was still empty and, with the binoculars, I confirmed that Ion Jones, off in the distance, was still dead.

I got Amy's gloves out of the back of the car and while I was pulling them on I checked the ground. The Freelander hadn't left any tyre tracks on the track because it was mostly shale and scree over solid rock. Looking down the hill, mountain or whatever it was, it was much the same material. Apart from an isolated boggy bit, all the top soil had been washed away a couple of ice ages ago and it should support the Freelander easily if I had to make a run for it.

I patted my jacket pocket to make sure my mobile was there and set to work, sliding the top off the coal bunker.

The cardboard box with the revolvers was still there under the sacking and there was another box under the first and then another. I had to climb on top of the bunker to reach in and carefully – very carefully – lift them out and transfer them to the back of the Freelander. They weren't packed in anything, just laid in rows. I presumed they were all loaded – it was safer that way. They were certainly heavy enough and though I wasn't going to handle them individually, I could see that they bore the trade mark Smith & Wesson. It made me think of the bumper sticker of the National Rifle Association in America: The West Wasn't Won With A Registered Gun. Neither was West Wales.

By the time I had the third box up I had counted sixty-odd guns. Assuming the box Ion Jones had been carrying held the same as the others, that was eighty or more pistols, all loaded for bear. Explain that away, Mr Solicitor.

But under the third box there were more, smaller boxes: ammunition boxes containing real live .22 ammunition. Four boxes each containing 100 rounds.

Planning a small war, were you, Mr Solicitor?

Except one of them didn't contain ammunition. I could tell that because it didn't rattle like the others. I opened that one and tipped it up on the top of the coal bunker. Nothing fell out, though it had some weight to it – it wasn't empty.

I looked inside.

I had never seen so many £50 notes curled up in such a small space.

Those went in the glove compartment of the Freelander and when I had stashed all the boxes of guns and ammo in the back, I took off my jacket and covered them as best I could, just in case a passing shepherd should peek in.

Then I took the Co-op carrier bag they had given me that morning and removed the torch batteries I had bought. In the house, in the living room where the lathe was, I clumsily used the long-handled broom to sweep up the pile of dust and metal shavings until I had filled the bag. Then I swept the remainder into a pile as neatly as I could.

Explain that, Sherlock.

I drove back to the road, paused and swept the horizon with the binoculars. I couldn't see a soul.

Now for the tricky bit.

I drove until I came to the turning for Brynteg and turned in. Like Bryngwyn, the track dipped so soon I was out of sight of the road, which was a relief until I realized I was in a dead end running off a dead end. Best not to think of these things.

The house, which I had only previously seen from the back, was a much more impressive building than Bryngwyn but made of the same black weathered stone. It had a front door in the middle, two windows downstairs and three upstairs. To the left was a garage with its doors open but the track went to the left of it, round the back of the house.

In fact it was difficult to tell where the track stopped and the mountain began. They didn't have to fence things off here; they didn't have direct neighbours.

For which I was profoundly grateful.

The house was taller at the back than the front, partly to level out the effects of the mountainside but also to accommodate a single storey brick extension. This I guessed would be Rees' workshop, built on below the level of the back door, incorporating some sort of cellar which had probably been blasted out of the rock when the house was first built a hundred or so years ago.

I put the binoculars to my eyes and scanned the slopes for any living creatures. Then I scanned the ground for dead ones.

I didn't see either but I think I located the dip in the ground where Ion Jones was. There were two birds, which could have been Red Kites, hovering way above it.

Next problem: access.

I checked my watch. Half an hour had gone by since I'd left Steffi and no phone call. I took that as a good sign. But then again I was trespassing on someone's property with a car full of weapons and a dead body within two hundred yards. Better get a move on.

Mrs Williams had said that no one in Tregaron locked their back doors. Haydn

Rees did, and the separate, lower door to the windowless brick extension was locked with a hefty hasp and a shiny new padlock.

If Ion Jones had been heading this way, surely he had a plan to gain access without making it too obvious a break-in if he wanted to plant the guns inside Rees' house. Just leaving them on the doorstep would look a bit weak, wouldn't it?

Then again, Ion Jones, fine precision engineer though he might have been had managed to shoot himself dead, so whatever he had planned, it wasn't rocket science, but I was damned if I could think of it.

Anyway, I didn't have time to think. I had to go and ask him.

The foxes had been back and the birds had started on him.

I tried not to look.

His body had slumped, or been pulled down and to the left, but he somehow had his arms still curled around the box of guns. The body looked pliable so I assumed that rigor had been and gone but I wasn't going to actually touch him if I could help it, as bits of him were moving slightly. Insect movement.

I gagged and took my eyes of his face, looking at the box of pistols instead, just to concentrate on anything that didn't actually make me feel nauseous. And there it was. A multi-head rotational screwdriver, nestling in between the replica Smith & Wessons.

When faced with a padlock, you don't try and pick it, you unscrew it from its hasp or hinge. Then you screw it back in when you leave. Oldest trick in the book.

I reached over his arm, trying not to brush his flesh and lifted it from the box, holding my breath until I was sure one of the guns wasn't going to go off.

'Cheers, Ion,' I said.

There was something I could do for him.

His torch had fallen face down and when I pulled it out of the moss, the bulb glowed weakly. I took the batteries I had brought for the Freelander and exchanged them for the spent ones, leaving the torch on. Then I rammed it upright into the one soft patch of earth I could find, directing the beam towards him.

No one would see it in daylight, but if he hadn't been found before nightfall he would have his own *son et lumiere* to guide people to him. If nothing else it might keep the foxes away from him for a while.

It was the best I could do.

I unscrewed the hasp and bent it back over the padlock. The door swung open.

It was a workshop, complete with lathes, benches down either side, drills, angle-grinders, you name it. There was a small model tank engine on one shelf, a disembowelled shell of another locomotive awaiting repair on another, radio-controlled helicopters, model aircraft and a scale working model of a traction engine. A single office chair on castors was the only furniture, and clearly designed to slide from one workbench to the other. The whole place was neat and tidy with tools put away, clean cans of oil and a laundry basket, for Christ's sake, containing bits of oily rag. There was also an open box of disposable rubber gloves. The guy was obsessive, and neat with it. Not an empty can of Coke, a cigarette butt or an oil spillage anywhere. You could eat your dinner off all the surfaces.

The only thing slightly out of place was a TV monitor hooked up to a video cassette player with a tape resting half out of the slot as if it had just been ejected quickly. Maybe they did 'Modeller's World' on instructional videos now.

There was a door at the far end, with a Yale lock, which presumably led into the house, but I had no intention of going there. I didn't have time. It had been an hour now since I'd sent Steffi back to the races, but at least there had been no phone calls.

I went back outside and reversed the Freelander up to the workshop door. That made unloading the guns easier and in no time at all I had them stacked in, on and under his workbenches. Then I spread the boxes of .22 ammunition about quite liberally, scattering one box on the floor. Finally, I emptied the bag of dust and metal shavings over the floor, sprinkling some over the workbench near the lathe and one of the drills.

I stood back to admire my work.

Get out of that one, Mr Solicitor.

The back of my legs collided with the poncy laundry basket of rags, a real 'Ali Baba' type thing, which I automatically reached out to catch before it fell over.

They weren't rags.

Well, they were in the sense that they were pieces of material that had been used to mop, wipe and no doubt polish because they were all covered in grease and oil and, from the smell, metal polish and methylated spirit.

But the curious thing was, they were all pieces of women's underwear.

Chapter Eighteen

Knickers. Mostly.

Cotton briefs for the majority, in white, pale blue and pink, sizes ranging from 10–12 to 14–16, but also a couple of pairs of thick black opaque tights, a single red stocking with a black seam, two camisole tops and one bra, size 36B. Analysed by maker, almost all Marks & Spencer, though there were two pairs of French knickers, one green, one red, from *Agent Provocateur*.

What was I doing? An inventory?

This surely wasn't regular practice for a model engineer. Oh, I could see the scenario where it was all-lads-together on the steam railway and one would pull out a pair of pink panties to casually wipe the oil off his hands and he'd say 'Ooh! Where did those come from?' or 'What on earth will the wife forget next?' for a bit of a laugh. But this was a bachelor model builder who worked mostly alone in a windowless workshop tacked on to an isolated house on the top of a mountain.

Maybe he threw wild parties, but there was enough underwear here to indicate that every eligible female (I discounted the

Daughters of the Dawn) in the town had attended at least once.

I looked at the door to the house at the far end of the workshop and wondered what went on in there. Then I began to wonder exactly where the door went because the workshop was built at a lower level than the back door and so if it actually went into anywhere, it must be a cellar. If it wasn't and it was just the outside wall of the back of the house, why build a door there?

And why put the Yale lock on this side? If you wanted to keep intruders out of the house, you put the lock on the inside. The only thing this lock would do is keep people in. As in a prison.

I hadn't got time for this, I thought as I turned the Yale and snapped the catch up so that it couldn't close behind me.

It was the cellar of the house with a door at the other end, but it wasn't the dank, dark cellar filled with household rubbish or even wine racks you might expect. The first thing that struck me was how warm it was, positively stifling and definitely sweaty. But it was windowless and dark though the light from the workshop door was reflecting off something.

I groped my hand up the wall and, sure enough, there was a light switch where I would have expected one. I flipped it and almost went blind.

The were six adjustable spotlights on a single track in the centre of the ceiling and they all seemed to have 100watt bulbs. One would have been overkill but the effect was multiplied dramatically by the fact that the walls were lined with sheets of kitchen foil, shiny side out. There was enough there to cook every Christmas turkey in Tregaron.

And it was *hot*.

There were two portable Calor gas heaters in the room and an electric fan heater, as well as a large curved iron radiator with pipes leading up through the ceiling to the domestic central heating system. I took off a glove and put my hand over but not on the radiator. It was on full pelt and I was feeling the heat now. The floor was covered in a bouncy grey carpet of underfelt which was probably insulating material. I couldn't imagine what it would be like if the gas heaters and the fan heater were on as well.

So the guy was a cold fish, or a reptile who needed to warm up before he could work.

Or he was a pervert.

Given that the only other objects in the cellar were a set of handcuffs locked around the downpipes to the radiator and a Canon digital camcorder on a tripod in the corner pointing at the radiator, I was going to go with pervert.

The camcorder was fixed to the tripod and

was powered through an adapter plug from the mains instead of the usual battery, which was unusual. So unusual, I unplugged it and had a look. It wasn't just a power lead, there was another small cable alongside it which continued through a hole drilled into the wall of the workshop. I knew instantly what that was and where it went.

I turned the camcorder on, fumbling at the switch with my gloved fingers, and then moved back into the workshop to turn on the TV on the bench on directly the other side of the wall. As the picture emerged it showed what the camcorder was focused on: the radiator in the cellar. The one with the set of handcuffs dangling from the pipe. They were just like the ones the Turner boys had used on me in the Armstrong II. They must get them wholesale in Wales.

I flipped the channels on the set which seemed to be for a/v input only. There was no aerial so he didn't use it to record *Pobol Y Cwm* while he was out. There was a tape half-in, half-out of the machine with just the number '17' written neatly in ballpoint on the spine label. I slotted it home and the machine indicated that it was on long play, giving six hours of running time.

The VCR hummed and whirred but nothing appeared on the screen to replace the live picture from the cellar. I stabbed the channel button again, flipping to 8, which was where most people put the video link.

Bingo. There was the picture from the tape. It was still the same shot of the radiator in the brightly lit cellar, although the camcorder had been angled so that it didn't show in the reflective tinfoil which coated the walls.

But I wasn't really looking at the fixtures and fittings of the cellar, I was looking at Amy.

Amy wearing the light blue woollen two-piece suit I had found in a dustbin bag back home, the skirt riding up to reveal a lot of leg and her red Jimmy Choo shoes.

Amy kneeling uncomfortably on the grey carpet of the cellar, turning her head to try and blow away the strand of hair that was falling over her eyes.

Amy itching and wriggling inside the suit jacket, trying to wipe the sweat from her forehead on the sleeve.

Amy moving position and touching the radiator with her knees and pulling away rapidly.

Amy handcuffed to the radiator pipes.

I stopped the tape and fast-forwarded it, then pressed Play.

Same scene, same Amy, same handcuffs; only by now the heat was getting to her. Her skirt was now around her waist and she had managed to unbutton the jacket so that the camera could see her white bra with darker damp stains where the sweat was running off her breasts. She had her eyes closed and was slumped, resting her head on her forearms, her hair hanging in damp strands like wet string.

I stopped the tape and ejected it.

It said it was Tape 17. That meant there were sixteen others.

I went back into the cellar and tried the far door. It wasn't locked and it revealed a flight of stairs up into the house with another door at the top which was not only unlocked but open.

There was a kitchen to my right and a hallway leading to the front door to my left. The first room was obviously used as an office, with a desk and a computer, a basic PC. I switched it on at the mains and while it beeped into life, I explored the other room.

This was the bachelor pad living room with two black leather swivel chairs, bookshelves with a few paperback thrillers, a low coffee table, a compact hi-fi system and a cube rack of CDs, another VCR and the biggest wide-screen television I'd ever seen. I've been in Odeons with smaller screens.

And he had three shelves of video tapes. I ignored the commercial ones and concentrated on the home video recordings. There in a neat row were tapes marked '1' to '16' all in one row. I turned the TV on and selected tape '4' at random.

It was a tall, slim redhead, aged about twenty, looking slightly bewildered and slightly amused by being handcuffed to the radiator. She wore a checked shirt and tight jeans and high-heeled boots. I fast-forwarded a good way and pressed play.

She was still handcuffed to the radiator, but had managed to strip herself of boots and jeans and had ripped open the front of her shirt. She wasn't wearing a bra and I thought I recognized her panties from the laundry basket in the workshop.

I ejected the tape and threw it across the room, selected number 6 and pushed it in, fast-forwarding to the end.

While the tape was running I charged back to the computer room. The desktop was up and I clicked on My Documents. There were a hundred or so files listed alphabetically. Fortunately for me, 'Amy' came near the beginning alphabetically. I clicked the mouse and it opened on to nothing. There was a blank space, clearly filed as 'Amy' but a blank space nevertheless.

I hadn't the time to go through the computer. A spotty sixteen-year-old nerd could have told me which files had been deleted and could have recreated them from the ghosting on the hard disc in ten seconds;

but there wasn't one available.

I didn't know how to do anything else and I was about to turn it off when I noticed the rewriteable CDs in a rack on the desk. They were a commercial brand, all in clear plastic wallets and some had written descriptions of the contents such as 'Property' and 'Ongoing Litigation' but several had just numbers. There was a number 4, a 10 and 14. There was no number 17.

I fed disc 4 into the computer and the screen jerked into life. It was the redhead in the check shirt and jeans in her initial pose of looking slightly bemused. I let the disc run, took the others with numbers on and threw them around the office.

The tape I had put on fast-forward had reached the end and was automatically rewinding. I stopped it and played. Girl Number 6 was a small straight-haired blonde who had probably looked frightened from the start. She wore a blue shirt with a fringe down the sleeves, long suede skirt and cowboy boots. She wasn't kneeling, she was standing, tugging at the handcuffs as they slid up the pipe. When she put one leg against the wall to try and get leverage, her skirt rode up to reveal stockings and a suspender belt. Red stockings with black seams.

I left that running as well and selected tape 10 to take into the workshop.

The only good thing about the tapes was that there was no sound. Whatever Rees was getting out of them, it wasn't the sound of women pleading to be set free. That was something, I supposed.

But nowhere near enough to save him.

The unmistakable sound of a diesel engine interrupted my train of thought and I rushed back into the office which had a window looking to the front.

Steffi Innocent was driving her cab right up to the front door and just in case I hadn't heard her coming, she was blowing the horn.

I ran down into and across the cellar and out through the workshop, to where she was pulling up behind the Freelander.

She lowered her window and stuck her head out as she braked.

'I knew you'd be here, you lying bastard!'

'You should have rung me. Why didn't you call?'

'There's no signal up here. No signal anywhere in Tregaron. Check your phone if you don't believe me.'

I pulled it out of my pocket and did so. She was right. The one time I had remembered to charge the battery and turn it on and I was in a dead zone.

'Where's Rees?'

'That's why I'm here. He decided to leave.

The train rides stopped about half an hour ago and he started to pack up. What have you been doing? It's been nearly three hours.'

It had?

'How much start have you got on him?'

'Five minutes maybe, tops. He wouldn't stay and talk to me, just ignored all my questions and said he was on holiday and to contact him at his office next week. Just cut me dead, but he was looking for somebody in the crowd. Probably you.'

'Probably. Look, stay in the cab, keep the engine running. If you see anyone coming down the track, honk the horn. I'll be back in two minutes.'

She started to protest but I was running back into the workshop before she could get a word out.

I slotted tape 10 into the VCR and set it to play, then ran through the cellar and up the stairs. Disc 4 was still on the computer screen. I gathered up the other numbered discs from where I had thrown them and then checked the living room, where the tape of Girl 6 was still running. I took as many of the numbered tapes as I could clutch to my chest, but leaving two or three scattered across the floor.

I looked around to make sure I hadn't left anything of mine and checked that I had Tape 17 safely in my pocket. Then I went back into the office where the phone was.

'Police, please.'

I was put through to a central control which could have been in England, so distant was the answering female voice, and so English the accent who asked me where I was calling from.

'Listen. I'm in a house called Brynteg on the mountain road going south-west out of Tregaron. That's T-r-e-g-a-r-o-n, north of Lampeter and south of Aberystwyth. The house is being used to keep young girls against their will. They have made pornographic videos of them. This is not a joke. There are also guns in the house. Lots of guns. A whole factory of guns. They might be terrorists. Check the cellar. Check the workshop. Get here fast. I repeat, this is not a drill.'

I hadn't bothered to disguise my voice. Keep it short and snappy and voice prints are rubbish as evidence. I had given them 'young girls', 'guns' and 'terrorists', three trigger words which should set wheels in motion in the remote call centre set-up. The phones would be manned by civilians but they would have been trained to act on any of those and channel the message to the appropriate Unit Despatch, or police station as we used to call them.

I hung up before she could say anything but if they wanted to trace the call, they were welcome. I ripped the receiver off its wire and replaced it carefully so the break didn't show at first glance.

Then I was tripping down the stairs into the cellar, remembering to close the doors after me. I dropped a couple of the tapes on the cellar floor near the camcorder, turned off the lights and snapped the Yale lock shut behind me as I reached the workshop.

The tape was still running, as it would for about six hours or however long Rees kept the girls for. I made sure that even a daffy Welsh copper could see the boxes of guns and I actually skidded on some of the loose .22 ammunition I had thrown around. I dropped another tape here and then dug into the laundry basket and grabbed an armful of underwear.

Outside I dumped the tapes and the knickers on the ground while I rescrewed the padlock hasp.

'Stop pissing about, come on!' shouted Steffi. Then: 'What the hell have you got there?'

I didn't answer, just concentrated on ratchet-driving the last screws home. It wasn't a perfect job but it would pass muster.

Then I dived for the Freelander, clutching the underwear and videos. I turned the keys with one hand and rammed tape 17 into the glove compartment just to make sure I didn't lose it. As the engine roared into life I checked I was in 4x4 drive and fastened my seat belt.

Then I lowered my window and shouted to Steffi to follow me.

'Down there?' she shouted back.

'No problem,' I yelled.

Well, it wouldn't be for me.

I moved off and aimed well to the left of where I reckoned Ion Jones was, dropping videos and bits of female underwear at twenty-yard intervals. Then I was concentrating on my driving and trying to lead Steffi down the gentlest path around and down the hill to the road at the bottom.

The sight of her TX1 swerving and bouncing and occasionally leaving space under all four wheels in my mirror was the best entertainment I'd had in a long while. I couldn't resist a chuckle at the thought of the state of her suspension by the time we got to the road. It was no more than a cat-kicker deserved, and it took my mind off the other things I'd seen that afternoon.

I grimaced in sympathy as I saw her hit one particularly savage depression and I swear I saw her head bang into the roof of the cab.

If anyone had been out walking the dog on the hillside across the valley and seen the two of us careering down the mountain like that, they must have thought it was a Eurofunded Welsh re-make of *The Dukes of Hazzard.*

Then again, it was the week of the races and they'd probably just shrug and put it down to the mad Irish visitors. Or again, someone might start a rumour that Jones the Farmer had got ideas above his station and had taken to herding his sheep with a London taxi.

In a way I regretted that I wouldn't be in the back bar of the Talbot that night to start some of the better rumours.

Eventually we hit the road and I turned right, back in front of the Talbot and right again, behind it into the car park, remembering to park ready for a quick exit.

About a minute later, the TX1 appeared and parked next to me.

Steffi was ashen-faced and she climbed out, leaving the door open, and bent over as if she was going to retch. She did retch, but nothing came up.

She had a massive bump on her head above her left eye and into the hairline and there was blood oozing from her bottom lip where she'd bit it.

'You're fucking insane!' she said when she got her breath back.

The car park was near deserted with everyone still at the races, so nobody but me noticed the steam coming out of the bonnet of the TX1.

'What car does Rees drive?'

'A silver Lexus.'

He would.

I walked to the entrance to the car park, ready to duck down behind the wall. Twm Sion Cati was sitting on it, as he had been this morning. I nodded to him and I think he blinked acknowledgement.

There was very little traffic through the town that I could see and from where I was I had a good view down the main street all the way to the garage on the bridge.

Steffi came up behind me, unsteady on her feet, dabbing at her lips with a tissue.

'What are we doing?'

'Seeing how close we came,' I said, then I grabbed her wrist and pulled her to her knees as I saw a silver flash of a car come over the bridge.

It roared by without a pause, only throttling down to take the narrow, twisty road up the hill.

'Was that him?' I asked her.

'I think so, I'm not sure. I think I might have concussion.'

'Nonsense. We've got to get out of here. Take the back road to Lampeter. That's the one we came down the hill on to.'

'Hill? that was a fucking mountain!'

'Whatever. Take the back road, that's important. There'll be police coming up the other road and a black London cab out here's just too conspicuous.'

'I think the suspension's buggered,' she said.

I knew it was but didn't want to depress her.

'You can't risk hanging about here to get it fixed. There's going to be some serious shit going down for Mr Rees.'

'What have you done?'

'Nothing. Just given the authorities a few pointers. Now go wash your face and let's get out of here.'

'Where are we going?'

'I'm going home, I don't know about you.'

She looked down at the ground and put a hand to the bump on her head. She would have quivered her lower lip if it hadn't been bleeding.

'I don't think I've got enough diesel left to get back to London,' she said quietly.

Don't worry about that, the suspension will give way long before then, I thought but I didn't say anything, just walked back to the Freelander, took forty quid out of my wallet and handed it over.

She didn't say thanks, she just limped off towards the public toilets.

As she raised her hands to her swollen head, the back of her jacket rose up and I saw the dolphin for one last time.

I suppose I sighed. How could someone

like that – fairly attractive, I had to admit, fairly resourceful too – with such a strong sense of right and wrong, kick a cat and never say she was sorry, nor even ask how he was?

There was a cruel streak in some people.

In the back of the Freelander I still had about a quarter of Mrs Williams' cream cake, now fairly well squashed and bounced around. I ripped the bag open and showed it to Twm Sion Cati, who proved there was nothing wrong with his long vision by dropping off the wall like a stone and then padding his way purposefully across the car park towards me.

'Come on, boy,' I said quietly. 'You've got a job to do.'

I moved over to the TX1, which still had the driver's door open, and I showed him the cake then plopped it into the luggage well next to the driver's seat. He didn't hesitate, he just took off and leaped by me and into the cab. He landed once on the driver's seat, then nose-dived into the cake.

Very carefully, so as not to frighten him, I closed the door.

'So long, pard'ner.'

I was by the entrance, engine running, signalling left when the first police car appeared in the town square and rushed up the mountain road across my bows, sirens

417

blaring and lights flashing.

I looked at my watch. Seventeen minutes since I rang. Response times were improving.

In the mirror I saw Steffi come out of the ladies' toilet, shrugging her way back into her jacket and wiping the palms of her hands down the legs of her jeans.

She looked once at the Freelander and saw that I appeared to be waiting for her, so she jogged the last few yards and quickly got into the TX1, slamming the door behind her and reaching for the ignition.

My mirror view was a bit blurred after that but I was sure the cab was rocking from side to side and it was due to internal motion as she hadn't even got to start the engine.

'Vengeance is mine sayeth the cat,' I said to myself as I pulled away.

Chapter Nineteen

About two miles out of Tregaron, heading south on the back road, I saw the flashing lights of two more police cars heading north on the main road across the valley of the River Teifi. There was no sign of a black London cab behind me.

I began to take in the scenery and it really was spectacular in a grey-green-brown sort of way. I passed through Nant Dderwen, Llandewi Brefi, Llanfair Clydogau and then there were roadsigns to Llawrda, Llangadog and Llandeilo. With The Dandy Warhols blasting out of the CD player I began to think maybe I could get to like the place.

But then I thought no. I'd never be happy in a country that didn't use enough vowels.

Just before the start of the M4, I pulled off the road and looked at my road map. The M4 running due east would bring me out after about 190 miles at a familiar landmark – the Fullers' brewery in Chiswick.

Or I could make a detour after Bridgend and drop down into the Vale of Glamorgan to the village of St Nicholas, see if Len Turner fancied coming out for a drink. Well, maybe I wouldn't go that far, but I'd earned the right to tell him he was going to need a new solicitor and if I could find where he lived, I might suggest to Malcolm Fisher that if he had any spare creosote...

Besides, I was sure I had Len Turner's money and I didn't want him coming after me debt-collecting.

I took the ammunition box out of the glove compartment, trying to ignore Tape 17 that was in there as well. It probably wasn't clever keeping the .22 cartridge box, so I took the money out, climbed out of the Freelander and walked ten yards in to the surrounding trees. I set fire to the box with my Zippo and lit a cigarette off the burning lid. When it had burned I trampled the ashes, partly to destroy them and partly to make sure I didn't start a forest fire. I didn't dislike Wales that much.

There was £7,600 in tightly rolled £50 notes and by the time I'd finished counting I was beginning to feel I knew Sir John Houblon (1632–1712) personally. Top geezer that Houblon, whoever he was.

Gareth Jones, Ion Jones' (no relation) former employer in Cardiff, had said he'd seen Ion with seven thousand quid to use as start-up capital. There was six hundred more than that, and he must have had living expenses, not to mention buying the old Oxford lathe and the soft steel bars, paying the rent on Bryngwyn and acquiring, if it was he who had, several hundred rounds of .22 bullets. Maybe Keith Flowers had slush-funded more than just the bulk purchase of Brococks. Maybe Ion had sold a few on the side to keep the wolf from the door. It didn't really matter now.

Then I had another flashback to Ion Jones lying on that hillside and I wondered if they still had wolves in Wales.

It was early evening when I found the village of St Nicholas, halfway between Cowbridge and Cardiff. It reeked of money – big houses, lots of burglar alarms, no obvious peasant dwellings – but it had a pub and this was Wales. If you wanted to know who lived where, who was working on what, or who was doing what to whom, check the pub first. For a nation with a reputation for Methodism, short opening hours and Temperance, you still had to drop in at the local to find out what was going on.

It was a pub of two halves, a bar and a restaurant which looked quite upmarket. There were only a handful of customers and nobody raised an eyebrow when I ordered a filter coffee from the bored barmaid in regulation white shirt and black skirt.

It took longer to produce the coffee than if I'd asked a for a cocktail in a hollowed-out coconut, but eventually she placed it gingerly on the bar along with a plastic tub of UHT cream and two sachets of white sugar. I smiled as I handed over the money and pushed away the cream and sugar.

'Is Len Turner in yet, love?' I tried as a conversational opener.

Home run. A fluke, but a home run.

'He's always in at this time. He's in the other bar,' she said.

I almost blew it by staring like a loon at her but I pulled myself together, said thanks, left my change (all of 40p) on the bar and carried my coffee next door.

I hadn't tried the restaurant bar because I had assumed it wasn't open yet. The lighting was subdued, the tables set for meals and no staff obviously around. There was a small bar with backlighting and three bar stools, on one of which sat Len Turner, dressed smart casual in a sweater and slacks and tasselled brown moccasins and pale grey socks – socks universally associated with men over sixty, but I didn't know why.

He was reading the *Daily Mail* and nursing what looked like a large scotch and water. I tried to stop the coffee cup rattling in its saucer as I approached. Thank God there was no sign of his offspring Huey, Dewey and Louie.

He didn't look up from his newspaper, but said:

'What the fuck are you doing here?'

'When in Rome, visit the Emperor,' I said and put the coffee cup and saucer on the bar so I could hear myself speak.

He continued to read his paper and didn't ask me to sit down. In fact he made a point of putting his feet on the rungs of the bar stool next to him.

'Sorry if I startled you,' I said.

Still reading he said: 'You couldn't begin to startle me.'

I believed him. It wasn't an idle boast. He wasn't startled, he wasn't disturbed and he certainly wasn't frightened. I pulled the third bar stool away from the bar and sat on it.

'I've got something for you,' I said when the silence became too much.

'Oh, yes?' He turned to the TV listings page.

'You mentioned a business partner when we ... met ... in London.'

'I haven't been up to London for twenty years,' he said, still reading.

'Right,' I agreed. 'I must have made a mistake. I'll be going, then.'

I made no move to go. He turned another page of the paper. How long did it take somebody to read the *Daily Mail?*

'Don't make two mistakes,' he said.

I didn't answer. I took out the wodge of fifty-pound notes and began counting them silently on to the bar on to a faded bar towel that advertised something called Hancock's Mild.

I was up to two hundred and fifty before he cracked.

'Put that away,' he said, folding the newspaper and climbing down from the stool. 'Follow me.'

He led me into the Gents toilet of the restaurant and before the door had swung closed he had turned on all four taps in the two sinks and then he went to the two unoccupied cubicles and flushed both toilets in turn.

'I'm not wearing a wire,' I said above the roar of running water.

'What's a wire?' He moved to one of the urinals and unzipped. 'I have a bit of a urinary problem.' He pronounced it 'yewerenery'. 'I need a little encouragement sometimes to make the waters flow.'

He should try the low-alcohol lager, but I didn't say it.

'You've got something to tell me?' he said over his shoulder.

'You had a business partner called Ion Jones.'

'Ah, you're wrong there for a start. He was Keith's business partner. I take it that partnership's dissolved.'

'You could say that.'

'No chance of a rescue operation?'

'Not unless you know a medium.'

'That bad, huh?'

He began to shake himself and I thought he'd finished but it was just 'encouragement'.

'Reckon so.'

'Keep talking, don't mind me.'

I don't know if he had trouble concentrating. I did.

'How much was your initial investment? If you don't mind me asking.'

'Nine thousand pounds,' he said quickly. A bit too quickly.

'I've recovered seven six for you. Best I could do.'

'That's mighty kind of you. Put it on the wash basin.' He groaned with pleasure. 'You can turn the taps off now.'

I did as he said.

'You do realize that the deal is off now?'

'What deal?' he said, looking down at the business in hand.

'Have it your way.'

I pulled open the inner door.

'Where you going?' he said without looking round. 'You've left me fourteen hundred quid short.'

I rested my forehead against the edge of the door and said nothing. Eventually he pulled away from the urinal and zipped himself up then patted his crotch to make sure everything was in place. He moved to the sinks to wash his hands.

'Will you take a cheque?' I asked.

'No.'

'Then I'll just have to get the money from Keith's real silent partner. Might take a while. I don't know if they have cash machines in Belmarsh.'

I saw his eyes in the mirror above the basin. They definitely flickered at that.

'Belmarsh? Where's that?'

'It's in London. They call it the creosote capital of the world, or so I'm told.'

He reached for a paper towel from the dispenser.

'Did I say nine thousand? My mistake. Seven six is what it was.'

'There's seven there on the sink.'

'What happened to the six hundred?'

'Legal fees,' I said.

As he dried his hands he said: 'I already have a very expensive solicitor.'

'No, you don't.'

We went back into the bar. It was still empty and it stayed that way until I left. He pointed to a table set for four and we sat down opposite each other. He didn't offer me a drink and my coffee was now stone cold on the bar.

'Start talking, I've got people coming for dinner at eight,' he said, 'and I daren't be late.'

I was relieved to see he was frightened of somebody.

'This has to be a trade. You tell me what I

want to know and I'll tell you what you really do need to know.'

He sniffed loudly.

'We'll see. You go first.'

'You were never going to get those...'

He held up one finger and I caught on.

'...that merchandise you ordered. It was going to be planted on a certain well-known solicitor who has won prizes for air pistol shooting. He probably has a few air pistols himself.'

'Bloody hundreds,' said Len with a sigh.

'Well, he's got even more now and I suspect that right this minute he's answering some very tricky questions about them up in Tregaron.'

'He's a good brief.'

'He'll have to be. There's a dead body within two hundred yards of his house. Dead as in shot.'

'He do it?' He said it throwaway as if he really wasn't interested.

'No, it was ... an industrial accident, I suppose you'd call it. But it'll take some explaining.'

'That it?'

'Then there's the girls and the kinky prison he's got rigged up and heated like a hothouse. Got quite a collection of videos, and CDs. Put some of them on to his computer, he has. Probably swapped some with other enthusiasts over the Internet. You know how the police love that sort of thing these days.'

'The stupid bastard,' Len said under his breath. 'I told him to cut that out but he said he wasn't even touching the girls and he paid them well.'

'Paid them?'

'Working girls from Butetown. I ... er... recommended a few. They'd go up there for the weekend. I didn't hear any complaints.'

As if they'd complain to this management.

'Didn't mind coming back without their underwear?'

'Aw, Jesus, he hasn't been collecting panties again?'

It suddenly occurred to me that *Pant-y-hose* was quite likely the name of a real Welsh village, but now was not the time to share my thought or to giggle.

'The place looked like he's been buying wholesale.'

'And the police have got all this?'

'They couldn't miss it.'

They had better not have.

He sat in silence for a minute, tapping the place mat – which incongruously showed scenes of Constable country in Suffolk – with the nails of both his forefingers. When he had made up his mind about something, he stopped.

'So you think I should look for a new solicitor?'

'If you think you might need one.'

'Don't be a smart alec.'

'If you can sign one up tonight, do it. And send an email to Rees' office right now cancelling all your business. Do it so you can prove you did it before the news breaks.'

I saw something in his cold, old eyes that I hadn't seen before: respect.

'That might be good advice,' he said. 'Why are you giving it? Why did you bring back my mon ... investment?'

'I'll be honest, Mr Turner,' I said showing as much respect for him as I could without throwing up in his lap, 'anything which stitched up Haydn Rees got the thumbs up from me, but there's no reason you should be out of pocket for that. I don't want you coming to London debt-collecting.'

'You show wisdom beyond your years,' he said and I half expected him to add 'Young Jedi'.

'Not wisdom, common sense.'

'What about our mutual friend in Belmarsh?'

'Now that's a bit more problematical.' He raised his eyebrows at such a long word. It was probably even longer in Welsh, with four 'g's or more, not that he'd know, being from the south. 'There's no doubt that our mutual friend's prime objective was to screw you around. I'm afraid he doesn't like you much, Mr Turner.'

I couldn't think why.

'What's between my brother-in-law and me is private. We'll keep it that way.'

Brother-in-law? And I thought I had the Oscar for dysfunctional families this year.

'Whatever you say, but I think it would please our friend to think that you were deprived of your merchandise, you lost your investment and, shall we add that you were thrown into a flat spin when you heard about your solicitor helping the police with their enquiries for the first time when it was on BBC Wales tomorrow morning? Wouldn't that satisfy him?'

'That might work, but he wouldn't believe it if he heard it through me.'

'I'll tell him,' I volunteered.

'You will?'

Well, maybe I'd write.

'If I have to, sure.'

'Do it. Now you said you wanted something from me. Better make it quick – I've got phone calls to make.'

I licked my lips because they had suddenly dried up.

'When we were in London, you said I didn't really know about Amy and Keith Flowers and something about her being "the old gang" or something. What did you mean?'

'I knew you didn't know,' he said and his face cracked into a grin. 'No, I shouldn't laugh, I suppose. Your Amy was a student here in Cardiff for a time. Keith Flowers was with a firm of accountants. I came across them because they'd rented some of my property down the docks. That was the old docks, not the tarted-up new one nobody can afford to live in.

'They'd got a nice little scam going with a company supposed to be making sundials.'

'Sundials?'

'Yes, sundials using recycled materials – bits of brass from the old collieries, Welsh slate for the bases.'

'Did they sell?'

'I dunno, 'cos they never made one, it was all a con. They got their start up money from the Common Market or the European Union or whatever the fuck they call it these days. Said Wales was a Third World country and needed aid. People were quite affronted by that at the time, didn't like to think of themselves as Third World. Now they call it "inward investment" and everyone's at it. Amy and Keith were among the first to get a grant, and they had a good solicitor.'

'Rees.'

'Spot on. When the company went belly-up they never found the cash, about £72,000 as I remember. It had been well squirrelled away. Young Amy had ambitions, you see. Needed some seed capital for a move to London. Rees did whatever she told him to

431

and they sort of cut Keith out of the loop.

'He was always a bit unstable, was Keith, but that tipped him over the edge. He threw a wobbler when two Inland Revenue investigators turned up and started asking nasty questions. He went for them, big time. Beat the living crap out of them. Both were hospitalized and took early retirement.'

'Two Inland Revenue inspectors? Maybe I've misjudged Keith Flowers.'

'Not funny, Mr Angel. They were both women. I don't like, nor do I approve of, violence towards women. That's why he got such a hefty sentence.'

'I didn't know,' I said contritely. 'Thank you for that.'

'She didn't tell you?'

'Not in so many words.'

'No,' he said with another sigh. 'She wouldn't. Women are such bitches.'

I didn't know whether to agree or not.

'Tell you what,' he said suddenly. 'I'll make a few calls, sort things out my end. You have a night in Cardiff on me. See some of the nightlife. Don't worry, I won't be with you. You don't want an old git like me cramping your style.'

What was going on? Any minute now he'd be adopting me.

'I hadn't planned...'

'Won't hear a refusal.'

I got the impression he never did.

'This wouldn't involve Barry and Huw, would it?'

'Not unless you wanted them to buy you a drink. I'd've thought you could find your own entertainment.'

'I can, I can, just I wasn't thinking of Cardiff for tonight.'

'I'll put you up at the St David's, the best in town.'

'They're probably fully booked,' I tried.

He gave me a look that said they were never fully booked for him.

'You do what you want. Make a night of it on the town or go to the health spa. It'll all be on my tab. Then you and I'll have breakfast together in the morning. How's that?'

'Do I have a choice?'

He wrinkled his nose as if thinking hard.

'Not really.'

'And if I just kept driving back to London, you'd come and visit me there? Maybe not tomorrow, maybe not next week, but some time, and I'd always be looking over my shoulder?'

He looked partly impressed, partly surprised.

'Good God almighty, you've got a vivid imagination on you. You don't realize how valuable you are to me, Mr Angel. I would wrap you in cotton wool if I could.'

'You would?'

'Of course I would. You're going to see my psycho brother-in-law in Belmarsh and tell him how I almost had a heart attack, thanks to his cunning plan. That way he'll stay cheerful for a while and give me a bit of peace. I don't want my living room creosoted. I've spent thousands on my living room. The wife would fucking kill me.'

I don't know how he did it, but there was a Master Suite waiting for me at the St David's. I only wished I'd had luggage to take up to it.

I didn't know why I was doing this. My hands shook as I raided the mini-bar. I should be a good proportion down the M4 by now. Len Turner was checking out my story, keeping me in town so he could put his hands on me if he needed to. I was being held on suspicion, albeit in a mink-lined prison. And it did have a health spa.

I charged a pair of Speedo swimming shorts to the room, hired a towel and relaxed in the pool, the sauna, the jacuzzi and then the pool again. When in Rome visiting the Emperor, it's always best to enjoy the decadence while you can. Tomorrow you might find yourself in the arena.

Back in my room – suite – I used my mobile to ring home to see if there were any messages. If Len Turner was getting the bill,

I didn't want to give him any itemized phone numbers I cared about.

There was one message for me. Amy asking me not to forget to pick her up at the airport.

That made me think of the confrontation that was coming round the corner and coming fast.

To hell with it, if I was going to be depressed I'd be depressed on a full stomach and the hotel's restaurants were good. From the Information For Visitors brochure I decided on lobster as it was the most expensive thing. I'd have it for starters, then see what I felt like for a main course.

I was putting on my least grimy T-shirt when there was a knock on the door, which was odd because I hadn't ordered anything for nearly fifteen minutes.

I glued my eye to the security spy-hole – the prisoner spying on the jailers – and there was a young, straight-haired blonde in the process of taking off a pair of octagonal wire-framed glasses and feeding them into a case in a small leather handbag.

I opened the door.

'Hello,' I said, making it upbeat and innocent, not fruity and lecherous like a bad Leslie Phillips impersonation.

She wore a white TALtop. Who'd have thought it? They had actually made it to Wales. And she'd set it off with a black leather waistcoat, a short red suede mini skirt, black tights and Victorian 'granny' ankle boots with three-inch spiked heels.

'Mr Angel?' she said politely.

'Probably,' I said.

'I've been told to keep you company for the night, do anything you want.'

She stood there with her hands on her bag, holding it to her stomach. Not nervous, not overly tarty as she could have been by putting her hands on her hips. Quite demure in fact.

'Anything?' I said. It was pure reflex. Old habits die hard.

She nodded, dead serious. 'Anything.'

I thought carefully about what to say next.

'Mr Turner sent you.'

'Yes.'

'And he'd be offended if I said no?'

It was her turn to think carefully.

'I could be in trouble if I didn't appear to come up to expectations, though I could order a replacement.'

'No, no, no problems in that area, it's just... Look, have you had guys say they just want to talk, you know, just sit and talk? And it usually turns out to be about their wives and how they don't understand them?'

'Y-e-s,' she said slowly, then she saw me grinning. 'All the time, actually. Sad fuckers, most of them.'

Oh, I had a feisty one here.

'Well, let me tell you...?'

'Julia.'

'Let me tell you, Julia, that you are in the presence of one of those sad fuckers, whose wife *does* understand him, but he's alone, in Cardiff for one night and is really, really hungry. *But* he's on expenses. So, the question you've got to ask yourself is do you like lobster?'

She was struggling against the smile, which was a pity, because she had a nice face which hadn't had much to laugh at.

'Let me get this right. You want to take me to dinner? That's all? No afters? It's OK, the afters are paid for. I just like to know where I stand.'

'Not quite correct. I want to take you for the *most expensive* dinner you've ever had, with the finest wines in Christendom. After which you can come in here and put your feet up – oops, bad choice of words there – what I mean is you can make it look like you stayed, if you think you need to, or you could get a taxi home at my expense. Well, not mine, but on expenses. Alternatively, we can sit and watch the Discovery Channel, because I'm pretty sure you can get that in a Master Suite and we can annoy Room Service until the wee hours. *Or* we could do the mini-bar shelf by shelf, seeing who finishes...'

'You're weird,' she said, smiling now. 'I think I'll take the expensive dinner option.'

'A wise choice, madam; you won't regret it,' I said giving her a low bow.

It was the least I could do for the girl on Tape 6.

By the time Len Turner showed up at breakfast I was on my third cup of coffee. I had restricted myself to couple of pastries after the blow-out of the night before. (There had been a minor fuss about me demanding fresh raspberries with shredded mint leaves to go with the *îles flotant* and the chef had been called for and had finally agreed, after the better part of bottle of cognac, that they did complement one another).

'I can't stop,' he said, not bothering to sit down. 'Got to go and sell a few shares to pay your fucking bill.'

'It was your idea,' I said nervously.

'Remind me not to have any more.'

He was dressed for business: three-piece suit, shirt and tie, clutching a briefcase. Well, one of his businesses.

'Going for an interview with my new solicitors, aren't I? Note that they're interviewing *me*, see if my business is worth having.'

'They'd be foolish to refuse,' I said. Foolish? Bloody suicidal.

'Oh, they'll see sense when the cheque

book comes out.'

Or when they see son Ron in dark glasses and leather jacket lurking at the entrance to the dining room, like I could.

'Just came by to say that everything you said has come to pass.'

'It has?' I said, trying hard not to sound surprised.

'Seven o'clock news. Helping the police with their enquires into a suspicious death. No charges yet.'

He sounded quite disappointed.

'So, that's that then?' I said hopefully.

'Not quite.'

He seemed uncomfortable, almost shifting from one foot to the other yet somehow not physically moving.

'I had some of my... Some of my associates visited the offices of a...'

'A mutual legal friend?' I supplied.

'Yes, well, there was a question of certain files to be recovered.'

'I thought there might be.'

'Well, they found this – and several dozen others.'

He rested his briefcase on his knee to open it and took out a video cassette in a plastic box. He put it carefully down on the table and closed the case.

'The fuckwit made copies for the office.'

I stared at the cassette. The sticky label on the spine said: '17 (Amy)'

Before I could say anything, Len Turner was leaving.

'Good luck,' he said.

Chapter Twenty

I never caught the news on BBC Wales. By the time I'd tried to retune the radio in the Freelander, I was on the bridge crossing the Severn and looking at Wales through the rear-view mirror. I found the national news headlines on Radio 4 at midday, but of course it didn't rate a mention there.

Just before the Chippenham turnoff I thought I saw a black TX1 cab pulled up on a garage forecourt, but I could have been mistaken.

I would get back to London with twenty-four hours to spare before I had to collect Amy from Heathrow.

I could tidy up the house. Maybe write a letter to Malcolm Fisher. Go see how Springsteen was. I could ring Stella – no, she'd still be on her honeymoon – or Veronica at Rudgard & Bludgen and ask if they'd heard from Steffi Innocent. I might just drop into the conversation that Steffi must be on some financial blacklist as she wasn't allowed a credit card. (And God knows, they gave them out to just anyone. Look how many I'd got.) Were they aware of that? Had they investigated the investigators?

And then again, I might watch a video.

I did all that except for cleaning the house.

Springsteen was fine. Fenella looked a little more harassed than usual, running around after him, tending to his every need, and she took it badly when I suggested we should get him a bell which he could bat along the floor with his good paw whenever he needed something.

'Did you ever find out who did this to him?' Fenella asked.

'Oh, yes,' I said. 'It's well sorted.'

When she'd gone I asked Springsteen if he had any relations in a place called Tregaron. He didn't deign to reply.

I wrote to Mr Creosote, or Prisoner HM8281 Fisher as I was supposed to call him, and told him in a roundabout way that his friend's idea for an adventure holiday in Wales had misfired (I liked that) and that the main backer had lost his investment fund. The matter was effectively closed.

I didn't have Mr Creosote's faith in the European Court of Justice ruling which said no one was allowed to read his mail.

I rang Rudgard & Bludgen and got through to Veronica.

Steffi Innocent had phoned in sick – eventually, she added huffily – and was likely to be off all week. No she didn't know where she was but she was such a strange girl, nothing would surprise Veronica. No credit rating? No, she hadn't heard that and she'd look into it. It was odd, wasn't it? They give those cards out to every Tom, Dick or Harry, don't they? My cat could probably get one if I filled in the form.

'Interesting idea, Veronica,' I said before hanging up.

She rang me back in the early evening to tell me that the basic credit check had come up immediately with Steffi's name on not one, but three, blacklists. An entire history of credit cards maxed out, one within twenty-four hours of being issued. A bit of a shopaholic, our Steffi, and therefore untrustworthy in a business which relied so much on trust. (It probably said that on her day-by-day tear-off desk calendar.) Sad though it was, when Stella got back they would have to review Steffi's contract.

That was sad and a bit like kicking someone when they were down.

But that's what she'd done.

Most of the night I spent watching a video – the same video of which I now had two copies – or as much of it as I could stomach at one go, which was about an hour.

And there was a fair bit of drinking involved.

A policeman ringing the doorbell got me out of bed just before noon.

He was by himself – his partner was in the police car parked in the street – and he wasn't wearing his hat. Good signs it wasn't serious.

'Mr Angle?'

'Near enough.'

'Sorry to disturb you, sir.'

I pulled the belt on my silk robe even tighter.

'What can I do for you?'

He pulled out his notebook and turned a few pages.

'Could you tell me if you were in the house on Tuesday night, that's Tuesday this week?'

'No I wasn't. I've been in Wales for few days. Since Monday actually and I only got back yesterday afternoon.'

'Wales? My sergeant's Welsh.' He flicked his head to the car where the other uniform was doing paperwork leaning on the dashboard.

'That's nice for you,' I said cheerfully.

'Not really. He's a bit of pain in the arse, if you know what I mean. However I've got to ask you because you're the last house on our list. Is there a wife…?'

'Yes, but she's in Spain. Comes back this evening. She wasn't here Tuesday either.'

'So it was a case of while the cat's away the mice will play, was it?'

Will somebody please protect me from

friendly policemen? There ought to be law against them.

'If I wanted to play away from home, do you think I'd go to Wales?'

'Fair point, sir, fair point.'

He wrote 'Mr and Mrs Angle not at home' and Tuesday's date in his notebook.

'What's this all about, officer?'

'The burglary,' he said putting his pen away.

'We haven't been burgled,' I said.

Well, not recently. In London it's bound to be your turn sometime.

'No, of course you haven't. It was just in case you'd seen anything. We were looking for witness statements. It was that house over there got done.'

He pointed.

'The Dunmores?'

He allowed himself a smirk.

'Yeah, and him the big cheese in the Neighbourhood Watch.'

'I bet he gave you lot some stick,' I said.

'He was about to, but we caught the guy. Though Mr Dunmore is going to tighten up procedures in the Watch ready for a rapid response, as he calls it.'

'Good for you, catching the bloke.'

'Wasn't difficult. He was a bit of an old boy, an old lag really. Had his pockets stuffed with Mrs Dunmore's jewels out of the bedside table. He should have legged it but he said he just couldn't resist the wide-screen television. Got as far as the end of the street there and sat down on it. Had a smoke under the streetlight. God knows how he thought he'd get it on the Tube. He was there when we arrived. Almost like he was waiting for us. Hard to believe, isn't it?'

'There's just no understanding some people,' I agreed.

I hoped Spider had a Happy Christmas.

Amy's plane was not only on time, it was early, and she had already swanned through Customs weighed down with bags, one of them chinking.

'You missed a treat!' she said, loading me up with shopping bags.

'Good time?'

'Excellent businesswise, and I've got a tan to prove I did nothing in the afternoons. It's far too hot to work out there except for about two hours a day. You'd love it.'

'Would I have to do the full two hours *every* day?'

'Not if you were sleeping with the boss. Don't drop that one. There's two bottles of a Spanish brandy that's even worse than that Italian stuff you drink. Do not light a cigarette after that.'

In Armstrong, which I'd parked in the taxi rank, she asked me what I'd been doing with myself.

'Touring around with the guys,' I said, remembering my cover story. 'We supported a Breton bagpipe band and a group called The Judith Charmers, would you believe.'

'Believe NOT!' she yelled in my ear.

'They're a good pub band,' I protested.

They did exist and they were.

For the rest of the journey it was mostly her talking about the Madrid fashion scene and which ideas she could steal, which trends she could start.

'You're very quiet,' she said as we neared Hampstead.

'Just impressed by the jet-set world of high fashion.'

'High fashion? Cut 'em low, price 'em high. That's all there is to it.'

She put her hand through the sliding partition and rubbed my shoulder.

'I wished you'd come. It'll probably be my last freebie abroad for a while.'

'It will? Why?'

There was a pause before she answered.

'A change of direction is called for. No, not called for, it's actually coming. We have to adapt to it.'

'That was a "we" wasn't it.'

'Yes, of course,' she said suspiciously. 'Why wouldn't it be?'

'No reason.'

'Oh, yes, there must be. What is it? Do we need to talk?'

'Probably.'

'Oh, fuck. When you say "probably" like that, it means you've been brooding.'

'I have not been brooding.'

'Yes, you have. I can tell.'

'I haven't, I've been busy.'

'Brood, brood, brood, brood...'

'We'll talk inside,' I said as I turned into the street.

I had a feeling two bottles of Spanish rotgut wasn't going to be enough.

We watched the tape together, or at least some of it.

Probably about fifteen minutes of it, but it seemed longer. The tape was silent, so were we.

Then Amy stood up and grabbed the remote control, froze the image on the television screen and then stood in front of it, hands on hips, staring at me.

She was wearing what she'd worn on the flight back, a white shirt and khaki cargo trousers with leg pockets that had never been used, and light brown suede shoes with kitten heels. With a military cap on she could have stepped out of a recruiting poster for Desert Storm.

'A long time ago...'

'In a galaxy far away.'

'Don't interrupt me! Just listen!'

I nodded an apology.

'This is something I was never going to tell you because it happened before *you*. Just like I don't want to know what you did before *me*. Can you understand? That should have gone – history. Good, bad history, it had gone. It was *before you*. OK?

'Keith and I got involved in a scam involving some European money.'

'In Cardiff.'

'I said, don't interrupt. This isn't easy for me. You've no idea how this isn't easy.'

'Sorry.'

'Yes, we were in Cardiff. Keith knew this solicitor on the make, a man called Haydn Rees. He would help us by making everything look legal. Long and short of it was, we were getting a grant for one thing but spending the money on something else. I thought we were spending it on developing what became the TALtop, i.e. one my fashion ideas. Keith had other plans, but then he was a psycho. When it all went ballistic, Haydn Rees had it so that Keith took the fall. He deserved to. He'd become unstable by that time – even violent.

'Years go by, right? Keith's in prison, I meet you. Things have moved on. There's *you* now.

'Then Keith gets out of prison and starts making a nuisance of himself. Then he gets himself rearrested and everything's back to normal. Well, it isn't. I know it's not the same, maybe it can't be.

'Because now this Haydn Rees comes out of the woodwork for some reason. He suspects Keith has some sort of revenge mission planned and he wants to make sure that Keith is stitched up good and proper this time. He's got too big, too important, to have shadows from his past embarrassing him in court. He wants reassuring that Keith isn't going to bring up old grievances.

'So I have to go and reassure him, because Haydn Rees has a long memory and so has his computer. He's got everything to do with our early business on file and that could damage me. Seriously. So I had to go and see him.'

She paused for breath. She was actually panting.

'He was cited as co-respondent in your divorce,' I said.

'How did you find that out?' she cracked back.

'By accident, just like I found out you were fucking married before. I didn't know that until a month ago.'

'I said, that was *before you*. Now is *with you*. Nothing else counts.'

Her face showed a half-hearted smile.

'You're jealous.'

'And you're pushing it.'

'Yes, I am, because it's so fucking stupid.'

I knew it would all be my fault, but there

was no stopping her now.

'Think, man, for fuck's sake. You've seen the tape, you've seen what Haydn Rees likes from women. He likes them to *sweat*. He does a bit of nominal bondage, that's true, but mostly he just likes to watch them sweat. He doesn't fuck them, he doesn't whip them, he doesn't verbally abuse them – *he's not even in the fucking room when it happens*. He films them and watches later at his convenience and creams his jeans in front of the video. Do you honestly think there could be anything between me and a so-solid perv such as that? Do you think I did that willingly? I did it to get the file from his computer. That was all. It was a business strategem, nothing more. That was the deal. I played his games and gave him my underwear – oh, yeah, he collects female underwear.'

'Just a minute. Where did you get this fucking tape?'

'It was with the others,' I said.

'Others?'

'There were sixteen in the house at Tregaron. He'd transferred the digital pictures from the camcorder on to his computer in some cases, but mostly they were video. He had a feed running through the wall into a VCR in the workshop.'

Amy put her hands back on her hips, looked at the floor and shook her head.

'The fucker.'

I looked at her and, bizarrely, all I could think was that she was putting on a bit of weight.

'Have you seen the end of this tape?' she said, looking back at me.

'No, not the end,' I said nervously.

She grabbed the remote and fast forwarded to what I guessed was about the two-hour mark. It took a few minutes. A few minutes of silence as she concentrated on the images flashing by. She was set on something and it was like I wasn't there.

'There!' she said triumphantly. 'Watch this bit.'

There was Amy in her super-heated prison in Tregaron, chained to the radiator. There was Amy, skirt round her waist, suit jacket half-shrugged off her shoulders, her bra totally grey with sweat, her hair hanging in ribbons.

I didn't see the point. I hadn't watched this far because ... well, because it was obscene. It was revelling in someone's powerlessness.

And then suddenly there was Amy, head up and alert, listening.

'I heard his car go,' she said and her voice startled me. I had almost forgotten she was here, live, in the house.

On the screen she waited, her head moving as if confirming something. Then she snapped the release button on the handcuffs – just like the Turner boys had done with me – and in an instant she was free and on her feet and marching towards the camera with a look on her face that would have frozen hell.

Then the tape went dark.

'I took the memory disc out of the camera,' she said. 'I didn't know the bastard had a video link-up.'

I eased my buttocks off the sofa and took out the tape I'd been sitting on.

'And he made a copy so he could watch in the office.'

She didn't take it from me. She sank to the floor, cross-legged and sat in silence.

'Cigarette?' I asked her, producing a pack.

'No, I've given up.'

That was news too.

'I thought I was doing everything right. I got the company files off him and then I thought I'd dealt with the camcorder,' she said as if trying to work out where she'd gone wrong.

'Are you sure you cleaned out the computer?' I asked.

'Yes. I know what I'm doing there. The record's gone. He's got nothing any more.' She looked up at me. 'Where did you get the tapes?'

'I had help.'

'You said there were more.'

'He used to hire girls to ... perform for him. Paid well, so I'm told.'

'There's not that much money in the world.'

Her head sank down again.

'I'm sure I've got the only ones with you if that was the only time...'

She flashed me a killer look.

'Yes, it was. And you know why I did it? Because it was the only way I could think of to protect *us*, what we have.'

I came out of the chair and put my arms round her.

'I think you did a damn good job,' I said. 'And it's over now. It's *then*, this is now.'

'I knew he was a perv; I just thought I could outsmart him.'

She looked me in the eyes and smiled.

'You can't out-perv a perv, can you?'

I smiled back.

'I've never met the geezer, but I could have told you he was a perv.'

'Yeah, right, Mr Smart Arse.'

No, I could.

Malcolm 'Creosote' Fisher had told me Rees was a 'panty-sniffer' when we were in Belmarsh.

Sole reason for going to Wales.

I wasn't going to have a panty-sniffer threatening my wife.

The doorbell rang.

'Who the fuck is that?' we both said

together from the floor, arms around each other.

It was the so-solid perv himself.

Stupidly, we didn't check first, we just opened the door together, arms round each other's waists, me trying to confirm that she was adding a few ounces here and there.

We stopped giggling – it was a laughter of relief rather than anything specific – as the door swung open and there was Haydn Rees.

He was dishevelled and unshaven and he had his hands in the pockets of a beltless raincoat with the two lower buttons fastened. He must have thought he was still in Wales.

'I want to speak to Amy,' he said.

I just gawped at him, but then I'd never seen him before, not really.

He had once had curly blonde hair, now thinning fast, and he was about five foot ten. He had the look of someone who needed to wear glasses, probably used contacts. In that raincoat he looked like Michael Caine playing Harry Palmer in *The Ipcress File*, but without the glasses and with none of the charisma.

I said nothing. I was gobsmacked, thinking things like: of course he's here, he would have got bail. He was a solicitor, after all.

Amy said nothing, but I felt her grip on

my waist tighten.

'I want to talk to Amy alone,' he said. Why was he talking as if she wasn't right there in front of him? This guy had real problems with women.

'Why?' I managed to say.

'Because I love her and I want her to come away with me to a new life.'

I looked at him in disbelief.

Amy looked at him.

Amy looked at me and I looked at her.

'You hold him. I'll hit him,' she said.

And that's what we did, right there on the front doorstep.

I did what Humphrey Bogart did to Elisha Wood, Jnr in *The Maltese Falcon*. I got behind him before he could move and pulled the shoulders of his rain coat down over his arms so he was pinned helpless.

Personally, I was surprised that it worked, but it did. Then Amy hit him with the best left upper/right cross combination I had seen outside of pay-for-view TV.

He staggered backwards, taking me with him, and I felt him frantically trying to pull his right hand out of the raincoat pocket. I got there first and wrestled from him the Brocock air pistol he was trying to draw.

This one was an air pistol. It was a frighteningly accurate model of a Walther automatic. I knew that because I could read

Walther CP 88 along the 4-inch barrel. It had a chestnut wood handle which fitted snugly into the palm of my hand and it had a safety catch. Beyond that all I knew was that it wasn't one of Ion Jones' specials which fired real bullets. They were revolvers, not automatics.

Well, I was pretty sure.

'He's got a gun,' I said as I struggled with him.

'Here we go again,' said Amy and she kicked him in the stomach.

I stood over him. It seemed a bit naff to point the air pistol at him. It was only an air pistol after all. Humphrey Bogart would have tossed it into the sage brush and snarled at him.

I looked down at him as he gasped for breath.

'Haydn Rees? I don't believe we've met.'

He didn't answer, just concentrated on getting to his feet and then stood there, panting.

I had moved back to be next to Amy, who was pumped up ready to have another go at him.

'I don't think you've got any business here,' I said.

'I'm not fucking finished with him,' said Amy.

'Yes, you are, because he simply doesn't

matter any more.'

'He doesn't?' she said quietly.

'He never really did,' I said. 'I just didn't see it that way for a while.'

Haydn Rees spoke.

'I've got nowhere to go.'

'Tough,' I said.

'My reputation's in ruins,' he said.

'Double tough,' said Amy.

He didn't say anything else, he just turned on his heels and began walking down the drive, head down.

'Let's see him off the premises,' I said.

Amy slipped her arm back around my waist and we followed Rees until he'd left the drive and turned right along the street.

About twenty yards down the pavement there was a silvery Lexus and he must have had a remote in his pocket because the lights flashed as he unlocked it.

'What do you think will happen to him?' Amy whispered.

'As if I cared,' I said.

But suddenly I did care because although he had unlocked the doors of the Lexus, he wasn't getting in it, he was opening the boot and then he was leaning into it and pulling something out which glinted in the street-lights.

'Oh, no.'

This was a revolver and I wasn't going to stop to ask if it was a specially adapted one.

I should have known he'd have at least one in his collection. He was a model freak and a collector. He was bound to have.

And there he was, calmly cracking the cylinder and loading the thing from a box of ammunition he balanced on the bumper of the car.

I had an air pistol. He had one too, but his fired real bullets.

'Run,' I said to Amy. 'Run for the house and lock the door. Now would be good.'

I knew I couldn't physically reach him in time. I had to shoot it out. But if he thought this was going to be some ten-paces-turn-and-fire duel, he was out of his fucking mind.

I'm not a bad shot, but I was outgunned from the start. I had to put my faith in local conditions and a lifetime's study of human behaviour. If I was wrong, that learning curve stopped here.

I raised the air pistol and made sure the safety was off. That was about all I was sure of. I didn't even know how many slugs the thing fired.

Out of the corner of my eye I watched Haydn Rees look at me in bewilderment as he saw me aiming not at him, but, as it must have seemed to him, up into the night sky.

It took two shots to put out the nearest streetlight. Then three to put out the next.

Rees watched in wonderment, not under-standing what I was doing, but then he didn't know Hampstead, did he?

Gun fire in the streets? No problem. Some vandal smashes a streetlight and – hey – the Neighbourhood Watch wakes up.

And they did by the time I'd smashed the third one. (Got it in one that time).

Two houses set their burglar alarms off and a siren began to sound – that would be the Dunmores, I guessed. They would have the local police on speed dial.

I shot at a fourth lamp, but it was an ambitious distance and I missed.

By that time though there were lights coming on and somebody waving a torch and the obligatory 'Clear off, you hooligans' being shouted.

Rees was suddenly gone.

He had slammed the boot and dived for the driver's door.

The engine revved and he was gone.

I put the air pistol down by the side of my leg and turned to walk down the drive. To all intents and purposes I had been a concerned citizen coming out to see what all the noise was about.

I took precisely one pace and walked into Amy who hadn't taken my advice at all.

'You should have gone inside, like I said.'

She grinned.

'Take orders from somebody who couldn't hit the side of a barn from ten feet?'

'That last one was a difficult shot and it's

dark, in case you hadn't noticed. All the streetlights round here seem to be faulty.'

'Bet you I could hit it.'

'What you got to bet with?'

'I'll think of something,' she said and her voice dropped a tone.

I looked over my shoulder. The neighbours were milling around in their doorways. In the far distance I could hear a police siren – but that meant nothing in London.

I handed Amy the pistol.

'Go for it,' I said.

Three days later there was an item on the local news that the London Eye had suspended operations whilst a body, believed to be a suicide, had been found bobbing up against Hungerford Bridge. Police believed it was a man they were seeking in connection with charges pending in west Wales.

But that night, much later that night, Amy confessed.

'There was something I've been meaning to tell you for a couple of days, weeks in fact. But this business with Keith and then Rees...'

'There's something else?'

I sat up in bed. Bolt upright.

'Yes, there is.'

'Go on, then. Do your worst. Stun me.'

She did.

'I'm pregnant.'

Being right about her putting on weight suddenly seemed little consolation.

When I didn't say anything, she said:

'You OK with that?'

'Oh yes,' I said. 'You know me. I love surprises.'

This Large Print Book, for people
who cannot read normal print,
is published under the auspices of

THE ULVERSCROFT FOUNDATION

... we hope you have enjoyed this book.
Please think for a moment about those
who have worse eyesight than you ...
and are unable to even read or enjoy
Large Print without great difficulty.

You can help them by sending a
donation, large or small, to:

**The Ulverscroft Foundation,
1, The Green, Bradgate Road,
Anstey, Leicestershire, LE7 7FU,
England.**
or request a copy of our brochure for
more details.

The Foundation will use all donations
to assist those people who are visually
impaired and need special attention
with medical research, diagnosis
and treatment.

Thank you very much for your help.